THE HUNT FOR KOMODO CRACKER

MICHEL CLOUTIER

Scripture taken from the King James Version of the Bible

ISBN: 978-1-7750-0330-4 (sc)
ISBN: 978-1-7750-0334-2 (e)

https://huntforkomodocracker.wixsite.com/michelcloutierkc

Published: October 2018

I dedicate this book to my lovely wife who inspired me to believe that I was capable of writing a novel and without whose support and patience I would have never achieved my dream.

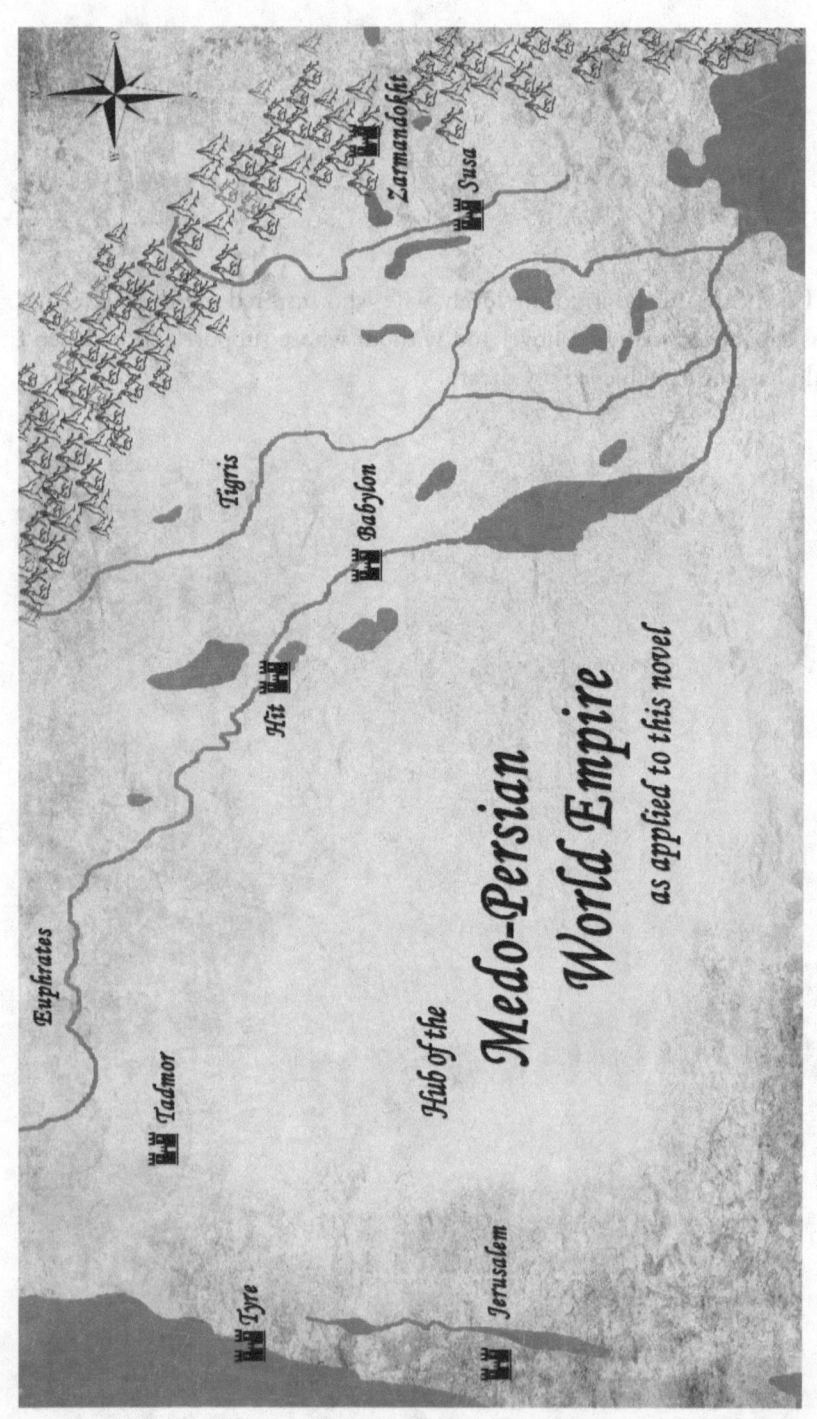

Euphrates

Tadmor

Tyre

Jerusalem

Tigris

Hit

Babylon

Zarmandokht

Susa

Hub of the
Medo-Persian
World Empire
as applied to this novel

PART 1
THE GATHERING

```
 1001011   0111101011
1000110010101001
101      110101011011011
1110101 HACKED 11   110
   101010010001011111
1001010101      01010100
1111   0111111011
```

CHAPTER 1

473 BC, Persia

"There's more dust in the light," Hutan said. "They're getting closer."

He was used to staring death in the face. It excited him. He felt cheated when given duties that kept him away from a battle. So when his best friend asked for his help working deep in the cave with the other troglodytes, he felt restless. He wanted more than anything else to be with his comrades on the battlefield.

"Then get away from the door and help me finish," Ramin said.

"We should be out there fighting, not digging holes," Hutan said. "Our brothers—and needless to say, my wife—need us now."

"For God's sake, Hutan, stop complaining and help me. The sooner we're done, the sooner we'll be out there fighting with them."

Hutan took one more look at the entrance of the cave before closing the door. "How do you know this stone will work, anyway?" he asked as he turned back to Ramin. He was already halfway through digging a hole.

"We've been through this." Hutan heard the annoyance in Ramin's voice. "You promised to help me bury this stela, and all you're doing is talking."

"I know," he said, grabbing a shovel. "And I owe you my life. But you spent all your gold in having this stone carved. It's an obsession with you. And still you won't talk to anyone about it. Why is it so important?"

Ramin leaned on his shovel. "Listen to me, Hutan. You know it's my only chance to get back home." He lifted his hand in a shrug. "Even if I went into detail, you could never understand. You'd think me crazy. Besides, I told you: once we're finished here, we're done. From then on it's in the hands of the god."

"Right—Chronos. Whatever you say," Hutan drawled.

"Thank you, Hutan; I knew I could count on you."

Hutan wasn't sure if Ramin had noted his sarcasm and chose to ignore it, or if he'd missed Hutan's skepticism altogether.

1

"I don't want to interrupt," Pantea interjected. Hutan's mother-in-law had taken up his former post at the door. "But I think the Amalekites have broken through our defenses."

Hutan rushed to the open door. "Mother, I told you to stay with the children. You heard the order. All seniors and children must stay in the cave during the battle. It's the safest place for everyone." He grasped her elbow and pulled her gently away from the door. "Now go back and sit down."

They both watched as she returned to her grandchildren. "She's right, you know," Hutan said. "The fight has reached the cave. They're bringing in the injured. We need to go, my friend. We can finish here later."

"Fine, I'm coming," Ramin said as he rushed to fill the hole with the last of the dirt.

Hutan kissed his mother-in-law. "Don't worry, I'll find your daughter," he assured her. "You and I both know she can fight as well as any man." He hugged his three children. "Stay here with your grandma, you understand? I'll be back with your mother very soon."

"Leave everything as-is," Ramin said. "We'll finish when we return." He hesitated, then retrieved a papyrus scroll from a leather bag at his waist and handed it to Pantea. "Just in case, this is the story to pass on—it is written in this document."

Pantea pushed the papyrus back at him. "You can explain it to us when you get back."

"We have to go," Hutan urged.

Ramin reluctantly pushed the papyrus back into the bag and nodded to Hutan.

They turned to the door, both unsheathing their swords. Hutan was first to exit the house. With a glance at the buried stela, Ramin followed Hutan, and they trotted through the maze of cave dwellings to engage the enemy out in the open.

• • • • • • • • • ● ○ ○ ○ ○ ○ ○ ○ ○ ○ ○ ○

January 2032, Zagros Mountains, Iran

For three hours the Persian sun blazed down on the old SUV. Barnaby Lancaster and the other occupants of the battered vehicle were traveling east at an average speed of fifty kilometers per hour. To Barnaby it seemed the sun had a personal vendetta against him. Salty sweat stained his matching safari shirt and trousers. To make matters worse, he had a heat rash developing in his armpits and burning sand induced irritations in unspeakable places.

Even at the advanced age of fifty-four and a height of only one point eight meters, Barnaby was irresistible to women. Knowing this, Barnaby took full advantage of his bachelorhood, wining and dining women of all ages as often as he dared. The only passion he put ahead of his desire for beautiful women was his love for archaeology.

Right now, however, neither women nor archaeology occupied his mind. He was contemplating an opportunity to teach Near Eastern Archaeology— or as some would call it, Biblical Archaeology—at England's prestigious Oxford University. He had been putting it off for almost five years, but this god-awful experience had convinced him that the time had come to consider the teaching position. He mused on this while being tossed in every direction without let-up.

Unable to contain himself any longer, Barnaby blurted at the driver, "Why in God's name did you rent a bloody convertible to take us out in this bloody dry, dusty furnace? Are you insane?"

The driver was a local Iranian with the body of a fifty-year-old wrestler. He wore a thawb the same color as the desert around them. He'd said nothing the entire trip. He looked at Barnaby with an expression that almost made him regret his outburst. Five seconds later, the man smiled and said in a strong local accent, "This only available. It goes there. Is good, yes—okay?"

Barnaby gaped at him, surprised he could speak. He had little respect for anyone he deemed ignorant or poorly educated. Discouraged, he rubbed a hand across his neatly trimmed salt-and-pepper beard and looked ahead at the never changing scenery. To his right, endless desert stretched to the horizon, broken only by rocks scattered like debris. To his left, the sheer vertical rock face of a plateau seemed to go on forever. It rose to irregular heights of at least one hundred meters, with no way up.

After yet another sigh, he held his hand over his shoulder. Without saying a word, a tall, thin man sitting in the back handed him a bottle of water. Barnaby groaned and shook his head as he realized the bottle was almost as hot as the dashboard in front of him. "Bloody hell," he said before he took a long, slow swallow of the warm water.

At this exact point in time Barnaby decided this would be his last trip in the field. He would remember this experience each time he found himself tempted to leave the comfort of his English home for yet another archaeological site. For over thirty years he'd been looking for the elusive Persian stela. The time had come for someone younger, someone with more zeal and enthusiasm, to take his place.

Reaching this conclusion, he felt a heavy load lift off his shoulders. *By tomorrow morning this will all be over,* he told himself. The thought of retiring from fieldwork relaxed him. He closed his eyes, bowed his head, and somehow over the next few minutes, he fell asleep.

"We are here," the driver said with an air of satisfaction. "I welcome you to Zarmandokht."

Barnaby tried to open his eyes but could not focus on what lay ahead, so he looked down at his watch. He had been sleeping for two hours. Cupping his hands over his eyes, he tried once again to focus. Now he could see the large opening as the plateau gradually materialized.

They passed through the gap in the ten-meter-high walls rising to the plateau and entered the small village under excavation. The driver stopped the SUV in the shade created by the walls, near the village square. Barnaby let his head fall against the back of the seat, exhilarated by the cool, refreshing breeze in this narrow passage protected from the sun.

"I can see Farshad," the driver said in a deep, commanding voice. "He waits. Look, he waits—you see? In front of big cave, under . . . how I say?" He muttered the word "canopy" in Arabic. "We must go now."

They moved straight ahead, into what Farshad had called in his communiqué "the Horseshoe." It seemed the endless plateau paused at this point, forming a horseshoe-shaped crater. The walls were of equal height all around. The only way in or out was through the narrow entrance.

For the last thirteen months, this had been an active archaeological site sponsored by the Iranian government. About one thousand people had inhabited this village in 473 BC. At the time a large, two-leafed wooden gate protected the village. In the open air within the horseshoe, tradesmen had their shops, with stalls for horses and other conveniences. Their homes were built deep into the cave located far back in the horseshoe, where water could be found.

"Welcome, Mr. Lancaster," Farshad said as the SUV came to a stop in front of him. "I hope the trip was not too difficult."

"You could have found a better guide," Barnaby said, ignoring the driver sitting next to him.

"You mean Samir? He's the best," Farshad replied. "You have no idea how difficult it was to find someone to come out here at this time of year. In fact, we were fortunate to have anyone at all. You would still be at the airport if it wasn't for Samir."

"Two peas in a pod," Barnaby quipped.

Farshad did a double take. "Excuse me?"

Barnaby ignored him. He was too busy fighting leg cramps.

"Anyway," continued Farshad, "would you and your companion like some ice cold water?"

"No," Barnaby snapped, grabbing the bottle out of Farshad's hand, "we much prefer a steaming hot cup of tea."

Barnaby knew Farshad had lived most of his adult life in the United States, but he seemed to be struggling with the snide comment, uncertain whether the remark was meant to be funny or sarcastic. Then his brows drew down, and Barnaby knew he realized he was being mocked. Barnaby didn't care.

"As we drove through the square I noticed a marble structure of some kind." Barnaby turned and pointed up the eastern wall. "Over there, up high. Is it a tomb?"

"Yes, it's a tomb. We found the body of a boy inside. The inscriptions over its entrance indicate the boy was some kind of war hero."

"A war hero boy, you say. I very much doubt that." Barnaby turned back to face Farshad. "I sure hope you found the real thing this time because this is the worst trip I've ever made."

"Please come with me and see for yourself. Don't forget to take your water with you. We don't have much time—you must be on your way before the workers return from their afternoon siesta." Farshad turned and led Barnaby and the tall thin man toward the entrance of the cave.

They paused just inside to let their eyes adjust to the light. Barnaby held his eyes shut, then opened them—and stood amazed at what he saw. "Bloody hell, this place is huge. It looks like a cathedral with most of its lights turned off."

"Be careful where you step." Farshad held out his hand to prevent Barnaby from stepping forward. "There are many trenches and tools lying around and they're hard to see in this light. Now, please be very careful as you follow me."

They shadowed Farshad through a maze of dirt paths, frequently crossing wooden planks spanning trenches thirty, sometimes sixty centimeters deep. After snaking their way over the broad network of trenches, they stepped onto solid ground at the back of the cave. It was nearly pitch dark. Farshad moved away; a moment later a halogen light came to life, illuminating the now helmeted Farshad standing at a large wooden table. He came back with two more security helmets. Barnaby put one on before giving one to the tall, thin man.

"There's no danger of falling rocks in this section of the cave," Farshad said, "but the ceiling is low in certain places. I wouldn't want anyone to crack their skull."

"How did you come across the stela?" Barnaby asked as he secured his helmet.

"Six days ago I was working in one of the trenches—that one over there with the marker B-14." Barnaby didn't look in the direction Farshad pointed. "Anyway, while clearing some debris in my assigned trench I came across a basalt slab. Since I happen to be working alone in this particular trench, it was easy for me to reveal a few centimeters at a time. I would then cover it up, only to start revealing more at a different place until I was able to identify with a measure of accuracy that I had the real thing. I reburied it, then came back that night to hide it deeper inside the cave. Two days later I called my contact in England to have someone come and fetch it."

"Why did you wait two days to contact us?"

"It took me most of two days to record its exact position," Farshad replied. "It's not easy doing it in secret. You have to properly survey and document a find like this for future analysis. To have removed the stone without recording its precise location would make me no better than a common thief, a relic hunter, a—"

"Bloody hell, Farshad, what in God's name were you thinking?" Barnaby blurted. "This stela will never end up in a museum. It's much too valuable to the League for your stupid dig protocols. Your delay could have cost us the stela."

Farshad stepped back and grimaced as Barnaby's spit sprayed over his face.

"So where's the stela now?" Barnaby demanded.

"Right over there, buried under a shaker screen."

They walked toward the shaker screens stacked at the back of the cave. "This is also where they stack all the discovered artifacts, right next to the expensive equipment," Farshad added.

Barnaby stopped to look around. "Shouldn't there be a security guard here?"

"Yes, of course."

"So, where is he?"

Farshad smiled. "I'm the one assigned security duties today."

Barnaby smiled for the first time. "Very good; well done. Now show me the stela."

Farshad used a shovel to displace a thin layer of dirt, revealing a jute canvas. He bent and scooped away the loose dirt around the edges of the object with his fingers, then lifted his head and nodded. Barnaby bent at the other end of the rectangular object to work his fingers underneath, and they lifted it gently and put it on top of one of the shaker screens. The three men paused, looking at it, then Barnaby stepped forward and peeled back the canvas, revealing a well-preserved basalt stela.

He gazed at it for a moment, then removed his glasses and cleaned them while he ran details through his mind. He pulled a tape measure from his pants pocket and checked the stela's dimensions: fifty-two centimeters wide, ninety-eight centimeters long, and eight centimeters thick. "The dimensions seem accurate."

Next he reached into his breast pocket and pulled out a piece of paper he'd folded and unfolded a hundred times. Unfolding it one more time, he compared the image on it with the stela. "There's no doubt about it. This is the stela we've been looking for all these years."

With great care he moved his hands over the surface, exploring it with his fingertips as if somehow it would communicate with him through touch. He analyzed the details found at the bottom of the stela. He began to decode the text in his mind.

"Mr. Barnaby, we must go now," Farshad said, his tone urgent. "The workers will return within the next fifteen minutes."

"Yes, yes," Barnaby murmured, his mind still in a cloud. He turned to the tall, thin man who waited nearby, his backpack open. "Put it in quickly, and let's go. And for God's sake, be careful—the future of the world is in your rucksack."

• • • • • • • • ● ○○○○○○○ ○ ○ ○

The morning after, en route to Aylesbury, England

Sipping on a tall glass of iced tea, Barnaby gazed absently out the window of the company's private jet as he waited, his cell phone pressed to his ear. The morning sun limned the dwindling Zagros Mountains in gold light. He was well quit of those, he thought smugly; life would be good, now that he'd found the stela.

After a short while, a woman's voice interrupted his reverie. "Mr. Harding will speak to you now, Mr. Lancaster."

Barnaby sat up straight as if the vice-president of the ULRA were sitting in front of him.

"What is it, Barnaby?"

"Good morning, Mr. Harding. I sure hope I'm not disturbing you."

"I don't have much time, Barnaby," Harding said, his voice tinged with impatience. "You said it was important, so what is it?"

"Well, Mr. Harding—" he paused for effect "—we found it."

There was silence for a beat. Then: "Are you sure it's the real thing?"

"There's no doubt about it. I've seen it with my own two eyes."

"If you're wrong, this will cause irreparable damage."

"Mr. Harding, I've been searching for this for almost thirty years. I'm not making a mistake; this is what we've been waiting for. I'm one hundred percent sure."

"Did you decipher the code?"

"No, not yet—that is, I did translate it, but I don't understand its meaning."

After a long pause, Harding said. "All right then, Barnaby, I will contact the others and begin the process." The dial tone droned in Barnaby's ear. Harding had disconnected.

Barnaby looked at his ice tea and smiled. "Hey there, sweetheart, would you please take this away and fetch me a martini?" He held his glass out to the hostess. "And don't give me none of that cheap vodka or gin; today I deserve the good stuff."

Relaxing back into his seat, Barnaby pulled his notepad from his breast pocket and flipped it open to the translation. "Who are you, Thomas K Faraday," he said slowly, "and why is your name on a twenty-five-hundred-year-old Persian stela?"

CHAPTER 2

February 2032, Montreal, Canada

Thomas Faraday had slept no more than one hour when the phone rang. On the third ring he fumbled for the handset, knocking over his clock radio. "Yeah," he said.

"He's back."

"What."

"I said he's back, Thomas."

As if the phone had never rung, Thomas dozed back to sleep with the handset still pressed against his ear.

The caller repeated his message. "Thomas, are you there? Wake up. You told me to call you as soon as he's back. Well, he's back. Thomas? Come on, man, wake up."

Thomas suppressed a yawn. "Hold on a minute." He forced himself to sit up. Rubbing the sleep from dry, itchy eyes, he drew a deep breath, then picked up the handset once more. "Michael, is that you?"

"Of course it's me. Who else would call at this hour of the morning?"

"What do you want?"

"My goodness, Thomas, I just finished telling you—he's back."

"Who's back?"

"Komodo, of course."

Now Thomas was awake. "Are you recording all his movements?"

"Yes, of course. He's been in the system for five minutes already; I'm trying to trace where he's coming from, but he's really hard to follow."

"Stay with him. I'll be there in forty minutes."

"You know I won't be here in forty minutes. I'm going home in ten."

"Who's taking your place?"

"Nobody. Mamoru is sick again so we're short staffed. I've already done

9

three double shifts this week. I spoke with Ménard after you left last night and he said we could do without a tech guy until you come in."

"Fine Michael, I'll be there as soon as I can. I'll let you know what happened. Thanks for calling."

Thomas hung up, then spent a few minutes gazing out the wall-to-wall window of his converted factory loft. He could see the makings of a blizzard outside. The streetlights lit up each fat flake as it floated by the window.

Thomas had moved to the big city a few months after the funeral for his wife, Amélie. He'd hoped the change would help him cope with his loss, that living in a new place would allow him to control his feelings. He did not want to forget her, so he displayed selected photos of Amélie as a reminder of the happy life they'd had together. Now he just wanted the pain to go away. Each night, when most people left their day behind and prepared for the adventures of dreams, the painful loss of Amélie would seize him. When it did, Thomas called upon his faithful evening companion, a bottle of fine scotch.

His eyes fell on the promotional poster his son Christian had made in high school as part of a class project to help the homeless in Montreal. He'd collected hundreds of photos of the homeless from a social media account and used the thumbnails to make a photo mosaic of a larger image: a hand holding two coins. All the proceeds from the sale of this poster went to helping the homeless. Christian had won first prize for his efforts, and Thomas felt the usual twinge of pride as he studied it now.

These reminders had limited positive effect on Thomas, so he indulged in many distractions to salve the pain of loss. When he wasn't working—defending a company called Northern Future Pharmaceuticals against computer hackers—he immersed himself in sports: hockey, baseball, and football, both American and Canadian. When there were no sports on television, he read volumes of books on the Middle East. He never understood his attraction to the subject. Perhaps it was his religious upbringing. He had memories of his mother reading to him from a Bible storybook each night before going to bed.

These distractions also claimed space in his loft. The left wall held jerseys, banners, autographed photos, and other sports memorabilia framing a two-meter LCD display, and the wall opposite housed replicas of Persian artifacts: the famous servant in the Achaemenid court, a golden lion, a replica of the Cyrus Cylinder, and a relief of Darius the Great sitting on his throne in the audience hall at Persepolis. On clear nights, Thomas would lie in bed and watch his Persian artifacts come to life as shadows created by the headlights of passing cars moved across them. The sculpture that Thomas valued the most was an Achaemenid griffin, with the body and legs of a lion and two eagle heads, one facing away from the other. Thomas wondered if this griffin protected some priceless treasure, as legend claimed, and imagined that the griffin was trying to communicate with him.

As Thomas sat staring at his artifacts, he smiled, thinking of Michael's words when he'd first visited him: "This place looks more like a museum than an apartment."

Michael was Thomas's only friend. In fact, Michael and the housekeeper were the only people who'd seen the inside of his loft.

Thomas took a deep breath and bent to pick up the clock radio and examine it. "Good, it's not broken. A small crack, that's all." He noted the time, two forty-five.

He threw on a white and blue football jersey, a pair of black denim pants, his baseball cap, and his all-purpose running shoes. He brushed his teeth but did not shave, grabbed his leather work bag, and headed to the basement garage to find his compact SUV.

At street level the snow blew much harder, traveling through the air tunnels created by the tall buildings. It gave Thomas the impression that he was moving at warp speed through a million stars. To avoid an accident he turned on his hazard lights and kept his speed to twenty kilometers an hour. Since he knew the way by heart, he had no trouble taking his mind off the road, instead concentrating on Komodo's attack.

A few months ago a hacker using the handle "Komodo" had succeeded in penetrating the LAN side of the network. What puzzled Thomas was how easily Komodo could breach the DMZ—the demilitarized zone—without leaving a trace. The DMZ was well monitored with honeypots, fake web servers designed to attract hackers and if possible trace them to their source. It also had firewalls with a minimum number of open ports to allow internet users access to the company's web page, which doubled as an email server. It blocked all access to the inside LAN network area where all the company employees had their workstations. This LAN area was where the main servers were located. It was next to impossible for anyone without the proper access codes to breach the DMZ from the internet and end up in the LAN side undetected.

As perplexing as Komodo's penetration was, Thomas was even more puzzled by his activities once he entered the network. It was clear Komodo was not interested in stealing information. The network logs proved this. Komodo would create a folder each time with files for Thomas to find. It would take

Komodo a maximum of twenty minutes to do this. Then he would erase his tracks and disappear.

Thomas was reflecting on this DMZ blueprint when he relaxed his grip on the steering wheel and stopped at a flashing red traffic light. The car behind him sounded his horn. "Sorry," he said and waved his hand apologetically as he moved forward.

When he arrived at Northern Future Pharmaceuticals, Thomas stopped in the lobby before taking the elevator to the server room. "Bonjour, Stéphane," he said to the security guard.

"Bonjour, Thomas. Coming in early again, eh?"

"No rest for the wicked, my mother always said." Thomas looked around. "Where's Natalie?"

"She should be back from her rounds any minute now."

"I bet things are much easier, now that there are two of you keeping guard," Thomas said, trying to kill time until Natalie returned.

"She's a godsend, that's for sure. While Natalie is doing her rounds, I can stay here and keep an eye out for people like you who come in at—" Stéphane looked at his watch "—ten past three in the morning."

"Salut, Thomas," Natalie said with a beautiful ear-to-ear smile as she stepped forward from behind him. "I guess you missed me so much, you just had to come in early again, didn't you."

Thomas grinned. "You know it, Natalie; can't hide anything from you."

They fell silent and exchanged awkward looks before Thomas continued. "Tell me, Natalie, did you and Stéphane have your coffee yet?"

"Ah, the true motive; it's not me you love, it's your coffee."

"If you don't mind getting one for me across the street, you know there's one in there for you." He glanced at Stéphane. "One for you too, Stéphane."

"I'll get one for you, Thomas," Natalie said. "You know I'll do anything for you."

Thomas smiled. "You're a sweetheart, Natalie. I'll take a double espresso—"

"Brown sugar," she interrupted. "And double it with hot whipped cream. I know."

"You're the best," Thomas said.

"Un double-double pour moi," Stéphane added.

As Natalie crossed the street and disappeared into the blizzard, Stéphane looked at Thomas. "She likes you, Thomas. You know that, eh?"

"No she doesn't; she's being friendly, nothing more."

Stéphane sighed. "When are you going to take a chance again, eh?"

Thomas looked at Stéphane. "Will you have it sent up to the server room when she gets back?"

Stéphane smiled, realizing it had been a dumb thing to say. "Of course I will."

To get inside the server room, Thomas had to pass through two security doors that opened with magnetic keys. Each door had its own key. He stepped through the second door into the cool atmosphere kept at a precise twenty-one degrees Celsius by the air-conditioning system to prevent the hardware from overheating.

He immediately went to his station to see if Komodo was still in the network. "Nope. Now let's see how many files you left for me this time."

Thomas opened the drive and the folder Komodo normally used and sure enough, there were three new files. He copied them onto his USB drive and then onto his laptop. He never opened the files while in the server in case they contained a virus. He always opened them in his laptop. If the files were infected, formatting his laptop was not a problem. Having to format a server, however, would be catastrophic.

He opened the files one by one. Still more encrypted text. The files themselves were not encrypted. They could be opened with a word processor. The text within the files resembled gibberish, random characters that filled the page from edge to edge. Thomas added the three files to a cloud server, where they joined the other fifty he'd collected so far. Even though he was an amateur cryptographer and would normally jump at such a challenge, he'd stopped trying to decipher them. He might find a pattern and figure out what the files meant once he thought he'd collected them all.

"Well, that's it for now." He looked at the clock. Three more hours before the phone starts to ring for forgotten passwords and lost access to network resources. *Sufficient time for me to take a short nap*, Thomas thought.

He reached for the framed photo of his wife and their son Christian that rested on his desk and kissed them both. Then he kicked off his shoes, tossed them under his desk, reclined back in his chair, and stared at the white tiled ceiling. The never-ending humming of the servers, with the occasional beep from the surge protectors, relaxed him. One thing left to do. He reached over to a desk drawer and retrieved a small flask of scotch concealed in a yellow paper envelope.

CHAPTER 3

In lecture room B at Oxford University, Queens College campus, fifty-five preselected students of theology, history, and archaeology listened to Professor Barnaby Lancaster sum up his two hour-lecture on the authenticity of the great flood.

"That is why we find similar historical accounts throughout history around the globe," Barnaby said as a slide appeared on a screen behind him. "Note the twenty-six countries where archaeologists uncovered teachings comparable to the biblical account." He gave them time to scan the chart before listing them out loud. "Australia, Babylon, Bolivia, Borneo, Burma, Canada, China, Cuba, East Africa, Egypt, Fiji, French Polynesia, Greece, Guyana, India, Iran, Italy, Malay Peninsula, Mexico, New Zealand, Peru, Russia, USA, Vanuatu, Vietnam, and Wales.

"They all describe a flood destroying the known world," Barnaby continued. "Eighteen believed it was by divine intervention, seventeen cited a warning before the flood, twenty-four mentioned animals being spared, they all recorded human survivors, and all but three listed a vessel used to spare their lives."

Barnaby turned to face his audience. "These ancient worldwide accounts confirm the Bible's authenticity. Now, are there any questions?"

As he said these words the door to the lecture room opened slightly. A woman discreetly signaled to Barnaby by tapping on her wristwatch that his time was up. Barnaby nodded. The woman retreated back into the hallway. Barnaby sensed her anxiety as she peered through the small window in the door

"I'm sorry, I thought I had more time." Barnaby gathered his manuscript into a neat stack and placed the papers in his briefcase. He took a few seconds to probe the audience.

"As I'm looking at you in front of me I am aware of those who think this is another lecture on reconciliation of the Bible with the sciences. I can tell who is as passionate on the subject as I am. I know who is open to the possibilities and of course, I also know who think I'm nothing more than a hopeless romantic."

His eyes locked on one rich kid sitting directly in front of him. "An old fart is one term that comes to mind." The young man smiled at Barnaby, knowing he'd made that derogatory remark only a few days ago.

"What if I have stashed away in a secret location a collection of genuine artifacts from each one of those historical events we've discussed in this lecture? What if I have the golden Ark of the Covenant hidden under a canvas, or King Solomon's crown? What if I show you King David's handwritten book of Psalms or one of the original letters distributed by King Ahasuerus throughout the Persian Empire giving the Jews the chance to defend themselves against hatred?" He paused for a moment. "What if I found Noah's ark? Would you then consider the legitimacy of the Bible? Could it even persuade you to consider that the God of the Bible is real and therefore has a purpose for humankind?

"Well, my prestigious future scholars, I now have in my possession the key that will allow me to uncover such artifacts. That is why I will be leaving the university for four years. During this time I will be recovering and also documenting the artifacts I mentioned, and so much more. When I return, I would like you, the most worthy students in your fields, to be the first to witness the public unveiling of a find that will change the way the world understands God. Maybe even the way the world worships."

The stunned audience remained silent. This bothered Barnaby. He needed a response. He needed to know they believed him or if they thought him mad. "Will you accept my invitation?" he asked.

The students looked at each other, trying to read the reaction of their peers. Two students sitting side by side rose and applauded. Slowly, steadily, more students rose to their feet, until all were applauding in a standing ovation.

"Please give my assistant your contact details before you leave so I will find you when I return," Barnaby called above the noise.

He maneuvered through the crowd of students now rushing to provide their contact information and left the room. As soon as the door closed behind him he peered through the small window, enjoying the enthusiasm of the students.

"Well, Professor," the woman waiting for him in the hallway said, "I'm hurt. You're keeping secrets from me. When were you going to tell me?"

"Sofia, thank you so much for giving me two hours of your lecture time," he said, still looking through the window. "It means a lot to me."

"Don't ignore me, Barnaby," she said. "Answer my question."

Barnaby said nothing, lost in thought. Realizing she was getting nowhere, she tried another approach. "Tell me, how did you get the university to fund this escapade of yours?"

Barnaby now looked at her. "They don't know anything about it. That's why I needed some of your lecture time. Otherwise, I would have reserved the room myself."

Her eyebrows shot up. "Don't tell me you're bankrolling this yourself?"

Barnaby snorted. "Of course not; I can't afford this kind of undertaking! I'm working for some powerful investors."

"Who?"

Barnaby looked around. "Come on, Sofia, let's walk."

"I can't, Barnaby. The students for my next class are wondering why I told them to wait in the corridor. I need to start my lecture right now."

Barnaby kissed her on the forehead. "Trust me, then. I'll explain everything as soon as I return."

She smiled. "Go, and be careful."

"Thank you, Sofia." Barnaby took one last glance through the window before leaving the building for a limousine waiting outside the complex.

The black limousine was in sight when a voice called out behind Barnaby, "Professor! Wait, Professor Lancaster."

Barnaby didn't need to turn around. He knew who was calling him. He could picture in his mind's eye the skinny twenty-one-year-old boy with his slicked-back hair that reminded Barnaby of a fifties biker gang member. He set Barnaby on edge, with his constant gum chewing and his inability to stand still or sit quietly even for a minute.

Barnaby stopped in his tracks, looked ahead at the black limousine, and sighed. "Bloody hell." He turned around. "What do you want, Mr. Derrek McCarthy."

Derrek stopped before Barnaby and bent over to catch his breath, both hands resting on his knees. "Professor," he gasped. "I almost missed you." He paused, gulping air. "You finished your lecture early. It's not like you. Wherever you're going, it must be important."

"What do you want, Mr. McCarthy? I'm very busy."

Derrek straightened. "I know you didn't invite me to your lecture because of my past mistakes, but since then I've matured. Surely you must have noticed?" Unconsciously, he squared his shoulders.

"Rest assured, Mr. McCarthy, I don't concern myself with your adolescent pranks," Barnaby replied. "Furthermore, those who were invited are not in your chosen field of study. They're archaeologists, historians, and theologians. You have chosen computer sciences."

Derrek took a step forward. "Professor, I would like to get straight to the point. I know what your quest is about—"

"I don't have time to waste with this nonsense," Barnaby snapped. "Good day, Mr. McCarthy." He renewed his march to the waiting limousine.

"Stop! Wait—I know about the time travel machine and the hunt for religious relics. I also know about the nuclear plant."

Barnaby continued his walk.

As he was about to open the limousine door, Derrek yelled out, "I also know about Komodo."

Barnaby turned to look at Derrek. "Why are you telling me this?"

"Because I want to be part of it. I want to come with you," He looked down to the ground. "I want to do something with my life that will make a difference. I believe this quest is what I'm looking for."

"First of all, spit out that ridiculous gum," Barnaby said.

Derrek complied.

"Who told you all these things?" asked Barnaby.

"Nobody."

"Then how did you come to those conclusions?"

"For the last few years my father has been working around the clock on different subjects—some that aren't even in his field of knowledge," Derrek replied. "He's reading about wormholes and time travel, things that are impossible. He also developed a new interest in biblical archaeology. He mapped out where potential treasures might be found, such as the Ark of the Covenant and the books of Kings—he seems primarily interested in the book of Esther."

Derrek shrugged. "I guess people get religious when they know they will soon die, but what mystified me most and got my attention was his sudden interest in nuclear technology. He seems to associate it with some ship. He's even given the ship a name: the *Kismet*. I don't understand what it has to do with nuclear technology, or ships, for that matter."

Derrek's voice softened as he continued. "You know my father is ill. He is dying of lung cancer and has only a few more years to live. Instead of resting or enjoying those few years, he concentrates all his time on research, almost like he's trying to solve a great puzzle before he dies."

"Have you read any of his research?"

"No, the results of his research are locked up in a safe, but I've seen enough material to know what he's doing. I think he's trying to create a time machine."

Barnaby crossed his arms and leaned back. "You know time travel is impossible, don't you?"

"Please, Professor, you once told me I'm wasting my life with stupid pranks around the university. I'm telling you I want to devote my efforts to whatever preoccupies my father. This way I can prove to him and myself that I can make a positive difference—"

"All you know about the project," Barnaby interrupted, "is nothing but speculation and guesswork over the research material you found in your father's study. You know nothing about what's involved."

"I know how much it means to my father. That's why I want to honor him while he's still alive. He never gave up on me. I would like him to know his efforts are not in vain. I can do this by being part of his project, no matter what it is. True, I might have guessed what it's about, but I promise I will do everything I can toward its success, no matter how long it takes or what sacrifices need to be made, and that's the truth," he asserted, the soft voice gone.

"You sound pretty sure for someone who six months ago put cayenne pepper in our football players' jockstraps."

"That has never been linked to me, Professor." Derrek smiled.

"Bloody hell, Derrek, it cost the team first place," Barnaby exclaimed, but he was unable to hold back his smile. "Anyway, I must go." He looked at his watch for the third time and turned to open the limousine door. Derrek didn't try to stop him.

Once inside the limousine, Barnaby rolled down his window. "What's this you said about Komodo?"

"Nothing, actually," Derrek replied. "My father has three new books in his library on the subject of Komodo Dragons. They were not there before so I thought I'd throw it in and see what happens. Does it have anything to do with the quest?"

"I have great respect for your father. He told me to keep an eye out for you after he's gone. Do you know what he said to me? In his deep, authoritative voice he said, 'Although he's young and immature he's quite smart and has a good heart. I think all he needs is an opportunity to feel like he's contributing to a cause greater than himself. I think he can make something good of his life, if given an opportunity.'"

Barnaby noticed Derrek's eyes glittered with unshed tears. "Because of this I will take your request into consideration. For the next three days, do not leave your house. If I decide to take you with me, I will call you there. I know the line is secure. And I'll call only once, do you understand me?"

"Professor, I will do that," Derrek assured him. "You will not regret it. You'll see—I will make both you and my father proud."

"I must be going now," Barnaby said. "I have someone to pick up in Aylesbury before I head for—" He hesitated. "Anyway, I must go."

He tapped the glass between him and the driver and the limousine drove away.

CHAPTER 4

Nicolas Knox was a short, chubby, jovial man in his mid-sixties with a fine-looking salt-and-pepper goatee and a full head of unkempt hair to match. He was not an educated man, but he was highly respected by everyone who knew him. He believed what he preached, and displayed a genuine love and empathy for the members of his small Aylesbury congregation. These qualities, along with his relentless search for accurate biblical knowledge, qualified him as an exceptional candidate for the League.

When Barnaby approached him with a lucrative offer, however, Nicolas declined. He argued that his skills were not organizational but humanitarian, and his congregation needed him.

It took most of two years for Barnaby to convince Nicolas that the League and its mission were theocratically inspired. He argued that such a League could never survive without God's blessings. He explained that its past success coupled with the recent discovery of the Persian stela was a God-given miracle.

The more Nicolas pondered Barnaby's arguments, the more influence they had. One night, while watching a documentary entitled *The Power Behind Atheism*, Nicolas wondered if the artifacts retrieved by this League could help people change their view of God. If so, maybe God wanted him to be involved after all. The next day he contacted Barnaby and said he'd changed his mind, but he needed three months to prepare his congregation for his long absence.

Barnaby was delighted to comply. In three months, he told Nicolas, they would fly to the League's secret base, a high-tech facility in North America.

Nicolas procrastinated, waiting until the last Sunday sermon before his departure to announce his plans to the congregation. "Today I have a special announcement," he told them. "Please open your Bibles to Hebrews Chapter 11, verse 1," He read the verse out loud. "'Now faith is the substance of things hoped for, the evidence of things not seen.'

"The word 'substance,'" Nicolas explained, "is taken from the Greek word 'hupostasis.' This word, hupostasis, is found in many ancient business documents. It was used to guarantee a future possession or service or property. As for the word 'faith,' well, it's taken from the Greek word 'pistis.' It impresses upon us the idea of confidence, trust, or strong persuasion. In some contexts, it also means faithfulness or fidelity.

"I know all of you here today have faith. It's evident by your weekly presence at our Bible study classes. However, we appreciate that some people sorely lack faith. Even veteran Christians sometimes display on occasion a lack of faith.

"The Bible has some examples of this. For instance, Judge Gideon was a man of faith. The Bible says he was one 'who through faith subdued kingdoms.' Despite this, when he faced the army of the Midianites and their allies, he challenged God with tests to make sure he would have success in the coming battle.

"Sometimes we too need assurances from God when facing difficult trials in our lives, but we have an advantage, we have faith in God. We have what the Bible says 'faith is the substance of things hoped for.' We understand 'the evidence of things not seen.' But what about those who do not believe in God? The atheists, for example—why are they unable to see what is so clear to us?

"Have they turned off religion because of the atrocities committed in the name of God? Or maybe they cannot accept the reasons given by God for allowing so much suffering and death. For many, the desires of the flesh are preferred over the strict laws and values of the Bible.

"I believe the main reason is a lack of accurate knowledge of God's word."

Nicolas paused to clear his throat, then continued. "I have some very good news for all here today—in fact, for all Christians around the world. I'm happy to announce that God has allowed us to stumble upon evidence that will solve this problem of faith once and for all time. Yes, archaeological evidence so strong, so irrefutable, no one will ever again be able to challenge the authenticity of God's holy Word the Bible. My brothers and sisters, what we have found will change the way the world views Christianity."

Although the congregation responded with animated applause, it quickly dwindled as they noticed an unfamiliar expression on Nicolas's face: sadness, concern, and uncertainty, all rolled up into one beautiful image. He looked like a classic Renaissance painting you admire yet never quite understand.

Nicolas wiped a tear from his eye and continued in a choked, cracking voice, taking long pauses between each sentence. "I'm so sad to say I will be leaving tonight for four years. I won't see you or even be able to communicate with you during this time. Please don't be sad for me, I will be thinking about you and praying for you every day. God, how I'm going to miss you all! But when I come back, I will be coming with all of God's glory. It will be in the form of incontestable evidence that will bring God's grandeur to the world.

"I have assigned Brother Walsh to take over for me while I'm gone," Nicolas continued. "He is, as you all know, very qualified to fill in during my absence. I know you will treat him kindly and follow his lead with the same love and devotion you give me.

"I will take with me Brother Brody Powell. His work in the congregation has assisted me greatly. Brother Powell never shirks or neglects his duties. His attention to details has turned our congregation into a profitable one. His humility and desire to serve God have led me to recommend Brother Powell for this mission." Brody, who practically worshipped Nicolas, was a young man devoted to his faith.

Nicolas smiled for a good long time. He wiped a few more tears from his eyes, then forced out, "In conclusion, let's all stand and sing a song of praise to God, after which we will invite Brother Walsh to conclude with a prayer."

He took one last look at all the faces in the congregation, burning the image into his memory. "God protect these people," he whispered to himself.

Satisfied, he stepped down from the pulpit and walked through a door behind him. He located a chair, sat down, and began a silent prayer.

A few minutes later Brody joined him, the singing voices of the congregation surging into the antechamber with him, only to be muffled again by the closing door. Brody paused, peering at Nicolas through his thick, black-rimmed glasses before moving into the room.

"That went well," he said. "You handled it like a pro."

Nicolas looked up. "Are you ready, Brody?"

"Yes. I have our bags ready. Our coats and boots are in the closet."

Brody walked to the fire escape door and opened it a crack. "The limousine is waiting," he said.

Nicolas walked a few steps toward the door, then hesitated. He turned toward the wall separating him from the congregation and stared at it as if he could see the people on the other side, singing that wonderful song. He would remember that song for the rest of his life. Whenever he heard it, he would associate it with this moment.

Reluctantly, he turned and walked through the fire escape door. Brody lifted their bags and followed.

• • • • • • • • • ● ○○○○○○○○○○

Barnaby was there to greet Nicolas when he entered the limousine. "Isn't this exciting, old friend?" he asked.

"Yes, it is," Nicolas said. "It's going to be quite the adventure. And with God's help, we will succeed."

"You're darn right we're going to succeed," Barnaby declared. "This has been in the works for a very long time."

"How do you do, Professor?" Brody said as he entered the limousine.

"I'm doing just fine, Brody, just fine."

The chauffeur slipped in behind the wheel after depositing their bags in the trunk and Barnaby tapped the window in front of him. "Off to Heathrow, driver." He pulled a cell phone from his coat pocket and dialed a number. "Hello, Carrot Top."

"Hello Barnaby, you old arsehole."

They shared a good laugh.

"Have you reached the airport already?"

"No Charles, I'm on my way there now. Nicolas and his sidekick are here with me." He looked at Brody and winked. "How's the health, Charles?"

"No change; at least the date of my death sentence is still the same."

"Don't talk like that, old friend; you're depressing me."

"Well, the doctors say it's terminal, no argument there. The debate centers on how long I have to live. The best estimate is three years. On the other end of the scale, it's ten months. It doesn't matter one way or the other, I had a good life."

"You're a great man, Charles," Barnaby said, his voice solemn. "You will always be remembered in the League."

"So to what do I owe the honor of your call, Barnaby?" Charles asked, briskly changing the subject. "There's no problem, is there?"

"There's something I need your advice on, Charles. A young man approached me this morning after my lecture. He said he wants to come with me and join the League. I'm impressed with how much information he acquired by snooping around. His facts are not all accurate but he did mention *Kismet*,

Komodo, and said he knows the mission involves some kind of religious relic hunting. I'm thinking of taking a chance with him, maybe taking him along."

"You surprise me, Barnaby. You're not one to take risks like this, especially with a stranger who has a few random facts."

"There's more, Charles," Barnaby said. "Not only did he figure these things out, but he wants to honor his father's work by continuing in his footsteps. He wants his father to be proud of him."

"Who is this lad?"

"Well Charles, it's your son."

"Derrek? I said nothing about the League or the mission to him. He must have poked around my research while I was sleeping or out of the house."

"If he's anything like you, old friend, he would eventually find out no matter how careful you are. Anyway, it doesn't matter. So what do you say, should I take him with me?"

"He has a tendency to get into trouble; you know that."

"I'm very much aware, but if I have your blessing, I will take him under my wing. I know he will live up to the McCarthy name."

"I can't ask you to take him. He's too great a responsibility."

"If you trust me with your son, I promise he will make you proud."

"All right, then," Charles said, sounding skeptical. "If you want to take him, one thing's for sure, there's no one I trust more than you. So I will let you make the final decision."

"Then it's done, I will send for him in three days. This should give you and Derrek time together before he leaves for the League."

After a long silence Charles said, "I sure wish I could be there with you, Barnaby."

"They invited you, yet you declined."

"I declined because the League is not a nursing home."

"After everything you did for them, they would consider it an honor just to have you present. It would be an inspiration for anyone, seeing the man who was there from the beginning."

"No, Barnaby, I would always feel like a burden. Well, good luck to you, old friend. I need to take my meds now, so I must be going. Keep in touch."

"I'll do that. Cheerio for now."

CHAPTER 5

Continuous beeping interrupted Thomas's snooze. He sat up, wiped his eyes, and squinted to focus on his LCD screen. He knew exactly what the beeps meant. Komodo was back.

A few selected keystrokes connected him remotely to an open source intrusion detection system. A few more commands and a packet sniffer took over his monitor with a steady stream of color-coded protocols. Most were green, some were blue, others yellow. The ones Thomas was looking for were blood red and there were lots of them.

He thought it unusual that Komodo had come back. He never penetrated the network more than once in any given day. This means something new was happening. He opened his desk drawer and retrieved a pad to write down his observations.

Thomas went to work. Every few minutes he took a snapshot of the data to analyze the results. Each time he came across important information and he would note it on his pad, hoping to detect a pattern that would lead to Komodo's IP address.

It bothered him that Komodo bypassed all the routers to get inside the network. That meant a Trojan had been downloaded and installed on one of the user's workstation. He would have to check all of them one by one until he finds the one that had been compromised. It would make finding the Trojan easier if he could find the source IP.

He took more snapshots and recorded more data on his notepad. He needed more, much more. He glanced at the clock; fifteen minutes had passed. *He'll be gone soon,* Thomas thought. He knew all too well Komodo's method of operation. He would leave his calling card, more encrypted files, then he'd erase his tracks from the logs.

Thomas looked for the folder Komodo usually created but found nothing. Five more minutes breezed by, then ten. He studied his notes to see if any pattern materialized. Still nothing. More snapshots, more analyzing, more notes.

And then Thomas noticed an IP address that shouldn't be there. He grabbed a binder from a nearby shelf and opened it to the IP mapping list of the network. "You bastard," he said. "You're attacking from inside the server room." He wrote down the IP address, studied what he wrote and noticed a pattern emerging.

He looked at the clock for the tenth time: thirty-five minutes. "I don't know what you're doing," he said to the screen, "but you're going to regret staying in longer than your usual twenty minutes, my friend."

Another eight minutes passed, then Thomas jumped up from his chair. "Gotcha." He grabbed the binder and flipped through the pages until he arrived at the source IP address.

When he found what he was looking for he straightened and remained motionless for a few seconds. "What?" Thomas's lips moved soundlessly. He double-checked to make sure. "No, no, no," he said, his voice rising with each word. He slowly turned his head toward an office door. "I can't believe it. Komodo is using Jean François's workstation?" Jean François Ménard was Northern Future Pharmaceutical's chief security officer.

Thomas now understood what was happening. Komodo was executing his final attack. *It's brilliant,* he thought. *Lull us with your routine intrusions, distract us with those meaningless files and meanwhile, pave a path to total control of all our servers. Then you can do whatever you want.*

Thomas now had a difficult decision to make. He debated shutting down the entire system. He understood that shutting down the servers had financial ramifications. He could never justify it—nor would he be forgiven for doing so.

Not sure what to do, he reached for the phone to call his supervisor but hesitated. It would take too much time to explain the situation before a decision could be reached. Meanwhile, Komodo could cause serious damage. He reached for a red binder titled *Emergency Procedures.* As he opened the binder, he noticed something from the corner of his eye. Under the chief security officer's door, a shadow moved.

Wondering if his eyes were playing tricks on him, he stared at the gap under the door for a good twenty seconds. He shook his head and was about to return his attention to the binder when the shadow moved across the opening again, this time in the opposite direction. Thomas stopped breathing.

He could handle electronic thieves, but real live physical thieves, that was a different matter.

He reached for his cell phone as he retreated slowly to the opposite end of the room. Slipping behind a row of server racks and content that he was well hidden, he selected a contact in his cell phone. "Stéphane," he whispered. "Can you hear me?"

"Yes, Thomas, I can hear you. What's up?"

"Is Natalie with you?"

"No. What's wrong?"

"There's someone here, an intruder in Jean François's office."

"That's not possible. The only person who entered the server room is you."

"I'm telling you there's someone in his office. I saw a shadow go back and forth under his door." That met silence for several seconds. "Stéphane, you need to do something," Thomas insisted. "Call the authorities or come up with Natalie. Maybe the three of us can confront him."

"Natalie is already heading up with your coffee. I'll radio her to stop and wait for me. I also need to call my supervisor. Then I'm coming straight up. You won't do anything until we arrive, eh?"

"Don't worry. I'm staying right here behind the servers." Now he felt like a coward.

Thomas hung up, put his cell in vibration mode, peeked through an opening big enough that he could see the clock, then rested against the wall and waited. He tried to figure out how this could have happened. *He must have been there before I arrived.* Perhaps he couldn't leave with Thomas in the server room so he tried to distract him by attacking the system again. *But why would he take such a huge risk by coming in person?* Suddenly a chill went through Thomas's body. *What if he's armed?*

Twenty minutes later the door to the server room opened. Stéphane entered with two police officers. Thomas emerged from behind the servers. Startled by his sudden appearance, the two officers pulled out their Glock 22s and aimed them at Thomas.

"It's okay," Stéphane whispered, putting out his hand. "It's Thomas."

Thomas pointed to the door where he'd seen the shadow. The police officers nodded acknowledgment and held up their hands, signaling him to stop. Thomas stepped back.

The officers positioned themselves on either side of Jean François's office door. One of them knocked hard on it, three times. "This is La Sûreté du

Québec. Open the door and come out with your hands in front of you where we can see them."

"La police?" a voice said from behind the door. "I don't know what's going on, but don't panic, I'm coming out. I'm doing as you say."

Seconds later the door opened slowly, and out came the intruder with his hands in the air.

"Mr. Ménard?" Stéphane said. "What are you doing here?"

"I'm working."

"But you're never here this early in the morning."

"So you called the police?"

Thomas stepped in. "I was working here at my desk when I followed Komodo to your workstation." He paused to gather his thoughts. "As I was monitoring his activities I discovered he was using your workstation to access the servers. That's when I saw a shadow move at the bottom of your office door. So I concluded he was here in person." He paused again. "So I called security."

One of the police officers turned to Stéphane. "You know this man?"

"Yes," responded Stéphane, looking embarrassed. "He's the chief security officer of the company."

"So everything's okay then," the officer said.

"Yes," Stéphane replied.

The officers lowered their guns. "Well then," said one officer, "we'd best be on our way."

"I'll see you out," Stéphane said. He looked at Thomas and shrugged.

Embarrassed at what had happened, Thomas apologized to Jean François. "I thought Komodo was in your office."

"You did the right thing, Thomas. The last thing we want is someone getting hurt." Jean François scratched the back of his neck. "So why do you think Komodo was hacking through my computer?"

"I don't know why. But I will show you my notes; they're pretty clear. You'll see how Komodo took over your workstation and penetrated the network. Come and see for yourself."

"No need for that, I trust you." He looked straight at Thomas. "Well, no harm done. Why don't we get back to work and forget about the whole thing?"

"Actually, we're not quite done yet," Thomas said. "We need to take out the hard drive and have it analyzed by forensics. We must gather as much information as possible on Komodo if we ever hope to catch him."

"I know the procedure, Thomas, but if we do this I won't have my computer for at least two days. Besides, I've not saved my latest work on the network. Can't we do this some other way?"

"You're the one who wrote the rules and procedures and since you had them approved by the board of directors, well, unfortunately, I'm under obligation to follow them."

Jean François held up his hands in resignation. "Okay, okay. Let's do it now so I can get my computer back as soon as possible."

Thomas called the security desk. "Stéphane, it's me again. I need you to come and sign as a witness for the hard drive we'll be sending to forensics."

"No problem, I'll send Natalie up."

After he hung up, Jean François was still staring at him. "I'm really sorry about all this," Thomas said. "It's just that we've been trying to catch Komodo for months now and when I saw the shadow under your door, well, I thought we caught him in action. He could have caused a lot of damage that would have taken months to repair, not to mention hundreds of thousands of dollars."

"Don't worry about it," Jean François said as he turned and retreated back into his office. He closed the door behind him.

Thomas checked on Komodo. Not surprisingly, he was gone. Only one file was dropped this time.

"Bonjour, Thomas," Natalie said as she opened the door. "You need papers signed?"

"Yes, Natalie. Come in. We need to get Jean François's hard drive first."

Jean François was on his cell phone as they walked into his office unannounced. "I have to go now," he said, looking as if he had just been caught cheating on his wife.

They removed the hard drive from the hot-swap port and put it in a security box, and Thomas sealed it with a plastic security seal. "Give me a moment to write down the date, time, and all our names on this sticker. After we sign I'll call forensics."

"No need to call," Jean François said as he looked at his wristwatch. "It's almost six thirty; the labs have been open for twenty-five minutes. Since I need to order another computer I might as well bring the box with me. I'll have them call you as soon as they get it."

Natalie nodded and she and Jean François left the room together. Thomas returned to his desk, where he spent the next hour and a half thinking about what had just happened. To make sense of it all, he examined his notes. The more he analyzed them, the more he felt something was wrong. He had an empty feeling about the way things had developed.

He jumped when a voice called from the entrance to the server room, "Hi there, Thomas."

He whirled in his chair, exclaiming, "God damn it, Michael, you scared the living bits out of me!"

Michael chuckled. "Good to see you still have a sense of humor."

Thomas relaxed back in his chair. "What brings you here, Michael?"

"I heard about what happened this morning so I thought I'd drop by to see how you're doing."

"Better than you," Thomas said, giving his best friend the once-over. "You look like crap." He smirked.

Michael waved that away. "Just tired. Anyway, I'm told you caught Komodo."

Thomas sighed and shook his head. "I don't think so. I might have scared him off, but caught? No, not yet."

Thomas knew Michael was not here to see how he was doing. Michael would have called first, and only if necessary would he come to see Thomas. But he played along.

"Come look at these notes I took," he said, turning back to his desk to retrieve his notepad. "I believe there's something shady going on here. I reexamined them and compared them to the data captured by the sniffer. That's when I found something disturbing. I think the attacks weren't coming *through* Jean François's workstation, but *from* Jean François's workstation." He turned to face Michael. "If I didn't know him better, I would have concluded he's Komodo."

Thomas stopped talking when he saw the expression on Michael's face. Thomas had seen it before. It was Michael who'd had the unpleasant task of bringing the news of his wife's death. The same look was on his face now.

"You didn't come here to see how I'm doing," Thomas said, his voice level. "Am I right, Michael?"

Michael's eyebrows rose. "What do you mean? Of course I did."

"Who told you about this morning's events, was it Jean François? It wasn't me, so why are you here?"

Michael's expression shifted to resignation and his shoulders sagged. He shook his head and pulled up a chair. He sat down and leaned toward Thomas then hesitated, looking away and compressing his lips, as if he had to force his next words out. Finally he looked at Thomas. "About an hour ago, I got a phone call from the forensic team working on this morning's events. They asked me to come in and replace you. I thought you were sick, so I asked what was wrong. They mentioned Komodo and your incident with the police and Ménard. That's when they said security will be coming to take your computer away."

Thomas saw Michael's Adam's apple bob as he swallowed. "Thomas, they said the hack didn't come through or from Ménard's computer as you claim." He looked Thomas in the eye. "They came from yours."

Thomas turned around to look at his monitor as if he could see evidence confirming what Michael had just said. He turned back to Michael. "Certainly you don't believe that. My workstation is the most secure in the entire building."

"I know, Thomas, but the forensic guys came to this conclusion and they want me to take over until they complete their investigation. They wanted to send Stéphane and Natalie, but I told them considering the work you put into this hacker, along with the events of this morning, it would be better to let me tell you than having security come as if you were some kind of criminal or something. So I asked if I could come and get the computer from you myself."

"What am I to do without my workstation?" Thomas said, dismayed. "I have all my tools installed in it. It will take at least a day before I can prepare another one, not to mention another two days to tweak all the software."

"You won't need another computer, Thomas," Michael said gently. He paused to compose himself. "They're sending you home."

Thomas gaped at him. "You mean they're firing me?"

"No, man, not fired," Michael replied. "They're giving you an indefinite leave of absence—with pay, of course—just until the committee can figure things out. Once they're finished you'll be back at your post. Think of it as a well-deserved vacation. How long has it been since you had a vacation, anyway—four, five years now? This will be good for you."

Anger made Thomas's face heat. "That's bullshit, Michael. Komodo attacked from Jean François's workstation and I can prove it. It's all here in my notes. And if they don't trust me, let them examine the intrusion detection system; it's all there."

"I'm sure they'll do all that, Thomas, it's just that they need to do it without you here. It's all a bunch of legal stuff, so don't take it personal, man. I'm sure they'll sort it all out and in no time you'll be back at work."

Thomas dropped his face into his hands. After a long moment of reflection, he looked up at Michael. "What am I going to do without work? You remember what happened after Amélie passed. I don't want to go back there. It's a very dark place."

"Just don't isolate yourself like you did back then. Besides, you have all the Komodo files to decipher. That will keep you busy till you get back to work."

"Yeah, I guess so." Thomas took a deep breath. "So this is it, then. I'm to give up my workstation and go home."

"They also need your passwords."

Thomas looked at Michael, eyes wide. "Why do they need my passwords?"

"I don't know Thomas, they just do."

"At least let me change them. You know I use a special algorithm."

"Sorry, man, I can't allow you to do that."

Michael reached into his pocket. A moment later he pointed to the floor next to Thomas's chair and bent, then straightened with a crumpled piece of paper in his hand. "You dropped this." He opened it. "It looks like a grocery list." He handed the paper to Thomas.

Thomas read: *The forensic team is recording everything we say through the monitoring camera system. Upload to your cloud the Komodo files and anything else you need. Do not forget to change your passwords.*

"It's not groceries," Thomas said, meeting Michael's eyes. "I'm working on a new word list for future passwords. I thought of using names of vegetables to start with. Then I would convert them into unique passwords." He crushed the paper into a ball and stuffed it in his pocket. "Guess this won't be good anymore since you won't let me change my passwords. Just let me retrieve my personal photos, then you can take the workstation."

"I'm not supposed to let you do anything." Michael paused for effect. "Okay, you have five minutes. I hope this won't get me into trouble."

Two minutes later Thomas got up and lifted his arms in the air. "Do you want to frisk me before I go?" he said for the benefit of the cameras.

"Come on, man, give me a break."

Thomas picked up his leather work bag and walked toward the door. "I'll see you later," he said without looking back.

"Wait!" Michael shouted. "Let me walk you to your car."

Thomas glanced back. "That won't be necessary."

"No, Thomas, I insist." He touched his magnetic ID card.

Thomas caught on. Changing his password nullified the old password on the door's magnetic smart card reader.

"Actually, Michael, I would appreciate it. He swept a hand toward the door. "Shall we go?"

CHAPTER 6

Two months later

"Thank you for coming, Mr. Griffin," the short, plump superintendent said as Michael walked into the lobby. "I'm very worried about Mr. Faraday."

"Don't mention it, Jocelyn. How long has it been since he last left his apartment?"

"Well . . ." She considered the question. "Every Wednesday he brings me six almond croissants from the Atwater market. It's been two Wednesdays since he came to see me. I guess that's about right." She pondered some more. "It's at least ten days."

"That is a long time. Do you have your keys?" She dangled her large ring of keys in front of him. "Good; let's see what's going on." Michael led the way to the elevator.

"Do you know when I started to worry?" Jocelyn said as they entered the elevator. "It was when the neighbors complained about a foul odor coming from Mr. Faraday's loft."

Michael looked at her sharply. "What kind of odor?"

"Well, I investigated, of course, but I didn't enter his loft. I would never go in without permission."

"No, of course not."

"Well, as I said, I investigated. I dropped to all fours, sniffed at the bottom of his door, and sure enough, there was an odor. It smelled like a football team's locker room right after a big game."

"That's quite specific," Michael said as they left the elevator.

"You see, Mr. Griffin? Am I right about the odor?"

Michael ignored Jocelyn and knocked on the door. "Thomas," he called. They waited a few seconds. "Thomas, its Michael. Is everything all right?"

Michael knocked hard three more times. "Thomas, please open the door. I need to speak with you. It's important, man."

One of the neighbors opened her door to see what was going on. Michael glanced her way and said, "Okay, Jocelyn, you can open the door now."

Jocelyn unlocked the door and stepped back. Michael slowly opened it and gasped at the odor that spewed into the hallway like a flood.

"Oh my," Jocelyn said, her hand flying to cover her nose and mouth.

Michael turned to her. "Go back to your apartment. I'll call you if I need you."

Jocelyn hurried to the elevator, her hand still covering her mouth. Michael waited until Jocelyn was gone before entering the loft. He closed the door behind him.

He saw Thomas sitting motionless on one of his two recliners, his feet kicked up, staring at the large LCD screen. Michael held his breath till Thomas raised a filthy glass of scotch and took a sip.

Good, he's alive. Michael breathed again.

The furniture had been moved against the walls to make room for sheets of paper that carpeted the floor; Michael peered down at one as he moved toward the recliner where Thomas sat—hardcopies of code. *The Komodo files.* In one corner of the room, empty pizza boxes had been stacked knee high. Dozens of empty scotch bottles lay beside the pizza boxes. Michael also noticed one unopened cardboard box of scotch.

He walked around the recliner to face Thomas. "Watching a soccer game, I see."

Thomas did not respond. Not wanting to rush things, Michael went to the kitchen, washed himself a glass, came back, and sat down on the second recliner, next to Thomas. He poured himself some scotch. A good half-hour passed before Michael took a sip.

"I thought you didn't drink," Thomas said.

"I don't."

"Then why are you wasting my scotch?"

"You seem to like it so much I thought maybe I'd try it. Perhaps I'm missing out on something."

"Put the damn glass down and go make yourself a coffee. I have some in the cupboard somewhere, I think."

Michael set the glass down but declined the coffee. "I missed you, Thomas. I haven't seen or heard from you in almost a month." After a long pause, Michael continued. "Did you fire your cleaning lady? Because this place smells like a cesspit."

"What do you want, Michael?"

"I want you to get off your ass and get on with your life. You don't call anyone. You don't answer your phone. You lock out those who care about you. No one knows if you're dead or alive."

Thomas showed no emotion. He kept staring at the soccer game.

"Did you look at yourself in the mirror lately?" Michael pressed. "By the look of things, you're always drunk and the food you're eating will give you a heart attack."

Thomas cast a glare in Michael's direction. "Do you know what month this is?"

"Yes, I know what month it is."

"It's been four years already. I still can't get over her. They took away my only real distraction when they sent me home from Northern F.P." Thomas took another sip of scotch. "Look at those files on the floor. They actually think I sent those to myself. I guess it doesn't help that Komodo never returned after that momentous day, either. But saying I'm Komodo, now that's not right. Tell me, Michael, why in God's name would I do something like that? What would be the purpose of it all?"

"I don't know, Thomas."

"No Michael, the deck's stacked against me. I'm going to send them a letter of resignation before they fire me." Thomas slumped back into his recliner. He stared at nothing with moist eyes. "Tell me, Michael—you're always trying to convince me of how great and just God is, so tell me—will I see Amélie when I die? Let's say I died tonight. Would I be reunited with her?"

"I don't like the way you're talking, man."

Thomas snickered. "I'm not going to kill myself, if that's what you mean."

"Why all the questions, then?"

"Because if I'll see Amélie again I would still have something to live for. I would try to make her happy, just in case she's watching me, just in case she's waiting for me."

"I can't answer your question, Thomas—how am I supposed to know what's in the next life? I'll tell you what I do know. I know the Bible promises we will have perfect happiness in paradise."

"Well, that settles it. Perfect happiness is waiting for me with Amélie." Thomas took another long swallow of scotch. "So you've encouraged me. You can be on your way now. Thanks for dropping by."

"Not so fast, Thomas," Michael said, not hiding his annoyance. "I do have a couple things to straighten out with you first."

"Why am I not surprised?" Thomas sneered.

Michael repositioned his recliner to face Thomas. "I know Amélie meant everything to you. I also cared for her." He reached out and touched Thomas's hand. "Are you listening to me? This is important, you know."

"Yeah, yeah, I'm listening."

"You better be listening. Now think on this for a minute. If you had passed away instead of Amélie, what would you have wanted for her?"

Thomas shrugged.

"Imagine you're looking down at her right now and she's drunk as a pig and full of self-pity. Is this the Amélie you know? What would you tell her if you could?" Michael paused. Thomas hunched his shoulders. "Would you want her to waste all her time chasing some mystery hacker and hiding in her apartment, isolating herself from everyone? Would you hope Amélie killed herself so you could both be reunited in death?"

Thomas's shoulders shook. He broke down and sobbed.

"That's right, Thomas, let it all out," Michael said, "let it all out."

Michael knew Thomas better than anyone else, with the possible exception of Amélie. He knew Thomas was a born leader, with the natural talent to inspire those around him. Normally he made friends easily. Seeing Thomas like this was difficult for him. Michael had pulled Thomas out of trouble before, but this time it was different. This was a matter of the heart. Michael had never had a relationship long enough to understand what Thomas was going through, so it took him a while to develop a strategy to help Thomas.

Now Michael was here to persuade him to follow a plan he believed would rescue his friend. For it to work, however, it had to appear spontaneous. He had to wait for the right opportunity. He did not need to wait long.

Thomas turned to Michael. "I don't know what to do, Michael. I have no strength left."

"Do you trust me, Thomas?"

"You know I do."

"Good. Now this is what I'm going to do," Michael told him. "I'll prepare everything for you. All you'll have to do is follow the itinerary I will give you." Michael stood up and paced the floor. "You're going on a vacation and I just happen to know the perfect place."

"Vacation?"

Michael stopped and turned to his friend. "Yes, Thomas, that's right: a long vacation where you can rest, somewhere far from the city. You like scuba diving, don't you." Thomas nodded. "Well, I'm sending you diving."

Thomas looked puzzled. "The only time I go diving is with Christian."

"I know that, but your son is somewhere in Asia trying to find himself, and we can't afford to wait for him to call. We don't have the foggiest idea where he is; Asia is a big place. You'll have to do this without him."

Thomas's shoulders slumped. "I wish he'd call. It's been three years since he left. I should never have given him that stupid ultimatum. So he found a new faith. I should have respected his right to choose instead of kicking him out of the house."

"I know, Thomas, but don't worry about him for now," Michael urged. "He just turned twenty-one; he can take care of himself. Besides, if he calls I'll contact you wherever you are to let you know, I promise."

Thomas frowned. "I don't know, Michael. I fail to see how this will help."

"Just trust me, Thomas."

"I need to think about this," Thomas said. "It all sounds kind of stupid."

"Hey, man, that's good enough for me." Michael looked around the loft. "Where did you hide your phone and what's your cleaning lady's phone number? If we're going to disinfect this apartment of yours, we're going to need reinforcements."

"It's a loft, Michael, not an apartment."

CHAPTER 7

Rain mixed with splashed mud made visibility difficult for Thomas. It did not help that he'd run out of windshield washer fluid five kilometers back. This, combined with the darkness of a country road, meant he struggled to stay awake. To maintain alertness, Thomas cracked the windows open a few centimeters to create a cold breeze. He'd also cranked up the sport anthems playing on the CD player.

Nine kilometers back he'd passed the village of Chisasibi. A member of the Grand Council of the Crees of Québec resides there. The Cree Regional Authority played a major role in managing parts of Baie-James. Thomas almost stopped to spend the night in Chisasibi but reasoned the hotel Michael reserved for him was less than three kilometers down the Route de la Baie James. Since he'd already covered fourteen hundred kilometers from Montreal in sixteen hours, another three kilometers was nothing.

"Nunavik," Thomas grumbled. "This is going to be my new swear word: Nunavik. The sip of scotch Michael took at my loft must have caused him brain damage. Who on God's good earth goes to Nunavik for a vacation? What does it even mean, Nunavik?"

Just then, as if he were in a horror movie, bright orange letters materialized in the dark up ahead:

WELCOME
HOTEL 993
Your last stop in La Belle Province, Québec

He pulled into the lot and parked his compact SUV in the reception area. Besides one new pickup truck, his was the lone vehicle. When he reached the shelter protecting the main entrance from the rain, he stopped to look around.

There were no lights in any of the windows. He thought this unusual, even at this late hour. He hoped the hotel wasn't closed.

The front door opened, much to his relief. Before he could say anything, a short, thin man behind the reception desk greeted him: "Bonjour monsieur, comment puis-je vous aider?"

Thomas answered in his broken French, "Bonjour, j'ai une réservation."

It was obvious French was not Thomas's native language, so the man answered in English, "Welcome to Hotel 993. I am expecting you." The man spoke with a strong accent that wasn't French; maybe Inuit? No, he looked more European than native.

"Did you say you were expecting me?"

"Yes, of course. You are Mr. Faraday, correct? If you'll just sign here, I'll help with your luggage."

"How do you know my name?" Thomas asked as he signed.

The man smiled. "That one is easy, Mr. Faraday—you're our only guest at this time. You might have noticed some parts of the hotel are still under construction. We opened to the public three days ago. You know, Mr. Faraday, not too many people pass this way."

"Then why build such a large hotel?"

"I don't know, Mr. Faraday; I only work here."

"I have but this one suitcase," Thomas said. "All I need is the key, the room number, and I will be on my way."

The thin man reached into his pocket and extracted a key ring with a fob in the shape of a Persian sphinx, fashioned in lead and colored glass. Selecting one of the keys, he opened a small box to retrieve a key card.

The Persian ornament caught Thomas's attention. "May I see your keychain?" The man handed him the keys without hesitation. "The details are remarkable." Thomas looked up at the man. "Where did you get this?"

"We have a flea market near town. There is a merchant who specializes in ancient Persian art replicas. I bought this from him last summer," the man replied as Thomas handed the key ring back, wondering why a Middle Eastern artisan would set up shop so far out of the way. "He has all kinds of replicas," the thin man continued. "Some small like this one, and others as large as a refrigerator. People place orders from all over the world. You should stop by tomorrow. If you like Persian artifacts, you can't afford to miss his stall. It's quite unique."

"I bet it is, but unfortunately I must leave early tomorrow morning."

"May I ask what your final destination is?"

"I'm going scuba diving at Puvirnituq. But first I'll do some fishing in Whoopmogoosty . . . Whoepmamagoosty . . . Whoopamagoosty? Sorry, I can't pronounce it," Thomas admitted with a sheepish grin.

"Whapmagoostui. It's a popular fishing and hunting destination."

"Yes, that's it. Sorry about the pronunciation."

"So you're going back to Chisasibi to take the plane, I presume?"

"That's right, I'm flying to Kujarpik—"

"Kuujjaarapik," the man supplied for him. "I know the airport. You're heading to Whapmagoostui from there?"

"That sounds about right."

"You know the plane leaves every day; if you're not in a hurry you should check out the flea market. You could take the plane the following day."

"Thanks, but I'm following a friend's itinerary and he has me on a plane tomorrow morning," Thomas said.

"That's too bad. Have a good night, Mr. Faraday. If you need anything, call the front desk. I'm here all night."

"Thank you. Oh—by the way, you know my name, but I don't know yours."

The thin man seemed surprised at the question. "My name? Yes, well, my name is Derrek, Derrek McCarthy."

Thomas accepted the key card and took the elevator up to the third floor. A new construction smell permeated the air of the room he stepped into. Dropping his bag on the chair beside the door, he turned on the television and was surprised to see that they had cable. After scanning for the sport channels, he looked at the double bed with its clean sheets and decided he wouldn't need to worry about bedbugs; he suspected he was the first occupant of this room. Next to the bed was a table that could be used for a laptop, but Michael had made him swear to leave his at home. Thomas shrugged; all he wanted was a hot shower and some much-needed sleep.

The bathroom had the usual complimentary soap, shampoo, and towels. He wondered if all the rooms were ready like this one, or if someone had made this room up just for him. He turned on the hot water, disrobed, and took his shower.

Refreshed, he lay on the bed to watch the sports updates and reached for the phone to request a wake-up call. He noticed the time—one forty-five in the morning. Frustrated, Thomas decided if Michael wanted him to relax, he should not have planned a sixteen-hour car trip and then forced him to take a plane early the next morning. *An extra day to wind down does not sound like such a bad idea*, he thought.

"Front desk."

"Hi Derrek, it's Thomas in room three hundred—of course it's me, I'm the only guest, who else can it be?" he said, feeling momentarily foolish. "Anyway, I thought it over and I've decided to take your advice. I will stay one more night after all."

Feeling as if he could finally relax, Thomas retrieved a large envelope from his bag and spread its contents on the bed. Returning to his bag, he pulled out a bottle of fine scotch. "Sorry, Michael, but this promise I can't keep." He unwrapped one of the glasses on the TV credenza and half-filled it from the bottle. After swallowing the scotch in one gulp, he took his time on a second, turning back to the papers on the bed. "Now, what are you trying to tell me, Komodo?"

CHAPTER 8

Thomas found the small flea market deserted of customers. The stalls that were set up offered new merchandise. He thought it unusual that no antiques or secondhand items were offered, as they were in the markets back home. Somehow it looked artificial, like a stage set for a movie.

He didn't walk far before coming across the stall with the Persian artifacts. Derrek had not been exaggerating when he said the merchant had a large and attractive collection. The stall was organized in a U shape with the large items in the middle. On two sides were tables full of smaller articles similar to Derrek's keychain. He could hear a spat between two men coming from a parked moving truck outside the belly of the U. It sounded like two adolescents arguing over a damaged toy.

"You wanker, you dropped it."

"Why don't you help instead of ordering me around?"

"Bloody hell, you know I can't lift heavy things. I have a bloody bad back."

"In that case I'm leaving it right here. I'll send for the dolly you forgot."

"I forgot? You old plonker, you're the one who was supposed to bring it."

Thomas listened to the childish back and forth as he inspected the merchandise. After a few more insults, a short man in his fifties came out to greet Thomas.

"Don't mind us, we're just pissing around." The merchant rubbed his hands together. "Well then, welcome to the Achaemenid Empire, my lad. What can I interest you in?"

"Actually, I did notice you have a few wall tablets from Persepolis," Thomas said. "How much do you want for them?"

"It depends on the size and how many you're interested in purchasing."

"I only want one. As for the size," Thomas looked at them again, "I like that one over there. It's a Persepolis bull head, isn't it?"

"Yes, it is. You seem to know your Persian history. Are you a historian?"

"Oh no, nothing like that; I'm just a fan of the time period, that's all. I did take an underwater archaeology course, but never practiced it."

"So you love archaeology, scuba diving, and ancient history," the merchant said. "You sure came to the right place."

Thomas smiled. "It would seem that way."

"Well, since you're my first customer today, I'll let it go for . . . let's see now." He pretended to think things over. "Three hundred. That's a real steal."

Thomas noticed the other merchant standing near the truck. He was waving his hands, signaling Thomas to go down on the price. Thomas pretended not to notice. "Three hundred dollars sounds fair; I'll take it. Do you have something I can use to bring it to my car? It looks quite heavy."

"No, I don't; my twit of a partner forgot to bring the dolly. But don't worry, I'll get some help and bring it to your car with you."

"I couldn't help overhearing your small disagreement back there," Thomas observed.

"Oh, that was nothing," the merchant said, waving his hand. "Nicolas and I are at each other like this all the time; it means nothing. We go back a long way." The merchant turned around and in a loud voice called, "Nicolas, get your skiver over here." He turned back to Thomas. "I'll place it out of view in case someone else sees it. This way it won't get accidentally sold to someone else. It can get pretty hectic around here sometimes."

Thomas looked around. There wasn't a customer in sight.

With the help of Nicolas, the merchant moved the Persepolis bull head, exposing another smaller tablet hidden behind it. "What's that?" Thomas asked. "I've never seen a Komodo dragon in Persian art before."

"Now how do you suppose this got here?" The merchant picked up the smaller, unfinished tablet. "This one is not for sale. It's not even a real representation of Persia. My nephew wanted to try out sculpting. He's actually not that bad. He's lazy in his research, though. It's surprising you detected it's a Komodo dragon. Don't tell me you're also a zoologist."

"No, not at all," Thomas replied. "I had an encounter with one this year—not a real one, of course," he added. "Just someone using the name. Never mind, it's complicated."

The merchant turned to Thomas. "Who did you say told you about this stall again?"

"Derrek, the clerk at the hotel."

"Will you be staying long?"

Thomas shook his head. "Just tonight; I'll be on my way tomorrow morning."

"Well, this makes it easy. Give me a deposit on the tablet and I'll personally deliver it to your hotel room. All I need is your name and room number."

"My name is Thomas Faraday and I'm in room number three hundred. Will one hundred do for a deposit?"

"Perfect. Tell the clerk Barnaby will be making a delivery tonight," the merchant said as he accepted Thomas's deposit. "Is eightish okay?"

"Sounds good, I'll see you then."

••••••••••●○○○○○○○○○○○

When Thomas was out of hearing range, Barnaby turned to Nicolas. "Did you get his name?"

"Good lord, I sure did. I guess Derrek forgot to warn us again. Do you think he might be the one?"

"I can't say. We've talked to so many with the same name."

"You want to know what I think?" Nicolas said. "He appears to have some knowledge of ancient Persia. He encountered someone or something by the name of Komodo. He comes to us at the edge of Hudson Bay three days before the training is about to start—"

"It does seem we're witnessing the fulfillment of the stela," Barnaby interrupted.

"It's God's will. It has to be."

"Don't get too excited, Nicolas," Barnaby warned. "We've been disappointed before."

"No Barnaby, you'll see, it's him. I can feel it this time."

"In that case, go to the hotel and contact the League. Let them know we might have the right man."

"Should we start to dismantle the stall? I'm tired of this mind-numbing assignment."

"No, not yet, just in case he comes back. We need to continue exactly as planned. Now move, Nicolas—go call the League."

••••••••••●○○○○○○○○○○

The phone rang, waking Thomas. He reached over and lifted the phone. "There's a Barnaby Lancaster and a Nicolas Knox here to see you, Mr. Faraday. Should I send them up?"

"Yes, Derrek, send them up please." Thomas hung up the phone and hurried to put away the Komodo papers lying haphazardly on either side of him. He looked at his watch: eight o'clock. He couldn't remember when last he'd slept so much.

As he put the envelope in a drawer, the two men knocked on his door. He pushed the drawer shut and crossed to open the door. "Come on in, guys."

"Thank you," replied Barnaby. He dragged behind him a wooden crate resting on a dolly. "Can I put it next to the bed?"

"Yes, that's good," Thomas said as he prepared the balance of the money he owed. He glanced at the crate and hesitated. "I think you brought me the wrong product. This box is too narrow for the tablet I chose."

The two men looked at each other. "That's correct, Thomas. I can call you Thomas, right?" Barnaby asked.

"Yes, of course."

"Please Thomas, sit down. What I am about to show you will most certainly amaze you." Barnaby turned and gestured for the other man to help with the crate. Nicolas produced a crowbar and opened the lid. Together they lifted out a linen-swathed slab and carefully set it on the bed.

"Get ready to be amazed," Barnaby repeated. He removed the protective cloth, exposing an ancient Persian basalt stela. He turned back to Thomas. "Before we examine it, I need to tell you a little about its history. This stela was discovered in a cave in the Zagros Mountains. We knew of its existence but didn't know exactly where to find it. For some two and a half thousand years a story has been told and passed down generation to generation to a privileged few. There's no written record of this story because its content is too unbelievable. However, very wealthy and influential members of a secret league donated large sums of money to find this stela and decipher its text. The list of scientist who worked on this stela alone runs something like this: bibliotists, cryptologists, lexicologists, semasiologists, semiologists—"

"Okay, okay, I get the picture," Thomas said impatiently. "A lot of important people studied this tablet. I get it."

"Yes, of course, you're right. I tend to get carried away sometimes. Sorry about that," Barnaby said. "For now, what's important is the message of the story. As I mentioned already, a stela has been carved. Its author prophesied that the one who deciphers its message could guarantee the success of a very special mission. So much rests on finding this person, the mission is on hold until we discover him."

"Why are you telling me this?" Thomas asked.

"Well," continued Barnaby, "the answer to your question is right here." He pointed at the stela lying face up on the bed. "Tell me what you see."

"This is the replica you're trying to sell me?"

"No, Thomas, you got me all wrong. This isn't for sale. It's the authentic Persian stela."

Thomas looked Barnaby in the eyes for a good five seconds. "I must have misled you earlier," he said. "I'm no epigrapher. Besides, if all those other scientists you mentioned failed, I can't see how I can be of any help."

"Please, Thomas, take a good look at it for me. You'll understand why I'm showing it to you."

Thomas reluctantly looked at the stela, making sure the two noticed his lack of interest. "It looks like a landscape with the horizon crossing through the middle. The top half must be water, perhaps the Euphrates River or the Tigris since there's a ship floating in it. The bottom half is sand so it must be the desert. I'm no expert, but there isn't enough information to determine a location, so I'm afraid I can't tell you any more."

"You're right about the horizon and the sand, but what you call sand is much more. Look closer."

Thomas leaned over, his nose almost touching the stela. "The grains of sand look like ones and zeros."

"That's right, Thomas. But look again, closer this time. Try to detect the smaller details."

Thomas examined the sand again, this time concentrating. "All I see is ones and zeros, maybe little pinholes here and there."

"That's precisely what you see. Those pinholes are spaced out evenly across the sand." Barnaby paused to make sure he had Thomas's attention. "After every eight combinations of ones and zeros."

Thomas snickered. "Bytes. Are you trying to tell me this tablet has a message written in binary code?"

"That's right, Thomas."

"The Persians knew nothing of binary. How could this be possible?" Thomas asked.

"I know, I know," Barnaby replied. "Yet here it is. I have here a paper with the translated code. Not only does the code make sense, but it's in English." He turned to Nicolas, who pulled a folded piece of paper from his pocket.

An angry frown creased Thomas's face. "Now you're making fun of me."

"Please, Thomas, stay with me for a few more minutes. I promise. This is very serious."

Nicolas stepped forward to hand him the paper. "Here's the translation of the binary code."

Thomas read the paper. He looked up. "'Thomas K Faraday.' Now would you look at that, my name is on a twenty-five-hundred-year-old tablet."

"Bloody hell, Thomas, it's a stela not a tablet," Barnaby snapped, then drew a deep breath. "I'm sorry. Please keep reading."

"'In Chris have faith.' Christianity was not for another five hundred years," Thomas said. "Besides, they misspelled Christ."

When neither of the other men spoke, Thomas continued. "'Never forget Komodo.'" *Komodo?* Now he concentrated. "'Step one, two, three, now we are ready. Five, eight, twelve. Two is better than one and three. Baboon.'" He read the last silently, for it seemed to be gibberish: *Rh!noc8ros.*

Thomas returned the paper to Barnaby. "This tablet—stela," he corrected himself, "is clearly a fake. The only way this could be real is if someone traveled back in time and made it, so someone could read it today. If you've finished with your little circus act, I would like my bull's head or give me back my deposit."

Nicolas let out a loud sigh. "Come on, Barnaby; he's not the one. Let's go."

Thomas looked at him. "What do you mean, I'm not the one?"

"When you told us your name at the flea market, we thought you might be the one mentioned on the stela. Your name does appear on it. So we thought you might want to see it for yourself."

Barnaby pulled an envelope from his pocket and handed it to Thomas. "Listen, I know this is difficult to believe. Being a serious archaeologist, I also initially found it difficult to believe. So here's your deposit. I put a copy of the translated binary code inside the envelope. I also added another two thousand dollars if you'll take the time to consider the information overnight. Tomorrow, no matter what you decide, you keep the money. I will give you the bull's head for free. We will walk away and you can continue with your trip."

"All right, I'll take a closer look, but I don't need your money," Thomas said. "I will take the Persepolis bull head, though."

Barnaby looked relieved. "Now that's bloody good news. I'll be anticipating your results tomorrow morning. Good night, Mr. Faraday." He and Nicolas moved toward the door. "Oh, by the way," Barnaby said, halfway through the door, "there's one more small detail I left out. The ship you identified—it's not in the water, it's in the sky." He threw up a hand when Thomas started to protest. "Now don't get excited, it's not aliens. This ship is the one and only spaceship to successfully travel back in time. You see, Thomas, I believe someone from that ship carved this stela especially for you."

Barnaby left the room before Thomas could respond. Nicolas followed him, but before he closed the door he turned around. "Are you a believer, Thomas?"

"If you mean do I believe in God, then yes I do, but I haven't as of yet found a religion that merits his name," Thomas replied.

"Good; yes, very good." Nicolas closed the door behind him.

CHAPTER 9

The next day, as Thomas walked toward the reception counter to pay for his extra night's stay, he noticed Barnaby and Nicolas in the breakfast cafeteria. He left his luggage with the receptionist, poured himself a cup of coffee, grabbed a cheese bagel, and joined the two men at their table.

"You're early this morning," Barnaby said as he sat down. "Leaving without saying goodbye?"

"When I travel I always pay my bills before having breakfast," Thomas told him. "And by the way, your stela is in my room. Do you want me to help you get it?"

"No, that's quite all right. We'll get it later."

Thomas took a bite of his bagel. "Your stela kept me up most of the night, you know," he mumbled.

Barnaby could hardly contain his joy. "So you did analyze the code. What made you change your mind? Because I seem to remember you saying something . . . now how did you put it again? Something about a circus act."

Thomas swallowed his mouthful of bagel before he spoke this time. "You must admit, it's quite a story to accept just because you say so," he said. "But then I got to thinking, this stela was carved before I got here. So either someone knew I was coming and planned all of this in advance as a joke, or I'm not the guy the joke is intended for. Either way, I can't ignore the personal information you handed me. Besides, a promise is a promise, and I did say I'd look at it."

"So, what do you think?"

Thomas took a sip of coffee. "Before I say anything, I want to make sure you both understand I don't believe this stela is two and a half thousand years old. Nor do I believe you found a way to time travel."

"Not time travel," Barnaby said. "Time hijacking. There's a difference."

"I don't care what you call it, I don't buy it. I do, however, give you credit

49

for figuring out all this information about me." Thomas looked at his watch. "Let's take a look at the list before I head for Whoopmogoosty."

"Whapmagoostui." Nicolas emphasized each syllable.

Thomas eyed him. "Do you want me to explain this or not?"

"Sorry, please proceed."

"The first line of the stela says 'Thomas K Faraday.' First of all, there's no K in my name. But I presume you already knew that. The K could, however, be relevant.

"Before my wife passed away, I sort of had a hard exterior as far as my personality is concerned. The only one who was able to tame me was my wife, Amélie. When alone together she would sometimes call me kitten—this was to imply that despite my hard exterior, I'm nothing more than a little kitten inside. You can understand why I told her not to use it around anyone, let alone explain the meaning. She agreed, but whenever she noticed I was getting a little too aggressive, especially in front of others, she would get my attention by calling me K. If I displeased her, she would mockingly call me Mr. Thomas K Faraday, usually followed by a comment like 'Now just relax, Mr. K.' It always worked. Now that she's gone, my son and I are the only ones who know the meaning behind the letter K.

"This can easily be chalked up to coincidence, if it weren't for the rest of the information. So let's go to the next line: In Chris have faith. I think it refers to my son. If so, then it's not a spelling error. My son's name is Christian, Chris for short. When my son was eighteen years old he joined a religious cult that demanded total loyalty. He attended meetings up to three times a week. There were also numerous conventions, some one day, others two weeks long. In no time, he began preaching to everyone and ignored all those who didn't agree with him.

"When he neglected his studies at college I put pressure on him to quit his faith. He took this as an attack. He even told me to stop persecuting him. So I proposed a compromise. I told him if he wanted to stay in this cult I would respect his decision, but he needed to do something for me: he had to get his grades back up in school. He told me he would think about it. Not long after, he dropped out of school to become a full-time preacher. I responded with an ultimatum. Quit this cult or leave my house and don't come back. He left the next day. I never saw him again. My friend Michael thinks he went to Asia since Christian often talked about going there."

Thomas took another sip of coffee to clear his throat. "So maybe the line 'In Chris have faith' refers to God after all." He looked at Nicolas for a reaction. "Maybe he wants me to make things right with my son; who knows. Anyway, back to the list.

"I might as well let the cat out of the bag on this next one. It seems the secret is out anyway. Komodo is a key. I've always encrypted my important information with an algorithm that requires an electronic key. This key always has 'Komodo' associated with it. It might vary in the way I spell it. For example, I can spell it with a C instead of a K, or I'll spell it using special characters that replace certain letters but look the same—like replacing an A with an "at" sign. But in the end it's always Komodo. I've been using this key ever since I became involved with network security. At least I used to; now I see this needs to change."

Thomas gave both an inquisitive look. "I'm not sure if a cracker I've been watching is in any way related to you guys, because he also uses the name Komodo. Do you have anything to do with this cracker?"

"What's a cracker?" Barnaby asked.

"You would probably use the improper term hacker instead of cracker. Do you know anything about the cracker Komodo who's been penetrating Northern Future Pharmaceuticals in Montreal?"

"We know nothing about any hacker, or cracker, as you call it," Barnaby insisted. "If there was an attack issued by us I would know about it, so your cracker is not part of our League. The only Komodo we know is the one found on the stela. Does anyone else know you use Komodo as a key—a close friend, perhaps, or a colleague at work?"

"Only my son Christian—as a matter of fact, it was his idea to begin with. He loves the lizard, so he suggested it as a password key, and it stuck." Thomas reached for his coffee but found it empty.

"Hold on, Thomas," Nicolas said as he reached for his cup. "I'll get you a refill."

"While we wait for Nicolas," Thomas continued, can you explain why you think all of this applies to me? It doesn't make any sense. I don't know a single thing about your organization."

"Let me be honest with you, Thomas. We haven't the foggiest idea. Everything about the mission is under complete control. Nothing is left to chance. With limitless financial resources we have the best of everything, both in materials and in human knowledge. So great is the intellect of our people, they keep coming up with innovations. No one else in the world knows about these inventions. It's mind-boggling.

"If you ask Nicolas about this he will tell you it's because God is behind the mission," Barnaby continued. "He keeps saying, and I quote, 'If God says we can't succeed without the man on the stela, we don't question it.' He says all things will be revealed to us in due time. His favorite quote is from the Bible's book of Proverbs. I don't know the verse exactly."

"I think what you're referring to is Proverbs 4:18," Nicolas said from behind Barnaby. "The path of the just is as the shining light, that shineth more and more unto the perfect day." Nicolas handed Thomas his coffee. "I hope you didn't continue without me."

"Of course not," Thomas replied. "Let's continue then, shall we? The next two lines have something to say about my son that has me petrified and captivated at the same time. How you came up with this information is beyond baffling.

"The first of these two lines confirms Chris to be my son. 'Step one, two, three, now we are ready.' These words refer to a progressive three-step program I implemented in his home education. I'm a big believer in puzzles helping the mind grow. They contribute to problem solving skills we need in everyday life. So being an amateur cryptographer, I tried to inculcate these skills in Christian in three progressive steps, each presented at different times in his young life.

"In the first step I introduced him to puzzles that reinforced the ability to decipher code. This was done with simple games I invented. In three short years we were having fun communicating with one another in written code. We started with the Caesar Shift, then the nomenclator followed by the homophones.

"After this we moved to step two, evolving to more difficult types of encryption. For this stage I created a replica of a nineteenth-century cipher disk developed by a man called Alberti. We had fun with this one. We continued with the Trithemius table, the Vigenère cipher, and the First World War ADFGX cipher. One cipher we practiced a lot was the World War Two Enigma machine, sometimes called the Hitler Cipher. Only twenty-four were ever made. The reason we used this cipher was because of its simplicity, and its use of binary, something we both mastered. Christian and I got so good at it, we used it right up to the time he left home.

"Finally, in step three, my goal was to introduce him to computer cracking software. This led to his interest in developing safer computer programs."

Thomas paused and took a drink of his coffee. Then he leaned forward, resting his elbows on the table. "To confirm what I just explained we must read the next entry on the stela. It says five, eight, and twelve. It was on

Christian's fifth, eighth, and twelfth birthdays that I introduced each consecutive step of the program."

Thomas frowned and shook his head. "I'm afraid I can't help with the following line. It says two are better than one and three. I have no idea what that means."

"It's possible you'll understand that when the time is right," Nicolas said. "When it's God's time to let you know."

"Yes, that's true," Thomas said. "It also applies to the last two lines, since I don't know what baboon or that string of letters and numbers mean either."

"Well then," Barnaby said, "I can see we have our man. What do you think, Nicolas?"

"I have no doubt you're the one the stela wants us to find."

Barnaby looked at Nicolas, who responded with a nod. "Thomas, how would you like to take the rest of your vacation with us?" Barnaby asked. "All expenses paid, of course. You'll learn about the mission and then, if you decide this is something you want to be part of, I'll tell you all about the training involved. I'll also explain the impact the result of this mission will have on all humanity."

"All humanity?" Thomas repeated. "Are you saying this has worldwide implications?"

"Yes, it's that big. And for reasons not yet clear, you're a large part of its success."

Thomas looked at Nicolas. "What would God want with a man who's without a temple to worship in?"

"I don't know what God wants with you, Thomas, but we can't ignore the facts." Nicolas counted on his fingers. "One, you can identify yourself on the stela. Two, 'Komodo' has significance in your life. Three, you end up at our League's gateway just days before the training process is about to begin. Four, you have knowledge of the place and period involved with this mission, the Medo-Persian world power. Yes Thomas, you're the one."

"It's true we don't have all the answers," Barnaby added. "But surely you can see the logic behind these events. In any case, what have you to lose? At worst you'll have free room and board along with great entertainment. At best you'll have the adventure of a lifetime. An experience other men can only dream of having."

"So this hotel, the flea market, it's all a front for your League and your mission?"

"Yes, Thomas, it is. So what do you say, are you in?"

Thomas stood and walked to the window. Closing his eyes, he envisioned Michael sitting in his favorite armchair back home. He tried to imagine his reaction to the possible change in his itinerary. Would he be upset? Would he be happy for him? Thomas took less than one minute to decide.

"Fine, I'm in, but be warned, I don't believe even for one second that this stela is part of some time travel story. The reason I'm coming is to learn how you came up with so much information about me." Thomas cast an exaggerated look around the cafeteria. "Since you went through so much trouble building this front, it must be important, this league of yours. I must admit I'm a bit curious about the mission."

"Now that's bloody good news. Trust me when I say this will prove to be the best decision you've ever made."

Barnaby turned as Derrek entered the room. "Derrek, get Thomas's luggage and prepare it for delivery to the facility."

"Yes, Professor," Derrek said, not taking his eyes off Thomas. "I knew as soon as I saw you, Mr. Faraday, that you're the man on the stela."

"What made you so sure?" Thomas asked.

"When you saw my keychain yesterday you immediately recognized the Persian sphinx."

Thomas smiled. "By the way, Derrek, whatever happened to your accent?"

"You mean my French accent?"

"I'm around French people every day. That was no French accent."

"Bloody hell, you two," Barnaby interjected. "We have a long trip ahead of us. Cut the chatter and let's get going."

"Let me get my work bag first," Thomas said.

"Don't bother with your bag," Barnaby told him. "It will slow us down."

"I'm not going without my bag."

"Bloody hell, Thomas." Barnaby threw his hands up. "Take your bloody bag, then."

Nicolas chuckled. "Welcome to the mission," he said to Thomas. "You'd better get used to him. It's all part of the package."

Thomas went to the reception and snatched his leather work bag from Derrek, then followed Barnaby behind the counter into a large employee rest area. They continued to the end of the room, where the others entered a large bathroom. Thomas stood outside.

"What are you waiting for? Come on, it's this way," Barnaby shouted.

Although surprised, Thomas did as he was told.

Barnaby and Nicolas entered a large shower cubicle with four showerheads. "Come on, Thomas, we can't keep telling you to follow us," Barnaby called.

"I beg your pardon?"

"Don't be so daft," Barnaby snapped. "We're not going to take a shower. Come on. You'll understand in a minute."

Once Thomas had stepped into the shower, Nicolas stood facing the wall under the left showerhead and gripped the hot and cold water knobs. Barnaby did the same under the right showerhead. Between them, Thomas watched as, on the count of three, they pushed in the knobs about three centimeters deep. Nicolas twisted the left knob a quarter turn clockwise. Barnaby turned his right knob three quarters counterclockwise. Next Nicolas turned his right knob counterclockwise half a turn, and Barnaby turned his left knob a full turn.

A thick, solid fiberglass door slid down, enclosing the shower area with the three men inside. Once the door was locked into place, the cubicle started to descend.

"A secret elevator," Thomas exclaimed. "You guys sure take this stuff seriously."

"You have no idea," Nicolas said.

As they descended, Thomas noticed numbers written on the concrete wall. They were counting down from forty meters. After five minutes the door opened to reveal a small, square concrete room. At the back of the room was a concrete counter with a metal roller shutter door. As he entered the room, Thomas felt as if he'd stepped into a tomb.

In response to Nicolas's knock, a man opened the shutter, revealing another bunker with preserved foods and camping equipment lining the walls. "Hello Lautaro, how are you doing today?"

"Muy bueno Nicolas," the man replied. He looked past Nicolas to Thomas. "Is this Thomas K Faraday?"

"Yes, it is."

Lautaro reached out to shake Thomas's hand with both of his, surprising Thomas. "It's a real privilege, Mr. Faraday, to meet such a man as you. Bienvenido a la misión, welcome to the mission. We have been looking forward to finally meeting you."

Thomas had to force his hand from Lautaro's viselike grip. "The pleasure's all mine, I'm sure."

"Give us our rucksacks," Barnaby said. "We don't have time to lose."

Lautaro lifted two large backpacks and set them on the counter.

"Take your rucksack, Thomas," Barnaby said as he hefted one onto his back. "We have a long way to go."

"Go where?"

The wall to their right opened like a revolving door in an old fashion hotel.

"Come on Thomas, let's go." Barnaby strode toward this new opening.

Nicolas and Lautaro waved goodbye.

The door closed behind them. Before him Thomas could see a concrete tunnel, three meters wide and four meters high. The walls were painted green to make it easy on the eyes. Running along the left side of the ceiling were three pipes of different sizes, for water and electrical wiring, Barnaby told him. A steady humming came from a round air duct on the right. Fluorescent lights spaced six meters apart ran in a straight line along the center of the ceiling. To the right, about half a meter from the floor, Thomas noticed a number.

"Please tell me this number says we have a hundred and seventy meters to go."

Barnaby smiled. "It's a hundred and seventy kilometers." Thomas looked at Barnaby in disbelief. "Don't give me that look. Eventually we'll be taking a monorail. But for now we will walk."

The two started forward.

"If we keep up this pace," Barnaby told him, "it will take fourteen hours before we meet up with the monorail."

CHAPTER 10

Thomas contemplated the situation he found himself in and wondered if he was being duped. The trip, the stela, and his identity were all losing their appeal as the kilometers went by.

Although they had only reached the eighth-kilometer marker, he had to admire Barnaby's stamina. What surprised him most was Barnaby's dedication; he tackled the walk as though nothing else mattered. He'd said nothing since entering the tunnel. So out of respect for the professor, Thomas stayed quiet. This was a serious problem. Silence equaled solitude and solitude equaled Amélie. To avoid becoming melancholy, he imagined himself a soldier on the march during the American civil war. He'd heard that during a long march, a soldier could close his eyes far enough that all he'd see was the heels of the man in front of him. His mind could be on his wife, his girlfriend, or if he was young enough, his mother. This state was similar to sleepwalking. Thomas narrowed his eyes to see only the floor in front of him and let his mind wander.

He was jolted back to reality when Barnaby decided to start a conversation. "Well, Thomas, instead of walking in silence like a couple of bloody monks, why don't we use this time to answer any questions you might have."

"I do have a question or two. For starters, what does this league of yours represent?"

"That is a good question. Why don't I start from the beginning of our modern chapter," Barnaby replied. "It began with an American soldier named Nathaniel Adams, who fought in the Mexican–American War. On the eighth of September, 1847, during the battle of Molino del Rey, Nathaniel and an unnamed soldier found themselves in the thick of the battle. At one point the unnamed soldier fell, mortally wounded, next to Nathaniel. Not wanting to abandon his friend, Nathaniel stopped advancing to stay with the dying soldier.

"When it became clear he would die on the field, the soldier gave Nathaniel a small notebook with instructions to visit his family in his native country of Iraq, which at that time was under direct Ottoman rule. He told Nathaniel to read the notebook and see if he could do something about its content. Nathaniel agreed.

"That night, when Nathaniel was alone, he opened the notebook and read an incredible story that began in the fifth century BC. The story is about a traveler and his companions who attempted to pass through a small city somewhere northeast of Babylon. They were arrested and accused of being spies from Athens. To complicate matters, one of his companions was of Greek heritage.

"They were held captive for almost a month, and one by one his companions disappeared. It was only a matter of time before his turn would come. So he planned an escape and succeeded in reaching the mountains, where he took shelter. He was found and nursed back to health by a group of cavalrymen, soldiers by trade who defended the disadvantaged people of Persia. Some call them the Persian equivalent of Robin Hood and his merry men. Grateful to this group for saving his life, the young traveler joined their cause.

"In time he became a skilled cavalryman himself. Over the next three months the traveler took advantage of their trips around Persia to learn about his missing companions. It did not take long for him to realize they were either killed by sadistic guards or died of illness due to poor treatment in prison."

"Did the notebook say what the traveler's name was or where he came from?" Thomas asked.

"Only that it was a far distant land. The story calls him Ramin but we believe it's not his real name. He most likely took on a Persian name. Anyway, without giving a reason why, the story goes on to say that the young traveler realized he would never be able to return home on his own. So he planned what would become a most unusual rescue. He used his share of gold to hire one of the best stone carvers of Persia to create the stela you examined yesterday.

"Once the stela was completed, he crafted an incredible story about the god of time, Chronos. Chronos would come back from the twenty-first century with a man who will correct the wrongs he and his companions suffered at the hands of the Persians. To ensure Chronos would not forget him or change his mind, the traveler gathered a collection of holy treasures. Some were made of gold and silver, others of precious stones, but his chief prize was a document with information on the whereabouts of significant religious relics. These treasures would be too much for Chronos to ignore. The only way Chronos could acquire these would be to go back in time with his rescuer.

"The next step was to arrange for his story to be handed down unchanged, generation after generation for two and a half thousand years. He gave this responsibility to a fellow cavalryman named Hutan. As it turned out, the traveler had saved Hutan's life three times during various incursions. Hutan's family would cooperate out of gratitude to the traveler.

"The story to be handed down was never to leave the family until the end of its journey. Also it was never to be written down so it could be kept a secret until the right time—our time.

"Now this is how you fit into the picture. The story concludes with the mention of a stela hidden in a small village called Zarmandokht. It goes on to say we will find on this stela information about a man who is indispensable for a successful rescue. It stressed that if this man is not present during the rescue, the location of the treasures for Chronos will not be revealed.

"The village was finally located two years ago. Our contact working on the dig located the elusive stela buried deep within a cave. We recovered the stela, converted the binary to text, and began our search for the rescuer."

"So the stela you showed me yesterday was the stela this traveler buried?" Thomas asked.

"One and the same," Barnaby said. "Now that I've told you the traveler's story, we'll go back to Nathaniel. He kept his promise and journeyed to Iraq. He was able to confirm the story with members of the dead soldier's family. After gathering as many details as he could, Nathaniel returned home. He recruited a team of scientists, historians, and archaeologists with the help of wealthy benefactors and the search for the stela began.

"I'm sure you can also appreciate that the sacred treasures spoken of by the traveler would attract religious leaders from all denominations. It's they who refuse to move ahead with the mission's launch until the mystery person is discovered. So you see, Thomas, now that we've found you, everything is in place for the launch."

"Don't get too excited about my role in your mission," Thomas warned him. "Keep in mind I'm a tourist in your world. If I don't like what I see, I'm out of here."

"I'm not worried. Once you see the facility, I know you'll want to be part of it."

Thomas looked at him askance. "How can you be so sure?"

Barnaby smiled. "I'm surprised you haven't figured it out already, being a code breaker and all."

"I said I'm an amateur cryptographer. I stress 'amateur.'"

"Then let me summarize it for you. Twenty-five hundred years ago a traveler knew that in the twenty-first century, a group of people will have the capability to travel back in time. He also knew this group will be seeking the whereabouts of lost religious relics. While in Persia, things went wrong. So he sent us a message only you would understand to make damn sure you will be on that ship. What do you think this all means?"

"It sounds like this traveler of yours is me sending myself a message," Thomas admitted. "But why?"

"Why? That's a bloody good question," Barnaby replied. "I don't know why. Perhaps you know what went wrong and by making sure you go back, you'll do something to prevent the wrong from happening all over again."

"That does not make sense. Why would I make sure I go back when the fact I was there to send myself a message indicates I will be going there anyway?" Thomas protested. "How else can I be there to send myself a message?"

"I understand what you're saying, and I wish I could answer you, but the reality is, we don't know for sure," Barnaby said. "Listen, Thomas, we'll have lots of time to debate this question later. For now let me go back to the soldier I mentioned earlier, Nathaniel Adams.

"As I said already, after hearing this story he put together a small group who began the hunt for the Persian stela. Over the years, more people contributed to the search. Eighty years ago the League stopped looking for the god Chronos. They understood the way back would be through a time travel machine. They looked into the technology of time travel, but as you insinuated, time travel is impossible. However, the idea of accomplishing the impossible drew more powerful contributors to the secret League. These influential people attracted other influential people until we had as members the smartest scientists in the world. Not being restricted by politics or money, they put their knowledge into action. Fourteen years ago we had our big break. A wormhole was discovered and we engineered it to be large enough to send a ship through.

"Seven years ago we started testing theories. We successfully sent a shoebox-size vessel with mice as passengers to 473 BC and back. All that was left was to gather volunteers to be trained in everything Persian—the geography, the costume, the language, and so much more."

"I suppose we are going to this training facility now?"

"Yes, we are. Everything I mentioned, including the ship and the portal, is also there."

"I must admit, I'm curious about all of this," Thomas said.

"Of course you are. You're the man on the stela."

Thomas noted the kilometer marker. "May I ask my second question?"

"Yes, go ahead."

"What do I do if I need to pee?"

Over the next seventeen kilometers they had detailed and sometimes heated debates over the plausibility of the story handed down to them. Thomas decided to go along with Barnaby's explanation, at least till they reached the facility. Exhausted by their discussion, Thomas switched the conversation to time travel. It seemed to him the time machine was the key connecting all the parts together.

"I've seen more than one documentary that made it clear time travel is physically impossible," Thomas said as they passed kilometer marker number twenty-five. "This makes it very difficult for me to accept your claim that I will end up two and a half thousand years in the past. Just saying it sounds wrong."

"Again Thomas, not time travel, time hijacking."

"Whatever. It's still impossible."

"There's a big difference Thomas. If we could time travel we could go anywhere at any time and come back as we please. Since this is time hijacking, we can only go where the wormhole takes us. We are under its control. We leave when it is ready and we come back when it chooses to come back. Thus the term time hijacking."

Thomas frowned. "That sounds risky to me. Is its timetable known, or do we wait and see?"

"We know when it will leave and when it will come back."

"How do you know that? Has anyone traveled through this wormhole to test it out?"

"Bloody hell, Thomas, I'm no time travel expert!" Barnaby exclaimed. "I just know they have a way to determine this. And no. You and your team will be the first to travel through it."

"Don't you mean time hijacking?" Thomas jeered.

Barnaby had enough. "It's already one o'clock," he said. "We've been walking for five hours. Why don't we stop for lunch."

They rested on one of the many recycled plastic benches placed along the route. The meal consisted of a chicken salad sandwich with fresh fruits and vegetables. A hazelnut raisin cake was for dessert. Barnaby took out a flask of hot tea to drink with his favorite biscuits.

"Do you want some tea? It comes from Assam, India," Barnaby asked.

"No thanks, I'm more of a coffee guy."

"Suit yourself."

Thomas thought of the half empty bottle of scotch in his bag but decided not to indulge. "How much farther?" he asked around a mouthful of his sandwich.

"Oh, I don't know. Another nine hours or so."

Thomas exhaled. "Why do we need to walk so much? Why not take the monorail right from the start?"

Barnaby put his sandwich back in its container and relaxed with his cup of tea. "Do you know anything about the James Bay Project?"

"I know it's a series of hydroelectric power stations that divert rivers into a large watershed. I also know Hydro-Québec runs it. It provides most of Québec's electricity."

"Good summary, Thomas, but it doesn't touch on the scope of the project. For instance, it covers an area equal to the state of New York, which makes it one of the ten most powerful hydroelectric power stations in the world. So far the cost is twenty billion dollars to build and it can produce over sixteen thousand megawatts. Not bad, considering it's not yet finished." He took another sip of tea. "Did you know the watershed covers an area the size of Florida? Think about it, that's twice the size of bloody Scotland."

Thomas smiled at the Englishman's reference. "That's all interesting, Barnaby, but what does this have to do with walking?"

"You sound like some of my students. Pay attention and you might not need to ask useless questions. Now where was I? Right—the size of the project. As I was saying, James Bay Two is in the process of being built. There is constant movement of large amounts of material needed for its construction. This allows us to slip in our own materials for the underground facility undetected.

"The Robert-Bourassa power station, which is three times the height of Niagara Falls, is only a few kilometers away from our site on La Grande Rivière. We're able to move large quantities of construction materials right under their noses without notice. This is the good part. The problem is, the James Bay Project attracts a lot of unwanted attention from the Canadian, American, and Russian governments. They all have sophisticated monitoring equipment to detect sound and, among other things, unaccountable movements.

"To avoid attracting unwanted attention, we walk until we find ourselves somewhere under James Bay, seventy kilometers from where we started. Once we reach that point we can make noise and still remain invisible. Does this answer your question?"

"Yes, Professor."

"Good. Shall we get a move on it then?"

By the time they passed the sixty-nine-kilometer marker, both men were fatigued. Each kilometer marker was looked for and noted. Thomas was sure the markers were getting farther apart, the nearer they got to their destination. To forget about the increasing pain in his calves and toes brought about by constantly walking downhill, Thomas broke his self-imposed silence.

"Whose idea was it to build this facility under James Bay?"

"The scientists, I guess. That's where the portal to Persia's located."

"How did they conclude it was under the bay?"

"I don't rightfully know, Thomas, but I'm sure happy someone figured it out."

"I was wondering how a portal gets found so deep under water," Thomas said. "Does it look like the effects in some of those sci-fi movies?"

"I don't know. I've never seen it. All I can tell you is what I learned from meetings I've attended. I already told you everything I know, except perhaps that the ship we will travel in will carry four hundred people, maybe more. I don't remember."

"Just one more question," Thomas said. "You mentioned I might be able to go back in time to correct what went wrong. How can you be sure we can do that? I mean, what about the paradox of the man—"

"I know, I know, the man who travels back and kills his grandfather," Barnaby said, waving a dismissive hand. "I believe that paradox is nothing more than an excuse to instill doubt in the possibility of time travel. The world is full of them. I once asked Nicolas a similar question when discussing God's role in the mission. He said there's nothing God can't do if he wants to. So I asked if God can build a rock so large, he can't move it. He refused to discuss it with me, saying he'd heard that question already. Anyway, the simplest way to explain it is like this: everything in the world today is a direct result of what happened in the past. Therefore whatever we will do in future trips to the past has already been done, in the past. It's called the Novikov self-consistency principle."

"Why would you bother making arrangements to ensure I go back if I can't change anything?"

"Bloody hell, Thomas, this time hijacking stuff is not my field of knowledge!" Barnaby protested. "You'll get all the information from the right people when your training begins."

Barnaby stopped walking to let out a long, slow breath. "Thank God we've arrived."

Thomas followed his gaze. Straight ahead was the long-anticipated monorail station.

"In the morning we will board the monorail to our final destination," Barnaby said. "Tonight we will stay here." He gestured toward a large enclosure with six metal doors on their right. "I'll be taking the last bunker on the left; it's my usual bunker. You can use any one of the other five. They are all the same. You'll find everything you need for a good night's rest." Barnaby did not wait to see which one Thomas would take. He disappeared into his bunker.

Thomas entered the bunker directly facing him to find a room that looked like a fifties bomb shelter. The walls were made of cinder blocks painted gray. There was an electric cooking plate on a counter next to a small fridge. A small aluminum table was bolted to the floor next to the bed. There were no chairs, no pictures on the walls, no alarm clock, and no carpet on the concrete floor. He set his backpack and leather bag on the floor next to the bed.

His first instinct was to investigate the closet. Inside were several pine-green uniforms neatly aligned on hangers. On the floor there was an equal number of black steel-toed shoes. A note was taped on the inside of the closet door: *Please leave your articles of clothing in the bin provided. Select a uniform and a pair of shoes. Your personal articles will be forwarded to you in three days.*

Thomas took one uniform from the rack and held it up. "You've got to be kidding me," he muttered, eyeing the jumpsuit. He examined the logo embroidered on the left pocket: a phoenix, its wings extended upward, protected by a Persian shield. Between the wings were the letters *ULRA*.

He put the jumpsuit back and opened the fridge to scan its contents, then made himself a tuna sandwich. To wash it down he had a couple cold beers. Needless to say, sleep came quickly.

CHAPTER 11

"Now you look like you belong," Barnaby said when Thomas emerged from his bunker the next morning wearing the uniform.

Thomas scowled. "One joke from you and I'm heading straight back to the hotel."

"Don't you worry. Every new recruit is wearing that uniform. Now if you're ready, let's get on with the final leg of our trip."

An eight-car monorail waited a short distance away, the League's logo painted on the sides of the open cars. They entered an empty car and settled in two of the six seats. Barnaby inserted an electronic card into a slot in the front of the car, and the monorail started to move.

"How fast does it go?" Thomas asked.

"Twenty-five kilometers per hour. We'll arrive in four hours, just in time for dinner," Barnaby added.

"Will we still be under James Bay when we arrive?"

"At the entrance to the bay, to be precise. It's eighty meters deep, but we're going to be another six hundred meters underground."

Thomas stared ahead at the blue lights passing hypnotically by on both sides of the tunnel and tried to compare six hundred meters to something he could relate to. His mind drifted to something Barnaby had said back at the hotel. "You mentioned this mission would have worldwide implications. What do you mean by that?"

"Well, think on this for a moment," Barnaby replied, leaning forward in his seat as he warmed to the subject. "Right from the start our main objective was to recover and share religious treasures with the world. This gained momentum when Charles Darwin's theory of evolution became popular. You can imagine what effect finding the Ark of the Covenant or parts of the original Hebrew scriptures would have on spiritual leaders of the world.

"Me, personally, I have no problems with this. The League benefits from this strong religious influence. We have as a result developed a solid sense of moral justice to the point where we have no criminals among our members. You'll notice this when you enter the facility. The guards have no need for weapons, nor is there any need for locks on the doors." Barnaby paused. "Now that I'm explaining it to you, it's actually quite impressive."

Thomas lifted an eyebrow but didn't respond to that. "What happens if someone does commit a crime?"

"We do have a cell for those unfortunate incidents. We also have a judicial committee to handle any conflicts. If a serious crime is committed, the offender will be imprisoned till the completion of the mission's objectives. You can see how it would be to the benefit of any conflicting parties to resolve their differences before it gets to the point of imprisonment."

"So the League's goal is to promote the worship of God."

"No, not really," Barnaby replied. "It's to convince the world that God exists. What people do with this knowledge is up to each individual. It is true that some are more zealous than others. A few believe this is going to convert the world to Christianity. Now, having said this, not all members are so spiritually inclined. Most who have been introduced in the last three decades are after scientific advancements. As for me, well, I believe everyone. Both the religious and the scientific groups could benefit from the discovery of these historical treasures."

"Once we arrive," Thomas asked, "should I adopt a pretense of godliness to be accepted?"

"Yes and no." Barnaby reached into his backpack to retrieve a flask of hot tea. "This might take some time to explain."

• • • • • • • • • • ● ○○○○○○○○○○○

They arrived at the facility at noon, as Barnaby had predicted. Two guards awaited their arrival on the monorail platform. One stayed next to a large freight elevator while the other came forward.

"Good day, Professor Lancaster," the guard said as he reached into the car to help with their bags. "Did you and Mr. Faraday have an enjoyable trip?" Before Barnaby could answer, the guard turned his attention to Thomas. "Welcome to the ULRA, Mr. Faraday. We are honored to finally meet you."

"Thank you," he replied, then added somewhat lamely, "and how's your day?"

"Exhilarating," the guard replied. "We've been eagerly anticipating your arrival."

As they approached the freight elevator, Barnaby leaned over to whisper in Thomas's ear, "Better get used to this. The news of your arrival has made you more popular than a rock star."

The guard beside the freight elevator pushed up its door to reveal a luxurious interior. With a smirk, Barnaby stepped to one side and ushered Thomas inside. They descended for almost fifteen minutes. *Six hundred meters,* Thomas reminded himself. When the car finally stopped, Thomas stepped out onto a balcony that stretched all the way around the walls of a cavernous open area. He walked to the edge to have a better look. The immensity of the facility took his breath away. The balcony he was standing on was one of many—Thomas estimated there were forty-five. *Forty-five levels!*

The lower floor of the facility was a mass of green—*a garden,* Thomas realized—with a small stream running through it to end at a pond where ducks and swans swam gracefully. People sat on benches situated along several cobblestone walkways, reading or just enjoying the profusion of plants and flowers around them. He noticed that the walls around the lower floor had been left unfinished, so the rough stone resembled the foot of a mountain. Embedded in the walls were many doors of different colors and sizes.

All doubts Thomas had about this organization disappeared. He turned around and said to Barnaby, "You weren't kidding when you said you had boundless resources."

"Bloody hell, Thomas, that's what I've been saying from the start!" Barnaby looked past Thomas. "Ah, and here comes your guide."

Thomas turned to watch a woman of average height and unremarkable features walk toward them. She had a small nose, a small mouth, and hazel eyes that were stunning despite her lack of makeup. He glimpsed a fine gold necklace that emerged from shoulder-length chestnut hair to disappear under a green tank top. She wore cargo pants and hiking boots and a man's wristwatch. Unlike the two guards earlier, she looked mildly annoyed, as if she'd been called away from something she would rather be doing.

Her face lit up as she greeted Barnaby, however. "Professor Lancaster, welcome back." She had a mild English accent. "How was your stay topside?"

Barnaby stepped back. "Let me take a good look at you. Yes, yes indeed. I swear you're looking more beautiful every time I see you."

"Now, now, Professor, don't start your smooth-talking with me. Save it for some of the more naïve women."

Barnaby chuckled. Then he turned toward Thomas, saying, "Let me introduce you to Thomas Faraday, the newest member of our family. Thomas, meet Anna Latimer. She's our linguistic specialist, among her many other qualifications."

"Pleased to meet you, Hanna."

"That's Anna, not Hanna. There's no H."

"Sorry—Anna. Pleased to meet you. You can call me Thomas."

"I prefer Mr. Faraday, if that's all right."

Thomas felt a chill down his spine. "If that's what you prefer."

"Well then," Barnaby interrupted, "I'll leave you two and get myself something to eat. I'll see you later, Thomas. Enjoy your tour."

Anna walked straight to the railing, gesturing for Thomas to follow. She wasted no time. "This is where all members get their introduction to the mission. It's the largest of three facilities connected by the tunnel you arrived in. Each of the two other facilities is half the size of the previous one. You and about eight hundred others will learn more about these facilities tomorrow."

Anna leaned over the railing. "Can't see it from here, but directly under us are the classrooms where you'll learn about ancient Persian history, their language, culture, and religion. Other types of training, such as martial arts and the use of ancient weapons, will be given on the top level." She pointed to a line of large, dark windows above them.

"Are we expected to fight battles?" Thomas asked.

"We need to be prepared for anything," Anna said without looking at him. "You'll learn more about these risks tomorrow at your introductory meeting. For now, I'm only explaining your new home.

"Now, if you look down straight ahead you'll notice several doors of different colors. Each one leads to a work area. For example, the fifth door from the left is where all the furnishings are made. This would be everything from the bed in your accommodations to the cockpit in the ship. In the middle is the hospital." She pointed to a red door bearing a white cross. "Next to it on the right is a recreational center equipped with a swimming pool, gymnasium, theater, and a reception area. Three doors from the left you have a drinking establishment where you can also find fast foods." Anna looked at Thomas with assessing eyes. "I believe brasserie is what you would call it in Montreal."

Ouch, Thomas thought, wondering if she knew about his drinking.

"I would like to bring your attention to the large and small doors almost touching each other on the far left. It's important you understand that you're never to enter those doors. That's the nuclear power plant that feeds all three facilities and provides the enormous amount of energy needed to operate the portal to Persia. You'll notice there's a large red border around them. That means Keep Out." She eyed him until he nodded.

Satisfied, she turned back toward the railing. "Still on the main floor, taking up the complete right side, we have the cafeteria. You must be there at seven a.m. tomorrow morning if you don't want to miss breakfast. Your table is already assigned to you. Now, if you'll please follow me, I'll show you to your accommodations." She led him back into the elevator.

Anna said nothing as they descended to the fourth floor. Thomas understood she preferred silence, but he had questions. "You said this is one of three facilities. What are the other two for?"

"Once again, you'll get all that information tomorrow. My job is to familiarize you with what you might immediately need." When Thomas continued to look at her, she rolled her eyes. "The second facility is also a training center. Those who make it to that center have graduated top in their class in the initial training. Only four hundred people will be transported to ancient Persia. Three hundred and seventy of those will never leave the ship. They are technicians, historians, linguists, healthcare personnel, management, and communications specialists, to mention but a few. They will give the foot soldiers the necessary support."

"Foot soldier?"

"That's what we call those who will be walking among the Persians. They have many responsibilities, such as recording events as they encounter them. They will also attempt to discover the location of many religious icons. Each foot soldier will have a ring equipped with a microphone and speaker for communication with the ship. They will also have a digital camera hidden in some form of headdress so everything the foot soldier sees will be sent to the ship to be stored in its massive data banks."

"If I turn out to be a foot soldier," Thomas interrupted, "I'll need to remember this when I take a leak."

His joke generated an irritated look. "I hope you'll take your role seriously, Mr. Faraday," Anna said. "By the way, what exactly is your role?"

"I don't know. I guess I'll find out tomorrow."

The elevator stopped and Thomas followed Anna out. "Once the training in the second facility is completed and your role is defined, you'll be sent to the third facility. That's where the final preparations are made—some call it perfecting. In this last stage of your training you'll need to get to know one another, as your life may depend upon it. You'll also see the ship for the first time. That's when you'll familiarize yourself with it. The ship traveling back twenty-five hundred years is located at the mouth of the portal."

"How far from the first facility is this portal?"

"Six hundred and three kilometers, which brings us almost to the middle of Hudson Bay."

Thomas digested that a moment, then asked, "How long will this training take?"

"Three years," Anna said, surprising him. "Two in this facility for basic training, eleven months in the second, and one month in the third."

"That sounds like a lot of work," Thomas said. "Three years is almost a university degree."

"It will pass quickly, at least for those who study diligently," Anna said, her tone sarcastic.

"Hold on there, Ms. Latimer," Thomas retorted. "I was practically bribed to come here. It's not my fault I don't know what my role is. For all I know, this is a misunderstanding and I'll be out of your hair in two weeks."

"What you don't understand, Mr. Thomas Faraday, is that everyone here has proven themselves worthy of this mission," Anna snapped, her hands on her hips. "They all have something to contribute. Like me, they all made huge sacrifices for the privilege of being among those who will be going to Persia. You, on the other hand, seem to have nothing to offer except maybe—and I stress maybe—you're the famous man on the stela. What's more, you get a free pass straight to Go. No matter how poorly you do in training, you'll be on that ship. So forgive me if I'm somewhat resentful of your presence here."

"Now that's unfair," Thomas protested. "You can't blame me for my situation. Besides, you don't know me. You have no right to judge me like that. And rest assured, Ms. Latimer, if I decide to stay, I will work as hard as everyone else to earn my spot. I've never in my life accepted handouts and I sure as hell won't start now."

Anna leaned forward until she was only centimeters from Thomas's face. "What will be your motivation, free scotch?"

This unexpected remark crippled Thomas. He was now sure there was a file on him. He felt naked and vulnerable.

Anna hesitated, then straightened. "I apologize. That was uncalled for. You're not what we expected. Or I should say what I expected. Everyone else is lining up to meet you."

"It's okay," Thomas said. "You're right about my drinking, but I also meant what I said about working hard."

An awkward five seconds passed before Anna continued. "Your accommodation is over there. Let me take you to it."

Anna opened the door and led the way in to stop in the middle of a small living room. Working clockwise, she pointed out the different features of his new home. "The kitchen is over there. Over here is the bedroom, the study, and the bathroom. You'll notice on the table a large envelope. In it you'll find the house rules, and the names of members of upper management, along with their responsibilities. I urge you to look at the document tonight since there's also a list of important contacts and emergency information you will need. Are there any questions?"

"Nope, I'm good for now. Thank you for giving me the tour."

"You're welcome," Anna said as she headed for the door.

"Oh, one moment," Thomas called out. "There is one more thing. I feel bad about the way things went between us. I would like a chance to start over. I might still have more questions after reading the contents of this envelope. Can we meet again, maybe later this evening?"

"Your meeting tomorrow should pretty much answer all your questions, Mr. Faraday." She turned and left.

Thomas counted to ten before stepping out onto the balcony. He watched as Anna entered the elevator. Oddly enough he felt attracted to her. Her mannerisms, her feistiness, were qualities he admired. But there was more to Anna than a few idiosyncrasies, and it took only a few seconds for Thomas to understand. She reminded him of his beloved Amélie.

After the elevator door closed, Thomas stood on the balcony and refocused on his situation. Despite all the qualms of the last three days, one thing became clear: this League was much larger than he'd ever imagined. There was no way so many resources and investments would be poured into such an enterprise without guarantees.

So the time had come to decide. He could always go back, but to what? The unemployment line, facing charges for hacking his employer, drinking himself silly in that poor excuse of a home? Or he could stay with these people, turn the page, and start a new chapter in his life. He would write a letter to Michael, who would take care of his things during his absence, and if Christian came back, he could look after him, too—presuming he even needed looking after.

Feeling liberated by his decision to stay, Thomas entered his accommodations, poured himself an ice cold beer, and opened the envelope. Inside he found a fifteen page Guide for All New Tenants. On the cover under the League's logo were the words *United League of Restored Axiom – ULRA*.

He put the guide down in favor of the contents of his leather work bag. He dumped everything onto the bed and shoved it all to one side except a worn yellow envelope containing the encrypted files left behind by Komodo Cracker. "Oh no, my friend, I've not given up on you just yet. You're a puzzle I'm determined to solve."

CHAPTER 12

Thomas was given a typical French Canadian breakfast—two eggs sunny side up, bacon, sausage, ham, beans, toast, some sliced fruit, and of course maple syrup. He might have chosen something a little healthier, but the elderly woman serving behind the counter had already pegged him for this hearty breakfast. Not in a mood to argue, he said thank you, grabbed his tray, added a glass of grapefruit juice, then turned to face the large cafeteria.

"You look lost," said a man who stood behind him in line. "You're new here, aren't you?"

"I arrived yesterday, actually."

"What's your table number?"

He looked at his place card to make sure he had the number right and said, "62-L."

The man pointed in the direction Thomas needed to go. "It should be about eight or nine tables from the end of that row."

At the table he was greeted by a tall, thin man in a navy blue pinstripe suit. As if the suit wasn't hard enough to look at, he also had on a full length, blood-red tie. "Well, well, well," the thin man said. "We were beginning to doubt your existence." Thomas couldn't take his eyes off his wide, toothy grin. "Look around, Mr. Faraday. You're the new main attraction around here."

Thomas forced himself to look. As the man said, all eyes were fixed on him.

"How rude," the thin man continued. "Please sit down. Let me introduce you to your dining companions. My name is Aldon McAllister and this is my beautiful wife, Yetta."

"Welcome to the mission," she said with a seductive smile. "We're all anxious to learn about you, Mr. Faraday."

Aldon was not exaggerating when he called his wife beautiful. She was also tall, with blonde hair, wide blue eyes, and full lips. She wore a tight white silk dress that left little to the imagination. "Yetta, that's an interesting name," Thomas said as he forced his eyes away from her ample assets. "It's very pretty. May I ask its origin?"

"The name is of Hebrew origin," Aldon answered on her behalf. "It means 'ruler of the house.'"

The others at the table giggled. Yetta tried but failed to hide her anger. She turned to spear Aldon with blazing eyes. Thomas pretended not to notice Aldon's discomfort as he asked him what his name meant.

"I think it's Italian or Old German. In any case, I know in old English it has many meanings—'old one, elder, old town,' or 'old friend.'" He glanced back at his wife. "Anyway, next to my wife we have Quincy Daramy."

Quincy stretched out his large hand. "Welcome to the mission, Mr. Faraday." He was a stout African American with a stylish goatee, clad in a black football jersey and a pair of blue denim pants cut below the knees.

"And to your immediate left—" Aldon began.

Thomas interrupted by putting out his hand. He smiled at Derrek, who mechanically stuffed potato chips into his mouth. "Are you a receptionist here as well, Derrek?"

Derrek extended his greasy hand to Thomas. "It's so nice to see you again, Mr. Faraday. I'm glad you're the man on the stela."

"Derrek and Quincy are both computer programmers," Aldon interjected. "And from what I heard, they're the best. They designed the ship's operating system."

"Actually," Quincy corrected, "we're not the ones who designed it. We tweaked the OS so it can be fully automated for minimal human interaction."

"Which was more challenging than it sounds," Derrek added. "We needed to read and understand the entire programming code before we could change anything. You see, Mr. Faraday, the real creators of the system can't be found."

"Can't be found," Thomas said. "Why can't they be found?"

"We don't know," Derrek answered. "No one would tell us what happened to them. All they said was that we're on our own. I wish we could meet them, though; their work is nothing short of genius."

Again Aldon interjected. "I'm sure Mr. Faraday finds all of this rather interesting, guys, but let's talk shop some other time, shall we?"

"No," Thomas said, "I'm curious about this."

"Aldon's right," Quincy insisted. "This is not the time. If you want we can meet later and I'll tell you all about it."

"I'd like that very much," Thomas said, though he was disappointed. He turned his attention to Aldon and Yetta. "What do you two do?"

"I'm a judiciary committee coordinator," Aldon explained. "As for Yetta, she works as a secretary for the members of the governing body. I still don't know how she got the job so fast." He looked at his wife with pride. "I guess she's good at what she does."

I bet she is, Thomas thought.

"The official title is administrative assistant," she corrected. "Not that it's important. Aldon is studying very hard to be part of the governing body. It shouldn't be too much longer, right, honey?"

"Yes, cupcake, it won't be long now."

Yetta turned her attention back to Thomas. "What about you, Mr. Faraday? What would be your contribution to the ULRA?"

"If I may ask, it would make me feel so much better if everyone just called me Thomas. I hope I'm not asking too much."

"Not at all, Thomas," Yetta said. "So, what is your assignment?"

Before he could answer, Anna appeared at their table with a rolling server tray. "Would anyone like some coffee?"

"Annie. How nice to see you again," Thomas said.

"It's Anna—not Annie, not Hanna—Anna. You're not too quick, are you, Mr. Faraday. Now, can I pour you a cup of coffee?"

Thomas felt his face heat. "Yes, please."

Anna poured him a cup. Everyone else at the table wanted coffee as well. Thomas held back from saying anything more. Since everyone else was quiet he assumed she was like this with everyone. Even Derrek's potato chip chomping stopped. Somehow this reassured Thomas.

Yetta put a wrinkle in his quick assumption when she said to Anna, "Will we be seeing you at tonight's cocktail party?"

"No, I need to be well prepared for tomorrow's class, but thanks just the same for the invitation, Yetta."

"Some other time, then."

Anna left to serve the next table. Thomas leaned forward and whispered, "She sure has many responsibilities here, doesn't she?"

"Yes, she does," Yetta said. "We all take turns doing the less glamorous jobs. But what we want to know is how you've come to be on that stela. We're just dying to know what all this means for the ULRA."

"You and me alike," Thomas answered. "This is all a big mystery to me as well."

Right on time, a musical chime announced the end of breakfast. "Well, I guess it's time for you guys to head to the auditorium," Aldon said. "Yetta and I are back at the office."

Thomas walked into a large multipurpose auditorium with a seating capacity of one thousand. There was eight hundred present. Everyone knew why they were there, except Thomas. He hoped this was where it would all come together.

At precisely eight o'clock, nine people walked onto the dais and sat down on the chairs behind the podium. A heavyset woman in her mid-sixties approached the podium with a small piece of paper in her hand. She had a short afro and wore dark-framed glasses. Her parents were from Haiti, she told the audience, but she was born and raised in South Carolina. "It is a great honor and a real privilege to welcome all of you to the ULRA," she said in a distinctive high-pitched, nasal voice. "My name is Captain Olivia Washington." She read from a set of cue cards. "You've all made many sacrifices to be here. Each of you has different reasons for embarking on the challenges the next three years will bring. All of you have proven your merit for this magnificent privilege. However, the next three years will be the most difficult you will ever experience.

"Many of you came from some of the top universities in the world; others came from more humble backgrounds, none of which is important here. You will be pushed in all areas of discipline. Most of you will fail to be among those going to Persia. I tell you this not to discourage anyone, but to prepare you for what's coming. Rest assured, all will be given responsibilities. But only four hundred will go to Persia and only thirty of those will be foot soldiers.

"Today you will be introduced to your leaders, your instructors, and your trainers. By the end of this information session, you will have all the tools necessary to succeed in your unique training." Olivia put down her cue cards. "I'm not here to make a speech, so I will introduce to you the leaders who will make the voyage with you."

The first one called to the podium was Lieutenant General Commander Callahan Rye. He was a man in his late fifties with a weather-worn face that commanded respect. He was responsible for the day-to-day activities of the mission once it left for Persia. In his twenty minute speech, he made sure all present knew he was second in command under Olivia.

Next up was Major General Nathan Kirkpatrick. He explained that the mental condition of those going to Persia would be his responsibility.

"I hope they teach us what all these ranks mean," Thomas said. "I've never been in the navy."

"Actually, they're army terms," Derrek explained. "US army terms, to be precise."

"Thanks," Thomas replied. "You made me feel much dumber."

"I now have the privilege of introducing your instructors and trainers," Olivia announced. She called to the podium Professor Barnaby Lancaster. In his usual self-confident way, he explained how the physical evidence collected during this expedition would change the way the world viewed God and the Bible. Thomas couldn't help but grin. He'd heard this speech before.

Next in line was Nicolas Knox. Although he'd said little at the hotel, Thomas knew his twenty minutes would be filled with quotes from the Bible. He wasn't disappointed. It was during the reading of Proverbs 3:5 which said "Trust in the LORD with all thine heart; and lean not unto thine own understanding," that Anna appeared on the platform and took her place among the others.

Now what's Anna doing on the platform? Thomas wondered. *She sure is a woman of many talents.* He glanced around hoping he hadn't said that out loud. Thomas found it difficult to concentrate while Nicolas delivered his lecture. He could not stop staring at Anna. Once he could have sworn she was looking straight back at him.

Next a perfect human specimen—tall and muscular without an ounce of fat, and a handsome, chiseled face—stepped up to the podium. He wore a white traditional Ethiopian shirt and pants with a colorful netela around his waist. He didn't list his qualifications like most of the others before him. In a deep, strong yet comforting voice he said, "Hello, my name is Kelile. I have been given the privilege of giving you the necessary physical training to stay healthy on the great mission to Persia. I will teach you to be proud of your body. I will teach you to defend yourself by applying techniques from differ-ent martial arts disciplines. I will teach you to skillfully use ancient Persian weapons of war. I will see you at four o'clock this afternoon. Thank you."

Olivia was in her seat only a few seconds before she had to get back to the podium to call on the next instructor. But before she did, she said, "As you can see, Kelile is a humble man. I will tell you about him. He is a world class ancient weapons specialist. He has trained with weapons from Rome, Greece, Africa, Asia, and Persia. He is also a master in Okinawan martial arts, notably karate, tegumi and kobudō. It is also noteworthy to tell you his name, Kelile, means 'my protector.' His father's name, Lemuel, means 'devoted to God.' You'll do well to learn all you can from this wonderful man."

Thomas sat up straight when Olivia announced Anna. "Hello and wel-come to our mission," she began. "I will keep this short. I'm a linguistic specialist. I can communicate in thirty-four languages, thirteen fluently, including modern and ancient Greek, Hebrew, and of course Persian.

"You will learn enough to communicate with our Persian hosts. Your vocabulary will be limited and you will have a strong foreign accent. This is acceptable since we will be portrayed as foreigners visiting their land. It will not be easy for you to learn this language. What's more, you must learn some Greek and Hebrew as well. No one said this will be easy. Well, that's it for me. I'm looking forward to working with all of you. Good luck to all."

For the next two and a half hours each speaker listed their qualifications and reiterated the challenges the next three years would bring.

•••••••••●○○○○○○○○○○

Over the next year, Thomas invested his time and energy in preparing for the ultimate prize, a trip to the ancient world empire of Medo-Persia.

Michael perhaps had said more than he knew when he visited Thomas back in Montreal and asked, "If you were the one who passed away instead of Amélie, what would you have wanted for her?" Thomas knew Amélie loved him and she would have approved, even encouraged, participating in this initiative, if for no other reason than to give him purpose.

But it wasn't all studies and training. There was the growing burden of being the famous man on the stela without a role. Although most in the ULRA trusted and supported Thomas, the few doubters proved to be the biggest challenge. As time went by they became bold in expressing their misgivings. Thomas held firm but inwardly, he might as well have hung a slab of basalt on a rope around his neck and disappeared. The burden of the doubters weighed heavy on his shoulders.

On the bright side, Thomas overcame the need to drink himself to sleep. He found solace in his small entourage of new friends. Even Anna softened her resentment toward him. As for the Komodo files, they spent most of the time in the old yellow envelope tucked away in his leather bag.

CHAPTER 13

One year later

"For the next item on our agenda," Ryan Moore, a very fat man with a full black beard, said, "I would like to invite Mr. and Mrs. McAllister along with Ms. Anna Latimer." Those summoned entered the room and took their positions at a large oval table.

Ryan opened the meeting by paraphrasing a prepared document. "Mrs. McAllister submitted a nine-page letter to this council explaining in some detail why we should investigate the legitimacy of Mr. Thomas Faraday's claim as the person referred to on the Persian stela." He looked at the McAllisters. "It's my understanding that you and your husband both signed this letter, but it's you, Mrs. McAllister, who wrote it. Is this correct?"

"Yes, that's correct," Yetta said. "But only after consulting with my husband."

"In that case, Mrs. McAllister, please explain to us in one minute or less the nature of your request."

"I'm suggesting the board should assign someone to investigate Mr. Faraday's claim that he is the man on the stela. My reason is—or should I say my husband and I agree—if he's the right man, we should know by now why he was chosen and what his role is in the ULRA. It's our understanding that this role is critical, so we don't want to put the mission at risk by blindly accepting the wrong person. Also, since he is given a free pass, he is taking the place of someone who has worked hard, someone who merits this position. This would be a miscarriage of justice, a lack of Christian quality—"

"Thank you, Mrs. McAllister, for your explanation," Ryan interrupted. "Does anyone have something to say on this matter before we invite Ms. Latimer's comment?"

Ridley Walker, a professor of Middle Eastern history, put both hands on the table in front of him. He spoke in a slow, deliberate tone. "I'm privileged to know Professor Lancaster. He told me that it was difficult to convince Mr. Faraday to examine the Persian stela. Even after he examined it, Mr. Faraday had misgivings about its authenticity. He was more concerned how the information about him was acquired than he was about the League. Furthermore, Mr. Faraday has not hidden his doubts about our organization. This would contravene the idea that he's bluffing his way into our League."

Scowling, Major General Nathan Kirkpatrick pushed his papers to one side. "As you know," he said, not trying to hide his annoyance, "I take my responsibility seriously. I personally get acquainted with all members of the mission. It's therefore my professional opinion that, despite not knowing his role, Mr. Faraday is not a fraud. I can assure all present that not knowing the role he's to play is harder on him than anyone else. He has expressed his own doubts to me, and I quote, 'maybe I'm not the man after all.' Yet despite this, he is one of the more industrious students in the program. I, for one, have no reason to question Mr. Faraday's motives."

"I agree with the major general," said Lieutenant General Commander Callahan Rye. "He has displayed a desire to learn and succeeds in all the subjects required of him. In my opinion, he has shown a high level of endurance. I say this because he has persisted despite the misgivings of others like Mrs. McAllister, who has not felt the need to hide her feelings. This has had a negative effect on Mr. Faraday, though not to the point of discouragement. I agree that no action on this matter is warranted."

"I would like to make one last point," Professor Walker said. "I remember a conversation I had with Nicolas Knox. As we already know, he was with Professor Lancaster in Québec when they approached Mr. Faraday. Nicolas confided in me his concern regarding Mr. Faraday's lack of faith in any organized religion. At first this bothered me as well. But after Nicolas explained his concern, he did say something interesting. He said the apostle Paul persecuted Christians before he became one of Jesus's most active apostles."

"Oh, please," Yetta cried. "You're not comparing Thomas to the apostle Paul?"

"Mrs. McAllister," Ryan interjected, "you are not permitted to participate in this conversation unless you're invited to do so. If you interrupt again, you will be asked to leave this conference room."

Professor Walker continued as if nothing had happened. "Nicolas Knox indicated that knowing what God has in mind for Mr. Faraday will be revealed in due time, even if it seems he lacks the faith we share."

"If there is no further comment," Ryan said, "I would like to invite Ms. Anna Latimer to share her opinion of Mr. Faraday."

"I'm afraid I don't have anything prepared," Anna said. "I was never told why I was invited to this meeting."

"Don't worry, Ms. Latimer; say whatever comes to mind," Ryan told her. "This is not a trial."

"Very well." She drew a deep breath and paused to gather her thoughts. "As you know, I'm one of Mr. Faraday's teachers. In my dealings with him, I have come to appreciate his hard work and his serious attitude toward his assignments." She hesitated as if unsure she should reveal something.

"Please, Ms. Latimer. Don't feel insecure about saying whatever needs to be said."

"Well," she continued, "I too had negative feelings about Mr. Faraday's role in the mission, but after hearing the comments at this inquiry, I must say I now see matters in a different light. I have been guilty at times of making it hard for him. I'm beginning to see my errors, especially now that I have his final grades for the first year's study period. I think Mr. Faraday has suffered enough at the hands of negative students. Some—not all, but some teachers and instructors like me gave him a difficult time. I'm ashamed, and I'm not shy to admit it. I recommend he should be left alone and the future will be his judge."

"First of all, Ms. Latimer, you don't have a vote in this committee, so please refrain from commenting on what we should or should not do," Ryan said. Anna nodded. "You said you have Mr. Faraday's academic results. You don't happen to have this report on you, by any chance?"

"As a matter of fact, I do. I was going to my office after this meeting to finalize the report to be sent to the other teachers and instructors. I'm the only one at the moment with the final results."

"Please tell us what the results are for Mr. Faraday."

Anna reached into her bag and pulled out a blue folder. She took about four minutes to highlight the results from his different classes. With the help of a calculator she compared his results with each program's average. When she finished, Anna had a hard time holding back a smile.

"Please note I'm doing this quickly," she said. "I have not double-checked the results. If my calculations are correct, Mr. Faraday's average of ninety-three percent puts him among the top ten students in our program. He won't need that free pass after all." She tried to stifle a giggle.

"Is there something else you need to tell us?" Ryan asked.

"Nothing important," Anna replied. "I just find it funny that a man who likes sports so much would score his lowest mark in Kelile's physical training class."

"Thank you, Ms. Latimer, for your cooperation," Ryan said, turning to address the table. "Does anyone have anything further to add on the matter of Mr. Faraday?" No one spoke. "Then I propose we take no action in the matter of Mr. Faraday's role in the ULRA. We will now vote on my proposal." All voted for Ryan's recommendation.

Anna, Yetta, and Aldon left the conference room. Ryan poured himself a glass of ice water.

"I don't like the attention created over this matter," Callahan said.

"It's getting too dangerous," Nathan added.

"Please, gentlemen," Ryan pleaded. "As far as we know all those involved with the stela are gone. We and a few others are the only ones who know the truth behind this stela. And we have all been sworn to secrecy. All we need to do is protect Thomas until the mission's conclusion. In time we will decide how much of the truth we will reveal. In the meantime, we stick with the plan. Very soon we will be in a position to do whatever we please."

"What do we do about McAllister?" Ridley asked.

"Nothing," Ryan said. "Aldon is too much of a coward to do anything. He will do whatever Yetta tells him to do. As for Yetta, I will call her tonight to emphasize the necessity of remaining quiet concerning Thomas. She will do what I ask of her." He took another sip of water. "I will reward her for her troubles, just to make sure."

• • • • • • • • ● ○○○○○○○○○ ○ ○

Anna stopped in front of the door to Thomas Faraday's quarters and composed herself before lifting a fist to knock softly on his door. Moments later, it swung open. "Ms. Latimer, what a pleasant surprise."

"How are you, Mr. Faraday?"

"Fine, just fine. What can I do for you?"

"May I come in for a moment?"

"Of course, please come in." He stepped back and she entered and stopped just inside the door. "Can I get you something to drink? I have coffee, milk, grapefruit juice—or perhaps you'd prefer a beer?"

"No thanks, nothing for me. I won't be taking too much of your time."

"In that case, why don't you sit down?" He indicated the sofa, but she looked around and decided to sit at the kitchen table. Thomas sat across from her and waited for her to reveal the reason for her visit.

"What I'm about to tell you Mr. Faraday is difficult for me to say, so I will ask you to refrain from making any comments until I've said what I came here to say," Anna said.

"All right."

She drew a deep breath. "Since you joined the mission one year ago, I've been acting in an unacceptable manner," she said. "I failed to show you respect. I even contributed to the difficulties you faced because of questions surrounding your role in the mission. I came here to apologize for my poor behavior. I hope you can find it in your heart to forgive me."

Thomas rose and went to the refrigerator for a beer. "Are you sure you don't want something to drink?"

"Yes, I'm sure, thank you."

He sat back down. "Listen to me, Ms. Latimer. I've come to respect you both as a teacher and a person. You're merely trying to protect what's close to you, the League and its mission. If I were in your place, I probably would have reacted the same way, so there's no reason to apologize and no need for forgiveness. You did what many here are doing, that's putting my presence into question. I don't blame anyone for that. It's up to me to prove I belong, not the other way around." He paused. "In fact, I have been looking for a way to tell you how much I admire you, as a professional, of course. You must admit, you can be a little difficult to approach, but since you're here and we're talking openly I think you should know."

Anna smiled. She gazed at Thomas for a few seconds then said, "You're a true gentleman, Mr. Faraday."

"Oh yes, one more thing," Thomas continued. "I hope I'm not overstepping my place. I know how you feel about this, but if you can be comfortable with the idea, it would mean so much to me if you call me Thomas instead of Mr. Faraday. It makes me feel old."

"Only if you call me Anna," she said.

Thomas smiled. "Okay, Anna."

Anna had hoped to feel relief after speaking with Thomas, but what she hadn't anticipated was feeling comfortable in his presence. Thomas's calm, caring reaction to her apology moved her in an unexpected way. She had a strong urge to stay and talk. So she pulled the blue folder from her bag and set it on the table. "I'd like to show you something, Thomas, but first you must promise not to reveal its contents to anyone until it has been made public. Can I trust you on this matter?"

"Of course you can trust me."

"I have here your final grades and your partial assignments."

Thomas held up his hand. "Wait just one minute. I'm going to need something a little stronger than beer." He pushed aside the unfinished beer, then rose and retrieved an almost empty bottle of scotch and two glasses from a cupboard. He poured the last of the scotch into the glasses and walked back to set them on the table.

Anna got the hint. Since the pressure was gone, she reached for a glass. "I believe this is a moment to celebrate, so why not." She took a small sip, looked at Thomas, and said, "Are you ready?"

"Yes, I am."

"Your final overall grade is—" she paused and smiled for a few seconds "ninety-three percent. That's good enough for ninth place in the entire academic program. This means if you continue like this you'll not only be going to Persia, but there's a good chance you'll be a foot soldier, as well."

She saw his fist clench. In a soft, controlled voice he said, "And I don't need that cursed free pass."

Anna got up, reached over to Thomas, and gave him a tender kiss on each cheek. "Congratulations, Thomas. No one deserves it more than you."

For the next few minutes they sat talking about his classes. Then she noticed a stack of papers on an empty chair. "I see you're busy doing paperwork, so I'll be on my way."

"No, please wait, Anna. Finish your drink, at least."

"All right." She glanced at the papers again. "So what are you doing, writing your memoir in some secret code?"

He chuckled. "No, that would require way too much work. I was thinking how much I missed the rain falling on the solarium roof back home." He glanced at a picture of a woman and a boy hanging on the wall beside the table—his family, Anna assumed. "So I thought of writing someone a letter telling them there should be rain once in a while, falling from the ceiling over our central park, of course. It would be a nice change from the perfect weather we get all the time."

"I think that's a great idea, Thomas; it would be romantic. But I was referring to those papers over there." She pointed to the small stack on the chair. "The ones that look like the computer is not compatible with the printer."

He looked at the papers. "Now I understand your secret code remark.

Those are a gift from a cracker I was tracking when I worked at Northern F.P. It's the encrypted message he left for me. I'm still trying to figure it out. I won't give up until I do. Along with a picture of my wife and son, these papers follow me everywhere I go. I'm convinced they have an important message intended for me."

"Maybe one day you'll let me have a look at them," she said. "I love puzzles."

"Then you'll love this one."

Anna finished her drink, got up, and headed for the door. "I guess I'll be seeing you in class tomorrow. By the way, why don't you give me your rain request when you're done, and I'll give it to the right people for you."

She turned to face Thomas before closing the door behind her. "Thank you for the drink, Thomas. Thank you for everything tonight."

"I'm glad you came by," Thomas said.

CHAPTER 14

One month before the trip to Persia

Three years of training came to an end with a great celebration. All were invited, from the maintenance staff to the governing body. The atmosphere was electrifying. All were in a festive mood. Rock classics of the seventies, eighties, and nineties—the music theme the League members had voted for—filled the air.

There was but one speaker this time, Mr. Ryan Moore, the rarely seen president of the League. In his congratulatory speech, he refused to give special thanks to any one person, feeling all deserved the same credit. He spoke for eight minutes before leaving a stage cluttered with musical instruments. As he walked toward his table, everyone stood to honor him with a standing ovation.

Thomas sat with his close friends Anna, Quincy, and Aldon at one table. Derrek had given up his usual place to be with his mentor, Barnaby Lancaster. Late in arriving was Kelile. "Thank you for having me at your table, I am honored," he said as he sat down.

"The honor is ours," Thomas insisted.

"The music is so loud," Kelile said, "I can't hear myself speak."

Thomas moved his chair closer to the table. "It's too bad Yetta can't be here with you, Aldon."

"It's hard for her to get away from her responsibilities."

"Still, you're her husband. You'd think she'd be here with you on a day like this."

"She did say she'll join us later."

"Well then," Thomas lifted his glass of fine red wine, "to best friends and to the success of the mission." They raised their glasses and responded with a loud "hear, hear."

"I too would like to propose a toast," Kelile said as he raised his glass of carrot juice. "To the health of all those I was able to help on the road to maximum physical fitness and the mastery of martial arts. And," he held his glass in Thomas's direction, "to Thomas for at least giving it his best shot."

"Hear, hear," they all said and broke into loud, boisterous laughter.

Quincy raised both hands to get everyone's attention. "If I may, I do have an important question for all of you. If you can answer this question I know your training is complete." Thomas smiled, knowing what was coming. "I still can't figure out the difference between the toilet and the microwave in my apartment; can anyone help me out with this one?"

"No Quincy, we have no idea," Thomas said, rushing the punch line.

"In that case, I won't invite you to my apartment. You might crap in my microwave." They all burst into laughter at his pointless joke.

Over the next two hours they ate till they could eat no more. As the waiter cleared the table for the next round of their preferred drinks, Yetta appeared behind Aldon. "Hello everyone," she said, lovingly resting her hands on her husband's shoulders before she leaned over to kiss Aldon on the lips.

"Come sit with us, cupcake," he said to her. "I'll order a Black Russian, your favorite."

"Don't bother, Aldon; I can't stay. I just came to say I'll be going to a private party held for the members of the governing body. Can you imagine? They invited me. I can't miss this opportunity to be with important people." She looked around with a superior smirk. "Not that your friends aren't important people, of course. You do understand, right honey?"

"Yes, of course, Yetta. Go and have fun. I'll be fine here with my friends."

Yetta turned and walked toward the exit. Aldon waited until she was out of hearing range. "I'll be all right. I have the best support system in the world right here." He raised his glass. "Hear, hear?"

"Hear, hear," they said with somewhat less enthusiasm.

Anna looked at her watch., "It's ten o'clock, boys—it's time."

Quincy rose and left their company. Thomas watched him go, his expression quizzical.

"Thomas, we have a surprise for you," Anna said. "It's someone we know you've been missing for the last three years. He made a special trip from the third facility just to see you. It was difficult to get permission, but being you're the stela man, well, in the end it was granted."

Thomas stood up when he saw Quincy approaching with his longtime friend. "Michael? Michael, is it really you?" They hugged in a tearful embrace. "Did you receive my letter?" he asked as they parted. "They allowed me only one letter, did you get it?"

Michael was beaming. "Yes Thomas, I got your letter."

"How did you find me? I mean, how did you know I was here?" Thomas asked as they sat down. "Wait." Before Michael could say anything, Thomas ordered him a cup of coffee. "You still don't drink, right? That's why I ordered you a coffee. So, how are you? How are things back home?"

"Everything is great, Thomas, just great. In fact, they want to know when you're coming back to work."

"So they realized I'm not Komodo after all. Well, they're going to wait a long time before I work for them again." The waiter arrived with Michael's coffee. "God, I missed you so much, Michael."

"I was never far away, Thomas. When the League contacted me, they sent me directly to the third facility. You know how strict they are about communication between facilities. That's why I was unable to let you know I was here."

"How long have you been here?"

"Nearly two years now."

"Two years, that long." Thomas shook his head. "I thought you'd just arrived. So tell me: what do you do for the League?"

Michael smiled. "I recruit people with specific skills for the mission."

"Sounds difficult, considering all the secrecy we have here."

"It's quite challenging," Michael agreed.

"How long have you been in Facility Three again?"

"Two years tomorrow."

Thomas was feeling hot. He ordered a double scotch. "So how long have you known about the ULRA?" He saw Michael stiffen. Thomas could always read Michael. He knew where Thomas was going with these questions.

"For almost nine years."

Thomas put his hand on his forehead as if nursing a headache. When his scotch arrived he downed it in one gulp. "Bring me another one," he told the waiter.

"Is everything all right, Thomas?" Anna asked.

Thomas ignored the question. "So let me see if I understand. You've been preaching religion all these years to me. And here I thought you wanted me to find God. Was it always for the League?"

"Not always, I do believe everything I said."

"The vacation you planned for me. You knew all along I was the man on the stela. Did you make that stela yourself, to trick me into accepting this mission?"

"No man, the stela is genuine. You should know that by now. I suspected you might be the one described on it, but I wasn't sure; I had to find out."

Thomas dropped his hand but glared at the tabletop. "You knew I was going through difficult times, yet you chose to keep all of this from me. We're best friends. We would die for each other. Damn it, Michael, I tell you every little detail of my life, even the personal stuff. And you do this to me."

Michael had nothing to say. After two agonizing minutes, Thomas looked up at Michael. "Are you Komodo?"

"No, of course not."

"Do you know who Komodo is?"

"No man, I have no idea who he is."

Thomas stood. "Thank you all for making these past three years a wonderful journey and for being my friends." The second scotch arrived. "Here's to real friends." He downed the drink. No one cheered this time.

Michael got up and approached Thomas. Thomas put his hand against Michael's chest. "Don't. Just don't."

Michael persisted. "Give me a chance to explain, man."

With his right hand Thomas punched Michael so hard across the cheek, he crashed into the next table. Kelile instinctively jumped up and held Thomas in one of his tegumi grappling holds. Michael stumbled back to his feet. The tables around them had fallen silent, as everyone watched. The band stopped playing. There'd never been a fist fight within the League before.

"Let me go," Thomas shouted.

"It's okay. Let him go," Michael insisted. "If he wants to hit me again I won't stop him."

Kelile released Thomas. He straightened up and looked around. "I've had enough celebrating for one night. I'll see you all in Facility Three." He looked at Aldon. "Or more likely at one of your judicial committees."

"Wait for me," Anna called out as Thomas walked away.

He stopped to face her. "How long did you know Michael was here?"

"I found out two weeks ago, after his seventh request for a visit to our facility to see you. Aldon found out about his last request and told me."

Thomas took a deep breath and said as calmly as he could muster, "You did what you thought was right. You had no way of knowing what Michael meant to me. Please go back and tell the others all is good, and I'll go to my accommodations and retire for the night."

Anna's shoulders slumped. After a moment she nodded.

Thomas stayed in his apartment until it was time to make the move to the third facility.

CHAPTER 15

Three days before the launch

Derrek and Quincy walked into a room that resembled the reception area of a medical clinic. There were no windows. The chairs were lined up in the center of the room. A beautiful young woman seated behind a small reception counter greeted them. She wore a uniform similar to that of an airline hostess, with the League's logo on the left breast. "Hey boys," she said.

"Hey," Quincy said as he removed his headphones.

"So you boys are here for the guided tour of the *Kismet*?"

"Yes we are. We were assigned to this morning's tour," Quincy said. "Are you going to be our guide?"

"That would be me, but first I need both of your names for registration."

"I'm Quincy Daramy and this is my friend Derrek."

"How do you do," Derrek said.

"Good, thank you." Her eyes remained fixed on Quincy.

"That's Derrek McCarthy," he added.

"You have us at a disadvantage. You know our names but we don't know yours," Quincy said.

"My name is Stephanie, Stephanie Emerson."

"It's nice to meet you, Stephanie Emerson. My name is Quincy."

"I know, you just told me."

"Oh boy," Derrek muttered. He looked at both of them. "I'll just go sit over there and wait."

"Before you go, sign right here and take your lapel card." She held out a clipboard. "You need to have the lapel card on at all times. As soon as everyone arrives, we'll be on our way."

Derrek sat down and watched as Quincy and Stephanie flirted like two teenagers. Five minutes later Aldon entered the room. He registered without saying a word. After taking his lapel card he took his place next to Derrek. "What's going on with those two?"

"They're under some kind of spell. They won't stop that embarrassing display."

"It looks like they're in love."

"In love? They just met."

"That's how it happened with Yetta and me. Yup, just like that—love at first sight. It's unmistakable."

Derrek looked at Aldon. "I think I'll just shoot myself right now."

"No, no, it happens."

"By the way, where is Yetta?" Derrek asked. "I thought she was taking the tour with us."

"She was supposed to, but she's not feeling well. I took her to the infirmary before coming here."

"It's not serious, I hope."

"No, it's not bad at all, probably food poisoning or something. Besides, she took the tour yesterday. She was coming to keep me company."

"Well, I hope she gets better soon."

"She'll be fine. She said she might meet up with us as soon as she leaves the infirmary."

Next to arrive was Anna, accompanied by Kelile. "It would seem Quincy made a friend," Anna said as they found their seats.

"Yes, you're correct," Kelile remarked. "Does anyone know her name?"

"Stephanie Emerson," answered Derrek.

Kelile turned his attention to Anna. "Have you heard anything from Thomas?"

"No. He leaves his accommodations for training, but that's about it."

"Does he not come out to eat?"

She shook her head. "Nope, only for training. I tried to visit him a few times, but he won't let me in. The last time, he told me he wasn't feeling well and not to come back until he told me to. He's supposed to be here for the tour. I sure hope he shows up." She released a deep sigh. "I blame myself for what happened. I shouldn't have surprised him with Michael. Had I told him about Michael before the party, he might have reacted differently."

"You should not blame yourself for what he did. He suffered much hurt in his life. Healing can take many years. He is not healed yet. Sometimes, when a person has lost a lot, they cannot accept the good that comes their way. So he hurts himself by chasing away the good, fearing it won't last, so why prolong the inevitable?" Kelile said.

"Michael was there for him all the way through his trials," Anna said. "Thomas has no reason to treat him that way."

"It's because of Michael's loyalty that Thomas reacted that way. It is our responsibility as his friends to help him realize he has the right to be happy."

Derrek turned to face Kelile. "How do you propose we do that?"

"We must stand by him without saying a word, without judging." He looked at Anna, expecting her to say something.

"What?" Anna said.

"You and Thomas seem to get along well. I think you more than the rest of us can help him."

"What do you mean, we get along well?"

Kelile hesitated. "I apologize, my words were inappropriate."

"No Kelile, you said something, now finish it," Anna pressed. "How are Thomas and I getting along well?"

"I am sorry, Anna. I misinterpreted your relationship with Thomas. When you're together you both seem so happy. You look comfortable together. Again, please forgive me for being presumptuous."

"Why all the long faces?" Quincy said as he joined them.

"Nothing," Anna said. "Go sit down."

Quincy shrugged. "Okay, just asking."

Before Quincy could find a seat, Michael arrived with Ashley Patterson, a successful general surgeon in her late thirties. She'd been on the ship many times before, helping to design the ship's infirmary. Anna assumed she was here due to the regulation requiring all members to take a tour before being allowed to leave for Persia. No tour, no trip.

"I would have arranged for a black eye myself, had I known the tour comes with a personal nurse," Quincy said, referring to Michael.

Ashley was not amused. "You want a black eye? Come over here, I'll be more than happy to indulge you."

Everyone stopped talking when Stephanie approached, accompanied by Nicolas Knox and Brody Powell. She paused to write some notes on a clipboard, then looked up. "Okay then," she said to the group, "it seems everyone but Mr. Faraday has arrived. Since we're already ten minutes behind schedule, we'd better get going without him. So, if you would follow me, we'll begin."

Anna hung back as everyone left the room, hoping Thomas would still show up. When she was the only one left in the room, she quickly wrote a note and set it on the reception counter before darting for the door. She was almost knocked over by Thomas, who was rushing into the room. They found themselves in each other's arms.

"Thomas! You're here. I was beginning to worry."

Thomas stepped quickly back. "I made it this far, Anna. I don't want to miss the boat, after everything we've been through."

Anna smiled at his "we've been through," rather than "I've been through." She handed him his lapel card. "I'm glad you made it, Thomas."

"Me too. Now let's go before we lose them."

• • • • • • • • • • ● ○○○○○○○○○ ○ ○

They caught up to the group as it followed Stephanie up a narrow steel staircase. They entered a large room filled with banks of electronic dashboards. It reminded Thomas of a photo he'd seen of the ENIAC Super Brain introduced in the forties when he'd been studying the history of computers at McGill University. What he was looking at, however, was no museum display. These were advanced beyond anything available commercially.

"So, as you can see, the technology here is the best in the world. In here, a small group of technicians will monitor the portal when the *Kismet* is launched in three days." Stephanie consulted her clipboard. "It's interesting to note that the time between the departure of the *Kismet* and its return is ninety minutes. So the observers will hardly have time to sit down when—bam!—it's all over. But for the mission's travelers, ten months will pass in Persia."

She walked over to a console where a man sat with his back to them. He didn't look up when Stephanie spoke and appeared to be ignoring the group, absorbed in whatever was on his screen. "At this point I would like to introduce you to Dr. Patrick Walsh. Patrick is one of five scientists who designed the portal and the mission control center we find ourselves in. Some people call him the Albert Einstein of Ireland. It must be because he's old." It didn't seem to bother Stephanie that Quincy was the only one who laughed at her joke.

"So anyway, he has a hearing problem. He has a tendency to speak very loud. I must also warn you, he considers himself quite the entertainer." Stephanie turned and stepped around to stop beside Patrick. Speaking loudly, emphasizing each word, she said to him, "They're all yours."

Patrick turned his chair around to face the group. "Welcome to the eyes and ears of the mission. I must say right from the start, I will be answering your questions, but you'll need to speak up. I refuse to wear those damn hearing aids. All they do is magnify the humming noise from these damn computers. Now please come over here. If you look through these large windows, you can see the *Kismet*. It is one hundred and thirty meters long, twenty-two point five meters wide, and fifty-five point five meters high."

The group leaned over to peer through the window but all they could see were two large doors at the bottom center of the ship. Since the only lights on were at the entrance of the portal, most of the ship was shrouded in darkness.

"You'll see the complete ship later," Stephanie said.

"This console in front of me controls everything related to the *Kismet* and the portal," Patrick continued. "If you look directly behind you, you see six rows of theater seats. That's where the mission's bosses will be when you beautiful people leave in three days.

"Now back to the portal. It was here that the large wormhole was discovered. Although it's as large as wormholes come, it must be enlarged even further for a ship like the *Kismet* to pass through it. You probably already know that in nature a wormhole is smaller than an atom. It's a billion-trillion-trillionths of a centimeter across. Imagine the power needed to enlarge one to the size of a ship." He paused to let them absorb that.

"That was not the only issue we needed to address. We need to keep the wormhole open long enough for a ship to pass through. To do this we have developed the world's first fully functioning negative energy plant. The blue and white electric field you see surrounding the ship is the actual walls of the portal, held open by negative energy. If you touch this energy, you'll be sucked into it. Who knows where and when you'll appear? Can I trust you not to touch the walls?" Everybody laughed at the remark. "If you look down again," Patrick continued, "you'll see the bridge leading to the *Kismet*. If you stay on that bridge at all times, you will not be in any danger.

"For the time being the ship is not connected to the portal. For send-off we need a closed circuit. To prevent an accidental launch, we keep the circuit open. To close the circuit we must do three things. First, the door to the portal must be closed. That's the entrance you'll be going through soon. Inside the *Kismet*, an umbilical cord must be attached. Once these are in place, I will punch down on this large red kill switch." He pointed to the kill switch next to him on the dashboard. "The switch is protected behind this Plexiglass box to prevent it from accidentally being pushed down." Patrick grinned. "So you see, from where I'm sitting, a monkey could send the *Kismet* on its way."

Stephanie clapped her hands to get everyone's attention. "So, thank you, Dr. Walsh, but time is moving on and I have no way of controlling time like your machine." There were mutters of disappointment. They wanted to hear more of what Patrick had to say. "Please follow me."

They retraced their steps down the stairs and stopped outside the portal entrance. Stephanie spent the next five minutes making sure everyone understood the safety rules before they entered.

"Stay within the yellow- and black-striped lines, okay? If you deviate from these lines you will get hurt or killed. As for the portal, it will not even notice." She looked at everyone to make sure they were paying attention. "So if you're ready, let's go in."

Stephanie led the group through the opening to the portal that was normally protected by a thick, vault-like steel door. "How are you doing, Igor?" Stephanie said to the diminutive man standing guard next to it.

"Very good, Miss Stephanie. How are you today?"

"Good, thank you." She turned back to face the group. "I would like to introduce you to Igor. We call Igor the gatekeeper. He, along with two others, Samir and Gopesh, are responsible for closing the door twelve times a day to disinfect the floor behind it. Remember, the smallest dust particle can affect the portal's performance." She scanned their faces. "Any questions? No? Okay then, please follow me."

Partway across the bridge leading to the *Kismet*, Stephanie turned and, walking backward, said, "If you look on either side of this bridge, you'll see a gap. It's actually a powerful vacuum that will suck in anything dropped into it. So ladies, hold on to your jewelry."

Thomas gave a respectful laugh and turned to Anna—but it was Michael walking next to him. He slowed down to let Michael walk ahead. Replacing him from behind came Anna. "It's okay, Thomas," she said as she slid her hand into his. All at once his senses exploded. He noticed every detail of Anna's presence, the gentle touch of her warm, soft hand, her hair brushing against his neck, the sweet scent of her perfume. If she had been any other woman he would have brushed it off as a harmless attempt at encouragement. But this was not any other woman. It was Anna, someone who captivated him, someone he respected, even admired, but not someone he was in love with. Or had he fallen in love? Not wanting to give in to those unexpected feelings, Thomas turned to her. "Thank you, Anna, it's very kind of you to care like this." He squeezed gently, then let her hand go.

The ship materialized as they approached. It looked like an oversized cargo container. As they got closer, the details became clearer. A line of small windows ran around the top of the ship and above these was a railing that curved outward like the lip of a pitcher. Above the hatch, a small sign no bigger than a tablet computer displayed the name *Kismet*.

Inside, Stephanie gathered everyone in the center of the small space. Thomas looked around. There were two elevators, one on each side. A sign on the wall identified the area as *Orlop Deck*. "Ladies and gentlemen, welcome to the *Kismet*," she said, then read from her notes, "The name *Kismet* is an Arabic word originating from ancient Persia; it means 'fate' or 'destiny.' We're not sure how it's pronounced in the original Persian language, but in English we pronounce it kizmet. Since the ship's destination is determined by the wormhole, it was deemed appropriate to name her *Kismet*."

Stephanie next directed them into the elevator. "Our first stop is the captain's cabin. As you see, the doors are closed; this means they're having a meeting as we speak. So, unfortunately I can't show you this section right now. Note the sign; it says *Captain's Cabin*. The truth is, behind those doors you will also find the lodgings for the *Kismet*'s entire management section. During the day the doors are usually open for administrative purposes.

"Let's now head up one level to visit the Boat Deck," Stephanie said.

They entered a large, almost empty room. On one side four objects that looked like large, silver eggs rested horizontally. "Here we have the pods used for transporting the foot soldiers between the ship and Earth. They're equipped with invisibility shields much like those on the *Kismet*, so the foot soldiers can leave the pods undetected on Earth."

Over the next hour Stephanie explained in great detail the seven remaining levels until they finally reached the hull of the *Kismet*. They followed Stephanie into a structure near the bow that resembled a wheelhouse you'd find on a large, modern ship. There, in the middle of the floor, was a man on a stepladder, his head hidden in an opening in the suspended ceiling. Stephanie noticed everyone was distracted by him, so she called, "Nasato."

A clean-cut young Japanese man dropped from the ceiling.

"May I introduce you to Nasato Nakamura," Stephanie said.

"Konnichiwa," Nasato said.

"So why don't you tell us what you are doing up in the ceiling, Nasato."

"In all humility," Nasato said, "what I'm doing here is historical." He looked at the soldering iron in his hand. "I will be soldering these two parts of the umbilical cord. This means, for the first time, all parts of the network will be amalgamated into one big system. You're fortunate to witness this momentous event."

• • • • • • • • • • ● ○○○○○○○○○○ ○

Down in the portal, Igor looked up to peer through the mission control window and gave the okay sign to Patrick. Because of his poor hearing, Patrick and Igor had developed a set of hand signals, rather than using the intercom next to the door. Patrick responded with his own okay sign, and Igor prepared to close the airtight door in order to clean behind it.

Patrick returned to his chair and relaxed into it with his fifth cup of coffee. He lifted the cup to his nose and inhaled appreciatively—and released the breath in a gasp as a tight pain clenched his chest. It felt like an elephant was standing on him! *Heart attack*— The thought flashed through Patrick's mind as his fingers curled into fists, crushing his Styrofoam cup. Coffee gushed over the dashboard in front of him. He fell to the floor, paralyzed.

• • • • • • • • • • ● ○○○○○○○○○○ ○

Igor finished his cleaning. He looked up to let Patrick know he was done, but didn't see Patrick. "Huh. Strange," he muttered. He called him on the intercom. Nothing.

He waited a few minutes, thinking Patrick had gone to the restroom. Finally, unable to reach him and unable to open the door, Igor called for help.

This gave the spilled coffee time to trickle under the transparent cover designed to prevent accidental depression of the red button. The button wasn't designed to be waterproof. The coffee dripped into the opening made for the red button and caused a short circuit—generating the same response as if someone had pressed down on the red kill switch.

• • • • • • • • • • ● ○○○○○○○○○○ ○

Everyone watched Nasato, who stood looking at the mission control window, waiting for the okay sign from Patrick. He waited thirty seconds and still he didn't see him in the window. Feeling somewhat foolish for making a big deal about the connection of the umbilical cord, he decided to go through with the soldering without Patrick's okay. He brought the two ends of the cable together to form a connection before soldering them—

A blindingly white flash filled the wheelhouse, followed by complete blackness.

PART 2
THE MISSION

ULRA

𒉀𒐰𒌋𒌋

𒁇𒈬𒌍𒍣𒁇𒌋𒐽𒌋

CHAPTER 16

Thomas gasped for air. He tried opening his eyes, but the light blinded him and his head felt like it was about to explode. He sagged back onto the floor. "Must find a way to get up," he slurred. "Must get up." He felt around for support but found only cold tiles. He forced himself into a sitting position with his back resting against the wall.

"Hello, is anybody there?" he called out. No answer. He tried to listen for familiar sounds, but heard nothing but his own breathing. He wondered if he'd been in an accident.

Someone groaned next to him. "Who's there?" Thomas asked, squinting toward the noise.

"Thomas? Is that you?"

"Anna! Thank God you're here. Are you okay? Are you hurt?"

"I feel sick, Thomas; I feel cold."

"Try not to move, I'm coming." He found moving difficult but managed to crawl toward the direction of Anna's voice. He gathered her gently into his arms.

"I can't see anything, Thomas."

"It will pass soon," Thomas said, hoping that was true. "Close your eyes and rest for a while."

"It feels like a hangover," she said and groaned again. Thomas smiled, pleased that she still had her sense of humor.

Ten minutes passed before Thomas could see again. He looked around, remembering that they were in the wheelhouse of the *Kismet*. Other members of the tour were lying on the floor like the dead on a battlefield. No one was moving. He remembered the Japanese man on the ladder. *Nasato*. It was all coming back. He gently nudged Anna. "You need to sit up. Can you do that?"

"Yes, I think so." He helped her. "What happened?" she asked when she too was leaning against the wall.

"I don't know. Some kind of explosion. I can't say for sure."

"Are the others all right?" She looked around.

"I can't say. They must have been rendered unconscious, like us." Thomas turned to Anna, cupped her face in both hands, and said, "I need you to help me with the others, Anna. Can you do that?"

Before she could answer, several groans and weak movements signaled that the others were regaining consciousness. *Break time's over*, Thomas thought, watching as one by one the others woke. The first to recuperate was Dr. Patterson. This was a good thing since she could help the injured. Derrek and Michael came to next.

"If you can hear me," Thomas called out, "you'll feel a headache and temporary blindness, but don't worry, it will pass. You might get nauseated, so stay where you are."

Two minutes later Quincy regained consciousness, then Aldon, followed by Stephanie. Another minute passed before Nicolas and Brody struggled to help each other off the floor. Thomas, now fully recovered, helped them get oriented.

It wasn't untill everyone was awake and seated that a painful cry rose from between two computer consoles. Thomas rushed to investigate. He found Kelile helping Nasato, who was in obvious pain. "What happened to him?" Thomas asked.

"He broke his leg."

Thomas turned to Ashley. "Can you move? Can you help him?"

Ashley stood to test her stability. "I'm dizzy, but I can help him." She tottered over and knelt to probe his leg while asking him questions. "Clear the table," she called out to no one in particular. "Come on, help me move him."

With the help of Kelile, Thomas laid Nasato on a table and placed a seat cushion under his head as a pillow.

"He broke his leg, all right," Ashley said. "I suspect he's also suffering from a concussion. We need to take him to the ship's infirmary for more tests."

"We can't do that," Thomas said. "We still don't know what happened. We have no idea if it's safe out there. Can't you stabilize him here while we investigate?"

Ashley agreed. As she made Nasato as comfortable as possible, Thomas stepped back to regain his composure. Things were moving way too fast for him. He looked around for a place to sit but found an audience instead. His actions seemed to have made everyone instinctively wait on him for further directives. "Shit," he muttered. He scanned their faces and forced a smile.

"Does anyone have any idea what just happened?" No one answered. "Fine then, sit tight and give me a minute to think."

Quincy broke the awkward few seconds of silence. "Excuse me, may I offer a suggestion?"

"Of course, all suggestions are welcome," Thomas said, relieved. "What is it?"

"Well, the servers on this ship are programmed to take control of navigation in the event human navigators are incapacitated. Why don't we tell the servers to execute the autopilot?"

"That's a great idea," Derrek added. "In order for the autopilot to take control, it must first do a total diagnostics of the ship's health. It then prints out the results along with a recommendation to let us know if it's viable to start the autopilot or not. Maybe the report will tell us what happened."

"Go then, see what you can learn," Thomas said. "Remember, make sure you do it from the consoles within this room."

Quincy and Derrek jumped to their feet and moved to keyboards. Thomas watched them tap in requests for information, working like a well-rehearsed, synchronized team. They knew what to do and what to look for, which reassured him.

Over the next hour, they kept themselves busy exchanging ideas. Stephanie helped Ashley with Nasato while Thomas and Michael pored over technical manuals. Nicolas and Brody were instructed to guard the exit in case anyone got the urge to open the door.

Anna and Kelile were looking out the window when Kelile said, "When I was a boy, I would love to lie on my back and watch the night sky. No matter what my troubles were, those sparkling stars would somehow bring me comfort. I wonder if that was the intention of the architects when they designed this portal."

Anna stared through the glass. "You're right, Kelile, I can see them too." She was silent for a moment. "Why would they waste valuable resources painting stars on the portal ceiling?" She and Kelile looked at one another. Then she called Stephanie over. "Did they tell you anything about a night sky simulation in the portal? Because we can see one."

Stephanie looked out the window. "That's strange. The portal ceiling is nothing but cut rock and steel supporting beams. It makes no sense that they would bother to simulate the sky. But then again, I never gave a tour with the lights off."

"Thomas, can you come here for a minute?" Anna called out. Thomas joined them. "Look out the window. What do you see up in the sky?" The words were barely out of her mouth when she gasped. "My God, Thomas, do you think—"

"That's sky all right," Thomas confirmed. He dropped his voice. "Don't say anything yet." He went to Quincy and Derrek. "Can you tell from this console if we're still in the twenty-first century?"

They both looked at each other for a moment. "Yes," Derrek replied. "We programmed the computer to track real time."

"Good. Now tell me the date."

It took but one combination of keystrokes to get the answer, but several seconds before Derrek could bring himself to press the enter key. When he did, the white characters on the black screen read:

Hīt, Mesopotamia, Persia, 8 Sivan, 473 BC

"That's what I thought," Thomas said. "Tell me, this autopilot you spoke of: can it get us back without our intervention?"

"Of course, but there's a small glitch," Derrek said. "It's also programmed to complete the mission, if you get what I mean."

"I understand. Be ready to answer some questions, okay guys?" Thomas turned to face the others. "May I have your attention, please? Everyone please sit down. I'm now quite certain what happened." He waited until everyone was seated.

"Somehow when Nasato attached the umbilical cord earlier—" Thomas giggled at the irony. "Well, to put it bluntly, we've been sent back twenty-five hundred years. So congratulations. As far as we're concerned, the mission has started."

Everyone was calm. There was some mumbling. Aldon bent over and spewed the contents of his stomach onto the floor. Vomiting aside, Thomas felt relieved by the group's positive reaction.

"So, can we override the system and head back home?" Stephanie asked.

Thomas gave Derrek a glance. He shook his head. "No Stephanie, we don't know how to steer the ship back, so we must rely on the autopilot to bring us home."

"Does this mean we're in Persia, then?"

"Yes, Aldon, we're in Persia. Somewhere over the city of Hīt. The year is as expected."

"How long will we be here for?" Nicolas asked. "Brody and I . . . we're not trained to walk among the Persians. I doubt we could last very long out there."

"The *Kismet* is suspended two kilometers above the Earth. Nicolas, you and Brody will most likely never set foot on the ground. As for how long, well, it's the full duration of the mission—ten months." Thomas held up his hand. "I know you have many other questions. I have many questions too, and we'll try to answer them all in due time but first, we need to find out if it's safe on the ship. Once we settle in we can get organized and try to answer these many questions. So without further delay, I propose Michael, Kelile and I leave the wheelhouse to make sure it's safe to be outside. When we come back, we'll see how we can make our temporary stay here as comfortable as possible."

He looked to the table where Nasato lay. "Ashley and Stephanie, stay here, look after Nasato. We'll come back with a wheelchair from the infirmary. Derrek and Quincy, continue your work on getting the computers operational. Anna and Aldon, stay here in case there's a problem to be addressed."

"I'm coming with you," Anna insisted.

"Me too," Aldon said. "I can't stay here. I need to do something."

"No," Thomas replied. "We need someone to stay and watch the wheelhouse."

"Do you think we're incapable of taking care of ourselves?" Ashley retorted.

"Brody and I will stay if you want," Nicolas suggested.

Nasato pushed himself up on his elbows, wincing in pain. "Wait a minute. Aren't we forgetting something? I remember seeing Captain Washington on the *Kismet* when I came in to work; did anyone see her leave?"

"That's right," Stephanie said. "There was an administrative meeting going on during our tour. I'm sure they're still on board."

"Then there's no time to lose," Thomas said. "Let's go find them. They may need our help." He pulled Michael aside to allow Kelile, Anna, and Aldon to enter the elevator. "Head for the captain's cabin. We'll be with you in a minute."

Thomas waited until the elevator doors closed before leading Michael to the ship's bulwark. "Wow, is it ever cold out here," he said, rubbing his hands together. "Do you think the invisible shield is working?"

Michael looked over the edge. "It seems to be working—I can't see the sides of the ship. It gives the impression there's nothing under the floor."

"Good, good, this means we can't be detected from below."

Michael pressed his lips together and looked at Thomas. "You didn't call me over to see if the shield is working. You could have done that yourself."

Thomas sighed and ran a hand through his hair. "You're right, Michael.

You're always right. I called you here to apologize for hitting you and for treating you . . . well, as a traitor. I have no excuse for my behavior. I wouldn't blame you if you threw me overboard; then you'd be done with me."

Michael said nothing.

"I guess what I'm trying to say is that I'm glad you're here. I could never survive this without you." Thomas looked over the edge to reflect. "You deserve better than this. I don't know why you care so much."

"Do you see a glow over there on the horizon?"

Thomas smiled at his attempt to change the subject. "Yes. It resembles the glow visible over a city when seen from a distance."

"It's probably the city of Hīt. I wonder if we'll have a chance to pay them a visit."

"If I have anything to say about it, you know we will."

"I thought that's what you'd say. Now shall we catch up with the others before they start rumors about us?"

• • • • • • • • • ● ○○○○○○○○○ ○ ○

"They were all knocked out when we arrived," Anna said as Thomas and Michael joined them minutes later. "I figured being deeper inside the ship must have had a stronger effect on them. But once they revived, their recovery was rapid."

"How are they doing?" Thomas asked.

"No one seems to have any serious side effects. That at least is good. You need to bring Captain Washington up to date on what we know. Aldon's trying to do that, but he's going in a direction I can't understand. He keeps asking if they saw others on board."

"What did she say? Are there others on board?"

"No one seems to know for sure, but all those she summoned to the meeting are here in this room. There might be maintenance staff or technicians on board. We just don't know."

"So we have no other choice, we must make a thorough search of the ship."

"Thomas," Aldon called out, "I spoke with Captain Washington about the situation but I doubt she understood much. You should speak with her."

Anna gave Thomas an "I told you so" look.

"They don't know if there are other people aboard," Aldon continued. "I'm going to look for signs of life."

"Wait a minute," Thomas said. "You can't just run off, we need to get organized for a search. There could be dangers out there."

"There's no time to waste, Thomas. I'm going now. If we wait till you're good and ready it might be too late. Besides, Ashley needs a wheelchair for Nasato—I'll get one at the same time." Not waiting for Thomas's response, Aldon disappeared.

"You see what I mean?" Anna said. "He's acting strange."

"He must have been affected differently than the rest of us. Let him go. He can't hurt anyone by himself."

"There you are, Mr. Faraday," Olivia said. "I'm told you have taken charge of the situation."

"Sort of," Thomas acknowledged.

"Then tell me what's going on."

"Well, this is what we know so far: as Nasato attached the umbilical cord, something went wrong. We don't know what, but we know it set in motion the *Kismet*'s travel sequence, so now we find ourselves in Persia, the eighth day of Sivan, 473 BC. That's in the months of May and June, if my memory serves me right. What's important, though, is that we'll head back to the twenty-first century in ten months. Quincy and Derrek said this can be done simply by executing a program."

"Quincy and Derrek?"

"Quincy Daramy and Derrek McCarthy are the main computer programmers."

"Good; they're the people we want for this situation. Please continue."

"Actually, there's not much more to say except everyone seems to be doing well health-wise, except for Nasato, who broke a leg. There may be some concerns about the effect of time travel on the brain. We noticed one of our travelers behaving mysteriously. I suggest Dr. Patterson examine him."

"Who is this passenger?"

"Aldon McAllister."

Olivia remained silent. This gave Thomas an excuse to continue. "We also know the invisible shield is working, which leads me to believe all or most of the systems are in working order. It's as if the mission started prematurely. Well, that's about it. Oh, Derrek—I mean Mr. McCarthy and Mr. Daramy are compiling more information for us as we speak."

Olivia looked at her wristwatch. "Is the time on our watches accurate?"

"I think so, but I can't say for sure."

"Let's presume it is. We have four hours before sunlight, so this is what we are going to do. We will organize a deck by deck sweep to see if there's anyone else on board; this should not take more than two hours. Afterward, we will choose our living quarters from the captain's cabin— there are more than enough apartments for all right here— this way we can stay together. The kitchen in the cafeteria is well stocked. You will have to prepare your own food untill we get better organized. If you get sick, report to Dr. Patterson at once.

"Lieutenant General Commander Callahan Rye and Professor Walker will stay with me." She turned to Kirkpatrick. "Organize a search of the *Kismet*; when you're done you will join us. The four of us have much to discuss. As for the rest, be present in the auditorium at twelve noon. At that point I will dictate our new strategy based on the information gathered. That's it for now."

Kirkpatrick divided the search parties into couples, each responsible for searching two decks. Thomas and Anna were assigned the infirmary and the Boat Deck.

They checked every corner of the infirmary. They looked inside all the rooms. There was no one to be found. Next, they entered the Boat Deck and again searched from room to room, looking for any evidence of life. The search completed, they sat down on a bench facing the launch area.

"I sure hope we get the chance to use one of those three pods to visit Persia," Anna said. "It would be a shame to have worked so hard only to abort the mission now."

"I'm sure we'll get the opportunity. We just need to get organized first." Thomas stretched his legs following that with a long, satisfying yawn. "It's hard to believe only a few hours ago we began our tour. And to think I almost missed it."

"Well, I'm glad you're here with me, Thomas. I want you to know that."

"Me too, Anna, me too."

Anna gently slid her hand into his. Her heart raced not knowing how he would react. Thomas responded by gently closing his hand. This is the moment everyone remembers: the first reciprocated contact between two people falling in love.

Thomas stood, never letting go of her hand. Anna reached up to him. She wished she could control her shaking. He put his arms around her waist. She put her arms around his neck. With their bodies pressed together, Anna surrendered herself to his strong, firm embrace.

Thomas tried to imagine something romantic to say, something meaningful, but when he looked into her hazel eyes, he understood there was nothing to say. All trembling stopped as their lips pressed together.

"There you are, Thomas," Derrek cried out. "We need to talk."

Thomas and Anna stepped apart, fazed by his sudden appearance. Derrek stared at them. He managed a wide grin while energetically chewing gum. "You want me to come back?"

Thomas diverted his attention to the pods in the room. "Tell me, Derrek. Were there not four pods when we took the tour?"

"Yes, why?"

"Because I count three pods, not four."

"That's right," Anna confirmed. "What happened to the fourth?"

"It's possible it never came with us. The smaller the vessel, the harder it is to control. Look, there's room for seven pods. Yet on the tour there were four. That's because the other three were sent off on their own somehow. We never did figure out why, but they managed to stop the disappearing of pods. Probably the fourth stayed behind. But never mind that. There's something much more important. You need to come with me."

"Can't you just tell me?" Thomas asked. "Do you really have to show me?"

"Very good, Thomas," Derrek replied in a "nice try" tone. "There's a password on the computer responsible for the return trip."

"A password? How can that be? No locks, no passwords, remember?"

"I know, but there it is."

Thomas turned to Anna.

"There's more, Thomas," Derrek said. "Knowing there shouldn't be a password, we pressed the *Enter* key, and a message appeared. It said we have three more attempts at getting the password right. The message also said after four failed attempts, the system will self-destruct."

"If the system is destroyed, how are we to get back home?" Anna said.

"Oh, there's one more thing," Derrek continued. "I know this will interest you Thomas. The message is signed Komodo."

CHAPTER 17

Those in the auditorium were bursting with anticipation. Some hoped for a relaxing cruise with food and games. Most hoped they would at least get the chance to visit the great Persian Empire.

"Thank you for being punctual," Olivia said. "I will be brief and straightforward. I will not sugar-coat the situation since we find ourselves in a difficult position. I met this morning with Mr. McCarthy and Mr. Daramy. To put it bluntly, the odds of our going back home are not good. Some malicious person or persons installed a virus in the server responsible for our return trip. This virus is programmed to destroy the server's software if we're unable to figure out the password. We have three more opportunities to get the password right.

"Mr. McCarthy and Mr. Daramy assured me they will work at deciphering the encrypted password. At the same time they will work on configuring a new server to take us back home. Apparently this is easier than trying to figure out the password. Keep in mind that it took six years to design this program; we have ten months. You do the math.

Now that you're aware of the situation, I'll disclose to you what the committee decided about our time in Persia. Even though we're grossly understaffed, we see no reason why we can't accomplish at least some of the mission's objectives. These objectives will be modified to coincide with our depleted staff.

"We've decided to send two groups, each with specific missions. One will compose of Nicolas Knox and Brody Powell. They will go to Jerusalem to discover the location of the Ark of the Covenant. We are aware they have no foot soldier training. However, Israel is not at war with the enemies of Persia, so there's little risk involved if they stick to the plan.

"The second group will be larger, composed of Michael Griffin, Kelile Lemuel, and Thomas Faraday, with Mr. Faraday being the team leader.

Joining them will be Aldon McAllister and Anna Latimer. Miss Latimer will study the Persian and Greek languages with great care so we can have a more accurate record for our archives.

"Team two's objective will be to observe and record the events found in the Bible book of Esther, as well as finding random relics of biblical significance. They will spend most of their time in Babylon with the last two months in Susa, where they will observe and record the conflict between the Jews and the Amalekites. We will not deviate from the original plan designed for team two. The rest of the staff will be given various tasks ranging from maintenance to ground support. We have three more days to get organized. On the fourth day we go to Persia.

"This concludes my announcement. On your way out please pick up an envelope from Professor Walker. Make sure your name is on it. Inside you will find a detailed list of your assignments. You will also find inside the date and time for a one-on-one meeting with Lieutenant General Commander Callahan Rye and I, at which time you will have all your questions answered. Thank you and good luck."

Olivia walked off the platform with the same detached demeanor as when she'd walked on. Now questions and speculations filled the room. Thomas was sitting at the back. He noticed the group's lack of concern with their mission assignments. *It must be their Bible training,* Thomas thought; *they believe God will see to it they make it back with the whereabouts of these religious relics, no less.* He wondered what it felt like to have such faith. It must be comforting. Yet, he couldn't bring himself to believe God was responsible for what was happening.

"You're coming, Thomas?" Anna called. "Michael and Aldon have gone to the cafeteria to eat. You want to join them?"

"You bet. I'm starving."

• • • • • • • • • • ● ○○○○○○○○○○ ○

"What took you so long?" Michael asked before taking a bite from a pickle. "We were so hungry we started without you. But don't worry, I made enough smoked meat sandwiches for all of us."

"That's great," Thomas said. "First there's something I want to show you before we leave for Persia. Can we clear a space here?"

Anna cleared a section of the table while Thomas reached into his ever-present leather bag, then held up the envelope he'd been carrying with him since leaving Northern Future Pharmaceutical. "I think this will be of particular interest to you, Quincy and Derrek, so listen carefully. It's important we keep this to ourselves. No one on this ship knows about these files. I can't explain why, but for now I would like it to stay this way. Can I count on you guys?"

"Can I count on you guys?" Aldon mimicked. "You sound like a secret agent or something."

Anna let out an audible sigh. "I don't know what's going on with you, Aldon, but since we've been here you've been acting like an asshole."

"Oh, really? Well, maybe it's because I'm the only one who left someone behind, have you thought of that?"

"This has been hard on all of us," Thomas said. "But if you can't take this seriously, now's the time to leave. No one will think less of you."

Aldon snickered. "I don't want any part of some secret that doesn't include our mission's leaders. So yes, I'm out of here, thank you very much."

Kelile gripped Aldon's arm as he stood up to leave. "Please reconsider. You are a valuable part of our friendship. Why don't you listen before you decide to go?"

"Sorry, Kelile, but I can't do that. We could never succeed if we have our own agenda, separate from the ULRA."

Thomas held the envelope in one hand. "This has nothing to do with the ULRA."

"Don't bother, Thomas, and don't try to include me again." Aldon jerked his arm away from Kelile and stalked out of the cafeteria.

"Don't be disheartened, Kelile," Anna said. "He'll come around in time."

"Yes, you are probably correct. It would seem he left more behind than we did. I will see what I can do to help him through this. So, you were saying, Thomas?"

Thomas opened the envelope and took out the thick sheaf of papers. He looked at them for a moment. "Before I give you these I need to explain something. About three and a half years ago, there was a cracker who penetrated my network at Northern F.P in Montreal. He was good at what he was doing; he seemed to be able to wander throughout our network, yet as far as we know, he never stole anything, nor did he cause any damage. He simply left fifty-four files in a folder where I could find them."

"Are those the files in your hand?" Derrek asked.

"Yes, these are the files, and as you can see," he handed them each a copy, "they're encrypted. I still can't break the code."

"Are these all of them?" Derrek asked.

"Yes. He stopped penetrating our network after I lost my job."

Over the next thirty minutes, Thomas recounted why he'd been accused of being Komodo and how Michael had arranged for him to see the Persian stela. He also told them his interpretation of the stela.

"Despite all of this, I still had serious doubts concerning my connection to the mission. That was until this morning, when you told me about the virus and the attached signature—Komodo."

"So let's see if I understand," Quincy pulled a pen from his breast pocket and began jotting notes on a napkin. "There's Komodo the hacker—that's one. There's Komodo on the Persian stela—that's two. The virus is signed 'Komodo' and your password is Komodo—that's three and four." He looked up at Thomas. "That's too many Komodos for it to be a coincidence. You think this cracker is trying to tell you something?"

"It sure looks that way."

"I have a theory," Anna interjected. "What if this trip in reality is a repeat of the same trip done before, sort of like history replayed? Maybe you've already been to Persia, Thomas, where something went wrong and you never made it back. So you carved the stela, put it where you knew it would eventually be found, and started the League to keep the message alive over the centuries. All this so you could tell your present self what you must do."

"I thought of that, but it's not possible. We can never change the past. Barnaby made that clear to me. So if this is the second trip I'm making, there's nothing I can do to change anything, just relive it."

"So the message would be worthless," Michael added.

"Yes. Also, the message on the stela would have been written in a different way if I had written it for myself. So I rule out this possibility. Besides, how could I have arranged for someone to crack the Montreal network, not to mention install a virus from two and a half thousand years ago? No, this is my first trip. Besides, the ULRA made it clear this is the first and probably the only trip possible."

"So you're saying the answer to this Komodo riddle is somewhere in these files." Derrek tapped his copy with a forefinger.

"I strongly believe so. These files are the only physical connection I have with Komodo. That's why I need your help. I feel our mission's success or failure somehow depends on deciphering these files."

"So how can we help?" Quincy asked.

Derrek snorted. "Crack the files, you dummy."

"That's right," Thomas said. "I need you to help me crack these files, and maybe we can find out what all this means. Remember, guys, I can't take them with me to Persia. So I need you to take a shot at them while I'm gone."

"Have you tried decryption software?" Quincy asked.

"Yes, that's the first thing I did. No success."

Derrek threw two pieces of gum into his mouth, then turned to look at Quincy. "Well, it sure looks like we have ourselves a challenge."

"So you'll look at them?"

Derrek nodded. "Yes, Thomas, you can count on us."

"This may sound corny," Quincy added, "but here it goes: one for all and all for one!"

CHAPTER 18

Everyone was preoccupied with preparations for the departure to Persia when Kirkpatrick called for their attention.

"Please gather around," he said. Only a few turned to face him. Normally he would have been offended at this lack of respect, but seeing the Boat Deck buzzing with activity, he knew the motivational speech would have limited effect. He satisfied himself with speaking to the few in front of him.

"The time has come to send you off on the biggest and most important adventure of your lives. The pods directly behind you have been loaded with your gear and they're ready to go. All that's left is for you to get into costume and board the pods."

Quincy, standing next to Kirkpatrick, stepped forward. "I spoke with Lieutenant General Commander Rye and Professor Walker about your suggestion of redistributing the items in your packs so that everyone has a pack for their own use rather than packs stocked for a particular purpose. This means, as suggested, that if anyone gets separated, they will have everything needed to survive independently of the others. Each pack has extra clothing and food for three days. We also added enough gold for exchange to the local currency, which should amount to one year's expenses. You also have in each pack a wooden chest of costume jewelry to present as a tribute to King Xerxes. Please keep in mind, although they're made of plastic, the Persians will consider them priceless treasure—they know nothing of plastic, so to them it's something rare and unique. So don't show them to anyone or you'll attract thieves.

"As for the extra communication devices you asked for, well, that was denied. There should be nothing taken that's foreign to the time period, except the costume jewelry, of course. You might be thinking of the problems we're experiencing with your communication devices, but don't let it worry you. They should be fixed shortly."

As Quincy was speaking, Nicolas and Brody exited the dressing room and walked toward the pod where Derrek was waiting. Nicolas wore a long white tunic with a fringe at the bottom. He also had a blue cloth belt tied around his waist and wore a pointed cap. This was a typical Hebrew nobleman's costume. A small dagger was visible on his belt.

Brody, who was playing the role of Nicolas's bodyguard, wore a Hebrew costume as well: a white top that resembled a modern t-shirt and what Brody called a skirt that ended just above his knees. His belt was of heavy leather, his headgear a turban-like leather helmet. He carried a small shield made of wood and leather. In his other hand was a spear.

"Thank you, Mr. Daramy," Kirkpatrick said when Quincy finished speaking. "There is nothing left to say, so I'll conclude with words that reflect the sentiments of the mission's entire administrative team. We wish you all a safe and successful voyage. May God be with all of you, and good luck."

"That has got to be the worst motivational speech I've ever heard," Michael said.

"What bothers me," Thomas added, "is the communication problem. What if it can't be fixed? How will we contact the *Kismet* if there's a problem?"

"You can always use smoke signals," Quincy said as he approached them.

"That's not funny," Thomas said. "If we can't communicate with you, we'll be stuck down there until we return ten months from now."

Before Quincy could react, the pod disappeared from view as the invisible shield was activated. Less than a minute later a large exit door opened, followed by a gush of cold air. Instinctively they backed away from the exit.

"Okay, people," Ashley called from the dressing room entrance, "let's get you all dressed for the ball."

Michael was given a wine red tunic with sleeves that matched the white and yellow floral border at the bottom of his tunic. He had a matching belt and a gold chain around his neck. On his head rested a red and yellow skullcap. His footwear, surprisingly reminiscent of modern casual shoes with laces, was also wine red.

Thomas wore a long-sleeved, mustard yellow, hooded shirt with a geometric pattern of white, blue, and red squares. The wide sleeves had blue-decorated cuffs. The hood was large enough to cover both his head and face during a sandstorm. His pants reminded Thomas of sweatpants; they were decorated with the same pattern as his shirt. A scabbard hung from the left side of a brown cloth belt, the hilt of the sword within easy reach of his right hand.

He stared bemused at his shoes—you'd think he'd stolen them from a Native American museum.

Once Thomas and Michael finished dressing, they came out and stood staring at each other for several beats before bursting into laughter, pointing helplessly at the other as tears of mirth ran down their faces. They stopped to catch their breath when Anna came out to join them.

She wore a double-layered silk dress that covered all but her hands and feet. The outer layer was sapphire blue and a little shorter than the ivory inner layer visible at her cuffs and hemline. A red silk scarf draped from her left shoulder down to her right hip. A winged sun disc hung around her neck on a gold chain, the symbol associated with divinity, royalty, and power.

"Anna," Thomas said softly. "You never looked more beautiful." What he wanted to say was that she'd never looked more seductive. He felt guilty for thinking that way.

Anna smiled and blushed. "Stop, Thomas! Quit clowning around." The laughter started all over again.

Aldon was the lucky one. Not feeling confident about his new role, Ashley gave him a low profile. He wore a short-sleeve, powder blue tunic that fell below his knees, cinched at the waist with a yellow cloth belt that matched the color of his sandals.

Kelile was the last to come out. He wore a short, Egyptian-style wrap-around knee-length skirt and eight-centimeter-wide gold cuff bracelets around his wrists, upper arms, and ankles. His skullcap was of gold cloth, his top a leopard skin that crossed from his left shoulder to his waist, leaving his right shoulder and midriff exposed. He carried a sword on his right thigh and a spear in his left hand. He did not look at all happy.

"They gave me the wrong outfit," Kelile said. "This is a Nubian outfit. I'm Ethiopian, not Nubian." He sighed in despair. "Since they did not have the right outfit to give me, you must refer to me as being from Kush, understood?"

"Correct me if I'm wrong," Thomas said, "but isn't Kush in Ethiopia?"

Kelile gave Thomas a stern look. "Did you know in my country only clowns wear what you two are wearing?"

Before Thomas could respond, the pod re-entered the *Kismet*. The door opened and Derrek hung halfway out. He gave them a mocking smile, chewing away at a pink glob of gum. "Whenever you're ready, ladies—the pod's hot and ready to go."

They entered the pod and sat down facing each other with their packs on the floor between their legs. Five minutes after boarding, Derrek announced their approach to the city of Hīt. "This city is much larger then I imagined. We'll have to find another place to land. As we passed over the forest I noticed a couple of clearings. Let's see if one of them is large enough for our pod."

As they hovered over the first opening in the tree canopy, Thomas glimpsed a clearing deeper in the woods. "What about that one over there?" he proposed. "I haven't seen anyone for at least half a kilometer."

Derrek took mental measurements of the clearing. "Okay, but just in case, you'll have to hurry when exiting the pod. I need to turn off the invisibility shield to open the door." They felt a slight thump as they came in contact with Earth. "Is everybody ready?"

With packs in hand, they exited the pod one by one in rapid succession. The first thing they did was scan the landscape for any observers. Even though the thick gray mist limited their view to fifteen meters, they were satisfied they were alone.

"Well, good luck to all of you," Derrek said from the pod's doorway. "I'll make contact as soon as communication is up and running. You'll probably hear from me before you go to sleep tonight. Oh, don't forget, your video recording devices work well. Keep this in mind when doing private stuff. Well, no time to lose, I must become invisible again." They watched as the pod disappeared from their view.

For the last three years, all their needs had been taken care of. They were surrounded by people whose responsibility was to make sure they were suitably trained, well fed, and happy. Now for the first time, they were alone. For a good long moment no one said anything. They had each other and that was it. Together they would succeed; together they would make history.

CHAPTER 19

The forest was lush with foliage and bursting with colorful flowers of every imaginable shape and size. Birds sang a symphony of music. The heavy, sweet scent of flowers and greenery enveloped Thomas and his team.

"Now I know where they get inspiration for their colorful arts," Anna said, pirouetting with excitement.

Michael took a deep breath. "Surely this rivals any modern day rainforest, but where does it all come from? I thought this was nothing but a big sandbox."

"It must be manmade," Anna said. "Persian nobles throughout the empire built huge gardens in the middle of the desert. Some even added animals for hunting."

"This is all very nice," Thomas interrupted, "but we'd better get moving. It's already late afternoon and we have at least an hour before we reach the city."

It took less than five minutes to find a well-traveled path. Along the way they encountered dozens of travelers, most going in the opposite direction. Since the locals took no note of them, they assumed their new costumes allowed them to fit in.

Then, as if they were exiting a botanical greenhouse onto a hot city street, the forest came to an abrupt end. It was as if someone had taken a giant knife and sliced away the forest, leaving a clean demarcation between living and dead. The cool air created by the shady trees lured them back into the forest.

Kelile, however, stayed a few steps away from the others, out in the open. He closed his eyes, held out his palms, and lifted his head to soak in the sun's rich energy. "Welcome to the Middle East," he said, ever so slowly.

"Man, it's hot. Is it always like this?" Michael asked.

Kelile dropped his hands. "No, of course not."

"Oh, good." Anna chuckled.

Kelile smiled. "It gets much hotter around noon."

Minutes later they all left the forest for Hīt. The closer they got to the city gates, the more numerous the merchants. Most sold livestock such as sheep, chickens, and pigs. Away from the khaki-colored canopies, larger animals like horses and camels waited. Occasionally they passed stalls selling pottery, tent materials, and garments. Also available were household supplies such as cutlery, lamp oil, and firewood, and foodstuffs: vegetables, dried fish, fruits, and nuts. But no wine—you had to enter the city for wine. Other products and luxury items such as spices, jewelry, and silks were also found in the city.

Something about this market seemed off. Thomas had expected it to smell like a farm. However, a distinctive, familiar city smell of hot asphalt overpowered the smell of farm animals.

"It seems the closer we get to the gate, the more guards we see," Michael noted. "They don't appear to view us as much of a threat."

"Why should they?" Anna said. "Of the twenty-five million inhabitants in the empire, only one million are Persians. They're accustomed to seeing people of different nationalities."

Despite her assurances, they all admitted to some apprehension as they arrived at the gates. Thomas pushed back his hood and after his eyes adjusted, he noticed wooden shelters housing a dozen guards. "Do we stop and talk to someone?" he asked.

"No," Kelile said. "If they want to talk to us they will let us know. Let us keep walking."

They passed through the gates without incident, entering an open space in the shape of a semicircle. Along its perimeter were houses of different shapes and sizes. Some were made of plastered brick with a single door and window. Most houses had two to three floors, reminding Thomas of a medieval paint-ing. On the roofs he could see colorful canvas awnings, gardens, and on some, the mud bricks of an oven.

"Which one of these roads do we take?" he asked, looking around the plaza. "I count five."

"We will take that one," Kelile said, pointing straight ahead. "There are more merchants that way, so it will be the safest. Besides, it will be among the merchants where we will find shelter for our first night."

"Halt!" a gruff voice shouted behind them. They stopped and turned to face a large bearded man. "Follow me," he ordered.

They were directed to a shaded area against an interior wall. Another large man in his late fifties, dressed in protective armor, approached them. He was flanked by three guards. Two of them wore white and orange robes and twisted head-fillets. Each carried a spear and a shield. The third guard caught Kelile's attention. He held a spear with both hands and hanging from his left shoulder was a bow, the arrows for it in a quiver hanging from his back. He had no shield, no armor, and only a simple turban on his head. "That guard is an Immortal, a member of the Persian elite infantry force," Kelile murmured excitedly to his companions. Thomas remembered what he'd learned about the Immortals: they numbered ten thousand, and their ranks were composed of ethnic Persians and Medians exclusively. "There are no better soldiers in all of Persia," Kelile said.

The man who approached them was the officer on duty. "Who are you and what are you doing in Hīt?" he demanded.

Thomas stepped forward to answer the question, and the guards moved in, though the Immortal stood still. Thomas stopped. The officer moved closer to Thomas, signaling the guards to stay back.

Thomas began his rehearsed speech in his best Persian. "We're travelers from a distant land. We understand your country to be an advanced society. One that is just to its inhabitants, a land with a noble king who believes in religious and cultural tolerance and who has implemented laws that are the envy of all peoples of the world. No wonder you refer to your great king Cyrus as Father. Just look at his building projects! Khorsabad, the gardens of Pasargadae, the magnificent palace at Susa.

"My people want to learn how you modified the land supporting King Darius's colossal palace at the capital, Persepolis. We would love to learn how to extract water from the rocks underground. This is why we were sent here by our ruler, so we can learn from you to improve our quality of life."

"Stop the horse manure," the officer interrupted. "Do you take me for an imbecile? Do you expect me to salivate over your words? I'm not some woman who loves to be told how beautiful she looks so you can do whatever you want with her. So shut your mouth and commit your words to answering my questions. Can you manage that?"

"Yes sir."

"Now, what country do you come from?"

Thomas realized they'd never decided what their fictional country would be called. His hesitation aroused suspicion.

"Well, do you or do you not know where you come from?"

"We are Canadians."

"You don't look Akkadian."

"Canadian, not Akkadian."

The guards looked at each other and shrugged.

"I've never heard of you people," the man said. "Where exactly is your country?"

"It's far west from here. We came by ship from the other side of the Sea of Atlas."

"So you say there's land beyond the ring around the world?" The guards laughed at the idea. "It's not possible," the man said. "Now again, where do you come from?"

"It's true. We came from a large continent by ship. We landed at Gades in the land of the Iberians. There we took a local boat through the great sea to Leptis Magna. At that point we traveled by land, following trade routes until we arrived in Egypt. From Egypt we passed through Israel and continued on to here. We want to stay for one or two days to get supplies and then we'll be off to Susa by way of Babylon."

"Are you all Canadian?" the officer asked.

"Yes."

"Is that man not from Africa?"

"Yes, you're right, he's a Kushite I thought you were referring to those of us who began the voyage together. We met Kelile when we stayed at Heliopolis in Egypt. He was recommended as a guide to help us get to Susa."

"How long did it take to get from Leptis Magna to here?"

"We stayed for many days at different locations on our journey. It's been almost three years since we left Canada, but from Leptis Magna to here, I would have to give it some consideration."

The man narrowed his eyes at Thomas. "How do I know you're not spies working for our enemies, like the ones we caught not two months ago? How do I know you're not from Athens or Sparta, coming to exploit our weaknesses?"

"First of all, from what we've learned, you have no weakness, which is why we want to learn from you. Also, our language and accents do not mark us as coming from those places you mentioned."

The officer stared at Thomas for a short while. Then he turned and spoke into the ear of one guard, who then ran out the gate they'd just entered. Thomas sensed something was wrong. No one spoke.

Eight soldiers ran back toward them. Kelile reached for his sword but froze when the tip of the Immortal's spear pricked his neck. Blood trickled down to his chest. Before the others could draw their weapons they were surrounded by Persian soldiers. Even the bowmen from atop the wall were in position.

The officer shoved through to face Thomas. "I don't believe your story. I think you're spies coming to steal our secrets."

No one moved or talked. Kelile kept a straight face, his eyes never leaving the Immortal. The officer lifted his hand and shouted, "Take these people into custody. Do whatever it takes to find out where they came from and what they're doing here."

"Stop, Officer Zubin," a woman's voice called out from behind them. "Release them immediately."

At once the soldiers obeyed the command. Even the Immortal stepped back. Thomas and the others turned to see who their savior was. A tall, stunningly beautiful woman walked toward them. She wore a blue blouse under a bright red sleeveless dress. Her white scarf covered long, charcoal black hair before sweeping around her neck.

"You know these strangers?" Officer Zubin asked.

"Yes I do," she replied with authority. "I've been waiting for them for weeks." She turned to Michael. "What took you so long? It's not easy keeping a house ready."

"I'm sorry?" Michael said.

The woman turned her attention back to Officer Zubin. "If there's nothing else, I will be taking them with me."

"No, we're done here," Zubin said. "They can go."

The woman looked at Michael again. "You'd better follow me. We have much to prepare before we talk business."

•••••••••●○○○○○○○○○○○

Officer Zubin watched them disappear into the city's busiest street. Once he was sure they were gone, he said to one of his guards, "Find Aridai the son of Haman and tell him more travelers from the west have arrived. Tell him they're a much smaller group this time, and we were unable to detain them. Tell him they suspect nothing and they're staying at Artemisia's house. Now be quick at it; we have no time to lose."

•••••••••●○○○○○○○○○○○

Anna sidled up beside Thomas. "Who is this woman?" she asked.

"I don't know."

"Why do you think she helped us?"

"I have no idea, but she sure has clout, did you see how the officer listened to her?"

Anna turned to Michael. "She seems to fancy you," she teased. "Why not speak with her and find out her name and why she helped us."

Michael nodded. Smiling, he approached the woman. "We're all indebted to you for your help back there. Those guards looked like they meant us harm. How can we ever repay you?"

"I will answer your questions later," she replied. "For now we need to purchase food for tonight's dinner."

"We don't have any local currency," Michael said. "But we do have some gold. Maybe we can make an exchange for the purchases."

"Please, sir, don't insult me," the woman said. "I don't need your gold."

"Forgive me, I didn't mean to insinuate, it's just—well, in our country, we share expenses for occasions like this."

"You often need rescuing?"

"No, I mean for dinner arrangements."

"I'm not a poor woman, sir. I can afford to purchase many things."

"Okay." Michael hesitated before he continued. "Well, since we're going to spend the evening together, you should know our names. The tall man who did most of the talking before you came is Thomas. Next to him is Anna. The Kushite is Kelile and finally the silent man is Aldon. He doesn't talk much. He's the only one who is married and he had to leave his wife behind—he's been melancholy ever since, I'm afraid."

"And you, sir, what do I call you?"

"My name is Michael. Can we have the pleasure of knowing your name?"

"Artemisia."

"Well Artemisia, we are glad to have made your acquaintance, that's for sure." He waited for a while before continuing. "May I ask you one question?"

"Do all the people from your country talk so much?"

Michael smiled and bowed his head. Artemisia resumed walking.

After collecting their needs, they arrived at Artemisia's large and spacious home. Seeing the house, Thomas knew she had wealth to go along with her authority. They were greeted by two young servant girls. One moved among them with a pitcher of cold water while the other provided sandals. After changing their footwear, they were directed to a large living area with many couches and tables. Before they could react to their surroundings, they were given dried fruits, dates, apples, and hot tea.

"I'll be right back," Artemisia said. "Please make yourselves at home."

"Take a look up," Michael whispered as he bent backward to look up at the five-meter-high ceiling. "I think those are cedar beams holding up the roof."

"That's the floor of the next level," Thomas said. "How long do you think it took to decorate those beams and the ceiling with all those colorful patterns?"

"Did you notice all the decorations, Thomas?" Anna remarked. "Statuettes of all kinds and some look like they're made of gold. And the carpets, the tapestries, and all the plants—it feels like I'm in an expensive luxury hotel. You know the ones I'm talking about, those fancy hotels in Dubai."

Thomas looked at Aldon, who still seemed shaken from the interaction with the guards at the gate. "What do you think about the house, Aldon?"

"It's very nice, Thomas. We must make sure to video record all of it." He rubbed his left arm with his right. "A little cold for me, though."

"Aldon's right," Thomas said. "If I didn't know better, I'd swear there's air-conditioning in here."

"Actually, Thomas, there probably is," Kelile said. "Did you notice on arrival the tall tower adjacent to the house? I think it's a wind catcher. Hot air is drawn in from the tower where it's directed to an underground water canal. The air is then cooled as it passes over the cold water before it is redirected up into the house."

They looked at each other in astonishment before they scrambled to find the openings.

"Look," Anna said with excitement. They joined her at a small set of niches, one on top of the other, half a meter wide and three centimeters high. "Feel that? It really is air-conditioning."

As they were all admiring this amazing technology, Artemisia walked into the living area. She held a decorated silver jar of wine in one hand and two golden cups resembling winged lions in the other.

"Which one of you is the leader?" Artemisia smiled at Michael, obviously hoping it was him.

"We don't have a leader, per se. We consult with one another. But in the end," Michael looked at Thomas, "he's responsible for us."

Artemisia looked disappointed as she addressed Thomas. "Please come with me. We need to talk." She gave Thomas the large silver jar, then waved for him to follow her up the stairs to the roof. Thomas looked back at Anna and shrugged. Anna waved back.

The view from the rooftop was magnificent. Seated on one of the chairs sheltered by a large and colorful canopy, Thomas scanned the entire eastern half of Hīt while Artemisia told the servant girl to leave them alone; she would call if they needed anything.

Artemisia turned to face Thomas. "Tell me, please: where did you really come from?"

Thomas assumed an innocent expression and quirked an eyebrow. "What do you mean? It's like I said to the officer, we came from a country called Canada. We are here to learn from you."

Artemisia smiled. "But you didn't come via the route you told Officer Zubin, did you."

"I don't understand. Why would I lie?"

She regarded him steadily. "That's a good question, Thomas. Why would you lie?"

Thomas concentrated on not shifting uncomfortably in his chair. "My friends and I are indebted to you for what you did earlier at the gate. I don't want to appear ungrateful, but I must insist you break from calling me a liar."

Artemisia sipped her wine. "Let me tell you what I do from time to time, whenever I'm feeling the need to be alone. I leave this hectic city to take a long walk inside the gardens. There's a place few people know about, an opening where animals sometimes gather to drink from a small, shallow natural well. Would you happen to know of such a place?"

Thomas got up and walked toward the edge of the roof. "Please go on," he said, eyes on the view before him.

"Well, this afternoon I happened to be in the mood to be alone, so I walked to my secret opening in the gardens. But when I arrived, there were no animals to be seen. What I did see was so impossible, I thought I'd been possessed by Ahura Mazda. A large oval container materialized right in front of my eyes. Out of fear I turned away and ran a short distance, but then I decided to look back. Not only was it still there, but people were coming out of its mouth. Fear again threatened to overcome me. All I wanted was to find safety. But yet, I needed to know what this was. You can imagine my surprise when the container disappeared, leaving behind the people."

She paused as if waiting for Thomas to respond. He turned back toward her but said nothing. She continued. "I tried to listen in on their conversation, but I understood nothing—they spoke a language I've never heard before. So I followed them until they arrived here." She stopped again, watching him.

"Tell me, Thomas. Would you happen to know who these people are?"

Thomas gazed at Artemisia for a few seconds. "Yes, I do."

She nodded. Then she asked, "What kind of magic is this?"

Thomas returned to his chair. "What you saw was not magic. It's a ship that can travel through air. I know that's hard to believe, but it's true. Just like you Persians could reroute rivers for irrigation, build glorious ziggurats, and travel around the world in magnificent ships, we have created a ship that travels through air." He leaned toward her, resting his arms on the arms of his chair. "You must believe me when I say that the rest of our story is the absolute truth. We brought gifts for your King Xerxes. We are a peaceful people. We want knowledge—that's all—and we're willing to pay for it."

She licked her lips and leaned forward in her chair. "Can you teach me how to build an air ship?"

"I can tell you how it works, but the materials can only be found in my country."

Artemisia pondered what Thomas had said for a good long time. "Okay, I believe you, but you must agree to take me with you to Susa. I will be a better guide than your Kushite. I also know people who can help you get your passports for the trip. This means you and your companions will be my guests wherever we go. In exchange, you must agree to share with me your knowledge of the technologies and military tactics of your country. We are always on the brink of war, and we might be able to use your experience to help defeat our enemies. Do you agree to these terms?"

Thomas leaned back in his chair. "You saved our lives today so yes, we will do as you say. Oh—there's one more thing." He leaned forward again. "The Kushite. He's not from Egypt. He came from Canada as well. So he will come with—"

Before he could finish a loud cry came from the stone-walled garden behind the house. They rushed to the edge of the roof in time to see an intruder jumping from the wall to land on the road outside. They watched him disappear into a maze of streets.

"What happened?" Thomas asked.

"I don't know," Artemisia replied. "Probably a thief. The rope he used is still attached to the wall."

"Look," Thomas cried, "it's Aldon! What an idiot. He's running after him."

Artemisia looked at Thomas. "Can your friend fight?"

"Aldon? God, no."

"Then let's hope he turns around. If he follows the thief he will likely get killed, by the thief or his accomplices."

They descended the stairs to the garden. One of the servant girls was hunched on the floor with her head buried between her knees, crying. Anna knelt next to her, trying to console her.

"What happened?" Artemisia asked.

"We're not sure," Anna said. "There was a yell followed by the crash of dishes. We ran to the garden, but before we arrived Aldon came running out, yelling, 'I'll catch the crook, I'll get him.' Then he ran out the front door. That's all I know."

"Is anyone hurt?" Thomas asked.

"No, I don't think so. This poor girl is scared stiff, that's all."

Artemisia looked around the garden. "Did he come into the house?"

"No," Anna said. "Aldon must have surprised him, so he climbed back up the wall."

"I'm going after Aldon," Kelile said.

"It's too late for that," Artemisia insisted. "If he doesn't come back soon, I'll send soldiers out to look for him. They know these streets. Besides, if anything goes wrong with your friend, it's already done."

Not fifteen minutes had passed before Aldon walked through the front door.

"Aldon," Thomas said, more angry than concerned, "what the hell got into you, running after the thief that way?"

"I thought I could catch him."

"And then what?"

Aldon shrugged. "Who knows. I just reacted, that's all. I made a mistake. It won't happen again."

"We need to stay together," Kelile insisted.

"I know," Aldon said. "It won't happen again. Look, I'm very tired. It's been an incredible day. Artemisia, can you please show me where I'll be sleeping tonight? I need to rest."

"That's a good idea," Thomas added. "We all need to rest. Tomorrow we have much to talk about."

"If you don't mind," Anna said, "I'll stay with this young girl for a while. I think she can use some company." She turned to face the servant girl. "By the way, what is your name?"

"Mani," Artemisia answered before the girl could. "It means 'angelic.'"

CHAPTER 20

Hot honey-glazed bread, warm milk, fruits, nuts and cheese greeted Thomas as he emerged from his room after a much-needed sleep. The first thing he did was sample an unfamiliar local tea. It wasn't coffee, but it was spicy and tasted good.

While he sipped his tea, Anna arrived. "Good morning, Thomas."

"And good morning to you, Anna; you slept well?"

"Like a newborn baby." She poured herself a glass of warm milk and gestured toward the laden table. "Do you believe all this food?"

"I know. And here I thought all we'd be doing is camping at discount inns."

"Count your blessings, Thomas," she warned. "We've just arrived. It might still come to that, sooner than you think." She reached for a piece of honey bread.

Mani walked into the room. "How are you feeling today, Mani?" Anna asked her.

"I feel much better, thanks to you."

"Did you just get up?"

"Oh, no." Mani giggled. "I had to prepare breakfast."

Anna glanced at Thomas. "After what you've been through, you still got up to work?"

"Yes. Why do you ask?"

Anna shrugged. "I don't know, I guess I figured you'd want some time to recover."

"Thank you, but I feel fine," Mani assured her. "I hope you like what I prepared."

"Of course! Don't be silly; everything's perfect."

"That makes me happy." Mani left the room, presumably to do more chores.

Anna watched her leave, then turned to Thomas. "Do you believe that, Thomas? She's acting like nothing happened."

"Maybe what took place yesterday is not uncommon in these parts."

"I see you've started without us."

The voice drew Thomas and Anna's eyes to the staircase, where Michael was descending accompanied by Aldon.

"Sorry, big guy, too hungry," Thomas replied.

Michael looked around. "Where's Kelile? I would have bet anything on him being the first one down."

"Don't know," Thomas answered before taking a bite of honey bread. "We arrived a few minutes ago ourselves," he mumbled around it.

Mani reappeared, this time carrying a tray of fresh fruits. Anna asked if she had seen Kelile.

"Yes, I'm bringing him his tea now. He was up even before me," said Mani. "Do you have a message for him?"

"Can you ask him to join us for breakfast?"

"I will relay your message to him."

Before she could, Kelile walked in from the garden. "And how is everybody today?" he asked.

"Good morning, Kelile," Anna said cheerfully. "Come sit next to me."

"Wait a minute," Michael interjected. "Shouldn't we wait for Artemisia before we eat? How rude of us."

Mani was listening. "Forgive me," she said apologetically. "I completely forgot to give you her message. Artemisia left for the market early this morning. She's making arrangements for your trip to Babylon."

"We need to get up earlier," Thomas said before popping a piece of cheese into his mouth. "It's—what?—seven o'clock now, yet it feels like half the day has been wasted."

Everyone muttered agreement, too busy eating—except for Aldon. Kelile looked at him. "Did you have a good night's rest, Aldon?"

"I slept okay. Just wish I knew what that thief wanted. Artemisia is doing so much for us, yet we couldn't catch a petty thief to help her out."

"We don't know for sure why the intruder was here. It could be for a number of different reasons."

"Still, I should have done something."

"You did your best, and you were very brave in pursuing him, but there's nothing you can do now," Kelile said. "Don't think about it anymore. Have something to eat. You need your strength for the day."

"Thank you, Mani," Thomas said as the girl set the tray down on the table, gently nudging other dishes out of the way. "Is it possible to leave us alone? We need to talk business."

"Of course," she said politely. "Please let me know when you're done, so I can come back to clear the table."

Thomas nodded. "We'll let you know."

He waited until the girl had left, then turned to the others. "Now, as you already know, Artemisia spoke with me yesterday on the rooftop. I now know why she's helping us, and her help is not free, so here's the deal. It turns out the drop location we chose yesterday was not so isolated after all. Artemisia uses that very spot to get away from the city. Guess what? She was there."

"Oh man," Michael groaned, barely loud enough to be heard.

"It's okay, it's not a problem," Thomas assured him. "It turns out she loves an adventure, so instead of running away, she decided to investigate us—even though she first thought we were demons from Ahura Mazda."

Anna put her hand on her neck. "My necklace—isn't it the symbol for Ahura Mazda?"

"That's right. That might explain her assumption. You'd better clear that up with her, the first chance you get. Anyway, last night on the roof, she wanted to know who we are and our purpose with the people of Hīt. After I explained where we came from and what our goals are, she asked questions about the pod. She called it an air ship." Thomas recounted the conversation he'd had with Artemisia.

"Did she accept your explanation?" Michael asked.

"It would appear so. I don't know if she's simply buying time before demanding more at a later opportunity, or if she really does accept what I told her. Anyway, she wants us to share our military knowledge to help her win the war against their many Greek city-state enemies. So I agreed to her terms. It's quite simple, actually. We share what we know about our technology, along with our military strategies. In return, she will take us safely to Susa."

"It sounds reasonable," Anna said. "It sure beats trying to do it ourselves. We found out yesterday how fast things can go wrong."

"I have a question," Aldon interrupted. "We have no military experience, and we're not engineers, so how can we satisfy her curiosity?"

"I think I have a solution for the military tactics," Michael chimed in. "We've all seen war movies; why not use some of the tactics in those?"

"I had the same idea," Thomas confessed. "In order for this to work, we need to decide which movies to use so we can coordinate our stories so they don't conflict. We just have to substitute the places and characters with our own."

"I also have an idea," Kelile said. "I have a large collection of documentaries that include great engineering projects. I could use some of the things I learned. This should keep her busy for a while."

"Did you forget we painted Kelile as a simple Kushite guide?" Anna remarked.

"Actually, I corrected that when I told her Kelile is not our guide, but a fellow traveler from Canada."

"That settles it," Kelile said. "I can play the role of an architect and engineer."

"Fine. I'll let Artemisia know we accept her proposal as soon as she gets back," Thomas said. "In the meantime, let's think on what information to share, and get together tonight to make sure we're all on the same page."

Aldon rose. "If this is the end of our meeting, I'd like to go out and explore the open markets."

"That sounds like a good idea," Kelile said. "I think I'll go with you."

"If you don't mind, I'd like to be alone for a while," Aldon replied. "I promise I won't chase any villains, and I'll be back in time for dinner."

• • • • • • • • • ● ○ ○ ○ ○ ○ ○ ○ ○ ○ ○

It was midafternoon. Thomas and Anna were enjoying the breathtaking view of Hīt from the rooftop.

"It reminds me of a vacation I once took," Anna said. "It was in the beautiful city of Dubrovnik. Strolling along the wall surrounding the city, you could see people relaxing or gardening on the roofs of their homes."

"Hello there, lovebirds," Artemisia interrupted as she stepped onto the roof. "Enjoying the view?"

"It's beautiful," Anna agreed. "Just got back from the market?"

"Yes, I made all the arrangements for our trip to Babylon." Artemisia sat down next to them and poured a glass of cold water from a pitcher. "We'll be ready to go in two days. My brother will meet us at the Buranuna River, where we will board a merchant vessel heading for Babylon. You'll like my brother. Like me, he loves an adventure."

"We both look forward to meeting him," Anna said. "What's his name?"

"Pigres. You'll find him to be a handsome man. Anyway, I have a question for you. While I was at the market, I came across this dagger." She held up her hand, which held an extravagant dagger about fifty centimeters long, its golden handle decorated with two lions heads looking away from each other and inset with colored stones on both sides. The double-edged blade was gold plated. She handed it to Thomas. "It's a ceremonial dagger. Do you like it?"

Anna felt threatened by Artemisia's overgenerous gift. "That's beautiful," she said, masking her concern. "It must have cost a fortune. But Thomas and I don't accept gifts that cost more than ten years' worth of our combined income."

Artemisia smiled and gave Thomas a flirtatious look to rub it in. "This isn't a gift for Thomas or you, Anna. I merely wanted a man's opinion before I give it to someone whom I find appealing. Even if I had feelings for your lover, I would never get between you two. I am a woman of honor."

Anna felt her face heat. "Thomas and I aren't lovers. We're in love, it's true, but we're not yet married—I mean, not that we made any definite plans or anything . . ."

Thomas came to Anna's rescue. "What she's trying to say is, we want to get to know each other better before we take it to the next step as lovers."

Artemisia looked as if she was enjoying Thomas's and especially Anna's discomfort. "So, do you think it would make a good gift for a man I hope to impress?"

"I'm sure he will be delighted with your generous gift," Thomas agreed.

Satisfied, Artemisia turned to head downstairs just as Aldon appeared from below. "Sorry for being late. I got carried away with all the different goods available in the market. You should go and have a look."

"We plan to," Anna said. "Perhaps tomorrow. Did you buy anything?"

"No, I don't have any currency. Just gold, and I don't know the value of it."

"I'll go with you tomorrow and exchange your gold for you," Artemisia volunteered. "By the way, who's the woman I saw you talking to?"

Aldon stared at her a moment before saying, "I wasn't talking to any woman."

"Yes you were. I was in the middle of negotiating a gift when I saw you talking to a woman. You were both in an alleyway. I remember because it's not often we see a tall, blue-eyed blond in this part of the country."

"You must be mistaken. I'm a happily married man; I would never—"

"Please, I'm not insinuating anything. I'm merely curious, that's all. After I finished my dealings with the merchant I saw you walking away with her."

"Oh yes, I remember now," Aldon replied. "We have many blonds in our country, that's why I forgot about the woman you're talking about. I was asking for directions to the latrine. When I didn't understand her directions, she was nice enough to show me the way."

"I see." Artemisia lost interest. "I must take care of a few things. I'll see you all at dinner."

Aldon waited till Artemisia was gone. "She can be persistent, that Artemisia. I had to pretend I was with that woman to shut her up." He looked toward the staircase. "She obviously saw someone who looked like me. Did I do the right thing—you know, pretending so she can think she's right? We need to keep the peace, right?"

"I guess," Anna said.

"Yes, I think I did the right thing." He paused. "You know something, I'm feeling tired from my walk, so I'm going to take a nap. I'll see you guys later."

Once Aldon had disappeared, they relaxed back into their chairs.

"Anna, I don't remember a Buranuna River in our studies."

"The modern name for the Buranuna is the Euphrates," Anna explained. "We will be going to Babylon on the Euphrates River."

"Nice."

"He's lying, you know," Anna said.

"Who's lying?"

"Aldon."

"I know," Thomas agreed.

CHAPTER 21

It was dusk—the perfect time for travelers and their horses to minimize the torture inflicted by the blistering sun. Michael and Artemisia were traveling side by side in front of the others.

"Desert sand, nothing but desert sand," Michael whispered to himself. He reached for a water bottle hanging from his belt. After taking a swallow of the lukewarm water, he seized a handkerchief to cover his mouth and nose. "Oh man, there's that god-awful smell again."

"You said something?" Artemisia asked.

"Yes! That smell—where does it come from?"

"Look around you. It comes from bitumen springs. We are a major supplier of the black gold. In fact, Babylon buys their bitumen from us."

Michael focused his attention on looking around. Workers were scooping up bitumen from springs of tar using palm leaves.

"You see?" Artemisia continued. "Naphtha springs are the most productive source of bitumen in this part of the empire. If you get close, you can hear the distinctive sound of the sulfurous liquid coming up in the form of gas bubbles. Do you want a closer look?"

Michael looked at the springs again. The ground was covered with yellow crystallized gypsum. "No thanks; let's just head for the river."

"Tell me something," Artemisia said as they urged their mounts forward. "What did you do back home in your country?"

"You mean, what did I do for a living?"

"Yes."

"Well, Thomas and I worked together as information security officers. This fancy title means that we had the responsibility of defending a large grid against pirates who want to steal our secrets." He paused to figure out how to explain this to someone who had no concept of computers. "Thomas had the day shift and I had the night. We used every advantage we had at our disposal to create a defensive wall. Thomas perfected a system called a demilitarized zone to monitor potential intruders."

"Did you have many pirates to deal with?"

"There is quite a large number, actually," Michael replied, "but few are skilled enough to be a real threat."

"It sounds like a lot of responsibility, Michael. Has anyone ever succeeded in penetrating your defenses?"

"There was this one pirate who went by the name Komodo who managed to penetrate our defenses whenever he wanted, without leaving a trace. Catching this pirate became an obsession for Thomas since he'd designed the security system. The funny thing about this hacker—I mean this pirate—he never stole or damaged anything. All he did was leave encrypted messages for Thomas to find."

"Did you ever catch him?"

Michael shook his head and heaved a sigh. "No, we never caught him. About three years ago, Komodo left and never returned. It almost ruined Thomas. That is until he met Anna. She's the best thing that's happened to him in years. She gave him his life back."

"She looks out for him," Artemisia said.

Michael looked at her. She looked thoughtful as if recalling something. "That too."

They paused at the top of a sand dune, taking in the view as they waited for the others to join them. Directly in front of them was the Euphrates River, flowing like a large serpent through the harsh landscape. They made way as the others came up and surveyed the landscape below.

•••••••••●○○○○○○○○○○

"Look, Thomas!" Anna exclaimed. "Along the river—Chenopodiaceae; wormwood plants. Do you recognize them from our studies? It's quite funny, actually. In our textbooks they're called Artemisia herba-alba. What an amazing coincidence. You can also see pistachio and palm trees scattered around those oaks over there. Do you see them Thomas?"

Thomas looked but could see nothing, not even trees big enough to be oaks.

"They're imported from Anatolia, you know," Anna continued. "You see them? Over near the pasturing sheep and goats." Anna moved closer to Artemisia. "Do you think we'll see any dangerous animals like lions, wolves, leopards, or golden jackals? Or a brown bear, perhaps?"

"No," Artemisia replied, giggling. "Not here. But if you're lucky, you might see a gazelle, or maybe an ostrich. That's about it, I'm afraid."

"If it's an Arabian ostrich," Anna whispered in Thomas's ear, "that would be something to get excited about. By the twenty-first century they were extinct."

Thomas glanced at Artemisia as he offered Anna his water bottle for a drink. "Is everything okay, Anna?" You're acting a little funny."

"I'm perfectly fine. I'm excited, that's all. And I'm famished. Are you hungry? You want a cake? They're quite tasty, in an exotic sort of way." She pulled two green cakes that resembled brownies from her bag and offered one to Thomas.

"Where did you get those?" Artemisia asked, eyeing the cakes with wide eyes.

"I noticed them in the kitchen before we left, so I took three for the trip. I hope you don't mind."

Artemisia broke out laughing. "You'd better give those to me. Once we're on the boat, you can have them back." Anna reluctantly handed the cakes over.

"Don't worry, Thomas," Artemisia said. "She's fine. She ate a hemp cake. Normally we smoke it, but sometimes we make cakes with it. Give her two or three hours and it will wear off." She rummaged in her own bag and turned back to Anna. "Here's an apple; why not take two." She held out two red fruits. "This should satisfy your hunger."

Anna accepted them and took a big bite. Her eyebrows shot up. "Wow, this apple tastes fantastic."

•••••••••●○○○○○○○○○○○

"Watch your belongings," Artemisia said as they arrived at the busy dock. Thomas and his companions stood nervously around their travel bags while Artemisia took a few steps away, eyes scanning the sailors, dock workers, and what Thomas assumed were passengers all moving with purpose up and down the wooden quay.

Although the dock was smaller than Thomas had envisioned, the rest was picture perfect. He stopped for a moment to take in the sights and sounds of the mingled cultures, and the people in their multicolored costumes. Fish merchants crammed side by side were selling their catch of the day amid a cloud of flies. He watched merchants and customers haggling over transactions, which produced a steady hullabaloo that made it difficult for Thomas to communicate with the others. Then peddlers surrounded them, hawking their goods and services. Thomas was reminded of the street hawkers in the cities of his time period, though these ones were more persistent, to the point of being aggressive in their desire to secure a transaction. No matter how much Thomas and the others frowned and waved their hands and pushed away proffered trinkets, the peddlers would not back off.

"I've got an idea," Kelile said. Drawing his long sword, he walked in a circle around their group, his chest puffed out like a rooster. With a few grunts of disappointment, the peddlers found better things to do.

"There he is," Artemisia called out. Without saying more, she ran to greet her brother, arms open wide.

The others followed, stopping a respectful distance away as the siblings embraced. After a few minutes Artemisia turned to face them. "Meet my brother Pigres," she said with pride.

"He is a handsome man," Anna observed. When Thomas frowned at her, she added, "Just kidding," with a mocking smile.

Thomas allowed that Pigres was attractive—tall and well dressed, with dark eyes, neat black hair, and a well-trimmed beard to match.

"It's an honor and a privilege to meet all of you," Pigres said with polished elegance. He looked directly at Thomas. "You must be Thomas." He stepped forward and gripped Thomas by the shoulders, then looked at Anna. "And you're much more beautiful than my sister said in her communiqué." He kissed her on both cheeks. Anna glanced at Thomas, who didn't hide his disapproval.

Pigres turned his attention to Kelile and Aldon. "I can tell right away that you're a man of wisdom, Kelile—it's in your eyes. And you must be the brave man who chased the intruder. I am indebted to you, Aldon."

He seemed to have intentionally left Michael for last, stepping past him to greet Aldon. Now he stepped back to look Michael over much as a football coach would a new rookie. "And you're the handsome man who stole my sister's heart."

"Pigres, what are you talking about," Artemisia exclaimed, her cheeks reddening. "There are some things in the communiqué that were not meant to be repeated." She looked at the others. "He's such a prankster, my brother."

"And quite the charmer, too," Anna said, glancing at Thomas again.

"Well, enough of this," Thomas said. "Where's this boat that's supposed to take us to Babylon?"

"Yes, of course," Pigres said. "Let me introduce you to the *Shireen*." He turned and indicated an old and battered-looking blue trireme, with a flourish.

Kelile sauntered ahead of the others. "I don't believe my eyes. I never thought I would ever see a real trireme so far inland."

"You like it?" Pigres asked. "It was confiscated from the Greeks."

Kelile didn't take his eyes off the vessel. "Yes, I do. She is magnificent."

"I don't know if I would call it magnificent, but it will take us to Babylon for cheap," Pigres said.

"It's been modified," Kelile said.

Thomas studied the ship, guessing it to be maybe thirty-seven meters long and six meters wide. The main mast with its square sail looked brand new. The smaller foremast was more weathered, and Thomas guessed it was original.

"Yes," Pigres answered Kelile. "Its owner converted it into a merchant ship. Only the thranite section is left. The two levels below that, the zygite and the thalamite, are sealed shut. And of course the ram at the bow was removed, for obvious reasons."

Kelile nodded. Since Thomas was still looking at the ship, he assumed interest and told him, "When in battle, the trireme would have carried about two hundred sailors and one hundred and seventy oarsmen, and forty-five tons of cargo. A trireme in perfect condition can reach speeds as high as seven knots."

Thomas just nodded. Kelile turned to Pigres. "How can such a large vessel navigate this river?"

"They were made for the open sea and shallow waters," Pigres explained. "In fact, this vessel's hull is made of both pine and fir. This is an advantage over the stronger oak-hulled vessels because it's much lighter. That's why it moves well on the river."

One by one they boarded the *Shireen* by way of a narrow plank. Thomas was somewhat surprised at its simplicity. It reminded him of a large canoe, with its deck covering the entire surface except for a gap in the middle that stretched from stern to bow.

Michael looked into the opening. "Great, more bitumen."

They were directed to the bow of the vessel and told to make themselves comfortable on the starboard side. There were no beds, just a designated spot on the deck to sleep.

"No matter," Anna said, dropping her pack to the deck. "I'm so exhausted I can sleep standing up."

"Settle yourselves in," the helmsman barked. "We'll be a leaving shortly."

"How do you plan to navigate at night in a river like this," Kelile asked him.

The man smiled, revealing a mouth full of missing or rotten teeth. "Have you not noticed her name, my good friend?"

"*Shireen*."

"So you did notice. Well, did you also know that her name means 'bright and luminous like the sun'? So you see, there's no problem." The helmsman executed an elaborate shrug and gave Kelile another proud smile. "Besides, we only have sixty parasangs to cover and we have torches every two cubits all around the vessel. So don't you be worried. I make one trip there and one trip back three times a week, and always at night—less traffic."

Thomas chuckled. "I guess traffic is not a unique twenty-first-century problem," he said in an undertone to Kelile as the helmsman walked away.

Anna, however, was not in a laughing mood. "I made quite the fool of myself today, didn't I, Thomas," she said, looking sheepish.

"How were you supposed to know the cakes were made of marijuana?"

She clasped Thomas's hand. "Come lay by my side, and the next time you see Artemisia, tell her she can keep those cakes."

Thomas looked at her with new appreciation. For the first time she needed him more than he needed her.

• • • • • • • • • ● ○○○○○○○○○○○

It was dark. Anna was asleep and Thomas was restless. He knelt on the bulwark to admire the shoreline, illuminated by the moonlight. The cool breeze reminded him of the many Mediterranean cruises he'd taken with Amélie. They'd loved sitting on their stateroom's balcony, looking for whales and other marine life as the ship traveled from port to port. He turned to gaze at Anna, wondering if she would enjoy a cruise when they returned home.

He was about to rejoin her when he caught sight of Artemisia, standing at the bow. He ambled down the deck toward her. "Can't sleep either," Thomas said, more as a statement than a question. "I noticed you've been quiet since we boarded the vessel. Are you feeling all right? You're not seasick, are you?"

"No Thomas, I would have to be super sensitive to be seasick on this river." She looked at Thomas as if trying to decide if she should tell him a great secret.

Thomas noticed her hesitation. "You don't have to say anything. It's none of my business anyway."

"No, it's all right." She paused to gather her thoughts. "Seven years ago, I was aboard a vessel much like this one. I was on a mission for King Xerxes at a place called Salamis. We had seven hundred triremes. The Greeks had three hundred or so. When our overwhelming force approached them, they fled before us. We expected this, so we pursued them into a narrow strait. We had them exactly where we wanted them.

"I knew Xerxes was watching from the shore and I would do anything for him. I loved that man." She looked at Thomas. "Anyway, I wanted him to be proud of me and my crew. But I was a fool. Like the others, I followed them into a trap. As soon as we entered the strait, their right wing, previously hidden from sight, attacked our flank from behind. The Greeks we'd pursued turned around and attacked us from the front. We were taken by surprise. It was a horrible defeat, a great humiliation. I managed to escape with my crew and the four vessels under my command. To my credit, I had advised Xerxes against such an attack. I was overruled by his chief admiral, who was so sure of victory."

Her voice grew softer. "Despite my failures, he still summoned me for my advice on another campaign. When the council was over, Xerxes asked me to accompany his illegitimate children to Ephesus. That was when I knew our love affair was over. Soon after that, he changed his wife Vashti for a new and more beautiful woman."

"Esther," Thomas said under his breath. For a long time they looked down at the river, saying nothing. "I think I saw a softshell turtle in the water before it got dark," he finally said, changing the subject.

"It's probably a Rafetus," she explained. "Don't ever try to eat it—it tastes really bad. But its fat is an excellent medication for many skin diseases."

CHAPTER 22

Susa, seven hundred kilometers away

"Thank you for coming, my brothers," Parshandatha said to his nine younger siblings. "Our father Haman would be proud of you. Tomorrow we will give him the proper funeral he deserves." He heaved a sigh and held his hands out, looking around the room before saying, "I apologize for this pitiful house. Since the king gave all our father's assets to that meddling prostitute, his queen, we now must work with the limited resources we have at our disposal."

"Please, brother," Aridai said. "In time we will get everything back, and even more when we get rid of her kind. We need to remain calm and concentrate on our objectives."

Parshandatha sighed again and nodded. "Yes, you're right; our plunder will be great. So let's discuss how we will deal with those demons that have reappeared. Aridai, tell us more about this threat."

"It's true—the demons are back, but they are fewer this time. I'm told they number five, and one of them is a woman. My spy in Hīt assured me that they are weak, so we can easily get rid of them, just as we did with the last group. The problem is, Artemisia of Halicarnassus has taken them under her wing, and we all know what she can do."

"Does she know they are demons?"

Aridai frowned. "I'm not sure, but I'm told Artemisia and her brother Pigres plan to bring them here."

"How long before they arrive?"

"Well, that's the thing. They're on their way to Babylon as we speak. My spy assures me they should arrive there tomorrow morning."

Parshandatha narrowed his eyes. "We need to find out how long they plan to stay in Babylon. Can you get the information for us?"

"Yes, that won't be a problem. My spy says there's a defector among them."

"Are you sure we can trust this spy of yours? Does she have a name?"

"She wants to remain anonymous so I don't know her name. Don't worry, my brother," Aridai assured him, "what's important is that she's motivated by revenge, and she has the powers of a prophet. She also said those demons could get in the way of her right to rule, whatever that means. She guarantees success if we do as she says."

Parshandatha smiled. "There's nothing more dangerous than an ambitious and scorned woman. What would she have us do?"

"She wants us to stop them from reaching Susa, nothing more," Aridai said. "If we are successful in keeping them in Babylon, all of our needs will be satisfied. This will give her time to steal the king's tribute of rare and expensive jewelry from the demons. To sweeten the deal, she will hand over to us half of the treasure."

Parshandatha grinned. "That's good—we keep those meddling demons away till after the slaughter and we get rich in the process. It's perfect. Can you go to Babylon and make sure Artemisia and her demon friends stay there?"

"Yes, I can do that, but there is another option," Aridai said.

Parshandatha chuckled knowingly. "Is that why Sadhanah is waiting downstairs?"

"Yes," Aridai admitted. His own smile faded. "But he won't come cheap. Do we still have access to the ten thousand silver talents Father left us for the cause?"

Parshandatha nodded. "Yes, the full amount is still intact."

"Then let me hire Sadhanah to stop those demons and maybe I can stay here in Susa where I can be useful."

Parshandatha nodded. "That's a good plan. But remember: whatever we do, don't say anything about the king's tribute, or that they are demons from Ahura Mazda."

Aridai responded with a curt nod. "I'll call him in, then."

The man who walked in was built like an ox. His hair was long, gray, and dirty. There was a scar across his left cheek and a patch over a missing right eye. The brothers ignored the fact that he reeked of urine.

"Thank you for coming, Sadhanah," Parshandatha said. "Please have a seat."

"Thank you, but I prefer not to sit."

Parshandatha hesitated. "Very well. We would like to hire you in the capacity of an enforcer. You'll need to make sure that a group of no less than five and no more than ten never leave Babylon. Can you do that?"

"The question should be, do I *want* to do that?"

"Of course. Do you want to do that?"

Sadhanah crossed his muscular arms. "Who are these people?"

"Five travelers from a distant land, Artemisia, and her brother Pigres."

"It's not Artemisia of Halicarnassus, by any chance?"

"Yes, that's the one."

Sadhanah looked at everyone around the table as if assessing how much they could afford to pay. He returned his eyes to Parshandatha. "Why do you want them to stay in Babylon?"

"As you probably know, our father Haman arranged to pass a law to annihilate the Jews from the 127 provinces of Persia. He convinced the king that the Jews are a lawless people who put a financial burden on the government. We have it on good grounds that those demons are trying to prevent this from happening, even though the king approved of our—"

"I know the story," Sadhanah interrupted. "The whole world knows the story. His plan miscarried." He looked around for a reaction. "Your father was unmasked, then put to death by hanging on the very stake he'd built for Mordecai. I also know Xerxes awarded all your father's possessions to Esther and promoted Mordecai to prime minister in his place. So how do you plan to pay me for my services?"

"We will give you three percent of the plunder we amass from the slaughter of the Jews."

"Don't you think I'll be doing my own plundering?" Sadhanah asked. No one responded. "Ten percent and five thousand silver talents."

"That's half the funds our father left for the entire venture," Parshandatha protested.

Sadhanah shrugged. "Take it or leave it."

"Five percent and two thousand silver talents. We can't afford more. If this is not acceptable, we will find someone else."

"Five percent, two thousand silver talents, and let me know where the plundering will be most plentiful."

"Done," Parshandatha agreed.

CHAPTER 23

Thomas woke up to a cool breeze and the smell of roasted fish. After rubbing the sleep from his eyes, he noticed Kelile talking with the helmsman. *The poor devil,* he thought. *I hope he loves talking about his vessel.*

"Do you smell that wonderful aroma?" Anna said as she stood up to stretch. "It's breakfast caught from this river. It looks like it's from the Cyprinidae family."

He looked at the fish being roasted by the chief cook. "It looks like a huge carp to me."

"I think it's a mangar, actually; if so, it's from the Cyprinidae family."

He looked at her. "How do you know this?"

"My father is a big-time fisherman. When I was young he would take me out fishing every chance he got, so I picked up a few things along the way."

Thomas noticed Artemisia standing once again at the bow. "I spoke with Artemisia last night after everyone was asleep. I suspect she's a lot more important than she's letting on. In fact, I seem to remember reading something about her. I can't quite put my finger on it." He looked at his telecom ring. "As soon as we can communicate with the *Kismet* I'll ask Derrek to look her up."

"What do you think she's doing?"

"I don't know. Last night she talked about some naval defeat she was a part of. I think this boat reminds her of it. Would it be okay if I talked to her for a few minutes?"

"No problem, Thomas, but be quick," Anna replied. "I don't trust her yet. Besides, breakfast is almost ready." She smiled.

Thomas walked over to Artemisia. "I hope you didn't stand here all night."

"No, of course not," Artemisia said. "I woke up a short time ago. Did you sleep well?"

"I sure did. A little cold on the deck, though."

"I know it can get quite cold at night." She released a deep sigh. "Thomas, can I ask you a personal question?"

"Sure, what is it?"

"I was speaking with Michael yesterday. He told me about the work you both did in your home country. He mentioned the pirates you were fighting and how you defended your country's secrets. He also told me about the one pirate that got away.

"Over the years I've come to know many warriors of different ranks. Few have a record as impressive as you. Yet you let this one pirate bring you down. If I were in your place, I would be very proud. If I had your record, I would be at the head of Xerxes's navy."

"What pirate did Michael talk about, exactly?" He hoped her answer would help him understand what crazy story Michael had dreamed up.

"Why, the pirate Komodo, of course," she exclaimed. "He's the one who penetrated your defenses."

"Oh yes, Komodo. Well, the reason he bothered me so much was, well, because I couldn't catch him, I guess."

"You guess?"

Thomas recounted the situation with Komodo and the encrypted files the best way he could. "Michael already told you all this, hasn't he?"

"Yes, Thomas, he did, but he didn't clarify why Komodo troubles you so much. It's not as if he caused you any damage."

"You're right." Thomas thought a moment. "Let me try to explain. You see, Komodo could never penetrate our defenses if he didn't have in-depth knowledge of our infrastructure. Only three people have this knowledge: me, of course; Michael, whom I trust with my life; and my son Christian."

"So it's personal, then. You think your son gave this pirate the information needed to break your defenses."

"No! Yes—" Thomas sighed. "I don't know."

Artemisia cocked her head and smiled at him. "You don't seem to be too sure, Thomas."

Thomas frowned in thought. "There is one more thing that bothers me: the name the pirate used. Christian and I used the same name to identify ourselves when working on what we called penetration testing." He struggled for a while, wondering how to explain. "We were sometimes hired by other entities to test the security of their defenses. If we were unable to penetrate, they could feel secure behind their walls. If we succeeded, we explained how we did it so they could fix the problem. Anyway, our handle, our trademark was 'Komodo.'"

"It could be a coincidence, you know."

Thomas decided it would be too difficult to explain the virus on the *Kismet* and the appearance of Komodo on a Persian stela. Besides, he'd gone over every possible scenario a hundred times; he had no doubts. It could never be Christian. "You're right, Artemisia. I should just forget the whole thing."

Artemisia got the message. "Why did you call yourselves Komodo?" she asked to change the subject. "What does it mean?"

"Komodo comes from the Latin words Varanus komodoensis."

"What's Latin?"

Thomas smiled. "Of course—never mind that. It also goes by the name Komodo dragon. It's the largest reptile in the world."

Artemisia looked concerned. "Is this dragon dangerous?"

"It can be, but in my opinion, it's the most perfect of all reptiles. It certainly is the most intelligent. It's about—" he stopped to calculate the conversion "—it's about six and a half cubits long. It can eat small animals like birds, mammals, and other lizards, but it can also kill large animals. In one documented case it ripped a hole in the abdomen of a water buffalo with its curved, serrated teeth. But the real reason we chose this reptile was because of its intelligence. Komodos make tunnels to hide in order to ambush their prey. Sometimes they even sever the tendons of pigs and deer to cripple them, and then they can take their time eating. They can even think their way out of traps. I can go on and on, but the point is, these same qualities are similar to those of a good penetration tester."

"Minus the eating of water buffaloes, I hope." Artemisia smiled.

"Thomas," Anna called, and when he turned, she held up two plates of food. "Come on, we're ready to eat."

"We'd better get some breakfast, Artemisia," he said. "I'll tell you more some other time."

• • • • • • • • • ● ○○○○○○○○○ ○ ○

"We're getting close," Thomas said, joining Michael at the bulwark. "We're beginning to see more agricultural land, and there are unquestionably more boats on the river. Now I understand why the captain chose to travel at night. We must have slowed our speed by half to avoid a collision."

Michael was too busy staring at Artemisia to answer. The breeze against her body revealed her curvaceous silhouette, leaving little to the imagination.

"She sure is a looker," Thomas said. "It's a wonder she's not married."

"Tell me, Thomas," Michael said, "do you believe in the cliché, love at first sight?"

"Come on, Michael, don't tell me you're falling for her," Thomas replied. "She must be—what? Five, six years older than you?"

"No man, of course not," Michael insisted.

"Good, because if you are, you know it could never work. In ten months you're going back home and she's staying right here."

"I know, but it feels good, getting some special attention." Michael turned back to look at Thomas. "All the way through college, you were the popular one. All I ever got were stories of your romantic dalliances."

He turned to look at Artemisia again. "I think she feels something for me. Ever since our arrival, she's been giving me that look. You know the look I'm talking about. When she thinks I'm looking at her, she moves her body in a seductive manner, as if to get my attention."

"How do you know she doesn't do that with every man she meets?"

Michael looked sharply at Thomas. "Why, has she done it to you?"

"No, of course not, but maybe it's because she knows Anna and I are together."

"Are you calling her a seductress?"

"No, Michael. I don't want you to get hurt when it's time to head back, that's all."

"Listen, man," Michael said, "if there's something here, I'm taking advantage of it. You were the one with all the girlfriends in school; you married Amélie, and now you have Anna. Don't try to take my first real chance at love away from me."

"Love! This is serious."

"I don't know if it's love." Michael sounded annoyed. "That's why I asked you if you believe in love at first sight."

"I love you," Thomas said with a smile.

"Stop kidding around. I'm serious. I want to experience love too, even if it's only for ten months. Was it Alfred, Lord Tennyson who said 'T'is better to have loved and lost than never to have loved at all'?"

No, it's not, Thomas thought.

Michael didn't wait for an answer. "Anyway, it's probably an infatuation.

Just be happy for me and whatever comes of it. Can you do that for me, Thomas?"

"Well, Michael, it's been five days since you first met her. You'll know soon enough if it's real or not. Just let me give you this piece of advice. Then I'll drop the subject and trust your judgment, okay?"

"I'm listening."

"Before we left for Babylon, Anna and I were sitting on the rooftop in Hīt when Artemisia returned from the market. She sought my advice on a gift she purchased for a man she wanted to win over. This man must have meant the world to her because the gift was a fifty centimeter-long, gold-plated dagger with some expensive stones set into its handle. It's probably worth hundreds of thousands of dollars back home. So I think she already has her heart set on someone else."

"She told you the dagger is for someone she liked?"

"Actually, I'm sure she loves this man, but she's not sure if the man loves her back."

"You're sure about this," Michael said, the question sounding more like a demand. "There's no mistaking her intentions?"

"Yes, Michael, I'm absolutely sure," Thomas said gently. "Ask Anna; she'll tell you. She was with me when Artemisia showed me the dagger."

Michael leaned over and rested his arms on the railing. He looked into the water for a good long time, then he looked at Artemisia, who was looking back at him. She waved. Michael waved back before he turned to face Thomas. "You really are a good friend. What you said has opened my eyes. I now know what to do. Thank you, Thomas."

"I'm surprised you're taking it so well," Thomas said. "I mean, the way you were talking earlier, I thought you would be disappointed."

Michael made sure he was facing Thomas. Then ever so slowly, he opened his red tunic just enough to reveal a fifty centimeter-long, gold-plated dagger. "Is this what she showed you?"

Thomas looked at the dagger. All he could do was nod in agreement. Michael tapped Thomas on the shoulder, then walked away.

Anna approached him with two glasses of pomegranate juice. She watched Michael swaggering away along the deck. "He looks to be in a good mood. What did you tell him?"

"You remember the dagger Artemisia showed us back in Hīt?" Anna nodded. "Well, guess who the dagger was for?"

"No—not Michael!"

"Yup, it was for him, and what's more, he's head over heels for her."

"My goodness, this is bad! What are you going to do?"

"Nothing," Thomas said. "I tried talking with him, but his mind is made up."

CHAPTER 24

Tadmor, nine hundred kilometers away

Though the first four days had been uneventful for Nicolas Knox and his assistant Brody Powell, they had discovered the frailties of the human body as they moved from inn to inn—dry skin, dry mouth, lightheadedness, and fatigue plagued them. Last night Nicolas had experienced heat cramps—all signs of dehydration.

They'd been unaware that passports were needed to travel within the Persian Empire. The Aramaic passport, written on pieces of animal skin, allowed travelers to access food and overnight accommodation. Since they had no passports, they stayed off the main road, in cheap, dirty accommodations made available by anyone with a spare room or a shed.

This night would be different. The next stop was not an inn but a city in an oasis on the northern edge of the Syrian Desert. It was also a popular caravan stop on the main route to Israel. King Solomon of the old kingdom of Israel had fortified Tadmor to serve as a garrison defending the northern border of his kingdom. Tonight they would get the comforts they longed for.

They had no trouble gaining entrance through the large open gates. Strangers came through every day. Inside, an array of commercial buildings lined both sides of the road—rather than open market stalls, these housed stores that shoppers entered to view the merchandise. The drinking establishments were easy to find—all they had to do was look for a gathering of drunkards, either lying on the ground or fighting over something or another.

"Just look at the size of this place," Nicolas said, looking around. "Some of these buildings are as large as the ones back home."

"That one looks like a church," Brody observed, jerking his chin toward an imposing stone edifice ahead of them. A wide walkway lined with pillars led to an entrance flanked by two life-size representations of the god Ishtar: two naked women with wings and bird feet.

"My young man Brody, that's not a church, it's a temple," Nicolas said. "I don't know enough to tell what kind of temple it is, but it must be Babylonian or Mesopotamian. Considering the location of this city, I'm sure we'll find temples from different areas of the Middle East."

"You think we'll see a synagogue?"

"It's possible. It's been suggested that synagogues had their beginning in the days of the prophet Ezra or Nehemiah—" Nicolas suddenly stopped walking. "Good lord."

"What?"

"If we're lucky, Brody, we might be able to meet the prophet Ezra in person." Nicolas looked at his companion, eyebrows high. "Imagine that."

Brody inhaled deeply. "That would be special."

As they continued on, they noticed the streets were almost empty. The few people visible were staring at them as if they were outlaws of the Old West entering Dodge City, Kansas.

"Hey, you two," a voice called from behind them. "Where do you come from and where are you going?"

They turned around to face two men and a teenager. "We come from Hīt and we're heading to Damascus," Brody said with a squeak in his voice. "We would like to stop for the night and be on our way tomorrow morning. Why do you ask?"

The three looked at each other and smirked. The younger one approached Brody and softly pressed his hand against his cheek. You're a beautiful boy, aren't you."

Brody backed away.

"Well, well," one of the other men said. "I don't believe we're good enough for them. What do you say we teach them proper manners, my brothers?"

Nicolas moved between Brody and the men. "I think you've mistaken our intentions. We don't want any trouble. All we want is a bath and a bed for the night. At first light we'll be gone."

The three men laughed as they approached Nicolas. Brody retreated, his spear held straight out in front of him. "Please, turn around and we will be on our way." A crowd started to gather, eager for excitement.

The crowd parted and a well-dressed man stepped forward, his massive frame wrapped in the traditional robe of honor worn by nobles and kings alike. This one was green with a floral border. An equally impressive tiara bound his long, thick hair. Unlike other noblemen, he had no beard. "What's going on here?" he shouted. His eyes fell on the three men. "Well, if it isn't the sons of Cedron. Now, why am I not surprised?" He walked over to them and sniffed, then turned his head away in disgust. "Been drinking again, haven't you, boys. Now go home before I call the guards." He faced the curious crowd. "There's nothing left to see here; go back to what you were doing."

The man turned his attention to Nicolas and Brody. "Are you all right, my friends? Did they hurt you?"

"No, you came just in time. Who are you, sir?" Nicolas asked.

"My name's JahanBakhsh. I'm the governor of this province, appointed by the great King Xerxes himself."

"You're the satrap of this satrapy?"

JahanBakhsh laughed loudly. "I've never heard it said quite that way, but yes." He looked them over. "You look Hebrew, but you're not; am I correct?"

"Yes, we're from a land far west of here."

Once more JahanBakhsh laughed. Then he looked them over for a moment as if weighing options. "Oh, why not. Since you had this humiliating encounter, I will insist that you be my guests tonight and dine with my family. I would not want you to have negative things to say about my city when you return home."

"Very well. Thank you," Nicolas said, deciding this would be the safest thing to do. "We look forward to meeting your family."

"Good, then. Come along."

They followed the formidable Persian to an enormous palace complex.

"This is your house?" Brody asked.

JahanBakhsh snorted. "No, this isn't a house, although as the provincial governor, I and my family live in a house inside this complex. This palace is a center for the government. Inside we have a courthouse, a tax office, and offices for many other necessary services for the citizens. When a governor or any other official visits, they stay in a stateroom here. You will be staying in one of those." He led them up the wide staircase to a set of bronze doors flanked by eight pillars, four on each side.

Ruining the otherwise perfect edifice were people kneeling on the stairs, throwing dirt on their heads. Brody was still staring at them as two guards stationed at the doors welcomed the governor. He tore his gaze away to ask JahanBakhsh, "Why are all these people tossing sand in the air?"

"It's not sand, it's dirt," JahanBakhsh answered. "And I'm a bit surprised that you don't know why, coming from Hīt."

"You know why, Brody," Nicolas interjected. "It's because the king issued an order to have all the Jews in all the provinces exterminated. They're Jews in mourning."

Brody looked back at the mourners. "That's sad."

"I don't know about that," JahanBakhsh said. "The letter bearing King Xerxes's seal says the Jews refused to obey the laws of the king and follow their own laws. We can't have everyone doing their own thing or there will be chaos. We would be no better than the divided Greeks. Our united peoples, the Meads and the Persians, defeated the Babylonian Empire because we're an organized and law-abiding people."

He too paused and looked at the mourners. "Besides, there's nothing I can do for them. The law is the law." He straightened his shoulders and turned back to the entrance. "Don't pay any attention to them. They won't be around for too much longer. Come, I want you to meet my family."

They followed JahanBakhsh through a cavernous open hall, its high ceiling bright with painted animals. Passing between two guards, the satrap led them through another door at the back of the hall into a long, narrow corridor, its whitewashed walls unadorned. At the end of the corridor they climbed a set of wooden stairs to a second-floor balcony with still another, much smaller door. As they approached, music filtered through the door.

"Oh no," Nicolas said. "You're entertaining. I feel bad for our intrusion."

"Nonsense," JahanBakhsh replied. "Besides, I don't know half the people here." He opened the door and they stepped into a large, decadently decorated reception hall packed with people of all ages feasting on a generous selection of food. At first glance, it reminded Nicolas of a wedding reception with relaxing background music but the somber, subdued tone of the conversations made it seem more like a funeral. "Now why don't you make yourselves at home—eat, drink, and much more, if you want." He gave them a wink and a lascivious smile.

"What we can use is a bath, before we join you and your guests," Nicolas said. "We've been traveling for four days."

JahanBakhsh nodded, peered around the room, and beckoned over two young slave women. "Takhat, Neferure, bring these men to the bath and see to it they get all the attention you would normally give to me, understood?" They nodded. JahanBakhsh turned back to Nicolas and Brody. "Before I leave

I would like to ask if you've seen a group of about forty or fifty cavalrymen coming this way."

"No, can't say that we have," Nicolas said. "Are they trouble, is that why there's hardly anyone on the streets?"

"No one knows for sure who they are. Their victims call them thieves but to their numerous followers, they are heroes. They steal from the rich and give some of the spoils to the poor. They stay mostly in the Ebir-Nāri province, but they've been seen in Phoenicia and Samaria. Rumor has it they're coming through here any day now. They must be expanding their territory. Anyway, I need to see to my guests. I'll see you both later."

The two slave women led them to the bath, a room of ceramic walls and a small pool inset in the marble floor. They brought towels and a bar of soap, then left the room.

"Can't believe the water is heated," Brody said before submerging himself.

"What did I tell you? Did I not promise luxury?" Nicolas said expansively.

Brody chuckled. "I don't think you meant this much luxury, I'm pretty sure. This is going to change everything I ever imagined about biblical times."

"I know what you mean," Nicolas said. "Bible classes will never be the same again."

As soon as they'd settled in, the young slave women returned, now clad in white robes. When they approached the side of the bath Nicolas tried to turn them away, but they looked at him blankly, as if they didn't understand, and continued with their assignment. One scattered sea salt over the surface of the water while the other poured oil from a tiny jar into the bath. Simultaneously covering their crotches with both hands, Nicolas and Brody could only watch in silence as the young women went about their duties.

"They can't be older than twenty years," Nicolas whispered, his face now flushed red.

The women walked around to the steps into the bath and dropped their robes, revealing beautifully toned bodies. Brody froze, gaping at the young women as they descended into the water.

"Stop!" Nicolas cried out. They looked at him blankly. "Good lord, if you don't understand my language, you'll understand this!" he exclaimed and rose to push them out of the pool. They sat on the marble floor a few moments, looking dejected, then rose and put on their robes. One woman started to cry.

"No, no, don't cry," Nicolas said in a calmer tone. "I know all you want to do is sponge us down—at least I think that's all you want—but we would rather wash ourselves. Do you understand?" He gave them a tender smile and nodded his approval. It seemed to work—they smiled back. Gathering Nicolas and Brody's dirty clothing, they left the room.

Nicolas sat back and sighed. "Do you believe what just happened?"

"You handled it like a pro; I'm impressed," Brody said. "There's no way I could ever have done what you did—you know, jumping up stark naked and pushing them out like that." They stared at each other a moment, reliving the embarrassment, then broke out laughing.

An hour later they entered the reception hall, bathed and dressed in clean clothing. They filled their plates with an assortment of meats and vegetables, found a place to sit, and gratefully accepted red wine offered by another slave. They enjoyed their meal while being entertained by the music of two flutists and a third musician playing a barbat, a lute that looked like a fat guitar with some of its strings missing.

"Did you notice that if we sampled a piece of everything here, we'd be sick for a month?" Brody said, studying a strange looking statuette on a small table next to him.

"That's why I put so little on my plate. I want to try as many of the delicious pastries as possible," Nicolas said.

"What do you suppose this tiny statuette symbolizes?" Brody asked, lifting the figurine. "It's kind of plain looking compared to all the other pieces."

Nicolas turned to see what Brody had in his hand. His eyes widened. "Put that thing back right now," he hissed. "Don't you know what that is?" He looked around to see if anyone was looking at them. "Don't touch anything, Brody. You can get us into serious trouble."

"Okay, I'm sorry." Brody replaced the statuette. "It's just that it looks like a child's toy." He looked at it again. "And an ugly one, at that."

Nicolas stared at him. "Are you telling me you don't recognize it?" He waited while Brody studied the statuette. Made of polished brass and about twenty centimeters tall, it depicted a man wearing a horned helmet, his left leg thrust forward as if he were walking. His right arm was holding a club over his head, while his left hand held a stylized lightning flash that ended in a spearhead.

"I'm sorry, Nicolas," Brody said after a moment. "I don't recognize it."

"Good lord, Brody, it's one of the worst gods mentioned in the Bible."

Brody looked at it once more. "Nope, sorry."

"What you're looking at is the god Baal."

"That little thing is the mighty Baal?" Brody scoffed.

"Yes Brody, every Baal worshipper has one in his home or a larger one on his rooftop. Each territory is represented by their own Baal god."

"So the name Baal represents many gods."

"That's right." Nicolas scanned the reception hall. "If there's a Baal god here, then there's probably something representing Moloch. They often go hand in hand."

Brody looked around. "What does it look like?"

"I don't know for sure. Look for a man with a bull's head."

As they swept their eyes over the reception hall looking for evidence of Moloch, a man approached them. "Hello there, my name is Rambax. Which side of the family do you belong to?"

"Actually," Nicolas answered, "we're not from one side or the other. Governor JahanBakhsh met us on the street and kindly invited us to be his guests."

Rambax smiled, nodding. "JahanBakhsh's always looking for ways to help others, he's a good man."

"Not to the Jews," Brody mumbled.

Nicolas elbowed Brody to shut him up. "So what's the celebrating for? There's a lot of people here."

"If you just got in, you wouldn't know." He looked at them for a moment, then pulled up a chair. He pointed to a woman in her twenties; she was smiling, but unmistakably uncomfortable. A number of people sat next to her, presumably family or friends, Nicolas decided. They seemed to be giving the young lady encouragement. "That young woman's name is Delara. Last week she made the most honorable sacrifice for her family. Now she has guaranteed their prosperity with the help of the great Moloch."

To hide his mounting anger, Nicolas took a sip of wine. "How old was the child?" he asked calmly.

"Six months," Rambax said, as if he were speaking about a farm animal.

"Where did the sacrifice take place?"

"It was to the god Baal Shamen of Tyre, in Phoenicia. That's where the temple is located." Rambax's eyes slid to Brody, who looked confused. "You don't know any of this, do you."

"My friend and I are not from these parts. Where we come from, there are no Baal gods or any human sacrifice," Nicolas interjected smoothly. Although he wasn't sure he wanted to know the details, he knew that for the sake of the mission and its biblical accuracy, he had to ask. "Since we've never attended a Baal sacrificial ceremony, can you describe the procedure for us?"

"Of course," Rambax said. He paused to turn and gesture a slave over with more wine. Then he settled back, cradling the goblet in both hands. "You found the right person to explain it since I was there," he said proudly. "It will be a privilege to tell you all about it.

"It was late afternoon when we arrived at the modest yet magnificent Baal Shamen. It is an enclosed building surrounded by columns, which inspires respect for the mighty Moloch waiting inside. The smoke from the rooftop reached up into the sky, indicating his glorious presence.

"We made our intention known to the priest, then waited anxiously for our turn. Not too long after our arrival, his assistant told us to get ready. He gave us a small bottle of inspirational tonic. I refused to take it since I wanted all of my senses sharp to experience the magnificent event. Delara and her husband took the tonic for courage, and the infant received an obligatory dosage."

Rambax leaned forward and whispered, "The tonic is opium, but few know this. It takes away any doubts the parents may have, and as for the infant, well, it would be cruel if the infant could feel the pain of the fire. You see, it's the life Moloch needs, not the suffering of the child. Moloch is a loving god, not a cruel god."

He straightened up. "Anyway, when our turn came we were directed through the front door into the dimness of the temple, sparsely lit with torches along the walls. I was positioned in a corner of the temple with Delara's husband, where we could observe the ceremony. Four large temple guards stood by, just in case someone changed their mind at the last minute.

"Delara and her baby were led forward. The priest and an assistant, a priest in training, stood one on each side of Delara. As the priest began to chant, the drums beat in a steady, slow rhythm. Already Delara was feeling the effects of the tonic. They walked slowly toward Moloch. The priest's chanting and the beat of the drums echoed off the temple walls.

"As they got closer to the image of Moloch, the drums and the chanting picked up in tempo. Delara's legs gave out under her. The assistant held her steady. Ten steps from Moloch's open arms, she could see in vivid detail what was waiting for her firstborn son."

Nicolas closed his eyes and retrieved a memory of this massive, monstrous idol. Archaeologists had reconstructed a statue eight meters tall: a man with the head of a horned bull, sitting on a throne, arms outstretched before him, with a staircase between his open legs that rose to his lap. In his lap was a hole.

Rambax animated the image in Nicolas's mind. "One could see the flickering light of the fiery furnace blazing under him. The furnace was so hot that Moloch glowed red, adding to his mighty appearance. Delara fell forward at this point. The tonic and the sight of Moloch must have been too much for her to handle." Rambax paused, then said softly, "What courage she had.

"They were almost at the steps when the priest took the infant from Delara's arms and prayed to Moloch with the now motionless baby in his outstretched hands. Two men dressed in black robes emerged from behind Moloch carrying a basket between them suspended on two long poles. The priest placed the infant in the basket."

Rambax grew animated as he added, "My heart was beating fast since this was the moment of sacrifice. As the drums and the chanting reached a peak, the basket was raised over Moloch's lap. It caught fire even before reaching Moloch's open arms. Delara, now on her knees, head lowered, raised her arms toward Moloch. She was unable to watch as her baby dropped into the hole.

"A moment later, everything stopped. There was complete silence. I can still see her husband's clenched fists as he watched every step. He was a brave man. He knew a sacrifice was necessary for the prosperity of his family; he also knew other children would come and bring them happiness.

"Delara was brought back to us and she fell into her husband's arms. Although she tried not to cry, I could see tears dripping down her cheeks."

He sighed and smiled, his eyes distant, reliving the memory. "They gave us a few minutes to regain our composure. Before we left the temple, Delara was given a representation of our god Baal. It's the one next to you on the table." He nodded toward the statuette. "After Delara and her husband left, I turned for one more look and saw the next couple and their baby already inside the temple, seeking the benevolence of Moloch."

Rambax took a sip of his wine. "I hope I explained the event properly," he said. "You really have to be there to appreciate it."

Nicolas felt nauseous. He looked at Brody, who regarded him with eyes wide with horrified disbelief. Brody looked away, rubbing his hands against his thighs as if to wipe off any taint from having touched the idol. "We get the picture," Nicolas said. "Thank you for the explanation." He looked at Brody again and put his glass of wine on the table. "I'm beginning to feel tired from our long voyage. I'm going to bed. Are you coming, Brody?"

Brody rose abruptly and thanked Rambax.

"We should find JahanBakhsh and thank him for his hospitality," Nicolas said.

Walking through the crowded room felt like they were walking through a party sponsored by the Devil himself. Nicolas wanted desperately to leave.

"There you are," said JahanBakhsh from behind them. "Enjoying yourselves?"

Nicolas turned, followed by Brody. "You've been an excellent host and we don't know how to thank you," Nicolas answered. "But I'm afraid all the food and wine has only increased our fatigue. I hope you won't mind if we head to our sleeping quarters. Tomorrow we must leave early."

"Not at all." He waved over the same two slave women who had taken them to the bath to lead them to their sleeping quarters.

Their original clothing, already cleaned and pressed, was laid out on the beds. Nicolas moved to the window overlooking the main street where they'd met JahanBakhsh earlier and looked out. "Do you see what's going on in the streets, Brody?" he said.

Brody joined him at the window and Nicolas nodded toward the fires built by people for warmth. They illuminated a fight farther down the street that had attracted a group of soldiers. Nicolas also saw the three men they'd encountered earlier. They were half naked, supporting one another.

"They're drunk," Brody said of them.

"I'm sure they are," Nicolas replied.

After a long moment of reflection, Brody broke the silence. "The people downstairs seem happy about the sacrifice. They don't show any more remorse for the child than they would a goat or a cow. Even Delara, the child's mother, though she seems to sense some kind of loss, behaves as if she lost a beloved family pet." His voice rose in anger. "I don't understand these people. I feel more for that child than most of them do."

"And this is why we must succeed in our mission," Nicolas explained. "The world must know that all religions are not accepted by God, and this is a perfect example. Do you remember what the apostle Paul said in his letter to the Ephesians, Brody? He said, 'There is one body, and one Spirit, even as ye are called in one hope of your calling; One Lord, one faith, one baptism, One God and Father of all, who is above all, and through all, and in you all.' This is why we must succeed."

"It's almost as if we were on a quest for God," Brody mused. "Maybe even a crusade."

Nicolas nodded eagerly. "We are. We are and don't you ever forget it. The evidence we bring back from Jerusalem is the key to opening the eyes of the world. We are doing God's will and for this reason we will succeed." His tone grew pedantic. "You see, Brody, the unbelieving world does not take the Bible seriously, just as the people here today don't. Don't you think they know how God, the real true God, feels about child sacrifice? Of course they do. The prophet Jeremiah told the Israelites before today that child sacrifice is a thing that God had not commanded, that it had not come up into his heart. So often, Baal worshipers were killed off because of what we witnessed today." He paused, gaze distant, lips compressed. "We will get the evidence we need, and we will find the location of the Ark of the Covenant so we can retrieve it when we get back home."

Brody looked skeptical. "Do you think it will be enough?"

"Yes I do, Brody," Nicolas said firmly. "That's why God has blessed this mission from the start."

CHAPTER 25

They stood at the bow of the vessel as it approached the city of Babylon. There were no more open fields to observe, no more grazing animals. Roads on both banks were filled with travelers coming and going, some on foot, others in horse-drawn carriages. Soldiers were everywhere, apparently keeping the peace. Beyond the roads were houses, mostly made of brick or clay. Almost all were whitewashed. The variety of colors seen in Hīt was absent. Thomas realized they were passing a suburb in one of the greatest cities of the ancient world.

"Look at the people, Thomas," Anna exclaimed. "They're from all over; you can tell by their garb—Egyptians, Africans, and Assyrians. And look! Those people came all the way from China."

"I see you're a people-watcher, Anna," Pigres said, resting his hand on the back of her neck. "Remind me to accompany you to the Ishtar Gate once we settle in. All the important people go through that gate, and you know how significant people love to dress up."

"That's very nice of you, Pigres," Anna replied. "Thomas and I would be delighted."

Pigres wasted no time in offering himself as a tour guide. "Did you know the Ishtar Gate was dedicated to the goddess Ishtar one hundred years ago by King Nebuchadnezzar? The gate is by far the most beautiful of the eight gates of Babylon. Its glazed bricks depict dragons and aurochs, symbols for the gods Marduk and Adad. Although the roof and doors are made of cedar, the gate itself is covered with the vibrant, deep blue color of lapis lazuli, a semiprecious stone that gives the gate a jewel-like appearance. Once inside, you can walk down the processional way, with its walls covered in glazed enamel yellow and black bricks. On the walls are one hundred and twenty lions, bulls, and dragons depicting the goddess Ishtar."

"Tell me, Pigres." Thomas inserted himself between Pigres and Anna. "What's that big building we're passing? Would that be the king's summer palace?"

"Sort of." Pigres moved over. "The first block you see, the one with the road going through it, isn't where the palace is. It's called the northern fortress. It's next to the main wall but located outside. The Ishtar Gate is out of sight behind it." He turned to look south. "In a minute we'll enter the city. The first complex we'll see is the southern fortress. Behind it is the king's palace. The two fortresses are separated by an aqueduct that surrounds the old part of the city. This was dug out to provide additional protection when the Babylonians ruled the world. It wasn't enough to stop us, though," he boasted.

The trireme, now inside the city, passed the southern fortress and three temples before it reached the focal point of Babylon, a colossal step pyramid that seemed to reach for the heavens.

"Do you think that's the Tower of Babel?" Thomas asked.

"We call it Etemenanki," Pigres said. "It means the temple of the foundation of heaven and earth and is dedicated to Marduk. It's said our ancestor Nimrod built the tower at the beginning of time. It's also said that all languages of the world had their origins here."

Thomas and Anna said in unison, "The Tower of Babel."

They were so captivated by the ziggurat they failed to notice the vessel was already moored on the opposite side of the now narrow Euphrates River.

"We need to hurry," Aldon called out. "We have to unload; the vessel needs to continue its journey."

Thomas noticed Artemisia, the helmsman, and Kelile were already on shore having a discussion with two officers. It didn't look positive. Thomas jumped off the vessel and approached them to investigate.

"I'm sorry, Artemisia," the officer in charge said, "but I don't make the rules. If anyone found out I let you pass without checking your companions' luggage, I could get into real trouble with my supervisor."

"Is there any trouble?" Thomas asked.

Artemisia turned to him. "They insist on checking all your luggage, even though they know you're traveling with me."

"That's okay," Thomas responded. "How long will it take?"

"I don't know, maybe an hour to search your luggage and half an hour to record everything," the officer said.

"Oh my, that is long." He looked at Artemisia, then at the officers again. "That's too bad. This means we'll be late for the ceremony prepared for

Shamash." From the corner of his eye, Thomas saw Artemisia look at Kelile, who shrugged. "You were right about these dock officers, Artemisia. They're dedicated to their work," he said to her, then he told the two officers, "It is told in my country that the laws of Persia are the best in the world. I can see for myself this is true. I'm so moved that I would like to submit to any search you want to perform. Not making it to the temple is not a big deal, don't worry about that."

Thomas hesitated for a moment. "If you're able to accept, would it be all right if I reward you for your loyalty? What I mean is, am I legally permitted in your city to give you and your fellow officer a small gift, a token of our appreciation for being such a good example, and afterward you could check our luggage?"

"As long as we're not prevented in any way from doing our work, I see no problem," the officer said. He looked at his partner, who nodded agreement.

"Wonderful, then." Thomas pulled two women's bracelets from a pouch and handed one to each officer. "These are made from a material unique to my country. I'm sure your wives would appreciate them, if you know what I mean."

The head officer frowned. "Thank you, but it's much more than we can accept."

"Nonsense! Honest, hard-working men like you deserve a break every now and then. Why should only the rich have good things?" Thomas said, pressing the bracelets into their hands. "So how does this work? Do we bring our luggage to you, or do you go on board to inspect our bags?"

The two officers looked at each other. "I suppose since you're on your way to the temple of Shamash, it would be wrong for us to stop you. Besides, we wouldn't want to have Shamash on our bad side now, would we?" The officer smiled. "We'll let you go this time, but next time, try to arrive a little sooner."

"You are true gentlemen," Thomas said. "We thank you both."

He and Artemisia watched the two officers walk away down the dock, then returned to the trireme and bade farewell to the captain. Their bags were already on the dock. Their small group watched the trireme disappear under the only bridge connecting old and new Babylon.

"Follow me," Pigres urged. "We still have a distance to cover before we arrive at the apartment—I mean the temple."

As soon as they were a safe distance from the river, Anna and Artemisia approached Thomas. "How did you know about Shamash?" Anna asked.

"I read about it during our training back home."

THE HUNT FOR KOMODO CRACKER

"What I want to know," Artemisia said, "is how you knew the temple is on this street?"

"I didn't," Thomas replied. "Is it really on this street?"

"What if they checked our luggage and found the gifts you brought for King Xerxes?" Anna said.

"I was betting those dock officers are as corrupt as the ones we have back home." Thomas grinned. "I was right."

Twenty minutes later they arrived at the dwelling where they planned to spend the next few months. Pigres opened a door and they walked along a narrow passage leading to a courtyard. On all four sides were buildings of different heights, all attached to one another. The only way into the square was through the one narrow passage. They climbed a staircase to the top floor of a five-story building and entered a spacious, seven bedroom apartment. It was well furnished and tastefully decorated. A second door opened onto a wooden balcony that overlooked the courtyard.

"Well," Thomas said. "This is going to be home for the next little while. It's a perfect base for our research. Thank you, Pigres; it's very nice."

"You're welcome."

"You and your sister will be staying here with us, I hope?"

"Yes, of course; our rooms are over there." He pointed to two doors next to the kitchen. "Now I will go to the market and get us some supplies. I'll see you in a short while."

After unpacking their luggage in their selected bedrooms the group gathered in the living room to await the return of Pigres.

Michael noticed a small wooden box with ivory squares glued on its top. "What's this?" he asked as he retrieved it from the shelf. Thomas came over to look at it too. There were twenty squares, each bearing one of five different patterns. The box was long, flat, and shaped like a small paddle.

Smiling, Artemisia took the box from Michael and opened the small drawer in its side. It contained three rectangular dice and what looked like seven white and seven black buttons with five dots on each one. "It's a game," she explained. "The objective is to throw the dice and move your tokens up the board and back down again. The first one to move all his tokens wins."

"That's it?" Michael asked. "Sounds simple enough."

"There's more to it," Artemisia warned. "Would you like to try it?"

"How about it, guys?" Michael said, looking around. "Anyone up for a game?" Everyone declined. He looked back at Artemisia. "Well, I'd like to try it. Show me how it's played."

While Michael and Artemisia faced off, Aldon and Kelile went to their respective rooms for a catnap. Thomas and Anna pulled up chairs to enjoy a view of the ziggurat tower over the Euphrates River from a large window.

"It sure is impressive," Anna observed. "I see how they must have been intimidated by its sheer size."

"I'm beginning to worry about—"

"Pigres?" Anna interrupted. "Well, don't. I'll tell him the first chance I get that you and I are together."

"Well, that too, but what I was about to say is that I'm beginning to worry about the *Kismet*. Quincy said they would fix the communications within a few hours of our departure." He looked at the camouflaged camera. He waved at it and smiled. "Even if we wrote a message for them to see, how will they reply?"

Anna looked at her camera. "Derrek and Quincy are the best at what they do. They'll find a way to fix the problem. At least they can gather the visual information until they repair the sound. Soon we will hear from them, I'm convinced of it."

Thomas frowned. "I hope nothing is wrong with the ship."

"Like what?"

"I don't know . . . . like, did the virus send them back home without us?"

"Don't think like that, Thomas. I'm sure it's only a glitch. And stop thinking about the communications; when they're ready, they'll let us know."

Thomas sighed. "Yeah, you're probably right."

CHAPTER 26

The temperature in the conference room was kept cool to prevent the participants from falling asleep while a lackluster, monotonous speaker babbled away on a tedious subject.

"We've been waiting for twenty minutes," Quincy moaned. "How much longer will she make us wait?"

Derrek controlled his nerves by chewing a gob of bubble gum and drumming his fingers on a polished mahogany conference table. He was blowing a large pink bubble when Captain Washington accompanied by Lieutenant General Commander Rye walked into the conference room and went immediately to their chairs opposite Quincy and Derrek.

"Hello Mr. Daramy, Mr. McCarthy," the captain said. "You requested this meeting to discuss a possible security breach. Please begin."

Derrek struggled with his gum so Quincy spoke. "We thought the meeting was between the three of us. The subject is delicate and confidential."

"I never meet alone, Mr. Daramy. This is as confidential as it gets."

"Very well." Quincy glanced at Callahan Rye. "Derrek and I have been alternating twelve-hour shifts to solve the virus situation while at the same time programming a new server to get us back home. Recently we've noticed changes not documented by either of us. At first, we thought it was absent-mindedness, but after considering these lines of codes, we suspect it was done by someone else. We therefore feel it's necessary to let you know that someone aboard this ship is sabotaging our progress."

Washington lifted an eyebrow. "Perhaps you're making mistakes and don't remember some of the codes you've programmed," she suggested. "Twelve-hour shifts can play tricks on the mind."

"Hell, no," Derrek said, now free of his gum. "We've been doing this for a long time. In fact, we usually work longer hours than this."

"So what do you want me to do?" Olivia asked.

"We need to secure the servers with passwords. The no locks, no passwords policy isn't working anymore."

"No." Olivia was unbending. "The policy was implemented because we're an organization of honest truth seekers. To keep this concept alive, we need to always display trust. No passwords."

"But how can we continue when someone keeps changing our work? The policy might have been good at one time, but now we have a dishonest person among us. We must take action," Quincy said.

"My decision is final," Captain Washington insisted. "It's non-negotiable. Besides, the changes are probably imagined, due to fatigue from working long hours combined with the stress induced by the possibility of never making it back home." She leaned forward, resting her elbows on the table and looking at Quincy then Derrek. "So this is what we will do. Cut your shifts to eight hours. When there's no one to work on the servers, shut them down."

"Shut down the servers?" Derrek blurted. "We can't just shut down the servers! They have important roles. Shutting down a server, even for a short period of time, will have devastating effects."

Olivia said nothing.

"Can we at least install alerts that will let us know if someone has logged into one of the servers?" Quincy asked. "Can we activate a monitoring system to track every activity in a separate log? This way we could examine them and report any abnormalities."

"If it does not involve passwords, then yes," Olivia said.

"There's one more thing we need to tell you," Derrek said. "We believe we know why we can't communicate with the foot soldiers."

"Let me guess: sabotage."

"Yes, but let me explain," Derrek said. "The first step in troubleshooting a communication problem like this is to use a signal analyzer to test the compatibility of frequencies. Nasato Nakamura, who has extensive experience in both electronics and telecommunications, told us where we could find one. However, the analyzer is missing. So he told us to do a physical check for damage on the antennas located on the wheelhouse. Nasato, of course, cannot climb up because of his broken leg and all, so we dismounted the antennas one by one and brought them to Nasato for inspection. He found nothing wrong with them. He concluded that someone is sending a phasing signal to jam both the incoming and outgoing signals, but without an analyzer we can't find its location."

The captain frowned. "Is there another way to solve the signal problem?"

Derrek shook his head. "Besides the physical inspection, no. We need this analyzer."

"Can you make one with parts available on this ship?" Callahan asked.

"We could program one, but it's the hardware that will cause a problem. We don't have the electronic parts to make one."

"Can they communicate with us any other way?" Olivia asked.

"The video feed is intermittent, but this was expected," Quincy said. "So yes, I suppose they could write the information down for us to read, but how do we respond?"

Olivia considered the situation. "You're telling me we can record the events they're witnessing. This isn't a problem, then. We could still fulfill our mission. As for their communication with us, well, that's not a problem either. We are able to see if they're in any trouble. They also know the location, day, and time to return to the *Kismet* at the end of the mission, so at that point, we will recover them."

She nodded to herself, then looked at Quincy, then Derrek. "Now this is what we will do. Abandon the idea of communicating with them for now. It's no longer a top priority. Focus on solving the virus password and the new server. We'd be no better off if we were able to talk to them, but could not get them home. Is there anything else?"

"No," Derrek said. "That's all."

The captain nodded and rose; Callahan Rye followed suit. Without saying another word, they left the conference room.

Quincy and Derrek shared an incredulous look. "Do you believe what just happened?" Quincy said. "I'm beginning to think they will be stuck down there forever."

"We can't allow that to happen," Derrek said. "They're counting on us. Besides, they need to know what's going on. Let's discuss this somewhere else."

CHAPTER 27

Seven days had passed since their arrival in Babylon and everyone had followed the mission's protocol in gathering information on every aspect of the Persian Empire. To ensure nothing was overlooked, they each had a specific feature to document that reflected their individual interests. Now it was time to share what they'd learned. They gathered around a table in the living area of their residence while Artemisia and her brother were away.

"I think the best way to do this is to give a brief overview of our research," Thomas said. "Afterwards we will be in a better position to know how long this will take. Kelile, why don't you start?"

"I began by befriending some soldiers on street patrol. I questioned them regarding their training and their weapons. Like many soldiers of our time, they take pride in their work and readily volunteered information. Some even allowed me to practice with their weapons. To get close and personal with the military, I volunteered to do mundane chores for the army. I can thank Artemisia, who used her influence to get me in." Kelile flashed a shy grin as if he'd done something wrong. "As you probably know, I never miss an opportunity to talk to our friend the helmsman each time he comes to Babylon with a new delivery of bitumen. Sometimes he carries weapons for the government. He has been kind enough to let me examine some of them."

"Very good, Kelile. I'm looking forward to more details," Thomas turned his attention to Michael.

Michael stood and repositioned himself behind his chair. "This city is not called by some religious scholars 'Babylon the Great' for nothing. Just about all religions of the world can trace some of their beliefs to this time and place. For example, the trinity taught in most Christian and many non-Christian faiths has its roots in Babylon. Sin the moon god, Shamash the sun god, and the goddess Ishtar comprise one trinity I discovered.

"I also found roots for the satanic cults. Among the over fifty temples I found within the city wall, magic, sorcery, and astrology play a prominent part in the Persian faith.

"Northwest of new Babylon, I found the temple of Enlil, who is known as the inventor of the mattock; she's also the god of weather. One of her teachings refers to a time when she was tired of the noise mankind made on earth, so she sent a flood to destroy mankind." Michael grinned. "Sounds something like the biblical flood, doesn't it.

"Next I crossed the Euphrates River to the busy northeast section of old Babylon, where kings and nobles spend their afternoons. There I found the temple of the Amorite god mentioned in the Bible as Nabu, the god of wisdom and writing. He is also the son of Marduk.

"Although most temples I visited confirm much of what historians believe, it's the famous Esagila, better known as the temple of Marduk the protector and principal god of Babylon, that intrigues me the most. The Bible calls him Merodach. Some say Merodach is the deified biblical Nimrod."

Michael stopped talking and returned to his seat. After a few seconds he looked at Thomas as if they were both alone in the living room. "I tried to locate people who might have come in contact with Bible prophets of this time. This proved to be much easier than I had anticipated. Thomas, did you know many grandparents and great-grandparents told their families firsthand accounts of prophets such as Jeremiah, Daniel, Ezekiel, Haggai, and Zechariah? I met this one man named Bel-Samu, who brought me to the house where Daniel lived. He also took me to the training facilities of Daniel's three companions, Shadrach, Meshach and Abednego. He even showed me the lion's den where Daniel was thrown in. He said his great-grandfather never talked down to the Jews again after seeing what Daniel did with the help of his God. Can you believe that?

"But that's not all. It's easier to find people ready to talk about prophets still alive today. You know the ones I'm talking about—Nehemiah, Malachi, Mordecai, and Ezra. Unfortunately, they are not here in Babylon at the moment. But we might meet Mordecai. I think he's in Susa." Michael sat up straight and looked around. "Well, that's it for now."

"That was inspiring, Michael. I sure do look forward to hearing more." Thomas looked to Aldon. "Aldon, it's your turn."

"I wrote everything down," Aldon said, rolling out a papyrus scroll. "Here are the highlights. The meetings I had with the few government officials who accepted a visit confirm what modern history books say about this government. I must tell you, though, that I learned more by speaking to common people at the marketplace."

Aldon stopped to make sure everyone was paying attention before continuing. "That's why I sometimes come home very late in the evenings. It seems people are more willing to talk at night. I can't explain why."

"We all appreciate your efforts," Thomas said.

Aldon nodded once and continued. "I learned about the judicial system enforced in Persia. I wrote down detailed notes on laws related to personal injuries and destruction of property. I also noted laws affecting the family and the treatment of animals. This empire has laws concerning theft, business dealings, and debts, as well as the amount of interest one can demand as a lender. There are laws applying to soldiers in the military, religion, and religious buildings. There are laws for the fair treatment of servants and slaves. So you see all citizens of the empire are protected. Next week I'll concentrate on taxation."

"Thank you Aldon, we're looking forward to more interesting details. Since I'm presiding, Anna, why don't you give the briefs on our assignment?"

"With the help of Pigres," Anna began, "we managed to gain access to some of the most beautiful palaces we've ever seen, like the celebrated palace of Nebuchadnezzar. I know Thomas is particularly fond of the place, so I'll leave him to tell you about it later. As for me, well, it's the hanging gardens. It took some doing, but Pigres managed to arrange for Thomas and I to visit the garden late yesterday afternoon.

"We learned that King Nebuchadnezzar built the garden for his Persian wife Amytis, a princess from Media. The garden was made to resemble the Zagros mountain range where his wife was born. She was homesick, so King Nebuchadnezzar thought it would make her feel more at home whenever she walked in the gardens.

The garden is built on what looks like a four-step pyramid, with the bottom step surrounded by pillars. In the middle of the west and east sides are wide marble stairs leading to the second level, with a terrace encircling the entire garden. From the bottom to the top we found sculptures of all kinds, fountains and waterfalls intermingled with trees, shrubs, and an assortment of exotic flowers imported from all over the world. We also encountered gazelles, ponies, and other small creatures walking about freely. Locked up in cages were lions and tigers, elephants, and a large variety of birds.

"It's a well-kept secret, just how the garden-keepers are able to pump water up to the ninety-meter peak to irrigate the terrace. I've estimated it would require at least thirty-seven thousand liters of water per day. I'm hoping Thomas and I can go back soon to learn more about the gardens. I sketched some of what we saw. I'll show them to you later. That's it for now."

"Thank you, Anna," Thomas said. "For the record, I found the gardens to be special as well."

What Anna didn't say was why the gardens were special for Thomas and her. The sky was clear the night they visited. He tried not to smile at the memory. Without a worry in the world, he and Anna sat holding hands, inhaling the sweet perfume of the exotic flowers, and gazing at the magnificent city that stretched out before them around the Euphrates River, which reflected the starry heavens as dancing crystals on its smooth surface.

A cool breeze had tickled their skin as Thomas dropped to one knee and asked Anna if she would be his wife. Anna said yes.

Returning from his reverie, Thomas was unable to suppress a grin. "Aldon, would you record everything on your papyrus rolls for us? I think you are the best person for this since you know how to filter out all but the important information required by the ULRA."

It took the better part of the next four hours before they concluded their reports. After a much anticipated dinner, Thomas and Anna went for a walk along the river. On their way back they stumbled upon a narrow lane they had not noticed before.

"Is it my imagination?" Anna squinted down the lane. "I see merchants with their goods laid out on tables."

"It looks like it, but I don't see any customers."

Anna walked a few steps into the lane. "I guess one needs to know they're here because it doesn't look like a good location for attracting customers."

"Do you want to check it out?"

"Sure, why not."

As they walked past the first few merchants, it became clear these were not ordinary booths. Each table had specific items representing a particular deity, and the vendors called out the names of the gods they represented as potential customers walked by their stalls. "It's a religious market," Anna said quietly. "Look at all the idols and other implements of worship. Look at that fish headdress, over there on that rack. And a cape for the Dagon priest."

At the end of the lane, one particular merchant who seemed to have paraphernalia for all the gods called out his inventory in an annoying, high-pitched voice. Although it was painful to the ear, it was effective. "I have more gods than the others. Come, come, I have your god for sure; come over here and take a look, come, come. I have Murdock—big ones, small ones—come and see. I have all the gods of Babylon, I have all the gods of Persia. Come and I will give you a good price! Come and see my bargains. I have all the gods of the world; come, come and see for yourselves. I even have Christians' god. Come! I will make it worth your while—come, come."

Thomas stopped in his tracks. "Did I hear him say he has stuff from the Christian faith?"

"All I heard was 'come, come,'" she mimicked in a high-pitched voice.

Thomas turned and stared at the table. "It's not possible. Christianity does not start for another six hundred years. I'm curious. I'm going to talk to him."

The man behind the table was small, with a round belly and fleshy lips. "Did you say you have something belonging to the Christian faith?" Thomas asked him.

"Yes, yes indeed," the merchant assured him. "Would you like to see it? It is brand new."

"Of course," Thomas said.

"Are you from Christian's faith? Because I can only sell you this object if you belong to Christian's faith. Otherwise, the god will seek revenge on me."

"Yes," Thomas assured him. "We're both Christians."

The merchant glanced around suspiciously before looking back at Thomas. "All right, then, wait here." He disappeared into the house behind his table.

Thomas tried to peek inside the partly opened door. "I can't wait to see what this guy is going to bring out."

"Imagine if he comes out with a cross," Anna said.

The merchant came back and whispered, "Hoshedar is waiting for you. You can go in now."

Anna hung back. "I don't like this, Thomas. It looks suspicious to me."

"I'll go alone. You stay here in case something happens."

"There's no way I'm letting you go in there by yourself," Anna said. "I'm coming with you."

They entered the house through the narrow door. A single oil lamp illuminated the room where a small old man waited. "Sorry for the secrecy," Hoshedar said, "but the man who gave me this wanted me to make sure only the one who is from Christian's faith can purchase this object. He gave me much gold to do this, so I ask you one more time: are you from Christian's faith?"

"Yes I swear to you, I am."

Convinced, Hoshedar turned to a cabinet behind him and pulled out a long, slender, cloth-wrapped object, which he handed to Thomas. Thomas unwound the protective cloth to reveal a cedar staff with a dragon carved into its top.

"That doesn't look like anything remotely Christian to me," Anna said.

"No, it isn't, but I'm not surprised. Disappointed, yes, but not surprised. I'd better buy it just the same since I made such a fuss." He looked at Hoshedar. "How much for the staff?"

"Six gold darics," the merchant said with a devious grin.

"Six gold darics! That's half a year's salary for most men."

"Just pay the man, Thomas, don't be so cheap."

Thomas gave Anna the staff while he paid. Then they stepped outside to have a better look at it.

"It looks like a lizard," Anna said.

Thomas could see the carving clearly now. "This isn't any lizard, this is a Komodo dragon."

Hoshedar had followed them out of the shop. Thomas turned around to ask him, "Excuse me, do you know what kind of dragon this is?"

Hoshedar looked at it carefully. "I don't know. I have never seen one before. Don't you know?"

"Yes, I do." Thomas hesitated. "Are you sure you've never seen this dragon before?"

"In my trade, I make it a point to know all the animals," Hoshedar said. "You never know when you might insult someone by trying to sell them something forbidden. So I'm telling you, this dragon is not from any place in Persia."

"Can I speak to the man who made this staff?"

"I don't know where he is," Hoshedar said. "He came to me once and I never saw him again."

"Where can I get a second one like it?"

Hoshedar shrugged, hands out. "If I knew, I would get more for you. No, this is one of a kind. That's why it costs six gold darics."

Thomas frowned down at the carving. Then he looked up at Hoshedar. "The man who gave this to you, did he look like me?"

"No, he was much younger. What kind of a question is that?"

"Come on, Thomas," Anna urged. "It's getting late, and I'm getting tired. Let's go home."

Thomas allowed Anna to pull him up the alley. "Fine, fine, but you need to know, Anna: I'm getting pretty tired of this Komodo popping up everywhere. All these appearances are related, and I'm going to get to the bottom of this before we leave Babylon, this much I can promise you. There's no way it's all a coincidence."

"Did you ask the merchant that question because you're rethinking the possibility that you might have been here before?" she asked. "You know what I mean, like the story that was told?"

"Maybe. I don't know anymore. It's so confusing."

They said little on their walk back home. Thomas tried to piece together the Komodo puzzle while Anna relived the marriage proposal.

"Thomas, can I ask you something?"

"Of course, Anna; what is it?"

"I've been thinking, even though our relationship isn't a secret, I think we should hold off telling people about our engagement. At least until we return to the twenty-first century."

"I agree. It might become a distraction." He stopped to face Anna, then gave her a long, passionate kiss. "Besides, I enjoy having a little secret, don't you?"

PART 3
THE TRUTH

𒁹𒈠𒀜 𒀭𒌋 𒐊𒀀

𒁹𒈠𒀭𒆠𒀜 𒀭 𒁹𒈠𒀜 𒀭𒌋

CHAPTER 28

Thomas tiptoed into Anna's bedroom. He stood next to her for a long moment, watching her sleep. She looked like an angel, so peaceful, so beautiful. He almost changed his mind about waking her, but Michael is waiting for him, so leaving was not an option.

Not wanting to startle her, he softly put his hand on her shoulder and shook her gently. "Anna," he whispered, "Anna, it's Thomas." He tried again but this time with a little more effort. "Anna, its Thomas; wake up. I need to talk to you." She let out a snort then shifted her position just enough to partially reveal her right breast. Thomas looked away.

"This isn't going to well," he said to himself. After covering her with a blanket, he sat down. He tenderly placed the back of his hand against her cheek and said in a soft but louder voice, "Anna, sweetheart, wake up. I need to speak with you."

She slowly opened her eyes, looked at Thomas, and smiled. "Hello, Thomas. What time is it?"

"I don't know—two, three o'clock, I guess."

She sat upright. "Is everything okay? Is something wrong?"

"No, everything's fine. I need to speak with you about something I figured out, that's all," Thomas told her. "But if it's not a good time I can wait—although I'd rather not."

"All right, Thomas. Let me put something on, then I'll be right with you."

Anna joined Thomas on the back balcony, where he sat on a wide wicker chair, waiting with Michael, who leaned on the balcony. A hot cup of tea was on an adjacent table. "Hello Michael," Anna said.

"Hi Anna."

"What's going on?" she asked. "What is it that couldn't wait another few hours?"

Michael shrugged. "Don't look at me, man. I just got up myself."

"I thought we can talk here without waking up the others," Thomas explained. "Please sit next to me." He patted the cushion next to him and waited while she complied. Then he took a deep breath and said, "I figured it out."

"You figured what out?" Michael asked.

"Komodo. I've figured out what Komodo wants with me."

Michael looked at Anna, then back at Thomas. "Okay, we're listening."

"First of all, I appreciate that you're here. I know it's early, but I need you both to confirm my conclusions before I say anything to the others. If I'm right, we need to move quickly and cautiously." Anna and Michael nodded.

"Let me start from the beginning," Thomas said. "Less than four years ago, I came in contact with Komodo for the first time as a cracker hitting our network. You know as well as I do, Michael, our network was as secure as Fort Knox. Yet he came and left without effort. Do you remember what our conclusion was at the time?"

"We thought he had the access codes and passwords belonging to one of our administrators."

"Good." Thomas nodded. "Next, I was let go because forensics concluded the attacks came from my desktop. If you remember, Michael, the attacks stopped right after that. It's as if Komodo set me up for the fall. That's when you came and convinced me to take a scuba diving trip to Nunavik, where the second Komodo sighting came to my attention, on the famous Persian stela." Thomas related his understanding of the text carved into the stela. "Once again I found myself facing information only Christian and my wife Amélie knew," he said.

"You think Christian or Amélie carved the stela?" Anna asked.

"It wasn't me, so I'm guessing it's one of them," he said. "Let me continue. The next Komodo sighting was in the form of a signature attached to the virus on the *Kismet*. At that point it became clear to me that these Komodo sightings were all related. But I wasn't able to associate them with one another until a few hours ago."

"Are you referring to the market we visited?" Anna asked.

"Yes, the market. Do you remember what the merchant called out? Do you remember what caught our attention?"

She thought back for a moment. "He claimed to have something belonging to Christianity."

"That's right, but it wasn't Christianity, was it?" He picked up the staff from the floor next to him. "It's another Komodo dragon. Well, last night it came to me. You see, the merchant was not calling out 'we have something from the Christian faith,' he was saying, 'we have something from Christian's faith,' as in the faith belonging to Christian."

"It sounds like you're saying Christian is here." Anna snickered at the idea.

"It's not funny, Anna," he said solemnly. "That's exactly what I'm saying. And I can prove it. Let me put it all together for you." Thomas repositioned himself in the chair. "Only Christian knew my passwords for the Montreal network. Christian also knew the information on the stela. Being he is a first class computer programmer, he, therefore, has the skills to make a virus like the one on the *Kismet*. Since these three incidents are all from the twenty-first century, he had to find a way to let me know he's here in Babylon. To do this he carved this staff and gave it to a merchant for resale, knowing I would find it while relic hunting for the mission. I'm almost certain that if we keep searching, we'll find more staffs."

Anna looked skeptical. "I don't know," she said. "I can't see this being possible."

"I agree with Anna," Michael admitted. "For this to be true, your son would have had to be here before we arrived." Michael looked at Anna. "It's not possible, right?"

"Yes, Michael, it is," Thomas insisted. "The League lied to us. We're not the first ones here from the twenty-first century."

"Why would they lie?" Anna argued. "There's no reason for it. I mean, I would have been part of the mission if it had been the first trip or the tenth trip."

"I thought about that too. I think something went wrong on the first trip so they decided to keep this information from us."

"Knowing the mission's members," Anna insisted, "I have a hard time believing that. They're all devoted Christians, and loyal to the cause."

"Then let's look at this more closely. Let's start with the secret facility back home. How long have you both been working in the facility?"

"About two months before you arrived," Anna said.

"I've been with the League a long time," Michael added, "though I arrived at the facility about one year after you arrived, Thomas."

"Who do you know was at the facility longer than you, Anna?' Thomas asked. "Take your time; think about it."

"The ones I know are the mission's governing body," Anna said, trying to think of others. "Maybe some old-timers, like Dr. Patrick Walsh from mission control. You already know Professor Lancaster. And oh yes, those in charge of the mission up on the *Kismet*: Rye, Kirkpatrick, and Captain Washington. I can't imagine there being more than twenty people."

"What about Nicolas?" Michael asked.

"No, he joined after me," Anna said.

"Don't you find it strange that those responsible for this titanic underground facility with all its ground-breaking innovations are missing? Where are all those people—the laborers, the architects, the scientists, all the masterminds behind this miracle facility? Do you remember, Anna, on my first full day when I was introduced to Quincy at the breakfast table, he brought to my attention the difficulties he and Derrek faced working on the *Kismet*'s operating system. He said the original programmers could not be found."

"I do remember the day, but I wasn't involved in the conversation," she said. "But now that you mention it, Aldon and Yetta have both been associates for much longer than me, maybe as much as ten years."

"Interesting." Thomas took a moment to reflect on this information. "Anyway, I'm telling you Christian is one of those programmers. That's why Derrek and Quincy could not contact the original programmer. He was left behind on the first trip."

"Oh man," Michael suddenly recalled, "I think you're right. Remember when we were stopped by the guard back in Hīt? What was his name again? Officer . . . whatever. He asked if we were part of the group of spies they'd captured two months ago. Do you think that was the first ULRA trip, and Christian was part of that group?"

"Yes, I see it now," Anna said. "This could be the story of the sole surviving traveler, your son. This would explain why the stela had all the pertinent information only you would recognize." She looked at Thomas. "Your son set this up to be rescued by you?"

"This is what I think happened," Thomas said, holding back a surge of emotion. "My son disappeared the night I gave him an ultimatum. I told him to slow down his activities with his new faith or leave my house. I never saw him again because he was picked up by the League. He was part of the original team who worked on the *Kismet*'s servers. Perhaps as time went by, he noticed or discovered something was not right with the League. To protect himself he began to hack into our Montreal network with the purpose of giving me encrypted files."

"Would it not have been simpler to call you?" Anna asked.

"No, he knew he was being monitored. The files were the right thing to do. Then he implemented a backup plan by creating a virus that would incapacitate the *Kismet* if things went wrong. Maybe he feared they might abandon him in Persia because of what he discovered, so a password would force them to take him back. If they left him there, the others would be left behind also."

"But the *Kismet* did come back."

"Yes, Anna, it did. He must have been working with an accomplice who knew the password and used it to get back home. Christian would need help for his plan to work. The only thing I can think of is that his accomplice must have betrayed him. But if I know Christian, he would have included a second password in case the *Kismet* made a second trip. He had the habit of making redundancies in everything he programmed." He paused. "And I know where to find the password. It's in those encrypted files. The files are part of his backup plan."

"This whole time travel thing is confusing," Anna said. "The ULRA exists because of the stela and its associated story, yet the stela and the story would not have existed if there wasn't a first trip to begin with. It's like the chicken and the egg—which one came first?"

"Come on, man, never mind that." Michael paused. "So what do we do now?"

"We rescue Christian, of course," Anna said.

"Yes Anna, once we find Christian we will know more about what happened back home, but we need to be careful. We need to be smart about the way we do this. Since I failed to decipher the files, we also need to get the password from Christian before time runs out on the *Kismet*."

Michael looked over the railing at the darkness below. "Somehow the mission's goal of finding biblical relics does not have the same appeal anymore."

"I don't know about you guys," Thomas said, "but one thing's for sure—they can all go to hell with their relic hunting. From now on my mission is to find my son."

"I agree," Anna said. "I'm with you, Thomas."

"Me too," Michael confirmed. "But what do we tell the others?"

"Kelile will cooperate," Thomas reasoned. "As for Aldon, he believes strongly in the mission's objectives. It's not going to be easy to persuade him. What worries me more is what we are going to say to Artemisia and her brother."

"Why don't I get us some fresh tea," Anna suggested. "Then we can work out a plan."

CHAPTER 29

"That's quite the story you're telling us," Artemisia said, glancing at her brother. "And you're absolutely certain it's your son trying to communicate with you?"

"There's no doubt about it. All the evidence leads to him."

"What are the others doing about this? Are they going to Susa with you as well?"

"Actually, I haven't spoken to them yet. Michael, Anna, and I spent all last night going over the facts. You two are the first we've approached since you're always gone by the time we get up."

"We're not concerned about their decision," Anna added. "They're very cooperative, so I'm confident they'll agree to come with us. But if they decide to stay, we three will still be going to Susa today."

Again Artemisia and Pigres looked at each other. This time Pigres gave her a nod signaling his disapproval. "My brother is not able to go with you," Artemisia said. "It's not because of any doubts; he has business obligations here in Babylon. But if you're willing to wait another two days, I can rearrange my schedule to accompany you."

"I don't think that will work," Thomas said. "I can't risk delaying any longer. We need to be back on the air ship before the twentieth day of Adar, or the ship will leave without us. Artemisia, please understand, I will not go back without my son."

"I do understand, Thomas, but also understand my position. I can't leave with you today. Believe me when I tell you there is a good reason for my decision. I can't divulge it to you right now."

Artemisia rose, retrieved a map, and consulted it. "It's just as I thought," she said. "If you go alone, I can give you horses and passports, but you'll be obliged to take the traditional routes. It will take at least twelve days to reach Susa, probably more. On the other hand, if you wait for me, I'll take you

186

through the back roads across the mountains. Even if we leave two days from now, we'll still arrive three days sooner than the traditional routes."

"Is that wise, sister?" Pigres said, not hiding his concern. "There are many risks in taking the back roads."

"If you're referring to the marauder bands, then that's not a problem. The weather has been unusually hot. If they're out there, they'll be in their hideouts, keeping cool."

"Oh, don't you worry, they're out there all right," Pigres said. "There are reports of activity in the wilderness as recent as yesterday. If they see a group of travelers, rest assured they will take advantage, especially if they recognize—" he paused to consider his words "—recognize you may be carrying valuables."

"I don't understand," Thomas said. "Why would the traditional routes take so long?"

"Because you're going at a time when the king will be in Susa—he has a palace there. So you'll be stopped at every relay station along the way. I don't know how many there are, but I can guess anywhere between fifteen and twenty stations. Keep in mind they like to take their time, and if they feel they can profit from you, they can further slow you down."

Anna turned to Thomas. "I think we should wait and go with her. It will be less of a hassle and it won't delay us."

"Fine then, we'll wait."

"Good. This will allow us time to prepare for the journey," Artemisia said. "Pigres, can you leave without me this morning? I'll be taking care of some things here. I'll catch up with you later."

"What are you guys talking about?" Kelile asked, wiping the sleep from his eyes as he entered the room.

"Kelile, I hope you rested well," Thomas said. "Please have some breakfast while I wake up Aldon. We have important things to discuss."

They were done with breakfast by the time Thomas summarized the situation. Kelile expressed his willingness to cooperate. Besides, he was happy for the chance to meet the elite force of soldiers who fought for the Achaemenid Empire, the Immortal guards protecting King Xerxes. But for Aldon, it was a different story.

"We shouldn't deviate from the original plan," Aldon argued. "Already we're handicapped by having been sent here prematurely, and now you want to abandon the mission? I'm pretty sure Captain Washington won't see it your way."

"Did you not hear what he said?" Anna pointed to Thomas. "The mission's leaders lied to us. We've been used and what's more, we've been put in the path of danger, not knowing what happened to the first team."

"We can't say for sure there ever was a first team. Your conclusions are based on speculations surrounding this stupid Komodo Thomas keeps bringing up. I'm sick of hearing about it. Besides, Komodo is your problem, Thomas. It shouldn't affect the mission."

"Aldon," Thomas said as calmly as he could, "I certainly don't want you to do anything you're not comfortable with. If you want to stay and meet us later in Susa, I won't put any pressure on you. As for the rest of us, we're leaving for Susa in two days."

"What about this," Kelile interjected. "Why don't we all go together? We can help Thomas find his son and still continue documenting and relic hunting. This way, if Thomas is right, we will have saved a life. If Thomas is wrong, we can still bring back enough information to satisfy the mission's goal."

They all looked at Aldon for several long seconds. "I need to think about this," he said as he got up and marched out the room.

Anna walked to the window to see where he was heading. "I can't say I'm surprised at his reaction."

Thomas joined Anna at the window. "He was just beginning to enjoy himself, then we hit him with more bad news. I'm sure after he's had time to think it over, he'll come with us. He needs some time alone, that's all."

As they watched Aldon disappear, a commotion rose from the opposite direction.

"It looks like a procession of some kind," Anna said.

"It looks more like a mob," Thomas said.

"I think you're right."

They watched the people waving sticks and farming implements and a few weapons.

Thomas tried to focus. "No, I'm pretty sure it's a celebration of some kind."

As they approached, Anna spotted someone familiar. "Artemisia, is that your brother running toward them?"

They watched as Pigres stopped to talk to someone in the crowd. He walked with a man for a short distance before he stopped, looked up at the sky, then started jumping joyfully. His gaze turned to their building. Seeing them all at the window looking at him, Pigres ran to the apartment building's entrance.

"It's wonderful sister," he shouted as he burst into the apartment. "It's the best news I've heard in a long time."

"Well, what is it?" Artemisia exclaimed.

"You know King Xerxes doesn't have the power to change any law sealed with his signet ring. Well, they found a way around the situation concerning the genocide of the Jews. He had another law passed that allows the Jews to defend themselves."

"That's wonderful, Pigres." Artemisia turned to face the others. "Don't you think so?"

"Yes, of course," Thomas replied. "Wonderful news indeed."

"There's more," Pigres said. "The new law says anyone else, meaning non-Jews, could take part in the defense."

"When was this law passed?" Artemisia asked.

"I'm not sure, but the news arrived in Babylon by courier sometime during the night." Pigres walked over to Artemisia and gripped her shoulders. "This changes everything. We don't need to hide our intentions anymore. Now we can openly recruit people and train them properly." He walked to the window. "Listen, I would like to stay and talk, but I must get back and start on a new strategy. Shouldn't you be there, sister? The participants we recruited look up to you."

"Yes, you're right. Go ahead. I'll meet you very soon."

"No wonder you've both been so secretive about your business," Thomas said. "You're organizing a form of resistance to help defend the Jews."

"Yes. It's a small, scattered group of Persians. In fact we come from many different backgrounds. There aren't many of us, but we feel Haman and the Amalekites are wrong in their dealings with the Jews. I realize we can't do much, but I'm sure our contributions will be appreciated."

"What you're doing is honorable," Michael said. "I'm convinced the assistance you give will go down in history."

"I don't know about that, but we will do what we can. My brother is the one who is involved in this endeavor. All I do is assist with the hard-to-reach contacts in the government."

"That's why he can't come with us to Susa?"

CHAPTER 30

The walls of the majestic canyon were closing in as they approached a passage less than a kilometer ahead. In under an hour they would squeeze through the narrow gap and camp on the far side for yet another night on their journey. For the past three days they'd traveled under the almost palpable weight of an unforgiving sun. As difficult as this was, no one complained as they followed Artemisia through a labyrinth of mountains, crevasses, and open desert.

Thomas looked ahead at the others who formed a single file fifteen meters long. "Just six more days," he said, wiping the sweat from his neck.

"If you're trying to encourage me, it's not working," Anna complained. "Would you believe Aldon hasn't said a thing since we left Babylon? I don't understand why Kelile has taken it upon himself to look after him."

"Maybe because he has no family so he sees in Aldon a child, someone to protect. God knows he acts like one sometimes."

Anna smothered a giggle. "Please, Thomas, don't make me laugh; it hurts too much."

Thomas slowed down to focus on Artemisia. "Something is happening ahead."

•••••••••●○○○○○○○○○○○

Artemisia allowed Michael to catch up before she spoke. "Michael, dismount and rummage through your bags; act as if I asked you to search for something important. Once you're done face me, all the while using hand gestures, pretending you don't have what I asked you for."

"Why am I doing this?" Michael asked as he dismounted.

"Play along for now," Artemisia said. "I'll explain in a minute."

"What are you looking for?" Kelile asked as he and Aldon caught up.

"Get off your horses and come over here," Michael instructed. "Act like you want to help."

"Why? What's going on?" Aldon asked.

"We'd better do as he says." Kelile dismounted.

As Thomas and Anna arrived, Artemisia gave them the same instructions. Soon, all were busy looking for nothing.

Artemisia approached to explain. "Good work; keep this up while I talk. Now listen to me, this is important. And whatever you do, don't look around, especially up the canyon walls, because we are being watched. So this is what we need to do. One by one, come to me and act as if you don't have what I'm asking for. Once the last person is done, Michael and Thomas, start pushing one another around and make a lot of noise. That's when I'll step in to break up the fight. At that point, we will pretend we're dejected and start remounting our horses. But don't go anywhere yet; wait for further instructions."

They played their roles like seasoned Hollywood actors. Aldon was shaking, so it looked even more real.

"You all did great. Now let's ride back the way we came," Artemisia told them. "Ride slowly, and remember, look frustrated. They're waiting for us to enter the narrow passage ahead. Once we're inside, they will have us trapped. To avoid this, we need to turn around and head back the way we came. If they think we know they are there, they might take a chance and attack us in the open. But if they believe we've forgotten something, they'll probably wait for our return."

By now Aldon was heaving hard, about to vomit. "Please Aldon, try to calm down," Kelile said. "Everything will be okay. Aldon, look at me; they're probably nothing more than common thieves. On the other hand, if they're professionals, well, they could be dangerous. So let's head back. I am sure there's another way around."

•••••••••●○○○○○○○○○○

From atop the canyon walls, the marauder band watched what was happening below. The leader was disappointed, but these men were not the ordinary thieves Artemisia hoped for, and they would not let this turn of events keep them from their prize. One man waved a flag to signal to their accomplices on the other side of the canyon. Together the ten men skillfully maneuvered their mounts down the steep walls.

•••••••••●○○○○○○○○○○

"They're coming," Artemisia shouted. "Let's go."

They managed good time before the marauder band reached the bottom of the canyon, but once on level ground, the thieves rapidly gained ground. Artemisia looked back. "They're catching up," she called. "We must go faster or we will have to fight."

Kelile, who knew their chances of outriding them were slim, dropped back to make sure no one fell behind, especially Aldon, who was a poor rider. He turned to peer through the dust cloud behind them. The band was no more than a hundred meters away and closing in fast. It was only a matter of time before they'd have to face their pursuers.

"Listen to me carefully," Artemisia shouted. "If we reach the mouth of the canyon before they reach us, we need to split up. Michael, Aldon, follow me to the right, into the mountains. The rest of you go left. There's a small village near the main road. Stay there. We'll come for you."

Kelile watched Artemisia pull out her sword to prepare for the upcoming clash. Following her example, he reached for his own sword. The distraction was just long enough for him to lose sight of Aldon. He slowed down to have a better look around. Where was he? Not seeing him, Kelile stopped to face the pursuers. The others had no choice but to do the same. That's when they saw Aldon charging the marauder band.

"What the hell is he doing?" Kelile exclaimed. "He can't fight worth a damn."

They watched in disbelief as the pursuers surrounded Aldon. There was a disagreement over what to do with him. Two men searched his bags before escorting him toward their rear. Kelile repositioned himself on his horse and prepared to charge.

Artemisia grabbed his reins. "No, Kelile, we're not strong enough. They outnumber us, probably out-skill us as well. It would be suicide."

"But they've stopped the pursuit; they're disorganized," Kelile protested. "Now's our chance to get him back."

"There is nothing we can do, trust me. If we attack, they'll kill us all. We'll organize a rescue later when we have a solid plan."

"We can't just leave him," Kelile said in a rare fit of anger.

Artemisia moved forward until she spotted Aldon among his captors. "They're not hurting him," she said, sounding surprised. "They're taking him prisoner. Very strange." After a reflective pause, she turned to face the others. "Let's go. We can't help him. We need to prepare before we could attempt a rescue."

"Look!" Anna cried out. "They're coming again."

"Stick to the plan," Artemisia repeated. "Let's go—hurry."

As soon as the party arrived at the mouth of the canyon, they split up as directed. It worked; their pursuers abandoned the chase.

•••••••••●○○○○○○○○○○○

They'd ridden for less than an hour when Artemisia spotted an opening in the side of a rolling mountain and pulled up. "Watch the horses," she told Michael and slipped through the opening to inspect the cave that lay beyond.

The cave proved to be a deep cavern; about halfway in, Artemisia located a flat shelf nine meters up the wall that they could climb to and spend the night. If anyone came through the entrance, they would have plenty of time to react. Farther back in the cavern, she found a subterranean river partially fed by a small waterfall emanating from an unseen spring. From this they could fill their drinking bottles and water their horses.

Satisfied the cave met their needs, she called for Michael to enter with the horses.

"Wow," Michael said after his eyes adjusted to the dim light. "This cave is enormous. Should we make a fire? It's really cold in here."

"No fire; the smoke might escape and reveal our location," Artemisia said. "Use your blanket. We'll be fine."

"I'm afraid I lost my blanket in the chase." Michael grinned.

Artemisia gave him a suspicious look. "Let me see your bag."

"Hey man, you don't believe me?"

"Just let me see your bag."

Several hours later, after they'd eaten cold rations and Michael had wrapped up in the blanket he hadn't lost after all, Artemisia lay under her own blanket, silently contemplating the day's events. It *was* cold, she had to admit, and the damp air within the cave intensified it. She looked at Michael, who lay with his knees drawn up, shivering from the cold. Without a word, she got up to lie next to him and add her blanket to his.

As she spooned her body with his and their hands made contact, she let out a short shriek. His hands were like ice! Michael reacted by pulling away. She turned over to face him. "Come on Michael, get over here. I promise I won't bite."

Michael relaxed and moved back in, though he crossed his arms and kept his hands firmly under his armpits. "Thank you," he said. "I was about to get up and start jogging."

"I can leave if you want."

"No, no, I'd rather have you next to me." His cheeks immediately flushed in embarrassment at the admission.

The trust his admission revealed made her feel guilty. She sat up. "Michael, I need to tell you something." Michael sat up next to her. "I haven't been totally honest with you or your friends. I need to tell you who I am."

"You don't have to say anything," Michael said, rearranging the blankets around them.

"Shhh," she put her finger on his lips. "Yes I do. Seven years ago I was involved in a major naval battle that didn't go well. We were defeated and we lost many ships. To save my crew, I rammed one of my own ships to deceive the Greeks into thinking I was on their side. I got away with it—as luck would have it, King Xerxes witnessed my actions. From his vantage point he thought I'd sunk a Greek vessel, and gave me honors for my bravery. The Greeks, however, were not fooled by the deception. They knew what I had done."

"I know all this," Michael interrupted. "You're Artemisia the First, a brilliant military strategist and queen of Halicarnassus."

She looked at him in complete shock. "You know who I am?"

"Yes. Your reputation has reached my country."

"The others—do they know as well?"

"Thomas knows some things, and if he knows, you can be sure Anna knows, as well. I think their knowledge is limited to what you told Thomas on the trip to Babylon. As for the others" —he shrugged— "I doubt they know anything."

"Why did you wait until now to tell me?"

"Because man, it doesn't matter who or what you are, I like you just the way you are."

Now Artemisia felt uncomfortable with the situation. She wondered what else he knew about her.

As if reading her thoughts, Michael continued. "I know your father's name is Lygdamis and your mother is a Cretan; I don't know her name, though. I also know you were once married and you have a twenty-year-old son. It was after your husband's death that you became queen." He looked at her stunned expression. "That's about it."

"I can't believe you didn't tell me this sooner," she said. She thought for a moment. "All I want is for you to notice me as a woman, not as a queen."

Michael pulled Artemisia close. "Artemisia, trust me, I noticed you as a woman—the most beautiful woman I've ever met."

Artemisia knew what she had to say next could change everything. "Since you know so much about me, I might as well tell you the rest. After the Battle of Salamis—that's the name of the battle I mentioned earlier—I had a long-running affair with Xerxes."

Michael nodded. "I know."

"I might still have some feelings for him." She paused and waited for a reaction that never came. "But now that he chose Esther as his queen, we both know our past affair is, well, the past."

"What's past is past," Michael confirmed.

"But that's not all. I'm so ashamed of what I did. I put you and the others at risk by taking you through the mountains. And now Aldon might even be dead because of me. I'm telling you about the Battle of Salamis because the Greeks think I'm some sort of war hero to our people. To kill me would be equivalent to killing an image of Persia. So they put out a reward of ten thousand drachmas for my capture."

"You think the attack earlier was because of this bounty?"

"What I said about the heat wave keeping the thieves away was true. So the only explanation I have for the attack is that someone told them we were coming, someone who wanted to collect on the bounty."

"You don't know that for sure," Michael told her. "You can't take responsibility for the raid."

"I know it is me they wanted, it's the only logical conclusion. So you and your friends must go to Susa without me."

"No," Michael said firmly. "We will do no such thing."

"But—"

"Now you listen to me, it's my turn to talk. We can't say for sure it's you they were after. So we say nothing about the ten thousand drachmas, okay? Besides, it was Thomas who insisted we hurry to Susa, not you. If he hadn't been intent on getting there so fast, we would have taken the main road and none of this would have happened. So we wait until tomorrow to get him back. Don't say anything about our conversation. It will serve no purpose, understood?"

"Thank you for listening to me," was all Artemisia could say. She turned to face Michael and rested on his shoulder. She gently put her hand on his chest and held him tight.

Michael held her back. "Let's get some sleep. Tomorrow is going to be a difficult day."

Artemisia slowly curled her leg over his thigh and fell asleep. Her warm, silky skin rubbed against his.

Michael was no longer cold.

CHAPTER 31

They found the small roadside community and waited there, exactly as Artemisia had instructed.

"Why don't you come inside and get something to eat?" Thomas asked Kelile. "It's getting late."

"I can't believe we left him behind," Kelile lamented. "We should have done something to help him."

"Artemisia knows her people better than any of us. She said we had no chance. I'm sure she knew what she was talking about."

"Still, we did nothing," Kelile insisted. "Poor Aldon. He must be so scared right now. He is probably wondering why we abandoned him."

"In the morning Artemisia will have a plan for us. Until then you need to eat. You need your strength for tomorrow."

"Stop telling me to eat, I am not a child." Kelile turned and looked away. "We could have defeated them; I'm sure of it."

"Maybe you have the skills to fight, but we don't. If you want to sacrifice everyone for Aldon, then your reasoning is askew. Aldon needs to take responsibility for himself. Every time he gets into trouble, you bail him out. Well, this time he put us all in danger, and that's where you should draw the line."

Kelile said nothing. Thomas took this to mean he didn't agree and the conversation was over, so he walked toward the inn.

"In about three hours I'm going after him," Kelile said in a calm yet determined voice.

Thomas stopped and took a deep breath before turning around to face Kelile. "Fine. And what are you going to do, exactly; take them on by yourself?"

"By the time I find their camp, they should all be asleep. All I need to do is look for the guards watching over a tent and rescue Aldon. I do not need an army for that."

"What if you can't find the camp, or what if they're not sleeping? What then?"

"I will cross that bridge when I get there. At least I will have tried."

"So you don't want to wait for Artemisia," Thomas replied in anger.

"They could be long gone by then—or worse yet, Aldon could be dead. No, Thomas, I am going tonight."

"Fine. I'm going with you. What's the plan?"

Kelile smiled. "Thank you, Thomas. I owe you a life."

"No, Kelile, Aldon owes you a life." *Maybe more,* Thomas thought. "Let me tell Anna what's happening. When I get back, fill me in on your strategy."

"You're crazy," Anna said. "We'll all be killed."

"There's no 'we,'" Thomas said. "This time you're staying here."

"Like hell I'm staying here."

"Listen, Anna, the more of us there are, the better the chances of being detected, and for this to work, it needs to be a stealth operation. Besides, if something goes wrong, I need you to tell Michael and Artemisia what happened. This way, they might be able to help us."

Anna reluctantly agreed. "Promise me you won't take any unnecessary chances. Promise me."

"Don't worry. Kelile will see to it that all goes well."

Anna forced a smile. "You're in good hands, that's for sure." Her face hardened. "If they come back without you, I'll kill Aldon myself."

"I'll be back, I promise. We have a wedding to plan, remember? Now let's go see how Kelile plans to do this."

•••••••••●○○○○○○○○○○○

They found the camp between the same narrow passageways Artemisia had avoided not seven hours ago. Thomas and Kelile hid among the rocks forty meters up the southern wall of the canyon. From this vantage point they could see the entire camp. Three men were drinking around a campfire situated in the middle of five tents laid out in a circle. None of the tents had guards. This made it difficult for Kelile to know where Aldon was being held. Although no one said it, it might also mean Aldon was already dead.

"How do we find him?" Thomas asked.

Kelile thought about it for a moment. "All the tents are dark except for that one." He pointed at the tent just below them. "If they have taken him prisoner, they will not leave him unattended. My guess is, they have him in that tent. If you look carefully, you can see four or five silhouettes inside. It must be Aldon and his guards."

Just then, two guards exited the tent. Only one had a weapon, a sheathed sword attached to his belt. "I don't understand," Thomas said. "They don't seem worried about being attacked."

"They have no reason to be concerned. We ran away from them without a fight, remember?" He gave Thomas a cold look. After scanning the camp once more, Kelile made up his mind. "Okay, this is what we are going to do. You stay here, and keep an eye on those sitting around the campfire. If they move, signal me with this handkerchief. I will look back from time to time. Once I reach the tent, I will take out the two guards."

Thomas was stunned at the casual way he talked about taking out those men.

"Once I am in the tent," Kelile continued, "I'll rescue Aldon. Then we will come running up this hill toward you. It's dark up here, so when I come out, keep waving the handkerchief until we start up the hill. If we head in the wrong direction wave the handkerchief again. But don't wave it unnecessarily. I don't want to expose our location."

"I understand," Thomas said. "Good luck."

Kelile disappeared down the hill. For the longest time Thomas lost sight of him. All he could do was keep an eye on the campfire. After what seemed an eternity, Kelile emerged from the brush below him. He moved to the rear of the tent, turned around, and waved at Thomas. Before Thomas could acknowledge, one guard left his post and walked toward Kelile. The guard made so much noise that Kelile was able to move out of the way. The guard walked past him to a shrub to relieve himself.

From his position, Thomas watched Kelile emerge from hiding. He grabbed the guard by the mouth with his left hand and slit his throat. Horrified, Thomas looked away. By the time he mustered enough courage to look back, the guard was on the ground and Kelile was trying to communicate with him. First, he pointed to his own eyes with two fingers, then he pointed left of the tent and then to the right. Thomas understood. He wanted to know the location of the other guard. In reply, Thomas waved his handkerchief to the right.

Kelile responded by picking up a stone before moving to the left. Once he arrived at the edge of the tent, he threw the stone over and to the right.

When the guard turned toward the noise, Kelile took him out as he had the first guard. He dragged the body away.

• • • • • • • • • ● ○○○○○○○○○○ ○

Kelile evaluated what might be waiting for him inside. All those years of ancient weapons training and combat techniques gave Kelile confidence. Add to this the element of surprise, and Kelile knew he had the advantage.

With his sword in one hand and a bloody dagger in the other, he entered the tent. He spotted Aldon, then instantly ignored him and prepared to assault the guard next to him. When he saw who it was, Kelile froze like a statue. Instead of attacking, he turned to Aldon.

"What—" was all he said. He forced himself to look down at a blade slowly retreating from his abdomen. Paralyzed by the sword that had pierced him through the back, all he could do was stare at Aldon. His eyes said it all: *Why did you betray us?*

Kelile hit the ground, dead.

Aldon leaped forward. "No," he cried out, then broke down in sobs. He turned his tear-smeared face away. "This is not what we agreed upon. You swore to me no one would get hurt." He looked at Kelile again. "You promised me and look, he's dead because of you."

Yetta looked at her husband in disgust. "You knew there were risks. It's not my fault Kelile came to rescue you. If you'd kept away from him like I told you, this would not have happened. But no, you had to be the weakling, so he took it upon himself to watch over you. If there's anyone to blame for his death, it's you, Aldon. Not me."

"This was a big mistake," Aldon said as he wiped his runny nose. "I should have never agreed to your stupid plot."

"My plot? Now it's my plot? You want this as much as I do."

Aldon said nothing. He took several deep breaths, then looked at Sadhanah still standing at the entrance with his bloodstained sword in hand.

"Don't look at me," Sadhanah said. "He killed two of my men."

Yetta, realizing this was not working, she tried a calmer approach. "Aldon, listen to me. You need to take control of your emotions. If Kelile is here, the others are probably outside waiting for him."

"No. I'm through," Aldon mumbled and sniffed.

"Aldon, if you don't go to them and pretend the rescue was successful, they'll come after us," Yetta explained. "Artemisia has friends and she will come with reinforcements. What will you tell them? How will you explain Kelile's death? Can't you see his death has sealed our fate? We have no choice but to go through with our plan. Aldon, look at me. Can you do this? Can you stop crying and be a man long enough to do what's needed?"

Aldon wiped his nose with the back of his hand. "Okay. What do you want me to do?"

"Go to them. Explain how Kelile died saving your life. When you reach Susa, find me in the far west side of the Imperial city." She retrieved a map and gave it to Aldon. "Memorize it, then go—before they send someone else. You don't want more deaths on your hands, do you?"

Aldon memorized the map and without so much as a goodbye, he left.

••••••••●○○○○○○○○○○○

"I don't understand," Sadhanah said. "How do you hope to rule your people with a baby like him?"

"That's none of your business."

"You're right, and my business with you is concluded. I and my men will be gone at first light. Don't forget to give Parshandatha and his brothers my love when you see them." Sadhanah laughed hard and loud.

"No, your work is not yet finished," Yetta retorted.

"It will cost more than you can afford," Sadhanah sneered. "How will you pay me?"

"How does half a king's tribute sound to you?"

••••••••●○○○○○○○○○○○

Thomas watched the three men around the campfire. By now they were too drunk to notice anything. Kelile had only to grab Aldon and get out of there. But what's taking him so long? His tension mounted. Something had gone wrong. He had to do something.

Just as he was about to move, Aldon appeared at the entrance of the tent. For a few seconds he turned in circles, looking for something. "He's looking for me," Thomas whispered. He waved his handkerchief to get Aldon's attention. It worked. Aldon waved back before rushing up the hill.

"Where's Kelile?" Thomas asked as Aldon approached.

"He didn't make it, Thomas." Aldon fell to his knees as if exhausted. "Kelile is dead."

Thomas tore his eyes from Aldon's stricken face to look down at the camp in disbelief. "Are you absolutely sure? Is it possible he's unconscious?"

"No, I'm certain of it. I saw the sword pierce him through the back."

"It's not possible," Thomas insisted as he scanned the camp. He looked for Kelile to step out of the tent, to wave back to him as he had before.

"We have to go, Thomas," Aldon whispered. "There's nothing more we can do for him."

CHAPTER 32

Michael woke to sunbeams piercing through openings in the ceiling. It was like nothing Michael had ever imagined. "You're right," he whispered. "If we had made a fire, we would have been spotted for sure." No answer came since Artemisia was already gone.

Michael smiled. He climbed down from the rocky ledge to the back of the cave to relieve himself. He spotted Artemisia's clothing laid out on a flat rock. Next to the rock the cavern wall curved inward, then away, concealing the small waterfall she'd spotted yesterday.

Curiosity led him to look around the curve. There she was, bathing under the fall of water. His first reaction was to leap out of sight and press his back against the wall. His first impulse was to leave, but his desire said otherwise. He struggled with his breathing as his heart raced. *Just one peek,* he thought. *She'll never know.*

As if by design, one sunbeam found its way into the otherwise dark cavern like a spotlight on a performer. It found Artemisia.

Her back was toward him so his quick peek became an entranced gaze. He watched as steam evaporated all around her body. His eyes followed the water flowing from her long black hair down her back and over her flawless bottom. Sparkling droplets of water were all that covered her dark, smooth skin.

Michael held his breath as she bent forward to massage her outstretched thigh with both hands. Without pausing she turned her head ever so slightly to peer through her draping hair in Michael's direction.

Like a spring let loose, he jumped out of sight. "What an idiot. What a stupid dumb ass," he muttered to himself. He returned to the ledge.

"Did I take too long?" Artemisia asked a few minutes later, returning from the waterfall. "I thought I should bathe before we find the others."

"Oh, is that what you were doing?" Michael tried to read her response. "I just got up myself."

Artemisia offered a knowing smile as if she were enjoying Michael's discomfort. "That is good, Michael. For a moment back there, I could have sworn someone was with me." She gave an elaborate shrug. "Oh well, I guess it was only me feeling vulnerable."

Ice water flowed through his veins. "I suppose so," he said, feeling his face heat when his voice squeaked. He cleared his throat. "Excuse me. I need some water. Where was it you took your shower again? I'll get some water for us and at the same time, I'll check to see if anyone is around."

Artemisia pointed toward the waterfall.

"Oh man, of course—you found the falls yesterday." Michael hurried in the direction she'd pointed. Behind him, Artemisia giggled.

• • • • • • • • • • ● ○○○○○○○○○○ ○ ○

Four hours later, they arrived at the small village where the others had spent the night and saw Thomas seated outside the inn. "I'm glad to see you're both okay," Thomas said when he saw them.

"Did everything go well with you guys?" Michael asked.

Thomas's face fell. "Can we talk for a minute? I need to tell you something before we meet up with the others."

Michael and Artemisia dismounted and they found a quiet place to talk. "Do you have any news on Aldon?" Michael asked. "Because we have a plan to get him back."

"Aldon is with us, Michael. We got him back early this morning."

"That's wonderful," Michael said. "How did you manage that?"

Thomas's smile sagged. "Kelile just couldn't wait another minute knowing Aldon might need his help, so we organized—I should say Kelile organized—a rescue. We left in the middle of the night to look for the camp and would you believe it, we found it exactly where Kelile said it would be. His plan was perfect. Only Kelile could make it work, with those odds against us."

With difficulty Thomas explained how the rescue took place. "But only Aldon met me at our designated meeting point."

Michael's blood went cold. "So what happened to Kelile?"

"Michael, Artemisia, we lost our good friend Kelile last night." Thomas could no longer hold back his tears.

From the corner of his eye, Michael saw anger raging in Artemisia's face. He knew she was blaming herself for his death, so he signaled her not to say a word.

"I wanted to tell you before you reached the others," Thomas said. "Everyone is disheartened about what happened."

"You did the right thing," Artemisia said. "We need to be strong now."

Inside the inn, they took the time to mourn Kelile. Thomas, Michael, Anna, and Aldon knelt down to pray while Artemisia, with permission from the innkeeper, prayed to her god Ahura Mazda from the rooftop. She was up there for almost an hour before returning to face the others.

She looked at Michael with determination in her eyes. "Do not blame yourselves for Kelile's death; the blame falls entirely on me," she blurted.

Anna was about to interject when Artemisia put her hand out. "I was not completely honest with you. In my battles against the Greeks, I made many enemies. I kept this from you because—" She paused to look at Michael. "Because I fell in love with Michael and did not want to scare him away. The attack by the marauder band last night was not a random attack to steal our possessions. The people who attacked us were after me, not you. There's a bounty on my head. So you see, I'm therefore responsible for your friend's death. For this I am forever remorseful. I've decided, for your safety, to head back to Babylon and not continue with you to Susa. I hope you can find it in your heart to forgive me for the pain I've caused."

"Get away from here, you murderer!" Aldon yelled, startling the others. "We never needed you anyway."

"Shut your big, fat mouth," Thomas growled. "If you hadn't turned to the pursuers, Kelile would still be alive today."

"That's right, Aldon," Anna said. "Why did you turn around? You never did explain it to us."

Aldon cowered back into his chair. "I don't know what happened. The horse took over; I had no control over it. I'm telling you the truth—it's not my fault." No one said anything. "I loved Kelile too, you know; he was my friend also. I grieve his death just as deeply as all of you, if not more."

"You see what I've done?" Artemisia said. "I've caused dissention among you. I'm a curse to your mission."

"You got that right," Aldon mumbled.

Michael, standing next to him, swung the back of his hand and struck Aldon in the face. The blow knocked him backward onto the floor. "I swear to God, Aldon, one more word from you and I'll strangle you right here, right now."

Aldon struggled to get up, picked up the chair, and wiped the blood from his mouth. No one helped him so he stepped backward until he reached the wall. His expression was unreadable.

"Listen," Michael said, shaking the pain from his hand. "There's no evidence this band of thieves was after Artemisia. For all we know, we were in the wrong place at the wrong time. So the blame for Kelile's death falls on the heads of those who pursued us yesterday and no one else." He looked around at their faces. "If we send Artemisia away, it's the same as if we blame her for his death when in reality we should thank her for saving our lives."

He walked over to stand next to Artemisia. "Now that we know the truth about this bounty on her head, I say we put aside what we can't change and concentrate on the rest of our mission. We need to get to Susa as planned—all of us, including Artemisia. Once we get back home, we will make sure Kelile gets the proper memorial he deserves."

"Well, what are we waiting for?" Thomas said. "We have a long journey ahead of us. I'm sure I speak for all of us." He glanced at Artemisia. "If you still want to, of course, we would like you to show us the way."

Artemisia smiled. "It would be my honor."

CHAPTER 33

"Konnichiwa," Nasato said as he limped toward the dining table where Derrek and Quincy were eating. "It's not often I see the two of you sitting together for a meal. Who's watching the servers?"

"Nasato, please join us. Can I get you something to eat?"

"No thanks, Quincy; I don't eat at ten in the evening."

"How much longer before you get the cast removed?"

Nasato grimaced in thought. "Let's see . . . it's been, what? Eight weeks since we arrived in Persia? So that means I have another four and a half weeks before it's removed." He sat down and placed his crutches on the floor next to him. "By the way, I have good news for you. I think I found a solution for your telecom problem."

"Great," Derrek said. "We still can't locate the transmitter that's sending the jamming signal."

"It's quite simple, actually," Nasato said. "Why don't you just change the frequency?"

"We already thought of that, but the foot soldiers' receivers have been programmed to receive on only one frequency."

"Are you sure about that?"

"I'm pretty sure," Quincy said. "Their communication devices are simple, with no moving parts—a ring, a necklace, a broach. You know what I mean, things like that."

Nasato looked skeptical. "Do you know this to be a fact? I ask because I distinctly recall a consultation meeting we had on the subject. The debate at the time was the portable devices." He frowned, straining to recall more details. "Yes, I remember. Kirkpatrick was there and so was Yetta, I think . . . yes, she was there too. I remember because I found it odd for her to be present at a meeting dealing with a technical subject. They must have changed their minds if you say there is only one available frequency."

"Are you sure it was Kirkpatrick?" Quincy asked. "Major General Nathan Kirkpatrick who is on the ship here with us?"

"One hundred percent sure it was Kirkpatrick," Nasato said. "I can tell you who else was at the meeting if you want."

"Anyone here on the *Kismet*?"

"No, there were mostly technicians."

Derrek looked at Quincy and managed a grin. He whispered into his ear, "I think we know who the bad guy is."

Nasato looked blankly at them. "Am I missing something?"

"Sorry, Nasato; we will explain it all as soon as we're sure ourselves."

"If you're talking about the telecom jewelry, there's an easy way to find out," Nasato said. "We have a box full of those devices somewhere on the ship. You know, the ones we would have given to the soldiers, had we not taken off prematurely."

Derrek's jaw dropped. "Of course! We could take one apart and check if it has the capability for more than one frequency. Then all we need to do is change the channel."

"Well, I'm done eating," Quincy said.

"Me too," Derrek agreed. "Let's go find that box."

Nasato looked around, dejected. "Here I am, alone again."

It took them fifteen minutes to find the box. It was in the changing room on the Boat Deck where the pod was launched. It contained the other devices and a single yellow envelope. Derrek picked up the envelope and handed it to Quincy.

Quincy pulled an electronic schematic from the envelope and spread it out on a workbench. They began studying it. The devices were simple in construction and could be easily understood by anyone with basic electronic training.

"Well, I'll be damned," Derrek exclaimed. "Nasato was right. They're equipped to transmit and receive in two frequencies. Look, each piece of jewelry has a stone, which works as a dip switch. They have only to set it to the desired frequency."

"How do we tell the guys down there to change the position of the dip switch?"

"Dammit, there's no way of doing that." Derrek tossed the schematic aside. "Oh well, it doesn't matter anyway. Some of the devices are starting to malfunction. Aldon's device keeps going off for long periods of time and

Thomas's and Anna's devices also go off more than they should. Sooner or later we'll lose all contact with them."

"I'm not convinced those blackouts are malfunctions, Derrek. Did you notice both Thomas's and Anna's devices always seem to go off at the exact same time?"

CHAPTER 34

Jerusalem, fifteen hundred kilometers away

"Are the relics we've purchased secured?" Nicolas asked.

"I hid them in the hole we dug under the bedroom carpet, as we discussed."

"Good; that's the best place for now."

"Are you sure the ULRA will approve of us bringing back these relics? They made it pretty clear we were to record the details of their location, not bring them back."

"Are you kidding me, Brody? We have the book of the wars of God. All we know of this book is found in Numbers 21 of the Hebrew scriptures. Surely you can appreciate the significance of this book." Brody looked puzzled. "It's a historical record of the wars of Israel. Think of the implications it will have on spreading the gospel. Besides, even if we record its location, it could never survive twenty-five hundred years. So how could they not be pleased with these acquisitions?"

"I guess you're right." Brody smiled. "It's quite the find, isn't it?"

"Yes, Brody, it's quite the find."

"It's a lot smaller than I imagined."

"What's that, Brody?"

"The city of David. I thought it was much bigger."

"From the temple wall where we're standing it does look small; I venture to say no more than half a kilometer long and maybe a hundred and sixty to a hundred and eighty meters wide."

Brody sighed with impatience. "You're sure Yissakhar said midafternoon? We've been here for over an hour."

"Not quite an hour yet, Brody."

As he said those words, a voice called out to them from behind, "Are you Nicolas, the traveler?"

Nicolas turned around to face a middle-aged Hebrew priest wearing the traditional multilayered dress, the hem of his white undergarment visible below a blue ephod cinched with a sash. He was not a high priest, so there were no Urim and Thummim. On his head was a turban. "Yes, that's me. And you are?"

"Yissakhar," the man said. "I'm to lead you to God."

"Good, we're ready to go."

Yissakhar took them through a door and down a set of stairs so narrow, they had to squeeze through sideways. "Why would anyone build such narrow stairs?" Brody asked.

"This isn't permanent," Yissakhar said. "It's been made for the rebuilding period. After we're done we'll block off this passageway. No one will know it ever existed."

At the bottom, they found themselves in an underground cave. "Grab one of those torches and follow me." Yissakhar pointed in the only direction they could go.

After ten minutes they arrived at a fork. "Now listen to me carefully," Yissakhar said. "Remember the following numbers: four, zero, one, and three. These are the numbers that will get you there and back."

"You're not coming with us?" Brody asked.

"No. I'm not a high priest."

Brody looked at Nicolas. "You're no high priest either," he said in English.

"Don't say anything, Brody," Nicolas responded in English. "I had to tell him I'm a high priest from a foreign land, otherwise he would not have shown us the way."

Brody glanced at Yissakhar. "How do we know he's a real guide? He doesn't even look like a Jew. Are you sure he's a Jew? And if he is, how can we be sure his accomplices aren't waiting for us inside?"

"Don't worry, Brody, I have everything under control." Nicolas looked at Yissakhar with a reassuring smile. "It's okay. My assistant is not a high priest like me, so he's naturally a bit nervous."

"It's understandable. Now you will need to pay my fee."

"I will give you half the original fee now, the other half when we return from the cave."

"Yes," Yissakhar said. "That's agreeable."

Nicolas paid the man. "Tell us about the number 4013."

"These numbers will direct you to your destination. Remember four, zero, one, and three, as well as left, right, left, right. This is how it works: as you walk down this tunnel, you will go left at the fourth tunnel that leads away from the main tunnel. Go straight to the end and turn right. Then go left again at the first opening in the tunnel you encounter. Finally turn right at the third opening. You got it? Four left, zero right, one left, three right. That's when you'll reach your destination."

"Right," Nicolas said. "Piece of cake. Come on, Brody, let's go."

Each lifting a torch, Nicolas and Brody entered the tunnels, walking carefully along narrow passages and ducking under low openings. Some were man-made. Others were carved out by nature over thousands of years and navigating their twists and varied heights made the trek difficult.

"Why did you have to say you're a high priest to get his help?" Brody asked when Yissakhar was well behind them.

"Because only a high priest could get close to the Ark of the Covenant. If I had not convinced him, all the money in the world would not be enough to get his help."

"Why is it so important?"

"Don't you remember the Bible account when King David had the Ark brought out of hiding? A man reached over to stabilize the Ark as it almost fell off the chariot. You remember what happened to him?"

"Not really."

"He was struck by lightning, Brody. And the reason why he was killed is because . . . ?"

"Only a high priest is permitted to touch the Ark?"

"That's right. Some believe the same rule applies for looking at it." Nicolas nodded ahead. "We've arrived at the entrance of the fourth tunnel. We need to go left."

"So how are we going to take pictures if we can't see it?"

"Actually, we can't look directly upon it, so to protect an onlooker that is not a high priest, there is a translucent cloth on top of it. This way, we can look but not directly at it."

Brody looked at him askance. "Are you sure about that, Nicolas?"

"Yes, of course I'm sure. Okay, we've reached the end of the tunnel. We did a left earlier so we need to go right. Now don't worry about it, Brody. If you're uncertain, let me go in first and when you see I'm not dead, then you can look at it yourself."

Brody considered that for some time before he answered. "Okay then, after we look at it as you say, we should video capture everything and leave as quickly as possible."

"That's the plan, Brody. Here's the first opening to our right, we must go this way."

"No. It's left." Brody stopped to retrace his steps. "Left then right then left again. We already did left, then the right, so we need to go left now."

Nicolas mentally repeated the direction change. "You're right, Brody, it's left. Good thing someone is paying attention."

"Why is the Ark hidden in these caves, anyway?" Brody asked.

"In the year 607 BC, Babylon, which was the world power, sacked Jerusalem. Many believe the Jews hid the Ark under the temple so the Babylonians could not take it away. No one can confirm for sure when it was hidden but our being here under the temple confirms where it was hidden."

"I read about this on the web. Wasn't it 587 BC?"

"That's what historians would tell you. Don't let people who have made science their god dictate what to believe, Brody. The Bible's chronology is clear on this matter; it's 607."

Brody accepted Nicolas's explanation. "Do you think it will still be here when we get back home?"

"That I can't say, nor can I say if God wants us to find it in the twenty-first century."

At the beginning of the third tunnel, they stopped. A foggy yellow light spilled from the entrance. Nicolas turned to him, eyes wide. "This is it, Brody. Are you as excited as I am?"

Brody grimaced. "I'm more scared than excited."

"There's no need to be afraid. Just follow me."

"Would you be disappointed if I waited out here?"

"If you don't come, you will regret it for the rest of your life. You know that, don't you?"

Brody thought about it for a moment. "If you don't mind, I'm going to wait for you here."

Nicolas shrugged. "Suit yourself. I'll be back soon."

Drawing a deep breath, he entered the tunnel, walking cautiously toward the light until he was about two meters from its source. A translucent blue silk curtain separated him from the Ark. Not knowing what to do next, he looked around and above his head. "Of course! I'm standing under the most holy, the only place to protect the Ark." Without turning around, he shouted, "You should see this, Brody. You'll never get another chance."

"Okay, okay, I'm coming." Nicolas sensed his approach, and his presence, although the younger man decided to stay behind him. "Wow, is that it?"

"Yes. You're looking at the most sacred object ever made. Isn't it magnificent? Look how the golden chest radiates God's glory. And the two cherubs facing each other on the lid—it's just as the Bible said."

Overwhelmed, Brody fell to his knees to pray. As for Nicolas, he moved forward to capture the Ark from the other side. He pulled up the silk curtain just enough to slide his hand under, aiming his video wristband at the Ark while keeping his eyes shut.

"No!" Brody shouted. "What are you doing?"

Startled by the sudden shout, Nicolas instinctively looked at his hand, thinking he was about to touch the Ark. In doing so, he inadvertently looked at the small area exposed by the lifted curtain.

Brody shielded his eyes with his arm as a bright light flashed, making him stagger backward. He tried to open his eyes, but the light rendered him blind. "Nicolas!" he cried, "Nicolas!" He got no response.

It took some thirty minutes before he could look toward the Ark where Nicolas had been standing. Nicolas was gone. He knew Nicolas would never leave him behind, so he sat and waited for him to return. That's when he detected an odor that was not there before. It smelled like seared pork.

Brody understood what had happened.

Without concern for his own safety, he faced the Ark. On the ground before the curtain he saw a heap of ashes. He stared at it for a while, feeling nothing. What he did next was all mechanical. He felt no more emotion than a robot. He gathered a few handfuls of the ash and dropped them inside a pouch, then retraced his steps to the exit where Yissakhar was waiting.

Yissakhar looked into the cave behind Brody. "Where is Nicolas the traveler?"

Brody said nothing. He handed Yissakhar all his money. "Thank you for your services, Yissakhar. I believe our business is concluded, yes?"

"Yes, it's concluded."

Brody squeezed his way back up the stairs and headed to his house.

Yissakhar followed Brody up the narrow staircase. "Yet another who presumes to know better than God," he murmured, watching Brody walk down the main street of the city of David. He looked at his pouch of riches. "This is the best deal for the temple treasury yet."

CHAPTER 35

They stayed in the shadows of the wall, where the air was crisp and cool. Susa was magnificent—not as majestic as Babylon, but just as important to the Persian kings. Here Darius had built a splendid summer palace where he and now King Xerxes spent much of their time.

The view over the top of the wall revealed an organized city grid. Southwest was the Acropolis. To the north was an impressive fortress. If you stood on top of the Acropolis and looked past the fortress toward Xerxes' palace, Michael imagined, you could probably observe people casually walking on its peaceful terraces. At night, Artemisia had told him, the lights glowing from Xerxes's audience hall reminded onlookers that their king ruled their world. East of the Imperial city were the dwellings of rich and important people in the government. As influential as Artemisia was, it was not for them to find residence inside the city walls. It was among the more affluent urban residences located outside the city where they would find their home base.

"You know what this reminds me of?" Anna said as they walked up the road. "A trip to Italy I once took. It looks like ancient Pompeii, with its houses of varying heights and painted graffiti." She indicated some of the messages. Some were genuine business advertisements, some were political slogans, and some, like modern graffiti, were gang-related badges.

They turned away from the Imperial city at the first intersection. Straight ahead, in the distant west, they saw the Shaur River.

"Wait here," Artemisia instructed, and approached a door where two guards stood watch. She spoke with them for a few seconds before signaling the others to follow her through the door one of the guards opened.

What they saw on the inside was no reflection of the neglected outer walls of the residence. They walked into a large open peristyle. Beyond the columns of its colonnade were tables set out for a banquet. The center of the peristyle

215

was given over to statues of Persians hunting lions and gazelles around a pool with a water fountain.

"Good gracious," Anna said. "Who would guess there was a paradise on the other side of the wall."

A well-dressed woman in her late sixties came to greet them. "Welcome to the home of Memucan, one of seven princes of Persia and Media. We've been expecting you. If you will follow me, I will show you to your lodgings, then later you can join us for dinner."

She led them past an atrium, then a small dining room. At the back of the house, interior balconies surround the three levels of guest quarters. "Please note the doors to your left are the servants' quarters. If you want anything, knock on one of the doors, and they will see to your needs. The large green door to the right is the entrance to Memucan's private residence. You're not to go there unless invited. Any questions?" They all answered no. "Very well then, please follow me."

The woman headed up the stairs. They stopped on the second floor at a door marked *12*. The woman said to Artemisia, "This room has been prepared for you and your lover."

Shocked at her words, Michael leaned over to protest, but Artemisia stopped him. "It's okay, sweetheart. I know you expected better, but this is all they had at such short notice."

Michael was confused, but he knew better than to argue with her. *She must have a good reason for making these arrangements,* he thought. "Okay," he said. "It will do."

After they entered their room, Artemisia explained what had just taken place. "When I spoke to Memucan, he said he had three rooms available. The only way we could stay here is if we pretended to be three couples. It was after he asked me if I'd remarried; I told him I had a lover. You must understand, I had no choice. There's a one week festival starting today—that's why his house is full."

Michael looked around the room. He saw one bed. "Three rooms . . . how did you explain Aldon and Kelile?"

"I told Memucan they were also a couple."

Michael thought about this for a moment, then smiled, "Oh man, Aldon sure would have liked that arrangement."

Artemisia smiled wickedly. "Come on, let's clean up before we meet the others and explain the accommodations. I failed to warn them, as well."

Michael and Artemisia were the first at their table, and what a spread it was. The tables were set for an international guest list. They could choose from breads and pitas of different flavors, fruits from Africa, Asia, and Europe, goat, lamb, beef, pork, poultry, and quail. Michael was certain they were about to feast on a dodo bird destined for extinction. There was wine—lots and lots of wine—served with cheeses and nuts from around the world. There were milk and juices for those who abstained from alcoholic beverages.

For the complete gratification of all the guests' senses, a small group of musicians played soothing compositions. It was truly a feast meant for a king and his guests.

"Artemisia," a harsh voice said behind them, "you have some explaining to do."

"Yes, Anna, I do," she said, turning. "Please sit down," Artemisia repeated the explanation she'd given Michael earlier. "So you see, I forgot to mention what the accommodations would be."

Anna looked around at the table. "How can I be angry? Just look at all this." She watched a servant girl fill their goblets with chilled white wine. "Forget it, let's eat."

They were having a good time trying to decide which dessert to take when Aldon joined their table. Without saying a word, he filled his plate.

"Is everything all right?" Thomas asked.

"Yes, thanks. And how are you guys?" he said indifferently.

"We were wondering where you were."

Aldon put his plate down. "Am I the only one here concerned about the mission? We're not on vacation, you know. We've been here in Persia for more than a month already, and we've accomplished nothing."

Michael's face flushed with anger. "Accomplished nothing? You say 'accomplished nothing' as if trying to find Christian is accomplishing nothing." Michael stood up. "Why you—"

"I have an idea," Artemisia interrupted. "Why don't we split up into two groups? I will use my contact to get us inside the Imperial city. His name is Carkas." She turned to face Aldon. "Why don't you come with Michael and me. You could ask him questions pertaining to your mission. Maybe, if we're lucky, we could get an audience with the king. This way you can give him the tribute you brought for him. In the meantime, Thomas and Anna will stay in the suburbs and with the help of the locals, try to find Christian. How does that sound?"

"You can get us into the Imperial city?" Aldon asked.

"Yes, I can."

Aldon thought about it for a moment. "Why can't you get us a visit with the king yourself? I thought you knew him well."

"Even his queen cannot have an audience with Xerxes without an invitation. The penalty is death."

"But this Carkas friend of yours can?"

"Yes, he can."

"Okay then, I'll go with you."

"That's just great," Michael said, dropping back into his chair.

Artemisia put her hand on Michael's thigh. "Come on, Michael, it will be all right," Michael said nothing so she turned her attention to Thomas. "Let me arrange the meeting with Carkas. He's one of the seven court officials and minister to Xerxes. He has many people working under him so he could arrange a search for your son. If he's in Susa, Carkas will find him." She smiled as she thought of Carkas. "He loves to talk about himself, so you can get from him information for your mission, Aldon."

"Fine," Thomas said. "How do you propose Anna and I start our search?"

"You should start with this city—that's everything west of the first street we entered. Then you cross over the Shaur River—there's a bridge not far from here, about one hundred steps from Daniel's tomb. On the other side you could search farther west—"

"Wait a minute," Anna interrupted. "Did you say Daniel's tomb?"

"Yes, that's right."

"This would not be Daniel, the minister to King Nebuchadnezzar, king of Babylon?"

"I don't know if it is the same Daniel you're referring to, but yes, he was a minister to King Nebuchadnezzar. He survived the Persian invasion of Babylon."

"I would love to see his tomb," Aldon said.

Artemisia smiled. "We must make it happen, then."

Thomas leaned forward. "I get the impression this is a large territory to cover. You mentioned we can get help from the locals?"

"Of course. For a small fee you can hire the people who know the city best; they will be your eyes and ears, I'm convinced if your son is in or near Susa, they'll find him."

"How do we come in contact with these people?"

Artemisia chuckled. "Just walk down the street—they'll find you. They're the city's orphans. No one knows what's going on better than the orphans."

A loud, boisterous voice disrupted their conversation. "Well if it's not the famous naval commander, Artemisia! Are you back with the king?"

Artemisia's expression darkened. "Zeno, who did you bribe to make your way here?"

Zeno laughed so loudly, the other guests stopped eating to see what was happening. "Still at war, I see. Now, who are these friends of yours?" He spread his hands wide and looked around at them.

"No one you need to concern yourself with," Artemisia replied stiffly.

He laughed again. "As you wish, Artemisia." He glanced around the table. His eyes lingered on Anna. "Enjoy the hospitality of my good friend and colleague, Memucan. I know I will." He walked away to start his arrogant display at another table.

"Who's that?" Anna asked.

"His name is Zeno. He fancies himself as quite the philosopher."

"Is he the Greek philosopher of Magna Graecia, a member of the Eleatic School?" Everyone looked at Thomas, surprised he knew who the man was.

"Yes, that Zeno. You know of him, I see."

"Only of his theories," Thomas said. "In our country, we study his views on a couple of paradoxes related to the perception of time. You know, the race between Achilles and the tortoise, the arrows meeting in midair?" He looked around the table. "What about the dichotomy?" It was clear no one had the foggiest idea what he was talking about. "No matter, it's not important."

Now eager to change the subject he turned his attention to the costume jewelry they carried for King Xerxes. "Artemisia, since we will be here for a while, can you recommend a place where we can deposit our valuables?"

"There are a few places I can think of, none of which are very secure," she warned. "I suggest we keep them with us until I get Carkas to arrange a visit with the king. If that will take too long, he may arrange for your tribute to be put in the palace coffers."

Zeno's obnoxious laugh disrupted them once again, even though it came from several tables away. Thomas stared at him for a while. It seemed he alone appreciated the man who understood how time works, thousands of years ahead of his time.

CHAPTER 36

Shevat 16, one month before the return trip

The mounting tension generated by the upcoming conflict between Haman's followers and the Jews had Persia on edge. Loyalties changed frequently between the two camps as Adar 13 approached, the day set aside for the actual battle. People became suspicious of their neighbors, their family, and friends. Not knowing who to trust made it impossible for Thomas to find assistance in the search for his son.

Since their arrival, Artemisia had been working on getting an audience with Carkas. The only way into the well-guarded Imperial city was through the Craftsmen City located outside the eastern wall. After waiting almost all morning for a confirmation, the guards finally let them through. They went directly to Carkas's luxurious home. Artemisia announced their arrival to the guards stationed at the entrance.

"You know what?" Aldon said. "I think it would be better if you two went alone. You need to make yourselves familiar on the first visit and you know the saying, three is a crowd."

"Nonsense," Artemisia said. "Men like Carkas are accustomed to meeting many people at a time. You have a lot to learn from being here."

"If it's all the same, I would rather explore the city. I'll meet with Carkas on our next visit."

"There might not be a next visit, Aldon."

"Oh, let him go," Michael said.

"Very well." Artemisia rolled her eyes. "We will see you back at Memucan's home."

"Good. I'll see you later, then."

"This Aldon, he's a hard person to figure out," Artemisia said to Michael. "First he wants to come, now without explanation he wants to be alone."

"Please enter," the guard announced from the doorway.

They entered a large reception area that resembled a museum lobby, with its vast marble floor and benches along its marble walls. Decorating the lobby were two paintings of King Xerxes. A ceremonial sword hung below a colorful tapestry. Four statuettes less than one meter tall stood on four marble pillars positioned around the room.

"Please wait here," the guard said before resuming his place outside the front door.

They stood silently for a good five minutes before Carkas entered to greet them.

"Artemisia," said an imposing monster of a man. His chest and shoulders were hidden beneath long black, curly locks and a full beard. "Artemisia," he repeated before he gave her a suffocating bear hug. "You look as beautiful now as you did when we were together. No, no, you look much more beautiful now." He hugged her again.

"Your memory is playing tricks on you, Carkas. I don't recall us ever being together."

"No, no—" He stopped and considered her remark. "Oh yes, oh yes, I remember—I proposed to you and you said no. You broke my heart when you said no, you know that, Artemisia? You broke my heart, I remember. It was so long ago."

"I said no to your proposal because at the time I was married."

"Yes, that's true. Yes, I remember. My bad luck, my bad luck. My god, you look beautiful. I'm so glad you came to visit me. Come, let's talk in the living room; it's much more comfortable in the living room."

"Are you getting blind in your old age, Carkas?" Artemisia said. "I'd like you to meet a good friend of mine. Carkas, meet Michael."

Michael smiled and nodded a hello to Carkas. "It's an honor to make your acquaintance, Carkas."

"Please forgive me for not noticing you, Michael," Carkas said. "You see, I was blinded by Artemisia's beauty. You do understand, don't you, Michael?"

"Yes, Carkas, I most certainly do."

They made themselves comfortable as a slave girl served them hot tea, dried fruit, and breakfast cakes. Carkas filled a plate, then took a sip of his tea. "How long have you been in Susa, Artemisia?"

"We arrived about seven months ago."

"What? Seven months, and you call on me only now? You break my heart, Artemisia. Seven months? Do I mean so little to you? Seven Months?"

"We tried to see you several times, but your secretary kept telling us to come back."

"Yes, yes, that's true. I did tell him to put official government business first. You understand, don't you? With everything happening with the Jews and all, you do understand, don't you?"

"The thing is, Carkas, I came to introduce to King Xerxes a foreign ambassador," Artemisia said. "He brings gifts, a tribute of materials not yet known in all of Persia."

Carkas looked puzzled. "Why did my secretary refuse you an audience, then?" He turned to Michael. "What do you want with the king?"

Artemisia answered for him. "They come from a land so far away, they're not even registered in our records. It's called Canada. They came to share their knowledge of advanced transportation; it is called an air ship. I've seen it myself. It's extraordinary. In return, they want to learn about our laws."

"We've heard many great things about the Persian laws and its benefit to your people," Michael cut in, annoyed that Artemisia had answered the previous question for him.

"When do you want this audience to take place?" Carkas asked.

"We must travel back to our country in one month, so the sooner the better."

"That's impossible." Carkas was adamant. "One month? No, no, not possible. With the upcoming conflict, all our efforts are concentrated on protecting ourselves from harm, and that includes King Xerxes. No, what you ask is impossible, especially in one month. No, get it out of your head, Michael. It won't happen."

"What if you make the request on our behalf?" Artemisia asked. "We tried to approach the proper authorities at Apadana, but they won't let us near the front doors. I told them who I was, but it was of no use; they turned us away every time."

"As I said," Carkas continued, "the upcoming conflict makes all contacts with the king difficult. The only chance you might have is through his beloved wife, Esther." He stopped to evaluate what he'd said. "No, no that won't work either. Xerxes has her practically in a vault—to protect her, of course, not as a prisoner. You know what I mean? Wait a minute, do you know her Uncle Mordecai? He's a high official at the court of the king. Maybe he can help you."

"No," Artemisia said. "I never met the man."

"That's too bad. Yes, too bad. I think your only chance will be after the conflict. I wish I could help, but it's a bad time right now."

Michael leaned over to come eye to eye with Carkas. "Are you talking about Adar 13?"

"Yes, of course; what else is there?" He bellowed with laughter. "Well, what else is there?"

"I know King Xerxes has given the Jews the right to defend themselves, and probably there will be much bloodshed, but why are so many people concerned? Should it not be the Amalekites who should be worried? After all, they're the ones who started all this."

Carkas straightened up in his chair and put his two large, hairy hands on his knees. "I don't know what you've heard concerning this conflict in this Kainada of yours, Michael—"

"That's Canada," Michael corrected him.

"That's what I said, Kainada. Anyway, the situation is much more complicated than Israelites versus Amalekites, you know. There are a lot of people outside of these two nations who have taken sides, you know—a lot of people. As information comes out, the Persian people, who love justice, understand what's really happening. That's right, the Persian people are not easily fooled and they love justice.

"At first it looked like Haman and his ten sons were responsible for the conflict, but as the full picture became clear, people asked questions, many questions. Many, many questions. For instance, is Haman alone to blame for starting the conflict, or is it Mordecai? That's right, don't look so surprised. Think about it for a minute. Why did Mordecai not bow down to Haman like everyone else? That's right, I said everyone else. There's no law among the Jews forbidding them to acknowledge superior authorities by prostrating themselves. Did you know that? Some say it's because Mordecai was too proud, or perhaps even his hatred toward the Amalekites started all this.

"Think on it for a minute. Did he not trick the king by hiding the fact that his niece is a Jewess? Did you know that 'Esther' is her Persian name, not her real name? That's right, her real name is Hadassah. That's right, Hadassah. I bet you didn't know that; now you do. But there's more. Is it possible Haman might have acted in self-defense? Did you know the Jews are determined to have war with Amalek from generation to generation? That's right, it is written in their holy books. I'm quoting directly from their holy books. Their King Saul and King David both attacked the Amalekites about six hundred and fifty years ago. So you see, Michael, there are many people taking sides with Haman and his sons, and they've made their intentions to participate alongside Haman known."

"May I ask you a personal question?" Michael interrupted.

"Yes, of course; please feel free."

"Would you happen to be an Amalekite?"

"Absolutely not," Carkas replied. "Besides, true Amalekites don't exist anyway—only scattered descendants can still be found. It's because Haman is a descendent of the Amalekites that we call him and his group that. It's probably the Jews who made the reference to justify their part of the conflict. Anyway, I'm one hundred percent Persian. And don't forget I'm also one of the seven court officials ministering to King Xerxes. I swore an oath to look at all sides of any conflict. So don't forget what I'm saying. What I tell you are facts. I'm hoping they will help you understand what's going on all over Persia. Do you understand what I'm saying? All over Persia."

"Yes, of course. Please continue." Michael sat back to listen.

"So you see," continued Carkas, "when the law was passed in the districts of Persia, no one thought the Jews stood a chance, especially since this law cannot be canceled. Did you know not even the king has the power to cancel a law? That's right, not even King Xerxes. So many made their opinions known publicly, to make sure they would not be viewed as taking sides with the enemies of Persia. However, on the twenty-third of Sivan, two months later, Queen Esther convinced King Xerxes of Haman's evil intention to eliminate the Jews from Persia. Of course the lovesick king believed her, and since he could not change the law, he passed a new one. This would allow the Jews to defend themselves. Do you see where I'm going with this?"

"Yes," Michael responded. "All those who spoke up against the Jews are now in fear of retaliation."

"That's right." Carkas looked at Artemisia. "This time you chose a smart one. Yes, this one is a real smart cookie." Artemisia couldn't help but smile at Michael. "The result is that many thousands will fight with Haman's sons, but most of those who spoke out against the Jews have no intentions of fighting at all. So now they fear they will be among those the Jews will try to kill. So you understand, Michael, that's why everyone here is so nervous about this upcoming conflict."

Carkas was getting more excited as he spoke. "There's something else. Did you know Haman's sons and their close supporters are right now here in Susa? Yes, that's right, right here in the Imperial city. Did you know that?" He rose to look out the window and pointed. "Right there. Look, can you see the Acropolis? Come over here and look, right over that way. In that big house right over there, that's where the ten sons of Haman are staying. I bet you didn't know that, did you? So Susa will be a target. If I were a Jew, I sure would hunt down Haman's sons. Wouldn't you, Michael?"

"I don't know, Carkas," Michael said. "I'm not involved in this conflict, but I can see your point about Haman and the Amalekites. Clearly there's a history there, but surely you don't think an attempt to eliminate the Jews from Persia is the right thing to do. The conflict between the two nations dates back six hundred and fifty years. You said it yourself. And don't forget, Haman did lie about the loyalty of the Jews to the empire in order for the initial law to pass. Is it possible King Xerxes is acting in fairness when he gave the Jews the right to defend themselves? Think also of the motive behind the first law. Haman and his followers would confiscate the property of any defeated Jew, whereas the Jews agreed not to touch anything belonging to those they will fight. Clearly there is no other reason than self-preservation for them to fight."

Before Michael could continue, another slave girl approached Carkas and whispered something in his ear. "I'm reminded of another appointment," Carkas said. "But yes, I agree with everything you say. You must also understand that having an audience with the king is impossible at this time. There's too much confusion right now. I recommend you wait until after the battle. Then I could do something for you."

Realizing their meeting was over, Artemisia abruptly changed the subject before it was too late. "We both thank you for taking time from your busy schedule to see us, Carkas, but there is one more thing I would like to ask of you before we go."

"Please do ask."

"Among the friends who traveled with Michael is one man who is looking for his lost son. We think he is somewhere here in Susa. We have neither the resources nor the time to find him before they must return to their country. Can you help us?"

"What's this man's name?"

"His name is Christian. He's a young man, early twenties. He's the same nationality as Michael."

"Does this young man want to be found?"

"Yes. He left us clues to help locate him. We believe his life is in danger, so perhaps he's in hiding."

"All right, Artemisia, I'll send word to my people. How can I reach you?"

"We're guests of Memucan."

"Really? Memucan? You're joking, right? Not Memucan! You see what I was telling you? He's hiding in Babylon, isn't he? He fears the coming conflict.

Would you believe it, one of the seven princes of Persia, and he's hiding in Babylon. Now you can appreciate why everyone is so hard to get hold of."

"We know you're a busy man, Carkas, so we'll be leaving," Artemisia said. "Thank you again for all that you're doing for my friends. I hope we will speak again soon."

CHAPTER 37

Aldon found the new dwelling Yetta had been forced to move into—a modest house with the entrance to the basement apartment in the rear. He descended the stairs and knocked on the door in the Morse code for SOS. Yetta greeted him with a short but affectionate embrace and invited him in. To Aldon's surprise, there were five men in the single room.

"Everyone, I would like you to meet Aldon, my contact with the travelers. Aldon, this is Parshandatha, Dalphon, Aspatha, and Aridai, sons of Haman. You already know Sadhanah."

Aldon's blood turned ice cold as he made eye contact with Sadhanah. It took all he had to force a hello. The others nodded back. Aldon turned to Yetta and said in a loud, clear voice, "I thought you said we would be alone."

"We don't have time for this," Parshandatha said, annoyed. He stepped forward to face Aldon. "You were supposed to have fifty percent of Xerxes' tribute. Why were you unable to fulfill your promise?"

Aldon searched for the right words. "It's complicated, and since your people killed Kelile, the others don't trust me anymore. So getting my hands on the treasure is not as easy as you may think."

Yetta stepped in. "That's why Aldon and I have devised a plan that will be much more agreeable to you. However, it will require your help in the process."

"Like I said, I have no time for this nonsense. You failed to keep your word. I have a good mind to cut you both to pieces right now." Sadhanah gripped his sword hilt and smiled at the thought.

Not knowing what Yetta was talking about, Aldon allowed her to continue.

"How would you like to have the entire tribute meant for Xerxes, all within the next thirty days?" she said. "Is this worth one day's work to you?"

Parshandatha looked at Aldon. "Your spy can't even get the promised half; how will he get the whole thing?"

227

"Not Aldon, Artemisia. I'll get her to bring it to you."

Parshandatha turned his attention to Yetta. "I'm listening."

"Artemisia visited Carkas today to arrange an audience with Xerxes. I know this because it is part of their mission strategy, but you know, as I do, that Xerxes is not entertaining anyone until the end of the coming battle. I don't need to be clairvoyant to figure this out. So this is what we will do, we wait a few weeks to eliminate any suspicion, then I'll have someone deliver a message to Artemisia in Carkas's name saying he found a way to have them meet with the king in private. All she needs to do is bring the tribute to Carkas's house. When she arrives you or your men will be waiting for her to take the tribute by force."

Parshandatha turned to Sadhanah for some hint of approval.

"What about Carkas and his guards?" Sadhanah asked.

"I'll keep an eye on Carkas," Yetta said. "When I see him leaving for the palace, I'll find you and let you know. As for the guards, I think you know what to do with them."

"We need to talk," Sadhanah said to Parshandatha. Parshandatha signaled the others to huddle in a corner.

"What are you doing?" Aldon whispered to Yetta. "You know what taking it by force means to them."

"Shush, they'll just threaten her." She watched the men talking. "That's all they need to do."

"What if she brings someone with her, like Michael—or anyone else, for that matter?"

"Michael and the others can't fight if their lives depended on it, so they'll hand over the jewels without resistance—you'll see," she assured him. "No one will get hurt."

"Artemisia can fight."

"Not by herself, and she knows that. Anyway, now is not the time to discuss this."

Parshandatha and the others returned to Yetta. "All right," he said, "have the tribute brought to the house. We'll take care of the rest." He walked over to Aldon and poked him in the chest with a meaty index finger. "If you fail me again, I'll come back and kill both of you myself, understood?"

Yetta moved between the two men. "Just make sure you send your best men, and we'll do our part. Don't ever threaten us again."

Without another word, the five men left the residence.

"I don't like this," Aldon complained. "If we do as you say, they will kill them without giving it a second thought."

"No, they won't; I have an arrangement with them. If any harm comes to you or the others, they'll lose the jewels."

"How can you guarantee that? If they have the tribute in their possession, they won't give a damn about your arrangement."

"Yes, they will. They believe I have supernatural powers; they're scared of me."

"They don't look scared."

"It's because they're terrified of the Jews. They never anticipated the numbers gathering against them. It's all a show to make them appear stronger. Trust me, Aldon, they're scared shitless. That's why the tributes are so important to them. They need to bribe the right people and that takes a lot of money—money they don't have."

Aldon frowned. "I don't get it. How does this make them scared of you?"

"To get Aridai and his brothers to cooperate I knew I needed more than the jewels, so I used our knowledge of this time period to make it appear as if I could peer into the future. They think I'm a wizard, a sorceress of some kind. It was the only way I could get them to cooperate with me in the first place."

Aldon grimaced and shook his head. "I don't know, Yetta. Everything we've tried so far has failed."

"Must I remind you again why we're doing this, Aldon? Have you forgotten already how the governing body treated us back home? For years we've been trying to get them to recognize our contributions. You know as well as I do that no one sacrificed as much as we did for the cause. What we're doing here will change all that.

"Once the world learns of our accomplishments, there won't even be the need for a governing body. You and I will be revered like gods. We will have the world to do whatever we want. We'll go down in history as the founders of what could be the greatest religion mankind has ever known.

"But fail, and we'll go back to being nothing more than a footstool to the ULRA. Nothing will have changed. Thomas, Michael, and Anna will get all the credit. Do you really think they'll include you, after what happened in the canyon? Have you already forgotten what happened to Kelile? And what about me, will you leave me behind when you're transported back home?"

Yetta searched Aldon's face for a reaction. What she saw was a broken spirit, a dark, empty shell. "Listen to me, Aldon. I know you care for the mission and its cause. I do too, but we both know that what God has in store for us is greater than the mission. Do you think it's a coincidence that while you were on the tour of the *Kismet* I came to meet you, and then we were both sent here? Don't you see God's hand in what happened? Think of all the good we can do in future trips back here when we are in control." No matter what Yetta said, she knew he didn't care anymore. "Do this last thing, Aldon. Bring back all the accumulated evidence and I'll make sure we are the only survivors."

Aldon looked up a Yetta.

"We don't have to kill them, Aldon. I'll see to it they stay here in Persia. They'll have each other; they'll be happy here, so don't worry about them. Please, Aldon, it's almost over. Just do this and that will be the end of it, I promise. When the time comes, you'll smuggle me back onto the *Kismet* and we head back home together, like the last trip."

"When you asked me to meet you here, I thought you wanted us to spend time together. I guess I was a fool to think you care about us. I should have known it was for this stupid scheme of yours. Well, don't worry, I'll do what you say—but take note, sweetheart. It's the last thing I'm doing. If this fails—" he paused for a deep breath of courage "—-f this fails, it will also be the last time you see me." Aldon left without waiting for her reply.

"You'll thank me later," she yelled after him. "You'll see. You'll thank me later."

CHAPTER 38

"Humble yourselves therefore under the mighty hand of God, that he may exalt you in due time: Casting all your care upon him; for he careth for you. Be sober, be vigilant; because your adversary the devil, as a roaring lion, walketh about, seeking whom he may devour: Whom resist stedfast in the faith, knowing that the same afflictions are accomplished in your brethren that are in the world. But the God of all grace, who hath called us unto his eternal glory by Christ Jesus, after that ye have suffered a while, make you perfect, stablish, strengthen, settle you. To him be glory and dominion for ever and ever. Amen."

When Brody opened his bloodshot eyes he saw the reflection of his campfire on the calm Sea of Galilee. For a moment he imagined Jesus walking on water toward his fear-stricken disciples. What a comfort Jesus must have been to his first-century followers, the men and women who witnessed his miracles.

Every day he repeated the words of the apostle Peter. Somehow it gave him the strength to carry on, to be made strong, to be made firm. He had only to throw his anxieties upon God.

Brody could not understand why the God Nicolas loved so much claimed his life at the most holy relic known to man. But perhaps it wasn't yet time to comprehend the greater good. There were many questions, but he always had many questions. That was why he'd loved his teacher Nicolas so much—he knew the right thing to say. Yesterday he'd scattered Nicolas's ashes in the Jordan River. He'd been instructed to do so if anything should happen to Nicolas. Now he was alone, alone in a foreign land, alone in a distant time.

Feeling depressed and lonely, Brody recovered his cup of chicory and poured into it a strong liquor smuggled in from India. Normally it was used in religious ceremonies, but Brody had found another practical use for it. He knew Nicolas would disapprove, but it numbed the pain. He took a sip of the hot, intoxicating beverage before making himself comfortable and closing his eyes. *Be sober, be vigilant; because your adversary the devil, as a roaring lion, walketh about, seeking whom he may devour . . .* The words of the apostle Peter echoed in his mind.

Brody still had vivid memories of the first time he met Nicolas. He was twenty-two years old, in search of a quiet place in a public park to smoke a cigarette, when he heard Nicolas lecturing to anyone who would listen. Out of curiosity Brody approached the small group sitting on the grass. Nicolas was lecturing on the teachings of Trinity in a way only Nicolas could.

"Do you know when the teachings of trinity entered Christianity?" Nicolas said in a nonconfrontational way. "It was at the end of the fourth century that this teaching took root in the form we know it today. That's right, friends, the first-century Christians did not believe in a trinity." Nicolas went on to quote both the *New Catholic Encyclopedia* and the *New Encyclopedia Britannica* to prove his point. Then he referred to his King James Bible.

"At Matthew 26 Jesus said, 'O my Father, if it be possible, let this cup pass from me: nevertheless not as I will, but as thou wilt.'

"At John 14, Jesus also said, 'Ye have heard how I said unto you, I go away, and come again unto you. If ye loved me, ye would rejoice, because I said, I go unto the Father: for my Father is greater than I.'

"What about First Corinthians 11, 'But I would have you know, that the head of every man is Christ; and the head of the woman is the man; and the head of Christ is God.' Does this sound to you like God and Christ are the same and equal? It sure does not to me."

The young and arrogant Brody had had enough. "You're nothing but a false Christian, a fraud," he called out. "You work for the Devil and everyone listening to you will join you in hell."

Nicolas smiled back. "I'm always looking for ways to save souls. If you can save mine, I welcome you to do so by calling out your scripture as evidence that I'm wrong. If you can do this, I'll admit my erroneous ways. So please, my friend, produce your evidence."

With only three words, "produce your evidence," Brody was defeated. Everyone stared at him, some anticipating a defense since he gave the impression that he knew something. Others smiled, enjoying how easily Nicolas could cut him down.

"I don't have any at the moment," Brody said, hearing a few giggles from the crowd. "But if you give me a chance, I'd like to meet you somewhere and hand them to you—the evidence, that is."

"It would be a privilege to meet with you at your convenience," Nicolas had replied before directing his next words to the audience. "And by the way, since you brought up going to hell, I'd like to extend to all of you an invitation to my sermon this coming Sunday, which happens to be on that very subject. The theme is 'Hell Freezes Over.'"

After Nicolas was done, he approached Brody. "I admire a man who comes to God's defense. You're indeed an exceptional young man. I think God might have plans for you. Why don't you come and visit my church on Sunday? You might like what you hear."

Brody had arrived ten minutes into the sermon. An attendant encouraged him to find a seat up at the front, but he declined. He wanted a quick way out, just in case, so he chose a seat at the back. He could see this was no ordinary church. There were no stained glass windows, no cross with Jesus nailed to it over the podium, no religious icons of any kind. Nicolas was wearing a three-piece suit with a blue necktie instead of a robe or some other gaudy costume. Brody was somewhat disappointed at the appearance of the place. He wasn't sure why he felt that way.

On a platform in front of the podium, Nicolas stood before a table on which sat a sand-colored puppy leashed to one of the table's legs. To his right were a fire extinguisher, a small fuel container, and a blowtorch. "Now, I would like to demonstrate what hellfire means to us," Nicolas said as he lifted the fuel container and squirted the puppy just enough to wet it, not soakA little girl sitting not far from Brody looked at her mother with fear in her eyes. "He won't hurt the puppy, right, Mommy?"

"No, of course not, sweetie; he's just trying to make a point."

Brody hoped she was right.

"You don't know this," Nicolas said, "but this puppy disobeyed my in-structions not to pee on the living room rug. So, because he disobeyed me, I will punish this puppy by burning him for five minutes. If I see he will die, I will save him with the fire extinguisher. What I want you to do while I set this puppy on fire is to think how loving I am in my method of punishment. Remember, this puppy was disobedient."

"Mommy, make him stop," the little girl pleaded. "Please, make him stop." She buried her face in her mother's bosom.

Nicolas lifted the torch, lit it with a match, then slowly approached the puppy.

"Oh my God," someone cried out. One father grabbed his two-year-old son and rushed toward the back. Throughout the church, mothers and their children cried.

"In the name of mercy, Nicolas, don't do it," an elderly woman shouted.

Three men stood up, fists clenched, ready to come to the defense of the helpless puppy.

Nicolas turned off the torch. He walked back to the podium and said nothing for a good five minutes, which was how long it took for everyone to calm down and the weeping to stop.

"I know this demonstration is a bit extreme, and I hope your children understand I would never hurt one of God's creatures. But think of this for one more minute. How did you feel about my suggestion to burn a puppy as a form of punishment, even if it would be for only five minutes?"

He opened his Bible. "Beloved, let us love one another: for love is of God; and every one that loveth is born of God, and knoweth God. He that loveth not knoweth not God; for God is love. In this was manifested the love of God toward us, because that God sent his only begotten Son into the world, that we might live through him. Herein is love, not that we loved God, but that he loved us, and sent his Son to be the propitiation for our sins.'"

Nicolas looked out over the congregation. "Answer me this question if you can, my brothers and sisters: if God is love and we're encouraged to have God's love, and none of you wanted me to hurt this puppy because you have God's love, then tell me, how can the God of love burn a human—even a sinner, which we all are—in an eternal hellfire as punishment? Is this what God's love means to you? That's why this teaching is not found in the Bible. It has been a means to control the population for centuries, not a representation of a loving God."

Brody was sold. He reasoned that Nicolas trusted only what he read from the Bible. If the teaching could not be supported with scriptures, then it should be rejected.

"Hey, hey mister, are you okay?"

Brody opened his eyes. In front of him was a soldier on horseback. Brody stood, dusted himself off, and took a good look at him. He seemed concerned about something and he wasn't alone; there were at least twenty other riders with him.

"I see you're a traveler," the soldier said. "Where, may I ask, are you heading?"

"My destination is a city called Hīt."

"Hīt." The soldier looked in the direction of the city. "You mean the small city just northwest of Babylon?"

"That's right."

"Well, this is your lucky day," the soldier told him. "It so happens we're heading that way. Do you wish to join us?"

Brody squinted up at him. "Why would I want to do that?"

"I'm sure you're aware of what's going to happen soon all over Persia. We're looking for people to join us in the fight against the Amalekites."

"I'm no warrior, I'm just a scribe. I'm afraid I would only slow you down."

"Too bad." The soldier seemed genuinely disappointed. "Well, keep safe; it's going to be dangerous outdoors when the fighting begins."

"I'll be careful."

The officer in charge gave the signal to move on, but the soldier remained in front of Brody. "Where do you come from? I can't figure out your nationality."

Brody hesitated. "Why do you ask?"

The young man looked Brody over. "It's your pouch over there. Its design looks like it came from my homeland—"

A log on Brody's campfire cracked like a gunshot and flames flared up. The soldier's horse reared and tossed its head. Brody stepped back and watched as the rider regained control of his horse. He bent forward to stroke its neck, saying in a soft, soothing voice, "It's all right, big boy, it's okay. I'm here. That's a good boy."

"Come on, let's go," one of the mounted men called from a short distance away. "We still have a long way to go before we camp."

"All right, all right, I'm coming," the man shouted back. He looked Brody over one more time, then looked at his fellows, then at Brody again. Without another word, he wheeled his horse and raced to join the others, who were already nearly out of sight.

"That was weird," Brody concluded as he sat back down. He wondered why the young man had been so interested in his bag. "Did he know what was inside?" Brody wondered aloud, contemplating the bag. *Maybe it's a sign. Maybe bringing these things back with me is contrary to God's will. Nicolas paid with his life, but God's giving me a chance to get rid of these relics. Maybe God will kill me as well if I bring these things back.* Without further thought, he tossed the bag into the fire. A heavy load seemed to lift off his shoulders, now that he'd stopped playing the role of savior of the world.

"God doesn't want people to worship because of evidence, he wants faith. Wasn't that the last sermon Nicolas gave? Faith, not evidence will bring us to God—wait a minute."

Brody jumped to his feet and ran forward to peer in the direction of the riders, but he saw nothing in the fading light. He looked at his own horse, wondering if he could catch up with them. No, it was folly. He relaxed his shoulders and dropped his head, focusing on the empty cup still in his hand. "Nah, it's not possible; must be the alcohol." He looked back toward the riders. "I could have sworn that young man spoke to his horse in English."

CHAPTER 39

As they walked toward Carkas's house, Anna read once more the invitation to meet with King Xerxes. Although she was happy for the opportunity, she'd revealed that she was suspicious of the timing. Carkas had made it very clear when Michael and Artemisia first met with him that no meeting could happen before the upcoming conflict between the Jews and the Amalekites.

"I need to tell you something, Anna," Thomas said. "I should have said something a long time ago, but I failed to muster enough courage. Time is running out, so here it goes."

Anna put the invitation back into her pouch.

"You know I love you, right?"

"Yes, Thomas, I know."

"Well, this is the situation. We have less than two weeks to rendezvous with the *Kismet* and we still haven't found Christian." Thomas swallowed hard. "I don't know how I could go back home without him. After all, he's the reason why I'm here. I can't just abandon him. I could never live with myself if I—"

Anna stepped in front of Thomas to get his full attention. "Stop talking," she said, sporting an encouraging smile. "I already knew this could happen. Don't say another word. If you stay, I stay."

"But—"

"My mind was made up a long time ago, Thomas. You see, I love you too, and I can't bear the thought of living without you. Nor can I see you unhappy, so let's not talk about this anymore. Besides, we might still find him. If not, I'm more than willing to make my home here if it is with you."

As Anna said these words, Aldon moved from the back of the group to catch up with Artemisia. "Don't you think it would be better if just you and I met with Carkas? Would that not speed things up?"

"No, Aldon, I'm sure he is expecting all of us."

"But it's almost lunch. If we all go in, won't it be an inconvenience for him?"

"Are you deaf?" Michael yelled. "She said we're all going in so why don't you back off, man."

"It's okay, Michael, he wants things to go well, that's all. Is that not right, Aldon?"

"Yes, of course." Aldon looked at Michael. "I hope they get you first," he mumbled.

"You said something?" Michael asked.

"Nothing, just talking to myself."

"That's odd," Artemisia said. "There are no guards watching over Carkas's house. Come on, let's see what's happening."

They gathered in front of the door, and Artemisia knocked. The unlocked door slid open a few centimeters. Thomas pushed his way forward to peer inside. "Carkas, it's Thomas and the rest of us." No one answered. "Artemisia is with me. May we come in?" Still no reply. He pushed the door wide open. "We're coming in, okay?"

Once they were inside, Aldon shut the door. "What do we do?" Anna asked.

"Let's wait here till the guards come back. Maybe they're inside with Carkas," Michael suggested.

"Wait!" Aldon cried out. "We need to get out of here—it's a trap."

They all turned to look at him. He looked miserable. "What are you talking about?" Thomas demanded.

"No time to explain; we need to go—now."

Michael marched in Aldon's direction. "What have you done, Aldon? What's going on?"

"I'll explain later." Aldon reached for the door, but it was too late. He stumbled back as the latch was ripped from his hand.

The door slammed open. Five men marched in, their faces and heads concealed by swaths of cloth, their swords drawn. Silently, swiftly, they spread out, forming a human barrier that blocked both of the room's doorways. Trapped, all Thomas and the others could do was back up against a solid marble wall.

Another masked man walked in. "You can go," he said to Aldon. Aldon glanced at Thomas before ducking past the man and running through the door.

The man in charge positioned himself between his men and Artemisia.

"Now look at what we have here. If it's not the war hero Artemisia, still trying to marry the king—or have your exploits at Salamis been forgotten already?"

"Sadhanah, is that you hiding behind a mask?" Artemisia sneered. Sadhanah said nothing. "No mask can disguise your hoarse voice, Sadhanah, not to mention your stench. Look at you: once a mighty commander in Xerxes's navy, now a common criminal hiding behind a mask."

"Enough!" Sadhanah barked. "The reason I'm here and you're there is because you killed your own countrymen to save your skin. That, Artemisia, is the worst kind of dishonor. I don't know how you live with yourself."

"What do you want from us?" Artemisia demanded.

Sadhanah removed his mask. "Give me Xerxes's tribute, and maybe we won't kill you."

Michael looked at the others before shrugging his pack off his shoulder. "Here, take it all." He threw the pack containing the jewels at Sadhanah's feet.

"Just one more thing," Sadhanah said as he picked up the pack, "Persian law says traitors must die, and that's what you are, Artemisia, a traitor. The rest of you can go."

Michael lunged toward Sadhanah but Thomas and Anna held him back.

"Michael, no!" Artemisia cried. "He's right. I must pay for what I did."

"No. Not here, not this way," Michael argued. "Does your law not require a trial?"

"Shut up," Sadhanah roared. "Your opinions don't matter here. If you don't want to die with her, you'd better do as I say."

As he said those words, one masked assassin sluggishly tilted forward, an arrow protruding from under his chin. Blood pumped out of his throat, one squirt with every heartbeat. He looked at Sadhanah, then fell to the cold, hard floor.

The assassins turned to face the threat. Two arrows in quick succession took out two more men.

Thomas took advantage of the distraction to grab a marble statuette from its pillar and swing it at the man in front of him. He heard and felt the man's skull crack upon impact.

Simultaneously, Anna snatched a ceremonial sword from the wall and swung it downward at the man in front of her. He blocked the blow, snapping the sword that had never been meant for combat in two. Tossing the pieces of the weapon aside, she retreated until her back was against the wall. The assassin lunged forward to pierce Anna but missed his mark. His lifeless body fell onto her, an arrow embedded in his spine.

Unarmed, Artemisia stood motionless. Still facing her was Sadhanah. As he thrust his sword toward Artemisia's heart, Michael threw his body against hers, knocking Artemisia out of the way. The sword missed her heart but penetrated her right shoulder. Together Michael and Artemisia hit the marble floor with an impact that rendered her unconscious.

Michael was on the floor looking up at Sadhanah, who loomed over Artemisia, his sword lifted high for a death blow. Michael rolled toward him and in one motion sliced Sadhanah's left calf with the dagger Artemisia had given him. Sadhanah screamed in pain. "You bastard rat," Sadhanah growled, turning to Michael, who waved his dagger back and forth. With one sweep of his sword, Sadhanah knocked it out of his hand.

Positioning his sword high behind his shoulder, Sadhanah prepared to slice off Michael's head. Michael covered his face with his arms. Several seconds passed before he heard a voice.

"It's okay, Michael. It's over." He opened his eyes and saw Thomas standing over Sadhanah's motionless body. In Thomas' hand was a bloody marble statuette.

The fight had lasted but ten seconds, though it had felt like an eternity. With the threat gone, Thomas started trembling. He still held the bloodied statuette high, the blood flowing from it down his wrist to his elbow in a warm rivulet. He let the statuette drop and crouched into a ball to avoid throwing up.

The others turned toward the door. Thomas turned around to look too. For the first time, they saw their hero: Pigres.

"Do not stare at me," Pigres said impatiently. "Take care of the wounded."

Thomas smiled. "Boy, am I glad to see you."

"How did you know to come?" Anna asked.

"I was heading to Memucan's when I spotted Aldon running toward me. He told me where you were and what was happening. So I came as fast as I could. You're fortunate Aldon was nearby."

"We'll talk about that later," Thomas said grimly.

Michael knelt beside Artemisia, who had regained consciousness. "Anna, give me a hand," he called.

"How badly is she hurt?" Anna asked, kneeling on the other side of Artemisia.

"It is only a shoulder wound," Artemisia said. "Some bandages are all I need."

Anna removed her scarf. "Here, let me take care of you."

Pigres moved closer to check on his sister. "I've seen worse," he said with a knowing smirk at Artemisia.

Artemisia smiled. "We could have handled it without you, you know."

"I wasn't going to let you have all the fun."

"Ouch," she said as Anna tugged the knot she'd made in her scarf tight.

"Sorry." Anna loosened the makeshift bandage. "This should stop the bleeding till we get proper supplies."

Artemisia had not noticed Anna's shaking hands until now. "You did a good job, Anna. Thank you."

"That's right," Pigres interjected. "You all did a good job, but the danger is not over. Michael, stay here with the women and make sure no one comes in through the entrance." Pigres gave Michael his bow and arrows. "Thomas, come with me. We need to see if there are others in the house."

Thomas took a sword from a dead assassin and followed Pigres.

They investigated every room of the three-story house, including a small cold room in the basement. Satisfied the house was empty, they retraced their steps, intent on returning to the others.

In the living area adjacent to the lobby, Thomas halted abruptly. "Look," Thomas whispered, pointing to the window. "Feet under the curtain."

Pigres signaled Thomas to sneak up to the curtain as he readied his sword. With a nod, Thomas crept forward and wrenched the curtain aside, revealing Carkas nailed to the wall, his throat slashed.

"My God," Thomas said. "They killed him."

"Yes, and they tortured him as well. Look here." Pigres pointed to burn marks all over the dead man's legs and arms.

"I wonder what they wanted from him."

Pigres shrugged and shook his head. "We'll never know. Maybe they tried to make him cooperate in getting the king's tribute."

"Should we take him down?"

"Yes, let's rest him here on the couch."

They removed the body from the wall as gently as possible and laid it out on the couch, folding the cold hands across the man's torso. Then they joined the others.

As they entered the foyer, Michael, Anna, and Artemisia were getting organized to leave. "The house is empty," Pigres said. "Except for Carkas."

"Is he all right?" Artemisia asked.

"No, I'm afraid he's dead."

"I thought so." She showed no emotion. "So what do we do now?"

"We hide the bodies in the cold room," Pigres replied. "If we leave them here they'll be discovered, and we can't afford to have the king's guards after us so close to Adar 13."

Thomas nodded. "We still need to find Christian and get back to the drop site."

"Oh yes, I almost forgot," Pigres said. "I came to Susa to personally tell you I found your son."

Thomas gaped at him in disbelief. "What did you say?"

"Your son, I know where he is."

"Well, where is he?" Thomas blurted. "Can I see him?"

"Yes—I mean, soon. He's with a group of mounted men. Your son is an honorable young man. He took up the fight against the Amalekites. I'm told he's been training in Israel, preparing himself for the upcoming conflict."

"When can I see him? We don't have much time."

"You can't see him for a while, Thomas. He took a position somewhere up north. I'm told that after the battle he will come to you at the air ship."

With no choice but to accept that, Thomas sighed. "How did you find him?"

"One of my scouts met up with him about twenty days ago. He tells me he's in good shape."

"So he knows I'm here, then."

"Yes, though my scout did say he looked surprised. Your son promised his support to his friends in return for their saving his life. He won't back away from his word."

"Well, what's the delay? Let's get back to Hīt," heading toward the door, all thoughts of hiding the assassins' bodies forgotten.

"Thomas, please wait. Before you head back, we need your help. We need all your help," Pigres said, eyes sweeping the group. "There's a small village of about one thousand inhabitants two days' ride from here. They have no defense against the Amalekites. They could use someone like you to help them prepare for a possible attack."

"How can we do that?" Thomas asked.

"You can use your skills and experience." When Pigres noticed Thomas's hesitation, he turned to Michael. "Did you not say to my sister that you're both professional security experts who successfully defended against pirate invasions?"

Michael looked at Thomas and shrugged.

"What Michael meant was, we're responsible for the defense," Thomas said. "We never actually physically fought the pirates."

"I know," Pigres said. "Witnessing your fighting skills today made that clear to me. I don't mean to be disrespectful, but you are not very good at combat. But that does not matter; I don't expect you to fight. All I want you to do is help the people of Zarmandokht fight for themselves as an organized unit. Your son and his group were assigned to help them, but then I remembered what Michael told Artemisia about your valuable skills, so I decided to send you there in his stead."

"I don't know if we're the best qualified for this responsibility," Thomas said. "Don't you have an experienced commander you could use?"

"The probability that a fight will take place in this village is low. I don't even think there are any Jews there. But the village was once a profitable exchange post between the eastern countries and Persia. When the inhabitants reclaimed the village they turned it into a trade center and in the process made many enemies. We are concerned some might use the coming conflict as an excuse to attack the village to turn it back into an exchange post. If they do, they will be few in numbers. So all we need from you is to get the villagers organized in case of an attack. Afterward, I will have a guide bring you back to Hīt at the speed of our most skilled couriers. You will meet your son there."

"We can do this," Anna said. "Think of everything they did for us. We owe them."

"You do not owe us anything," Pigres said. "Do not feel obligated."

"No, Anna's right," Thomas said. "It would be a privilege to help."

"Count me in as well," Michael said. "Tell us what to do."

Artemisia reached for Michael's hand. "I'm coming with you—that is, if it's all right with you, my brother."

"Thank you," Pigres said. "I will send a message to have your son and his companions join you at Zarmandokht if they can be spared, but I would not count on it. Our defenses are thin in the north."

He looked around the room. "For now we must take care of these bodies. Then we can get your materials from Memucan's house and head for Zarmandokht. We will camp about one hour east on the Khorasan highway, just off the Royal Road. That's where I will leave you. The next morning you'll head to the mountains. You should arrive at Zarmandokht before nightfall. They expect someone to lead them, so tell them I sent you. They will look after all your needs."

"What about the traitor, Aldon?" Michael asked. "What do we do about him?"

"I doubt we'll see him again," Thomas said. "He knows what will happen if he ever tries to contact us."

CHAPTER 40

Thomas felt like he was on one of the many camping trips he'd made with Christian as a young boy. Before nightfall he would arrange the chopped wood in a heap with lots of newspaper and add a little lighter fuel for the evening fire. Christian's job was to find two long, green branches for marshmallows. Thomas had never mastered the art of making a campfire, so by the time the flames were blazing it was already dark. Amélie would join them until she was overwhelmed by the persistent army of mosquitoes. Then Thomas and Christian would sit in front of the fire, Christian eating toasted marshmallows while Thomas enjoyed his fine scotch.

Tonight, warm beer purchased from a passing Egyptian caravan was his drink, and Christian was preparing for battle somewhere in northern Persia.

"Look at my hands," Thomas said, holding his hands palms down over the campfire. "They're still shaking from this morning's fight."

Anna moved closer to have a look. "It's okay, Thomas. It's over now."

"I know, but it's not that. It's just, well . . . I can't believe I've killed another man. I never would have agreed to come if—"

"If you knew you would end up saving my life," Michael interrupted from behind them. "Not just my life; Artemisia's life, as well."

Anna reached over to hand Michael a beer. "Is Artemisia not joining us?"

"No, her shoulder is swollen and she is in pain. The ride from Susa didn't help."

"I'll go see if she needs any assistance."

"No need; Pigres gave her some kind of medication before he left for who knows where. All she needs is rest. Let her sleep. She'll be fine in the morning." Michael noticed Thomas's hand. "Why don't you get rid of your telecom ring? It's ruined."

Thomas took a closer look and tried to reposition it. "It's the stone, it turned ninety degrees. Look—it's not broken, it's made so you can change the stone's position."

Anna and Michael looked at their own rings and tried to move the stones. "You're right," Michael said.

"Me too," Anna confirmed. "What do you think it's for?"

"I think it's an on and off switch or something like that. Here, let me reposition mine in the opposite direction and see what happens." Thomas then held the ring a few centimeters from his mouth. "Hello?" He looked at the others. "Hello, is anybody listening?"

"Hello?" a voice replied.

"Hi! Hi, can you hear me?"

"Is that you, Thomas?"

"Oh my God, Derrek! Yes, it's me."

"Thomas, don't move, just stay where you are."

"Where's he going?" Anna asked. Thomas shrugged.

"Thomas, its Quincy Daramy. How did you figure out to change the frequency?"

"Change the frequency?"

"Hi Thomas, it's me again—Derrek. Sorry about Quincy. How's everybody doing?"

"Most of us are doing fine, Derrek."

"That's good. Listen Thomas, who's there with you? I mean right now?"

"Michael and Anna."

"Is Aldon with you?"

Thomas took a deep breath. "No. Why?"

"You need to stay away from him. We don't know what his motivation is, but he's doing everything to stop you from completing the mission."

"Man, I knew it," Michael spat. "He's been fighting against us ever since we arrived in Hīt."

"We noticed something was wrong with him," Thomas added. "We thought he was anxious about the mission—you know, not being trained for it and all."

"Oh, he's ready for it, all right," Derrek said. "We suspect Aldon and Yetta planned this from the start. It would seem they've been working together since we arrived. Yetta must have been on the ship when we left the twenty-first century. We know this because after Kelile's death, Aldon became lazy with his concealed video jewelry, and at times he forgot to turn it off. Perhaps Kelile's death affected his judgment. As a result we witnessed some troubling things."

"Wait a minute, did you say Yetta?"

"Yes Thomas, Yetta. We don't know how she made the trip, but it's definitely Yetta."

"You must be mistaken. How could that be possible?"

"We're not sure. Maybe it has something to do with that missing pod," Derrek replied. "Remember the missing pod?"

Thomas looked at Anna. "Yes, I remember. But Derrek, are you sure it was Yetta? I mean, how can you be sure?"

There was a long moment of silence.

"Hi Thomas, its Quincy again."

"What's going on, Quincy?"

"Do you remember when you and Kelile rescued Aldon from those thieves?"

"Of course I remember."

"Well, we saw what Kelile saw through the video feed received from his concealed camera. When he entered the tent, Kelile let his guard down because of what he was looking at. Sitting next to Aldon was his wife Yetta."

"Are you saying Aldon killed Kelile?"

"Not directly, but the shock of seeing Yetta disarmed him. That's when he was stabbed through the back by one of the thieves. Aldon might as well have killed him."

Thomas looked at the others. They should feel overwhelming anger or crushing sadness at the news, but he felt nothing. Michael and Anna's expressions were blank. An empty detachment prevailed in all of them.

"Michael," Artemisia called from her tent, "can you come for a minute?"

"I'll be right there," Michael shouted back.

"Listen Quincy, we should avoid talking for now," Thomas said. "We'll be in Zarmandokht for the next five or six days. I'll contact you when we arrive."

"That doesn't give you much time to reach the drop site," Quincy said.

"I know, but we have a plan. We'll be there, I promise."

"Well, don't be late. We still need you to crack the Komodo password."

Thomas smiled at Quincy's comment. "Of course, I forgot. Don't worry about the password anymore. It's no longer a problem."

"You cracked it?"

"Not exactly," Thomas explained about Christian, Komodo, and the ULRA's first mission.

"We knew something was wrong when we discovered the frequency on your telecom rings was being jammed."

"Quincy, don't tell anyone we can talk. There's a good chance someone is working with Aldon from your end. Let's keep this to ourselves."

"Will do," Quincy replied.

"Have the others switch the frequency on their rings as well."

"Yes Derrek, we did," Michael said. "Can you hear me?"

"How about me?" Anna asked.

Quincy failed to respond. "It would appear only my ring is working," Thomas concluded.

"We have to go," Quincy whispered. "Someone is coming."

"Fine, we'll contact you after we arrive in Zarmandokht."

CHAPTER 41

They arrived at the small, isolated village of Zarmandokht late in the afternoon, after following a high plateau for most of the day. There was a break in the plateau before it continued east, and the small community had sprung up in the gap. Two massive wooden gates ten meters high and six meters wide protected its inhabitants from any outside threat. The village was a natural fortress, impregnable to anything but a professional army. In the hands of skilled soldiers, battering rams would make toothpicks of the gates.

"It's strange there are no guards to check us at the entrance," Anna said with some concern. "Everywhere we've been, the security borders on paranoia."

"There's no need for guards," Artemisia said. "They close the gates and no one can get in."

Thomas looked up at the soaring walls and was reminded where he'd heard the name Zarmandokht before. "Professor Barnaby Lancaster! He called it the horseshoe. This is where he found the Persian stela with my name on it." He looked around, half expecting to see someone sculpting a stela. "I wonder if it's here now."

"I don't think so, Thomas. Christian would have had to make it long after he realized he was not returning home."

"You see, Anna, that's what I don't understand," Thomas said. "If we rescue Christian and bring him back with us, does that mean he never makes the stela? Yet it had to be made for me to be here."

"Oh man, not that again," Michael said with exasperation. "Here's a better question. How do we find our contact?"

"I'm sure they'll find us," Thomas said.

Just then a boy no older than twelve approached Michael. "Greetings," he said with a cheerful smile. "Are you Thomas the security wizard?"

Michael raised his eyebrows. "No, I'm not. The wizard you're looking for is over there." He nodded toward Thomas.

The boy turned to face Thomas, then fell to one knee. "Good day, Hazarapatis. We have been expecting you."

"Please get up, young man. Can you take us to your village elders?"

"Yes, I sure can. Please follow me."

They followed the boy across a large square with workshops all along its edges. There were stalls for carpenters, leatherworkers, sculptors, blacksmiths, jewelers, tentmakers, and other trades and craftsmen. In the center there were more stalls for carriages and their horses. On the eastern side of the square, a wooden staircase held together with thick rope zigzagged to the top of the wall. It was the only way up to the flat, empty expanse of the plateau.

"Those stairs are very narrow," Thomas remarked.

"It will take you to the top," the boy said with excitement. "Do you want me to take you?"

Thomas laughed. "Maybe some other time."

"You're sure? Because I can take you up there, you know. From the top you can see forever in all directions. No one ever goes up there anymore. There is little vegetation, mostly just sand and rocks. Not good for much. But I like to go up at night and study the stars. One day I will become a Zoroastrian magi."

"Maybe you should take us to your elders," Thomas insisted.

"Okay; it's this way."

He led them to an opening at the rear of the square. It was five meters high and stretched the complete length of the rear wall.

"Your elders are inside this cave?"

"Yes. It's very comfortable. It's cool both night and day, and there's plenty of room for everyone to have a private room."

"You're saying the entire village lives inside this cave?"

The boy looked surprised at the question. "Of course. Why?"

"How many are there?"

"I don't know." The boy stopped to think for a moment. "About five or six hundred, I guess."

"And they all fit in this cave?"

"Yes. Come and I will show you."

Their eyes had to adjust before they could see the enormous maze of wooden structures filling every centimeter of the massive cave. *Only the ancient Persians could have put this together,* Thomas thought.

"Over here," yelled the boy, already standing at the entrance of one dwelling. "Here is the home of Paeshatah."

The boy entered. A few seconds later Paeshatah came out to greet them. "Welcome, welcome my friends. Please do come in."

They entered the home and found themselves in a two-room dwelling with chairs and tables placed on a collection of beautiful colored carpets scattered on the floor, covering it completely. Strategically placed candles illuminated the room with a soothing glow. As they removed their footwear, two young girls with basins of water and towels hurried to clean their feet. Artemisia was the only one at ease with the ritual.

"Please make yourselves comfortable," Paeshatah said. "My home is your home."

As they sat down, a servant laid out pitchers of wine, juice, and water on a small table. They all took something to drink and thanked their host for his hospitality.

"We are grateful you agreed to come and help us defend our village," Paeshatah said. "We would be lost without you."

"We'll try our best to help you get your army organized for the defense," Thomas said.

Paeshatah laughed. "Pigres did say you have a sense of humor. I made arrangements for the four of you to stay here in my home. Your army will camp outside the village."

Thomas looked at the others. "Our army?"

"Yes, your army." Paeshatah looked at them, eyebrows raised. "Certainly you did not think we have room for them in here." He hesitated. "You did bring your army with you?"

"No. We were under the impression that you had an army and we were to help them with strategies to repel your enemy."

Paeshatah stood up and walked in circles for a while, head bowed in thought. Finally, he looked up. "I guess we're in deep trouble, aren't we?"

Artemisia calmly stepped in. "Do you have men capable of fighting? Perhaps some who have experience in Xerxes's army, or even the navy?"

"We might have a dozen or so, but not much more. We are tradesmen, not soldiers. Most of our population are women and children."

"Let's take a moment here and think about this," Artemisia reasoned. "I have battle experience. I know for a fact we are in a good position of defense, with these high walls surrounding your village. We have two experts in defensive strategy with many years of experience, I might add." Thomas and

Michael looked at each other. "So all we need is a few hundred men and we are in a good position."

Paeshatah looked at Thomas for confirmation.

"Yes, that's right," Thomas said. "We will need a census of the population for our planning. With this information, along with knowledge of the terrain, we can do this."

"I can get this information for you," Paeshatah confirmed.

"Good." Thomas stood and the rest followed. "We'd like to thank you for offering us a place to stay in your home, but I think we'll better serve you if we stayed in tents on top of the plateau. From that vantage point we can see the terrain below, both inside and out. Can you provide us with the proper camping materials?"

Paeshatah smiled. "We have the best tentmakers in the empire. What is it exactly you need?"

"We will need one tent large enough to hold meetings for ten people at a time, and some smaller tents for sleeping. It would also be nice if we can have a runner to communicate with you and the others."

"I will have all of this before nightfall."

After polite goodbyes, they left and made their way up the narrow stairs to the top of the plateau. There they looked north, at the never-ending desert that covered the plateau. Looking over the southern edge, they saw the road they'd traveled on earlier.

"Wow," Anna said, looking out to the horizon. "You sure can see a long way from here."

Thomas stepped closer to Anna. "This is good. We can see them coming, giving us time to react."

"If they come at all," Michael said.

"Oh, they will come," Artemisia said. "My brother is a smart man. He would not have sent us here if he was not sure of a battle. Otherwise, he would have sent us somewhere else."

"But he said it's a precautionary measure."

"You're right, there is a small chance they will not come." Artemisia paused. "No, they will come. So while you start preparing a defensive strategy, I will head down and see what materials are available. We will need weapons, and maybe Paeshatah has the information you asked for."

"I'll come with you," Michael insisted.

Anna walked up to Thomas as they left. "What are we going to do?"

"I'll be damned if I know."

Over the next two hours the tents were put in place with the table, chairs, and everything else Paeshatah had promised. Thomas admired their unexpected enthusiasm as he observed the work. He expected these people to be resourceful, being tradesmen and -women, but they showed no fear, only zeal to do whatever they could to defend their home.

•••••••••●○○○○○○○○○○○

"So, how does it look?" Artemisia asked eagerly as she joined them. "Is the strategy all worked out yet?"

Thomas turned to her. "Good, you're back. I was waiting for your report before making any definite plans. What do you have for me?"

"Paeshatah said there are 275 able-bodied men who can fight, and 330 women, 250 of whom can participate in the field; the rest, about 250, are elderly and children. I think this is good, don't you agree?"

"Yes," Thomas said. "It's much better than I expected. What about weapons? Is there anything we can use?"

"There are no weapons, but plenty of quality wood," Artemisia replied. "There is a large quantity of leather and different types of metals. I'm sure we can create the spears, swords, bows, and arrows we will need in the next three days. We can also make shields with the wood and leather."

"Can you take care of having the weapons made?" Thomas asked.

"Yes, I can do that," Artemisia said. "There is also plenty of food and a natural well inside the cave, so food and water won't be a problem. They even have large barrels of honey, right next to two hundred barrels of processed bitumen."

Thomas walked to the edge of the plateau and looked down at the village. He saw the barrels of honey. Then he walked to the other edge, looking at both the land outside the village and the village itself, within the gates.

"What is it?" Anna asked.

Thomas held up his palm to stop Anna from speaking.

"I've seen this before," Michael whispered to Anna. "That's what he looks like just before coming up with a brilliant idea to stop a cyber-attack."

Thomas walked back and forth along the edge, stopping periodically to challenge his thoughts. After twenty agonizing minutes, he turned to face the others. "I've got it. Quickly, Artemisia, find Paeshatah and have him send me three of his best military minds; also bring me his best runner." Artemisia left to comply with Thomas's instructions.

"You have to tell us what you're thinking, Thomas," Michael said impatiently. "Don't make us wait for the others."

"Come," Thomas said as he walked to the edge. "Look." He pointed to the barrels of honey. "It's the honey that gave me the idea. I don't know how much you know about computer networks, Anna, but the honey is the solution."

Michael looked at Thomas and nodded his understanding. "What a genius you are." He looked at the terrain, trying to put everything together.

"Can someone explain to me what honey and computers have to do with the coming battle?" Anna said in frustration.

Thomas walked over to Anna, leaving Michael with his thoughts. "It's like this: in network security we need to defend against crackers. So what we do, among other things, is set up a DMZ between the internet and the intranet."

"What's a DMZ? It sounds like something from the military."

"Actually, it is. It's a demilitarized zone." He paused, frowning in thought. "How can I explain it to you? We have firewalls with selected communication ports open so the public can access our web servers. But these same open ports would be a security risk if they were added to the firewalls protecting our intranet. That's where our main servers and workstations are located. So we separate the internet from the intranet with a DMZ.

"We also use the DMZ to trap crackers and try to trace them back to their location. The way we trap them is by setting up a false server with holes they can easily exploit. So they think they've penetrated our network, but they don't realize they're in a trap. Do you know what we call these servers?"

Anna looked at Michael, who was still looking down at the village. "Honeys?"

"Close. Honeypots. Much like honey attracts bears, electronic honeypots attract crackers."

"Okay, I understand the technical terminology, but how is this going to help us here?"

"I'm not a hundred percent sure how we'll do it, but if we could lure the enemy into the village, we could close the doors behind them and they will be at our mercy."

"I see . . . they can't get out and we'll be on high ground shooting down at them."

"That's the idea."

"But that would be a slaughter," Anna protested.

"Anna, if they come here, it will be to kill women, elderly people, and children. This has nothing to do with fairness; this is war and war is ugly, no matter how we look at it. I know it sounds cliché, but it's true when they say it's them or us."

Before Anna could respond, Artemisia returned with the information Thomas required. "We'll talk about this later," Thomas said to Anna.

"Here are the military minds you asked for," Artemisia said, using the terminology Thomas had used earlier. "This is Omid and Parshan, brothers who both served in the navy. This is Sheeva. She was in the navy as well, until her father was discharged for a blunder against the Greeks."

Thomas looked at Sheeva. She was so petite, she looked like a schoolgirl. "Don't let her looks deceive you, Thomas," Artemisia said. "She is highly decorated for bravery. She is no longer in Xerxes's navy because she felt her father was unfairly treated, so she resigned in protest."

Thomas smiled and welcomed the three soldiers. "Thank you for volunteering. I need people with your experience for the coming battle. Artemisia, were you able to find a runner?"

Artemisia pointed to a boy standing near the entrance of the large tent. "Come here, boy." The boy ran as fast as he could, demonstrating his speed to Thomas. "You're the boy who greeted us earlier. What's your name?"

"My name is Arsalan, it means lion."

"Is that right, Arsalan. Can you run like a lion?"

"Faster! And one day I will be as strong."

"That's plenty good for me," Thomas said with an encouraging smile. "Welcome to the team."

The boy stood tall. "I will not disappoint you, Hazarapatis."

Thomas put his hand on the boy's shoulder. "I know you won't, Arsalan. Now, let's enter the tent so I can explain our strategy."

The three soldiers, Artemisia, Michael, and Anna gathered around a table with a papyrus sheet on top. Thomas picked up a charcoal stick and hastily drew a map of the village.

"This is the village and here is the entrance to the village." He pointed to the opening of what looked like an omega sign. "Our enemies will be coming from the west and will be positioning themselves in front, facing the entrance doors. There's no other possible position. They cannot climb the plateau; the walls are too steep. they won't come from up here; it's too difficult to get down and capture the village. So this is where they'll make their attack." He tapped the papyrus, indicating the open area facing the entrance to the village.

"So we'll begin our defense in front. We'll dig a small trench, about one handspan deep and one handspan wide. It will begin at the left side of the gate and form a semicircle out from the entrance, ending at the right side of the gate. We will fill the trench with bitumen and cover it with a sand-colored cloth.

"When the enemy is detected, we will deploy one hundred armed men and women in battle formation outside the village but inside the semicircle. Some will have bows and arrows and some will have spears. All must have their best shield to protect them from enemy missiles.

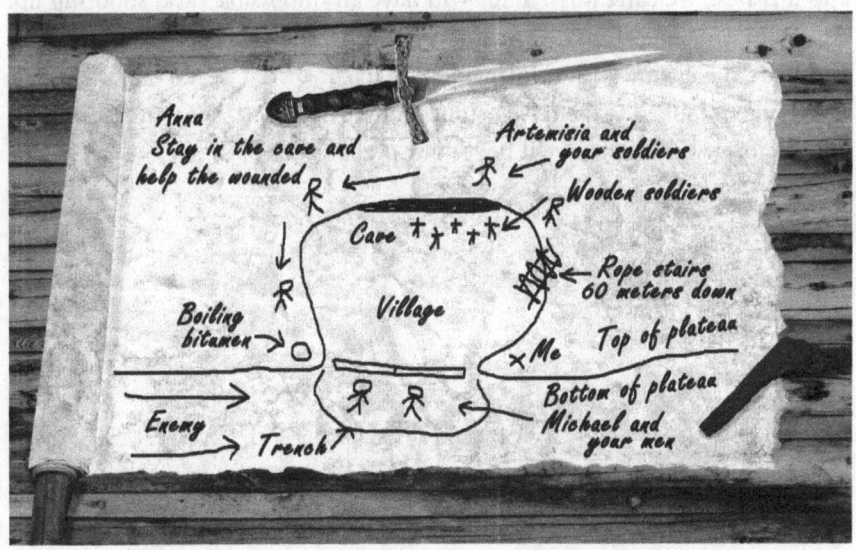

"The enemy will be positioned in front of our soldiers when they begin their attack. It is at this point we will light the bitumen to make a temporary firewall separating them from us. I will give the signal from up here, where I will have a full picture of the field. The fire will not hold them back for long. In fact, when they see the fire they'll probably laugh at our efforts. We want them to think we are weak and disorganized. This is our strategy. This is our honeypot. As soon as the fire engulfs the entire half circle, our soldiers will retreat back into the village and into the cave, leaving twenty of them positioned among wooden soldiers placed at the cave's entrance. This way, when the enemy forces find their way into the village, they will think we are out in the open waiting for them. This should move them to concentrate on the cave's entrance, rather than on our archers positioned up above." Artemisia murmured her approval.

"The battering ram they are sure to bring with them will make a small opening in the gate," Thomas continued. "They don't need a large one to get everyone in. As the enemy enters the square, the twenty soldiers visible at the cave's entrance will move back and forth to simulate activity. Once they have all entered, two things need to happen at once. Our remaining twenty soldiers will retreat and rejoin the others inside the caves. At the same time we will drop boiling bitumen down on the wooden gates and set it on fire. The enemy will be trapped inside the village square. That's when our soldiers positioned on top of the plateau will rain down on the enemy a storm of arrows and missiles. We can't miss. They will have an impossible task, shooting up. And with only one flimsy staircase to reach us, they won't succeed. We will eliminate the enemy with minimal loss to us."

Thomas looked at them. "Any questions? No? Good. We will rest tonight and tomorrow at sunrise we'll begin our preparations."

CHAPTER 42

Adar 13, three o'clock in the morning

Thomas strategized on the events of the coming day all night long. He had hoped a good night's rest would replenish his energy, but that seemed unnecessary now. He was revisiting his plan one more time when he noticed the unmistakable silhouette of a small boy at the entrance of his tent.

"Can't sleep either?" Thomas asked.

"No, Hazarapatis, I'm much too excited. I've never fought in a battle before."

"My name is Thomas, not whatever you said."

The boy giggled. "Hazarapatis? Its means chief of security, commander of one thousand."

"Well, call me Thomas, okay?"

"All right. One of your pickets is waiting to talk with you; should I let him in?"

"No, I'll meet him outside." Thomas got up to dress. "Tell him I'm coming but first, you're not fighting in any battle, is that understood, Arsalan? I need you as my runner."

"Yes Hazarapatis, I know; it's just that I feel like a real soldier. This is the most exciting day of my whole entire life."

"No fighting," Thomas insisted. "Let me hear you say it."

"No fighting."

In a torchlit circle in front of his tent stood a well-dressed man armed with the traditional lance and shield of a Persian soldier. Artemisia wanted the volunteers to look the role to encourage professionalism. "Please come closer," Thomas told the picket. "Do you want something to drink?"

"What I have to say is urgent."

"Yes, of course. What is the message?"

"An army of about eight hundred men is coming. Maybe five hundred infantry and three hundred cavalry—we're not sure yet. They're moving at a slow pace. At this rate, they should arrive at sunrise."

"So this is what Pigres was afraid of. They're here to retake Zarmandokht. Do they look well-equipped?"

"It's hard to tell at night—all we see are silhouettes. But they're not marching like a mob—they seemed well-disciplined. We'll know more as the sun rises."

"Thank you for your report. Go back and keep me informed of their progress at regular intervals," Thomas told him.

"Yes, Commander." The picket turned and left.

Thomas walked beyond the illuminated area. To avoid walking off the edge of the plateau, he stopped after a few meters and allowed his eyes to adjust to the darkness. Following him was Arsalan. Thomas smiled. "Are you frightened, boy?"

"No, Hazarapatis." He sounded hurt that the question was even asked. "I may be just a boy, but I'm no coward. You'll see. I will prove myself today. I will show you what I'm capable of."

Thomas forgot that Persian children were different from the children back home. While modern children played video games, Persian children dreamed of being part of the greatest empire of their time. "That's not what I meant, Arsalan." Thomas crouched down to look him in the eyes. "The people I work with back home are not as brave as you. I can tell you have the courage of a lion." The boy smiled. "Now go wake up the others, all of them. Tell them to meet in the conference tent. Then go tell Paeshatah to get everyone ready for battle. And one more thing, if we are to be friends, you must call me Thomas. Is that okay with you?"

"Yes, Thomas." Arsalan ran off as fast as he could.

With his eyes now adjusted to the darkness, Thomas walked to the edge of the plateau. He prayed to God for the first time since his beloved Amélie died, not for himself, but for the others, for Anna and Michael, for the boy Arsalan.

"So they're really coming?" Michael said as he approached Thomas.

"It would appear so."

"I must admit I never thought when I signed up with the ULRA that I would end up fighting a war."

"Me neither, Michael, me neither."

"This is going to be a short meeting," Thomas assured everyone. "This is the information we have: we will be facing around eight hundred soldiers, of which three hundred are mounted. They should arrive in about four hours.

"Artemisia, prepare your bowmen and women up along the edge of the plateau. Keep them hidden until you see my signal. Michael, go down and wait outside the gate but stay back; make sure everyone knows what to do after I give the signal to retreat. Anna, you take your position inside the cave and wait for Michael, who will let you know when the retreat has begun. This way you can watch out for incoming enemies who might make it all the way to you.

"As for the rest, see to the preparedness of your troops. The success of our defense relies on your ability to move your people efficiently and swiftly. Now if you're ready, to your posts."

••••••••••●○○○○○○○○○○○○

Over the next three hours, the enemy's movements were reported to Thomas. From his position near the top of the gate, he could see both inside and outside the village. As he looked west for the approaching enemy, he was grateful the sun rose in the east. Until noon the sun would be behind him. This would be an advantage to his defense.

Thomas tried to determine the time when he saw two of his cavalrymen approaching. One dismounted and walked to Michael. Thomas watched as Michael sent a runner inside the gate, who gave Arsalan instructions, then retreated into the cave. While he waited for Arsalan, Thomas noticed a dust cloud in the distance, moving fast.

Arsalan ran up to him. "I have a message from Michael," Arsalan said breathlessly. "The cavalry will arrive any time now, well in advance of the infantry."

Thomas could see the horses and their riders. He turned to Arsalan. "Quickly, go to Michael and tell him to keep me up to date with everything as it happens."

The boy ran back down to deliver the message while Thomas found the signalman. "Signal them to get into defensive position. Have them light the torches but wait for my command before igniting the bitumen."

The signalman waved his flag. Thomas looked down and saw Michael looking up at him. In less than a minute the villagers-turned-soldiers positioned themselves for battle.

Thomas watched as the cavalry slowed down to assess the situation. He could see their faces now. These were not a mob of people randomly put together, these were veteran cavalrymen. Their horses' noses and chests were protected with metal mesh. The riders varied in dress and style, but most had bow and arrows, many had long spears, and some had both. Their headgear reminded Thomas of their dual empire, the Medo-Persian world power.

His attention switched to a much larger dust cloud coming from the west. *The infantry.* In less than ten minutes they'd be positioned in front of the gates.

The wait was agonizing. Thomas felt sick to his stomach. Doubts were creeping in as the moment of truth approached. His thoughts flashed back to the moment Pigres had asked for his help. What a mistake that was! Now everyone was relying on him—no, much worse—their lives depended on him.

"Anna, Michael, what have I done?" he groaned. The signalman turned, thinking he was giving an order. Thomas, unable to speak, waved him off. He thought how selfish he was for placing everyone in the dragon's mouth while he stayed up on the plateau, shielded from any danger.

"They're getting ready to attack," the signalman said.

Before Thomas could react, a loud cheer came from below. One of the cavalrymen had positioned himself front and center of the cavalry, his sword held high. A bellowed order sent archers forward through the line of horses to kneel and draw their bows. Michael, seeing what was about to take place, did not wait for Thomas's signal. He gave the order to take position behind their shields. The shower of arrows was so thick it looked like a cloud of smoke. Three defenders fell to the ground, but their shields protected the rest.

Thomas looked to the officer commanding the enemy cavalry in time to see the man's sword sweep down. As the horses surged forward, their riders screaming battle cries, he gave the signal to light the bitumen, then start the retreat. Within seconds the fire was blazing, throwing up a curtain of heat before the charging horsemen. This gave Michael just enough time to get his men back into the village. As expected, the flames did little to deter the enemy. Without hesitation the horsemen moved through the flames unharmed, though the infantry charging in their wake slammed to a stop. Once through, the horsemen lobbed arrows at the retreating villagers but otherwise split ranks and veered off to the sides to watch as Michael and four others closed the village gate. As the line of fire burned down, the enemy infantry again charged forward. Thomas spied the long bulk of a metal-tipped ram being hauled forward just behind the front ranks.

Thomas was satisfied. The plan was working. All he could do now was wait to see how long it would take for them to smash through the gates. He did not wait long. Those hauling the battering ram reached the gate and without missing a beat, began swinging it against the massive barrier. The deep thuds from the repeated impacts reverberated throughout the village.

The gate splintered within five minutes. The opening they created was all the enemy foot soldiers needed to stampede their way into the village.

Michael and some of the others were still racing to the cave as enemy arrows found their mark. Artemisia was supposed to wait for a signal before shooting, but the enemy was moving too quickly toward the cave. She had to slow them down until the rest of the enemy entered the square. She gave the order. All it took was one volley of missiles to slow the momentum.

Thomas watched as the last of the infantry entered the village. "Okay, it's your turn," he said, staring at the cavalry. But they failed to move. He moved to another vantage point to see what was happening inside. Artemisia's archers were keeping the enemies at bay with scattered shots but Thomas knew this would not hold them for long. Once more he turned to look at the cavalry. They had not moved from their original position.

Thomas could wait no more. "Pour the liquid bitumen over the gate," he ordered. The signalman waved his flag.

Before the pouring was complete the bitumen was ignited by four well-placed fire arrows. The thick black smoke reached for the heavens. This was the signal Artemisia was anxiously looking for. Thomas heard the hollow blast of a horn followed by an explosion of battle cries.

Like a breach in a dam, arrows poured down from the plateau heights onto the unsuspecting enemy. Sickening moans rose from the village square. Thomas refused to leave his position facing those still outside the gate. The cavalry heard the cries as well. When they realized what was happening, one man urged his horse toward the plateau to have a closer look at Thomas. There was no disappointment in his eyes. He saluted Thomas, then wheeled his horse and galloped away.

In the canyon below, the brave stood up to the archers atop the plateau. The rest fell where they stood, dead or wounded. Others scrambled for whatever shelter they could find while those who made it deeper into the village raced for the cave entrance. That was when Michael gave the order to attack. The villagers positioned themselves in the shadow of the cave's mouth. From there they hit their mark with every shot.

• • • • • • • • ● ○ ○ ○ ○ ○ ○ ○ ○ ○ ○ •

Anna moved forward to witness the carnage. What she saw was not a battle, but one-sided butchery. Unable to stomach it any longer, she searched for Michael, hoping to convince him to stop the fighting.

Anna found him giving orders to his combatants. "It's over, Michael. Tell them to stop." He ignored her and moved closer to the fighting. Anna followed. "Please Michael, they're not even fighting anymore. Look, they're begging for mercy."

Michael turned to face Anna, his face red, his eyes black. "Get back into the cave, Anna. I know what I'm doing."

Anna took a few steps back. "But—"

"Get her out of here," Michael shouted. Two men responded. They dragged her deep into the cave and threw her on the ground. Not far away, Arsalan witnessed what happened and came to see if she was all right.

"He sent you here as well, I see," Anna said to Arsalan.

"No, he sent me to see if you're all right." Arsalan looked at her. "Are you all right?"

"Yes Arsalan, I'm okay. What about you? Aren't you scared?"

Arsalan tipped his head, curious. "Scared of what?"

"The battle, the killing."

"No, I'm not scared—we're winning. If Hazarapatis allowed it, I would be out there fighting with them."

Anna was stunned by Arsalan's response. "Don't you think it is terrible, killing all those people now that the battle is won?"

Arsalan thought about it for a moment. "No. If we were losing they would not hesitate to kill all of us down to the last man. This is war. This is how it is."

Anna abandoned that conversation. "Do you have something I can write on? I'd like you to give Thomas a message for me."

"Yes, but I have an excellent memory. You can tell me. I won't forget, no matter how long your message is."

"I know, Arsalan, but I need to send this in code."

"I understand; you're afraid I might get caught and tortured. There's no need for code, though. There's nothing they could do to make me talk."

"I know. You're the bravest boy I've ever met. But this message is for Thomas's eyes only. Not even you can know it."

Reluctantly Arsalan gave Anna a pouch containing everything she needed to write her message requesting that the fighting stop.

"Cowards," Thomas said as he watched the cavalry retreat east. He returned his attention to what was happening inside the village. From his vantage point he could see the battle was almost over. The center of the square was littered with the dead and wounded. Michael and his soldiers were now streaming out of the cave to finish their work.

That's when Thomas detected a new, distinctive odor coming from the battlefield. It was an awful, acrid odor, not what he'd imagined the smell of death would be.

"I ordered the cessation of hostilities," Artemisia said as she located Thomas. "If we continue, we risk hitting our own people."

"That's good," Thomas replied. "Are there many casualties—on our side, that is?"

"Very few. I'll get the numbers for you once the fighting is done."

Thomas put his hand over his nose and mouth. "Does a battlefield always smell so bad? I thought the bodies had to decompose before they stink."

"The odor comes from the fire, Thomas. Look." She pointed to the burning gate. Out of desperation, some of the enemy had attempted to escape through the flames. The reality of frantic men at war registered as Thomas stared at the burning corpses. "Thank God it's over," he said.

"Yes, it is almost over." Artemisia looked down at the square. "Michael and his men will finish them off."

Thomas approached the edge to have a better look at what had become the focal point of the battle. To see as much as possible while avoiding falling over, he stood on the landing and held onto the wooden railing around the staircase leading down to the square. A small group of the enemy, no more than thirty, were making a last stand. Some were trying to race up the zigzag staircase while others engaged Michael's men. He spotted Arsalan, trying to push his way up the stairs. Being so much smaller than the others, he wiggled through and ran up the stairs—until a wayward arrow thunked into Arsalan's left thigh.

With a muffled exclamation, Thomas dashed to the top of the staircase to help the boy, only to be restrained by two burly soldiers. Unable to free himself, he stopped struggling and looked into their eyes. "Listen to me. I'm giving you an order to let me go. If you refuse, I'll have you both executed."

The soldiers reluctantly complied. Thomas grabbed one of their swords and stepped onto the first step—then scrambled to grab onto anything within reach as the staircase collapsed from under his feet. His hand found the thick cable that had supported the staircase and grabbed it, stopping his fall. His arm felt like it was being ripped out of its socket, but the cable saved him. Despite the blinding pain, he swung his other hand up and held on. Blood from his palm scraped raw, trickled down to his elbow.

Thomas tried to focus. He looked up, then down. He'd fallen a third of the way down the cliff face. He decided it would be easier to climb down rather than up.

Every movement he made crippled him with increasing pain. He was weakening fast. With ten meters left, he was losing his grip. He was about to let go when he spotted Arsalan lying on his back amongst the rubble. Now fighting to save another, Thomas continued with renewed strength. With no more than a meter to go, he dropped and crashed into the jagged debris beneath him. Unable to find his footing, he pitched forward, his head striking something hard.

When Thomas regained consciousness he found himself on the ground with Michael kneeling over him. "Where's Arsalan?" Thomas asked.

Michael pointed. "Over there."

"Help me up."

Leaning on Michael, Thomas reached Arsalan despite the pain gripping his entire body. He fell to the ground next to the boy.

A fragile-looking old woman sat with Arsalan's head resting on her lap. "How is he?" Thomas asked her.

The old woman turned her attention to a soldier standing next to her. The soldier bowed his head. "He's dead," she said in a calm voice before she set Arsalan's head gently on the ground. "He refused to meet the gods until I promised to give you a message." Thomas focused on the old woman's lips as she told him word for word what the boy had said: "'I'm sorry, Hazarapatis. I failed you. You trusted me with a simple task and I failed. Please forgive me.'"

Thomas hunched forward, dropped his face into his hands, and wept. The old woman put her hand on his neck. "You must be strong, Hazarapatis. I will continue to fight next to you until the battle is won."

Thomas lifted his face to the old woman. "What did you say?"

"I said 'I'm sorry, Hazarapatis. I failed you. You trust—'"

"No, after that, just now—what did you just say to me?"

"That is what I said," she replied, frowning as she tried to understand what Thomas was asking her.

"After that," Thomas said as he looked around at who was watching. "After I began to cry, when you put your hand on me."

"Nothing. I remained silent, seeing your grief."

Thomas became confused. He tried to stand but his legs felt like they were made of lead and his head spun. Determined not to show weakness, he straightened to face the crowd gathered around him. Michael helped him back to his feet.

He was holding onto Michael's shoulder when Paeshatah pushed through the crowd. "Well done," he exclaimed. "What a success the battle was, and it's all thanks to you, Thomas. We're all indebted to you, yes indeed."

"Find me Arsalan's parents," Thomas snapped.

"Whose parents?" Paeshatah asked.

"Arsalan."

"Who is Arsalan?"

Thomas thrust a forefinger toward the small body on the ground. "The boy you sent to greet us when we arrived; my runner."

"Oh yes, that boy. He has no parents. He showed up one day and never left."

"The boy is an orphan, then."

"That's correct."

Thomas walked pass Paeshatah and beyond the crowd to have a look at the battlefield. From the direction of the cave he saw Anna coming toward him. She had to maneuver carefully to avoid stepping on the dead and wounded. Even from this distance Thomas could see the concerned look on her face.

"We should have all of this cleaned up by nightfall," Paeshatah said, catching up to Thomas. "Then we will appropriately thank you and your companions."

"Did I not do everything you expected of me?" Thomas asked.

"Yes, and much more."

"What have I asked in return?"

"Nothing, but rest assured, we will gratefully give you all you ask. Just tell me what you want."

"I want you to build a stone tomb. It must be large enough to lay two adult bodies inside. The tomb must have a marble engraving that reads 'In memory of Arsalan, a lion warrior who fought with a brave heart in defense of Zarmandokht.'"

"But this kind of memorial is reserved for kings and very important men," Paeshatah protested. "Not orphan boys."

"I know," was all Thomas said.

"Okay, if that's what you want, we owe you. Where do you want it built?"

Thomas looked around. He tried to think of where the boy would want to rest, a place Arsalan was proud of. Then he remembered the first time they met. He'd wanted so much to bring Thomas up to the plateau. He pointed. "Up there, on top of the plateau. I want him to rest facing the stars."

Paeshatah agreed.

Anna caught up to Thomas and jumped into his arms. "Thank God you're all right."

"I'm so sorry I've put you through this Anna," Thomas said, hugging her. "I should have kept you with me. I don't know why I sent you down here in the middle of the carnage."

Paeshatah once again stepped in with no regard for who was speaking, "As I told Thomas, by tonight we will have cleared the field and then we can celebrate."

"No," Thomas said. "There's no time to celebrate. Use all your resources to help the wounded and bury the dead outside the village. I don't care if it takes all night. We need to prepare for a second attack tomorrow."

"That's not possible," Paeshatah said. "King Xerxes permitted only one day of battle. A second attack would bring the king's indignation."

"I know for a fact King Xerxes sanctioned one more day for the Jews to finish off the Amalekites."

"How could you possibly know that?" Paeshatah asked.

"Because I'm a damn time traveler, that's how," Thomas blurted. "I know everything about this cursed time period and I'm telling you there is going to be more fighting tomorrow."

Michael stepped between them. "Watch what you're saying, man. We still need their help to get back home."

Thomas pushed Michael aside. "Get the people to build a rope ladder so I can get back up to my post. Afterward have your best carpenters rebuild the stairs."

Paeshatah turned to the others and yelled out, "You heard him, there's another fight tomorrow. Get to work."

•••••••••●○○○○○○○○○○

Thomas and Anna watched as smoke escaped from the gate's ashes. Beyond, men were diligent with the burials. Sunset signaled the end of the most life-altering day Thomas and Anna would ever experience—at least that's what they thought.

"I'll never forget this day," Michael said as he pulled up a chair next to Thomas.

Artemisia arrived soon after. "Your plan worked like a charm. You both lived up to your reputation."

Thomas was in no mood for praise tonight. "Do you have the casualties for the battle?"

"Yes," Artemisia responded. "We lost thirty-eight. Most died as they retreated from outside the village gate. Another thirty-six wounded. I don't have the death toll for the enemy, however. We have nine prisoners." Artemisia moved to face Thomas. "A messenger arrived from Susa. He said King Xerxes extended the fight for one more day. How did you know this was going to happen?"

"As I said, I'm a time traveler."

"I don't understand, what do you mean you're a time traveler?"

Thomas took a deep breath. "We are from the far west, as we've told you, but we're also from the future." He looked straight at Artemisia. "You heard me, we're time travelers. That's how I knew there's more killing tomorrow. God knows we need more killing, don't we? Isn't killing what you people live for?"

Michael leaped from his chair. "What the hell do you think you're doing, Thomas? You're not the only one suffering, you know."

"It's okay, Michael," Artemisia said in a calm voice. "I've seen this before. It's battle fatigue. All he needs is time to himself, so let's leave him alone."

"You know something? You can be a real asshole sometimes," Michael said as he watched Artemisia walk away. "I was going to tell you after the fighting, but I guess now is as good a time as any. I'm not going back with you to the *Kismet*. I've decided to stay here with Artemisia. Paeshatah's qualified to marry us, so after you're gone Artemisia and I will get married. So now you know." Michael walked away.

Without changing his position, Thomas yelled, "You can't do that, Michael! It will never work." Michael never looked back. He raised his arm and gave Thomas a one finger salute.

"Well," Anna said. "That went well."

"Is he serious? Does he really want to stay here?"

"It sure sounds like he does."

Thomas lifted his hand. "Calling *Kismet*, calling *Kismet*, do you read me? Over."

"What are you doing, Thomas?"

"I need more information on Artemisia. I know there's more to her than she's letting on. Calling *Kismet*, calling *Kismet*, do you read me? Over."

"She told us everything about herself," Anna insisted. "And we know from history she's telling the truth."

"Damn it, is this thing broken again? Calling *Kismet*, calling *Kismet*, do you read me? Over."

"Thomas, listen to me. Michael had lots of time to think about this. If he wants to stay, then let him. He's not a child."

"This is *Kismet*; is that you, Thomas?"

"At last. Yes, this is me. Listen, Quincy, I don't have much time. Is there a library on board?"

"Yes, a digital library. Why?"

"I need you to look up everything you can on Artemisia the First of Halicarnassus. She's some kind of war hero. She's known for her role in the Battle of Salamis. Can you do that for me?"

"Sure thing. Can I ask why?"

"Michael wants to marry her."

"Marry her? Doesn't he know we can't take anyone back with us?"

"He wants to stay behind. I can't let that happen."

After a moment of silence, Quincy said, "I don't think it's ethical to spy on Michael."

"I'm trying to save him from ruining his life, Quincy. Is there anything unethical about that?"

There was another pause. "Okay, what I am looking for?"

"I know the basic history of what she did. However, there's something missing, something I don't remember. Can you please check and let me know as soon as you come up with something?"

"Okay, Thomas, I'll do this for you." After yet another long pause, Quincy continued. "By the way, how's everybody?"

"Everyone's fine, Quincy. Listen, I need to go now. Call me as soon as you have the information. Over and out."

"Over and out."

"I sure hope you know what you're doing, Thomas," Anna said. "He's your best friend, remember that."

"I'm tired," Thomas said. "It's been a long and bloody day, so I'm going to bed. I suggest you do the same." As he walked by the chair where Arsalan sat while waiting for his assignments, the tears came again.

CHAPTER 43

Adar 14, day two

"What would you like me to do, Hazarapatis?"

"Arsalan?" Thomas sat up on his cot. "Is that you?"

"Of course it's me. I told you I will stay next to you until the fighting is done. The fighting is not done yet." The boy stood at the foot of his cot.

"But yesterday I saw you next to the old woman. You were dead."

"That was yesterday. Today I'm back. I still need to prove I can be a good soldier." The boy took a step back.

"Wait, Arsalan, don't move. I have something for you." Thomas reached for a medal, a Cross of Valour resting on a small table next to his cot. As he reached for it, though, it displaced itself farther away.

"I'll wait for you outside, Hazarapatis."

"No Arsalan, stay here, please. I have something you need." Thomas again turned to retrieve the medal, but it was gone.

"I'm heading out now, Hazarapatis; I'll keep the tent flap open so I can hear your call."

The boy turned to leave, and Thomas froze in horror. An arrow was sticking out of Arsalan's thigh.

"Thomas, this is *Kismet*, do you read me?"

Thomas felt the night air cold against his sweat-drenched body. He focused his attention on the tent flap. It was closed.

"This is *Kismet*, do you read me? Over."

"Yes, hello, this is Thomas," he blurted, lifting his hand. "Is that you, Quincy?" Thomas shook his head free of sleep as his breathing returned to normal.

"Yes, it's me. Derrek is here also. It's not too early, is it?"

"No guys, your timing couldn't be better. What's up?"

"I have the information on Artemisia. It would seem her information is historically accurate. She has been telling the truth all along. Do you want me to summarize just the same?"

"Yeah, why don't you do that?"

"Okay, I made some notes, so here is the rundown. She is the queen of Halicarnassus, or Caria, but as a proxy for her young son, Pisindelis. She did say she has a son, right?"

"No, I don't think so...I'm not sure."

Quincy seemed to be enjoying his role as historian. "Anyway, according to Herodotus, she did fight as a commander and tactician in the Battle of Salamis. That's when she rammed her vessel into one of her own to escape the Greeks. This made her a hero. Since there were no survivors in the vessel she rammed, there was no one to challenge her actions. The king saw everything from a distance. He seemed not to care that she'd rammed her own people since he was reported to have said 'My men have turned into women and my women into men.' Maybe the king failed to understand what had happened. The Greeks knew what she did, though, and placed a bounty on her head of ten thousand drachmas, dead or alive. That would be about four hundred thousand US dollars." Quincy paused for a reaction but got none, so he continued.

"She's also known for giving King Xerxes military advice. For instance, she was against that naval battle I just mentioned. When the king didn't listen to her, she fought in it anyway. The next time Artemisia expressed her opinion was on a confrontation that turned out to be another defeat for the Persians. This time King Xerxes was saved from blame due to Artemisia's counsel. She instructed the king to send one of his generals instead of going himself. This way, if the battle went wrong, the king could blame the general, leaving him free from reproach. For this she gained favor with the king.

"I'm not sure if she was pleased with the king's decision to give her the responsibility of escorting his illegitimate children to Ephesus."

"Everything you're telling me I already know," Thomas said as he opened his tent flap. He glanced at the empty chair once used by Arsalan.

"There's not much more said about her," Quincy responded. "Except maybe the way she died. However, it's not from a reliable source. It was written by Photius some thirteen hundred years later."

"Tell me anyway."

"Okay." Thomas heard Quincy tapping away at the keyboard. "Here it is. Photius says Artemisia blinded the man she fell in love with because he failed to love her back. Afterward she followed the advice of an oracle and committed suicide by jumping off the rock of Leucas. I wouldn't read too much into this story," Quincy added. "It's more a legend than anything else."

"Does this man have a name?"

"Dardanus."

"What does it mean?"

"It doesn't mean Michael if that's what you're thinking. It means 'strong and immortal' in Persian and in Greek, 'all the gods' or 'all the flowers.'"

"Is that it, Quincy?"

"There's some unreliable random information, bits and pieces of different battles. For instance, Thessalus, a son of Hippocrates, describes her as a coward, a pirate sailing under different flags, depending on who she's attacking. It's also said by some that she had an affair with Xerxes. Others say she fell in love with him but did nothing about it. Who really knows?"

"Thanks Quincy, you did well."

"Thomas," Derrek interjected, "to change the subject, you wouldn't happen to have that password, by any chance?"

"No Derrek, I don't. I'll get it at the same time as you—when Christian meets us at the rendezvous."

"One more thing," Derrek said. "Be careful with your transmitter. It would appear it's the only one working."

"Will do," Thomas responded, only half interested. "I'll contact you if anything happens between now and our trip back to you. Over and out."

"This is *Kismet*, over and out."

Thomas exited his tent and walked toward the edge of the plateau, where he met Michael and Artemisia. Thomas knew he had to make things right with them over last night's events. "Hi guys," he said. "May I join you?"

"Certainly, Thomas," Artemisia answered with a genuine but concerned smile. "You know you're always welcome."

After a long moment, Thomas spoke. "I would like to apologize for the way I treated both of you yesterday. It was wrong and it's not how I feel."

"Please, Thomas," Artemisia interrupted. "We say and do many strange things when in battle. I've been there, remember?"

"I'm still sorry. I should have been more professional." He paused. "Listen, Artemisia, may I have a moment alone with Michael?"

"Of course." She rose and gave Michael a kiss on the cheek before leaving.

"If I promise to never bring it up again, can I say one last thing about your decision to stay in Persia?" Thomas asked. Michael agreed with a nod.

"I want to make sure you know who Artemisia is—according to history, that is," Thomas repeated most of what Quincy had told him.

"Thomas," Michael said as politely as he could, "I appreciate what you're trying to do. But there's one thing all your history books can't get right: they fail to understand Artemisia as a person. The time I've spent with her since our arrival is all the history I need."

"What about the part where she blinded her lover? What about her suicide?"

"Thomas, you know better than anyone, history is dynamic. It's rewritten all the time. Besides, my mind is made up. I love her and she loves me. That's all I need to know."

"Fine, Michael. As I promised, I won't bring this up again. But I'm sure going to miss you."

"No you won't, you have Anna now. From what I can see, she's not only beautiful, she's also an intelligent woman who happens to love you back. I don't know how you got so lucky. Hell, I bet the first thing you're going to do when you get back home is take her on that scuba diving trip to Egypt you've always wanted to do, where you'll frolic in the Red Sea. You won't give me a second thought."

"That's not possible, Michael. I mean about not thinking about you. As for the Red Sea, you bet I'm going, right after Anna and I get married."

Michael waved his index finger violently at Thomas. "Don't you ever forget me."

They stared at each other for a few seconds before breaking out in laughter.

"Come quickly! we're under attack," a high-pitched voice called behind them.

Thomas turned, half expecting to see Arsalan. Instead it was an older boy, shaking with fear. Thomas jumped from his seat and ran to the edge of the plateau. "I don't see anything."

"Not there," the boy shouted. "They're coming from that direction." He pointed northeast, to a point somewhere behind the tents. "They're on top of the plateau."

Thomas looked at Michael. "A back door."

"I'll get Artemisia," Michael said and ran toward her tent.

Thomas turned to the boy who'd delivered the message. "Are you sure about the attack?"

"Yes, I'm sure. Pishan told me."

"Who's Pishan?"

"One of the pickets assigned to watch the left flank."

Thomas took one more look toward the enemy. "Can you tell me their formation?"

The boy frowned. "I don't understand."

"Are they on foot, or on horses?"

"On horses."

"Why the hell didn't you say so earlier?"

"I'm sorry," the frightened boy said. Urine dripped down his leg.

"Listen to me. Did the picket say anything else?"

"No, that's it."

"Now think again; it's very important that you remember. Did the picket say anything else?"

"No, there's nothing else."

"Fine. Go down and locate the woman I came here with; her name is Anna. Tell her to come up here directly. Can you do that?"

"Yes," the boy said, staring at Thomas.

"Go then."

The boy slid down the makeshift rope ladder that had replaced the stairs.

"Do you see them?" Artemisia said as she arrived with Michael.

"No, not yet."

"I'll redeploy our soldiers from the other side of the plateau to face the enemy here."

"Michael, this time you're staying with me. Instruct the signalman to have the soldiers from below come up and form a defensive position."

Soon after Michael left, a picket on horseback arrived. "I have a report," he shouted. "It's cavalry—about three hundred. They're not moving fast. They look determined, though. I think it's the same cavalry from yesterday."

Thomas nodded. "So they were not running away, they were redeploying. How long before they arrive?"

"At this pace, I think very soon. They're about a quarter parasang away."

"One and a half kilometers; we have fifteen minutes, no more," Thomas whispered.

Anna was the first to arrive. "I got your message. The others are coming, but it will take a while. The rope ladder is fragile. About five men can come up at a time. They're working on the second rope ladder, but it's not ready yet." Anna stepped out ahead of Thomas. "Is that them?"

Thomas squinted. "Yes, that's them. How long will it take for our people to come up?"

"Twenty to thirty minutes."

"We don't have that much time."

Artemisia returned to report on her deployment. "Our defense is in position," she said, eyeing the cloud of dust."

"How many are we?" Thomas asked.

"About one hundred, but we're being reinforced from below."

Thomas grimaced at the approaching riders. "This doesn't look good. We're outnumbered three to one."

Artemisia unsheathed her sword. "I expected this, so I have prepared a way to improve the odds. Wait for my word, then drop to the ground like dead fish."

Anna looked at Artemisia, then back at Thomas. "We'd better do as she says," was all Thomas could say.

Now they could see the enemy's faces. Thomas recognized the man who'd saluted him not twenty-four hours ago. This time he could see a controlled fury on the man's face. It was clear this man had a killer instinct. Thomas knew from Kelile's training that survival meant he had to eliminate all traces of fear, hate, and anger from his consciousness. If he failed at this, he would become indecisive and vulnerable.

Thomas stepped forward to face his soldiers, who were now in their defensive position. "Today will define who we are. For better or for worse, today we must be brutal. Today we must be explosive and efficient with our weapons." He turned his attention to Michael and Anna. "Remember Kelile. If he were here he would remind us of the need to stay unified, to work as one, to rid ourselves of all distractions and fully focus on the enemy. Do this and we have a better than good chance of winning this fight."

Thomas moved to stand ten meters ahead of his soldiers to face the enemy. In a low, controlled voice he said, "This is for you, Kelile. This is for you, Arsalan."

"Now!" Artemisia shouted. She, Thomas, Anna, and Michael dropped to the ground. The charging horses instinctively leaped over them and plunged straight into the soldiers positioned behind them. The first rank had dropped to one knee to meet the attack and anchored the butt ends of their four-meter-long spears into the ground. The front line of invaders slammed into this deadly wall. Fallen horses thrashed amid their broken riders, piled into a heap of squirming flesh and blood.

Artemisia stood to engage the enemy. Thomas, Michael, and Anna followed her lead. The fighting was bloody and brutal. To Thomas, everything seemed to be happening in slow motion. Because of this he could inflict upon his opponents a deadly injury with every violent thrust of his sword.

After what seemed an eternity, the enemy retreated and the surviving defenders gathered. Thomas scanned the battlefield, hoping to see the cavalry fleeing. Instead, he saw what remained of his own small force with their backs to the edge of the plateau, surrounded by a barrier of determined and proficient executioners.

"Why did they stop?" Thomas asked.

"I don't know," Artemisia responded. "It makes no sense."

Thomas looked toward the ladder, hoping for reinforcements from the village. The rope ladder was on fire so no one could come up to help. There were about twenty fighters left to face two hundred or so enemies. The only avenue left was to fight to the death.

Breaking away from his cavalry, the commander rode forward several paces. "You have fought bravely, but surely you can see the folly of any further resistance," he called. "Surrender the village and your lives will be spared."

Thomas glanced at the remaining defenders. There was no fear in their eyes. It was clear they would rather die than surrender.

The commander nudged his horse toward Thomas. "What's there to think about? Surely you can see fighting is suicide."

"If our death at your hand is suicide, then that makes you a leader of murderers." Thomas tossed his shield on the ground. With both hands he held his sword in front of him and called out as loud as he could, "Hold your positions, soldiers, and let it never be said the people of Zarmandokht surrendered to a mob of murderers."

The commander backed away before giving the order, "Finish them now."

The cavalrymen nocked arrows in their bows. They took their time aiming. It did not matter who shot who, the sheer number of them guaranteed at least two or three arrows in the heart of each soldier. The commander lifted his hand, about to give the final order.

The earth rumbled. Before anyone could grasp what was happening, a tidal wave of missiles hurtled from the north to smash into the enemy.

The commander was hit so many times, he flew from his horse as if struck by a wrecking ball. He'd barely hit the ground when a second wave of arrows found their mark. Without their commander, the army wheeled and fled at full speed back the way they'd come. Seconds later, a new band of horsemen appeared, riding in pursuit of the enemy. Like a roaring train the men rode by, seemingly oblivious to Thomas and his soldiers.

One rider broke away from the pursuers, his face was hidden behind a head scarf designed to protect him from the choking dust. He approached Thomas and stopped just long enough to reach inside his cloak and pull out a leather cylinder. He hurled the cylinder at Thomas's feet, then offered a military salute.

"Wait, who are you?" Thomas shouted as the rider turned and rejoined his comrades, leaving Thomas standing there.

He waited until the last of the cavalry rode away before bending to retrieve the cylinder. "Who were those men?" he asked Artemisia.

"I don't recognize them, Thomas."

"You're sure it's not your brother?" Thomas asked.

"I am sure. Pigres's men carry the banner of Simurg. I did not see any banners bearing her symbol." Artemisia exposed her right hip to Thomas, revealing a tattoo of a creature with a dog's head, a peacock's wings, a lion's claws, and a body covered in scales. "She is a guardian and protector with healing powers."

"So as far as we know, they could be competing for the village," Thomas reasoned. "And as soon as they're finished with our enemies they could return for their prize." He turned to scan the plateau. "Do you know what happened to the second rope ladder?"

"It is down in the village," Artemisia answered. "But we do have strong rope up here. I will throw one end down to retrieve the rope ladder, then we can bring people up here to fight."

"Good. Once we have a hundred or so with us, send out help to the wounded."

"I will do this at once." Artemisia left, accompanied by Michael, to prepare for a potential renewed attack.

Thomas and Anna now stood alone. "Do you think this was divine intervention, Thomas?" Anna asked.

"At one time I would have." He took a deep breath of the dusty air. "But now, with all this death and suffering, I'm afraid I don't have your faith. And when I think this will go on for thousands of years, well, it's hard to have faith."

"If it's not God's hand and it's not Pigres, then where did the mystery cavalry come from?" she wondered.

Thomas looked at the cylinder. "Maybe the answer is in here. But since I can't read Persian, we'll have to wait for Artemisia."

• • • • • • • • • • ● ○ ○ ○ ○ ○ ○ ○ ○ ○ ○ ○

"I'm sorry for being late," Paeshatah said as he joined Thomas, Anna, Michael, and Artemisia at the table. "I guess I'm a little out of shape." No one responded to his poor attempt at minimizing his tardiness. "It being so dark didn't help either."

Thomas had enough. "We're glad you were able to make it, Paeshatah. While we were waiting, we dealt with most of the day's more pressing necessities. I thought you would want to know how the battle affected your people."

"Of course I do," Paeshatah gasped. "Would it be all right if I sat down? I can hardly breathe." He pulled up a chair and sat down. "So tell me what the damage is."

"As far as the enemy is concerned, there are twenty-six prisoners. We don't know how many are dead. As for our soldiers, we have forty-seven wounded with thirty-three dead."

"I see," Paeshatah said, genuinely affected by the news. "Do you have their names?"

"Yes. I will have them brought to you before you head back down. I suggest you have someone visit every family of the dead and wounded tonight, so each will know what happened to their loved one."

"Yes, of course I'll do that."

"Did you find out where the cavalry who helped us came from?"

"Not yet," Paeshatah answered. "May I ask you one question?"

"Yes, of course."

"Is the fighting over? I ask because yesterday you knew there was more to come and you were right."

"I'm sure the fighting is over, Paeshatah."

"Good, that's a relief." He looked around uncertainly. "Can I organize a celebration for tomorrow, then?"

Thomas's blood pressure spiked. Anna tilted over to whisper in his ear, "This is a different time, Thomas, a different place."

Thomas took a slow swallow of cold water and worked to compose himself. "Yes, Paeshatah, you may begin to organize your celebration, but don't schedule it until Anna and I are gone." He glanced at Michael. "We have little time left to reach the ship that will take us back home, so we'll be leaving at sunrise tomorrow morning."

"But how will it look if you leave without proper recognition?"

"Sorry, Paeshatah, this is non-negotiable. Our decision is made. However, there is one thing you can do before we go. Tell the people of Zarmandokht that it has been an honor fighting side by side with them. It's to them the honor of victory rightfully belongs. Tell them we are sorry we couldn't stay to celebrate, but Michael and Artemisia will represent us. Can you do that for us?"

"If that is your wish, Thomas."

"Thank you. Now, if it's fine with you, we still have some things to discuss." Paeshatah took the hint and left for the village.

"Okay Thomas, where is the cylinder?" Anna asked.

Thomas retrieved the cylinder from under the table. "I can't read Persian," he said. "To me, it looks like an army of chickens marched across the papyrus."

Artemisia held out her hand. "May I read it?"

"Please, Artemisia, won't you?"

Thomas handed her the cylinder, she opened it and unrolled a small papyrus scroll. She looked at it, then up at Thomas. "I'm sorry, Thomas, but this is not Persian." She handed the scroll back to Thomas. Thomas looked at it and his head spun.

"What is it, Thomas?" Anna asked. "Are you feeling sick?"

"It's—" He hesitated. "It's English."

"English?" Michael said, looking at Anna. "It must be Nicolas or Brody. It's probably the *Kismet*. That's right, I bet it's Derrek who sent the cavalry."

"No Michael, it's none of them. It's my son. It's Christian." Flashbacks of the young man on the horse came to him.

"Well, Thomas," Anna said impatiently, "what does it say?"

With shaking hands and a cracking voice, Thomas read the letter.

Hi Dad,

I just found out the unbelievable news that you're here in Persia. I had a hard time believing it at first, but when Pigres told me you and Michael are looking for me, I knew it had to be true. I want to let you know I'm all right. The friends I've made have taken good care of me. I know you don't want to hear this, Dad, but God has looked after me.

It seems like just yesterday we were thirty foot soldiers newly arrived in Persia. Needless to say, we were all very enthusiastic about our journey, but almost immediately we were arrested and accused of being spies. They took us somewhere in the desert and incarcerated us in the filthiest holes you could ever have imagined. One by one my comrades started to disappear. With God's help I alone escaped into the desert, where I was rescued by a small group of vigilantes. I have been with them ever since. I'm sure the others are dead.

That's why I was surprised when Pigres said Aldon is with you. He was with us also. Please be careful, Dad. Back at the ULRA I overheard him and his wife Yetta discussing a plan to take credit for the mission's success. They said something about becoming godlike and having the world as their footstool.

Anyway, since you were not on the ship with me, I could only assume the ULRA made another trip. I knew they would, so I planned for this eventuality by putting a virus in the server's return trip. This way, if they did come back, they wouldn't be able to leave for home without you, as they did with us. I didn't know then I would be the lone survivor. I also sent you encrypted files by hacking into your employer's servers with a password to deactivate the virus hidden inside. I'm sure you figured it out quickly. I made it easy for you. I figured if you were not on this trip then the Kismet *would be lost to the twentieth century forever and the ULRA will die with it. I tried to stop them but I failed.*

I intended to send more files explaining my involvement with the ULRA and their intentions, but I was discovered. They locked me up until the day of our departure. I was allowed out only to work on the Kismet. *During the time I spent alone I tried to figure out how I would communicate with you from Persia if something was to go wrong. I guess one of those ideas worked. Can't wait to find out how I did it.*

I have so much more to say to you, Dad, but I'm running out of papyrus. Besides, we're about ready to go. I'm told there is a small village somewhere in the mountains that needs our help. Pigres says if something goes wrong, he will deliver this letter to you for me.

Thomas stopped reading to look at Anna. The horror on his face said it all. "The man who threw you the cylinder was a younger man, correct? So it was not Pigres, it was your son." Thomas accepted her explanation and went back to reading the letter.

Pigres tells me you have a girlfriend. He tells me she's very pretty and her name is Hanna.

Thomas smiled. "He said Hanna, with an H." Anna smiled back, remembering her first encounter with Thomas at the mission's underground facility.

I'm looking forward to meeting her when I see you again on the Kismet. *Don't tell them the password until I arrive, okay?*

Love you,
Christian

CHAPTER 44

A large crowd watched as Thomas helped his guide prepare their horses for the return trip to the rendezvous. Thomas understood the villagers' need to express their gratitude, but did they all have to be there in the middle of the square? There was the elderly standing side by side, mothers with babies in their arms, and the men and woman who had fought with him. Some supported themselves with homemade crutches; others, too broken to walk, struggled to gaze at him from their cots.

Thomas finished loading the last of his supplies. A thin young woman in a simple white dress and bare feet presented him with a loaf of bread. She stood out from the crowd like a single unharmed flower on a bloody battlefield. She gave him a tender kiss, her dark brown eyes swimming in tears as she looked straight at him. "You should let go of the sadness and embrace the life that awaits you."

"Thank you," Thomas said as the young woman backed away to rejoin the villagers.

"What are all these people doing here?" Anna said as she arrived with Michael and Artemisia.

"I think they feel the need to see us off."

"All of them?"

"I know, it's ludicrous, yet here they are." Thomas turned to their guide. "Can we go now?"

The guide smiled at Thomas. "There is one more thing you need to address before we leave."

Thomas was about to ask what it might be when an unmistakable voice pierced the deafening silence. "There you are, Thomas. And look at what we have here: Anna, Michael, and Artemisia. I was hoping you'd all be here."

"Paeshatah, how nice of you to see us off," Thomas forced himself to say.

"Of course I came to see you off, the entire village is here. We all want to witness the handing over of this special gift. It took all night to make."

The villagers began to chant a victory song in a low, somber tone. A small girl and a small boy no older than ten years emerged from behind Paeshatah. They were dressed for the occasion in glamorous multicolored costumes and a large assortment of gold jewelry.

Paeshatah knelt before Thomas and his companions. The two children gave them each a package wrapped with snow-white silk cloth. Thomas looked at Artemisia for guidance. She gestured with her hands to open it.

Inside was a medallion in the shape of a silver ring surrounding a gold disc. Etched into the gold disc was the village's symbol, a hammer and a chisel. Protruding from the top were the famous Persian wings with three feathers representing good words, good thoughts, and good deeds. Under the symbol was an inscription written in cuneiform.

Artemisia whispered to Thomas, "It's the name of the village. It means 'daughter of time.'"

Thomas thought it ironic; the village they saved, the same village where Christian hid the stela, was named after the daughter of time.

Paeshatah spoke in a voice that carried throughout the square. "We would like to honor you with this medallion symbolizing our small community. It's the highest honor one can receive. It denotes the sacrifice and risk you took on behalf of Zarmandokht. Normally, this is given in a ceremony followed by a seven-day festival. But knowing you must leave today, we will give it to you with gratitude, witnessed by all our people, great and small."

Thomas spoke as loud as he could to the gathered crowd. "You, the people of Zarmandokht—you are the true champions. It's you who sacrificed everything for your home and your people. When you tell this story to your children, don't mention us. Tell them how you, the villagers, came together and won the day against evil." The crowd broke into a loud and raucous cheer.

The guide approached Thomas and tapped him on the shoulder. "It's time to go."

Thomas kissed Artemisia on both cheeks. "I will never forget you, Artemisia. You're the reason we're alive."

He turned to Michael. No words were said; none were needed. They embraced for a good minute. Thomas put into Michael's hand the last working telecom ring with a note that simply read, *Just in case.*

Thomas mounted his horse and Anna followed suit. The people of

Zarmandokht parted and they rode toward the charred remains of the gate. The chanting continued as they headed west toward the king's road.

•••••••••●○○○○○○○○○○○

Over the next five days, the guide used the horses positioned along the route for carrying the king's mail to transport them to the rendezvous. He bragged that a single rider could go from Susa to Sardis in seven days, a distance of about twenty-seven hundred kilometers. The distance they needed to travel was somewhat shorter, but it was also more difficult. The hot, dry desert reduced their speed, as the horses needed to rest more often during the journey. The devastation left by battles prompted them to show respect by dismounting and walking through each village they encountered. Yet they reached their destination on time, as Pigres had promised. They arrived at the very spot on the Euphrates River where they'd boarded the trireme to Babylon almost ten months previous. They were seven then; now they are two.

The guide returned to his people despite a threatening storm that turned out to be the heaviest downpour in a generation. It was as if God was washing away the blood spilled during the conflict. Thomas and Anna were forced to stay in a traveler's inn overnight as the rain flooded both the Euphrates and the road leading to Hīt.

It was not yet noon when they arrived at the outskirts of Hīt the next day. Despite the ground being saturated and muddy, the merchants were out selling their goods to travelers and locals.

A hoarse but familiar voice called out from a nearby food stand. "Before you go, I need to caution you about something. Why don't you have a seat?"

Thomas clenched his fists. "Aldon, you have balls the size of Europe, approaching us like this." Aldon was sitting on a bench with a blanket covering his legs. The left side of his face was bruised many shades of blue and black. His left eye was swollen shut and his right arm was in a sling. Despite his appearance, Thomas sneered, "Where's Yetta and the rest of your thugs?"

"Please, spare me the muscle talk and sit." Thomas grabbed his sword while Anna scanned the area. "You don't need that," Aldon assured them. "I'm alone."

"No," Thomas replied. "If it's the jewels you want, we don't have them anymore. We left them with Michael."

"And where is Michael?"

"None of your damn business."

"Listen," Aldon said. "I know you're heading to the rendezvous. It's time to head back. But I'm not the only one who knows you're here. There are people waiting, intent on killing both of you."

Aldon paused for a violent cough. He struggled to catch his breath, wheezing as he inhaled. It took all of thirty seconds before he could breathe normally again. He stuffed his bloodstained handkerchief up his right sleeve, then gently massaged his leg with his good arm. "I know it means nothing to you, but I truly regret everything I did, and I'll be damned in hell if I don't try to do this one last thing right."

"There's nothing that will keep you out of hell," Thomas said.

"Let's hear what he has to say," Anna said.

"Thank you." Aldon smiled at Anna as she dismounted, and waited while Thomas did the same. "The same day after I left you at Carkas's house, Sadhanah came to Yetta and me, accusing us of setting him up."

"Wait a minute," Thomas interrupted. "Sadhanah's dead. I killed him myself with a marble statue."

"You should have paid more attention, Thomas. All you did was knock him cold. He woke up in the basement with his dead friends next to him. He sure was alive when he approached Yetta and me, ready to hack us to bits.

"Anyway, the only reason I'm still breathing to tell you this is because of Yetta's one good asset, saving her own skin. She told Sadhanah everything went as planned until I got cold feet and warned you of the trap. Sadhanah believed her, so he tied me to a post and tortured me for information on your whereabouts. I said nothing since I had no idea where you were. That's when he broke my arm and knocked me unconscious.

"When I regained consciousness, I was tied to a chair. Everything was blurry. I could hear Yetta crying somewhere in the room, but I couldn't see her. Scared shitless, Yetta told him about the rendezvous. She told you two, along with Michael, would meet in Hīt before going back home, so if he still wanted the jewels, this would be his last chance."

"After all this," Thomas said, "he's still after the stupid jewels?"

"Greed has no reason," Aldon replied. "But that's not his only motivation. He wants revenge. He wants to kill you all."

"Why are you telling us this now?" Anna asked.

"Because I want to go back home with you."

Thomas moved closer to Aldon. "What makes you think we want you back?"

"I'm not asking you to take me back as a friend. I'm not stupid. I know it will never happen. But I'm appealing to your conscience. I'm telling you this to save your life and in return, you can save mine." He took another deep breath. "Listen to me. If you leave me here I'll be dead by nightfall. Help me, and I will submit myself to the judicial committee back home. I'm asking you to give me life, not to forgive me. I assure you I will answer for everything I've done. Don't let me die without an opportunity to atone for my sins. Please."

"What about Yetta, is she coming too?"

"No, she's not."

Anna looked at Thomas, signaling her approval. "How do you propose we get past Sadhanah?" she asked.

"They're expecting four people on horseback. They think Artemisia will accompany Michael. What we need to do is give them something else. I'll dress as a woman. You, Thomas, will be my husband. I'll be sitting on a horse being led by you through the market. You, Anna, will dress as a young boy, our son. You'll be pulling behind you the other two horses. Once we've passed the market and we're in the woods, we'll mount the horses and head for the rendezvous."

Thomas glanced at Anna, then back at Aldon. "Why do you get to be on a horse while we're on foot?"

Aldon removed the blanket from his lap, revealing his left leg.

"Oh my God," Anna cried out. "What happened?"

"Before we left Susa, Sadhanah wanted to make sure I would not run away, so he smashed my knee with a sledgehammer."

"It's infected," Anna said. "It must be three times its normal size, and the white and green pus . . ." She grimaced. "You need a doctor."

Aldon looked at Thomas. "And that's why I'm the woman on the horse."

"Fine," Thomas agreed. "We need to go; the pod is probably waiting for us as we speak."

"One more thing." Aldon struggled to stand. "Take this note, just in case I don't make it. It might answer some of your questions."

They walked by the main city gate. The same gate they'd walked through when they first arrived in Persia. They could see Sadhanah with six other burly men, sitting at an outdoor table drinking and eating. Their horses were tied to nearby trees. The men looked bored, but Sadhanah carefully scanned everyone passing by. Not far away, Thomas saw Yetta sitting alone under an umbrella.

They managed to fool Sadhanah with their costumes. But a few yards before they would disappear into the forest, someone recognized Anna. She looked her in the eyes. Anna smiled. Artemisia's servant girl smiled back nervously.

"Hi Mani, it's nice to see you again."

"It's nice to see you, too."

"Out for a walk in the woods?"

"Yes, but my mistress is waiting for me at the house; I must hurry back."

"What mistress would that be?" Anna knew Artemisia was still in Zarmandokht.

"Artemisia," Mani lied. "I really need to head back. I wish you a safe trip home." Mani did not wait for Anna's response. She walked past them and made a beeline to the market.

"She's a lookout," Thomas said. "Come on, let's get out of here."

As soon as they entered the large manmade garden, Thomas turned to look at Hīt. The servant girl was halfway between them and Sadhanah. This was close enough for her to get Sadhanah's attention. Within seconds Sadhanah and his men dropped everything, mounted their horses, and began the pursuit.

"They're coming," Thomas called. "Hurry, let's go."

It was difficult to sustain a steady speed on the muddy trail. Low-hanging branches laden with raindrops whipped them in the arms and face, leaving burning welts. Aldon tried not to let his crippled state slow the others. They knew it would be a miracle if they reached the rendezvous before Sadhanah caught up with them.

One hundred meters ahead, they could see the clearing where the pod should be waiting for them. They rushed toward it, passing a fork in the road. Thomas's heart thunked in his chest—they were going to make it.

Suddenly his horse stopped dead in its tracks, throwing him clear over the animal's head. He landed face-first in a pool of water. Sputtering, he sat up in the knee-deep water and looked back at Anna's riderless horse.

"I'm over here," Anna said, emerging from the water a few meters away.

"Are you okay?" Thomas asked.

"I think so."

"Good," Thomas said as he struggled to stand. "This pool must have been caused by the rain. I'm guessing the horses won't go through."

Anna was already on her feet and moving toward the open field when Thomas saw a large snake swimming in his direction. "Wait for me," he cried out.

The first thing they did after stepping out of the water was locate Aldon. He had not followed. Somehow he'd managed with only one arm to tie the other two horses to his saddle. All they could do was watch as he galloped away down the other fork in the road.

"What's he doing?" Anna asked. "It's suicide."

Thomas put his arm around Anna's shoulder. "He's atoning for his sins."

Not one minute passed before Sadhanah arrived. Thomas and Anna dropped to the ground. They were well hidden in the tall grass, but if anyone approached, they'd be seen from horseback. Sadhanah and his men stopped at the fork, unsure which direction to go. Sadhanah moved closer to the water but stopped when one of his men called, "The tracks of the horses lead this way." Sadhanah scanned the water once more before returning to his men.

Just then Yetta arrived. Thomas and Anna could not hear what was being said, but it appeared Yetta was telling them to follow the tracks. Sadhanah looked once more at the water before giving the order to move onto the other fork in the road. With a quick look at the water, Yetta followed Sadhanah.

"Come on, Anna," Thomas said. "If we hurry we can still find Aldon with the help of the pod."

They reached the middle of the clearing as the long-anticipated pod materialized. The hatch opened, revealing a beaming Derrek, his jaw working at the ever-present wad of gum. "Welcome back."

Thomas and Anna rushed in so fast, they almost knocked Derrek over.

"Hurry, let's go," Thomas yelled. "We need to find Aldon."

Without hesitation Derrek jumped into the pilot's seat to start the pod. "Where is he?"

Thomas looked out the cockpit window. "There's a fork in the road leading here. Can you follow it?"

"Probably, if there's not too many trees covering it."

"Let's go then."

As Derrek bent over the console to begin the five-minute liftoff sequence, Thomas joined Anna, who was already seated in the passenger area, trying to regroup her thoughts. He wrinkled his nose at an offensive odor. He was about to ask Anna if she knew where it came from when Anna shushed him and pointed to the rear of the pod. Sleeping in a sitting position was a small, dirty man with long hair and a greasy beard. He looked like a down-on-his-luck tramp waiting for a handout. Thomas looked to Anna for answers but all she could do was shrug.

"Okay, we're ready," Derrek called out. Thomas and Anna rejoined Derrek in the cockpit.

Following the road was easy. In five minutes they passed over Sadhanah's men and spotted Aldon entering an open field a few dozen meters ahead of his pursuers.

"We're too late," Thomas said.

Anna leaned forward to have a better look. "Why do you say that? All we need to do is land right there, you see? Right there in front of him."

Thomas directed Anna's attention to the edge of the open field. "Look at Sadhanah. Like I said, we're too late."

Realizing he had been duped, a scowling Sadhanah had his bow drawn, poised to loose an arrow at Aldon's back. No one in the pod saw the arrow in flight, but they saw Aldon's lifeless body drop like a ragdoll to the ground.

Yetta, riding a short distance behind Sadhanah and his men, led her horse to the front. Seeing Aldon lying on the ground, she kicked her horse into a gallop, then hauled on the reins beside his body and slid to the ground. She fell to her knees to tend to her husband. Those in the pod saw her reaction as she realized he was dead. She lifted helpless hands, then her shoulders sagged and shook with her sobs. She dropped on top of Aldon's chest, sobbing inconsolably.

Sadhanah and his men reined in a short distance away. Sadhanah dismounted and approached the body and the weeping woman, then stopped as if allowing Yetta time to mourn his death. He waited until she noticed him standing next to her and looked up at him. She saw the sword in his hand and understood her time had come. Those in the pod glimpsed the resignation on her face as she accepted her fate, positioning herself so when the blow came, she would fall lying next to Aldon. It took Sadhanah but one swing of his sword.

"Come on, Derrek," Thomas said, his voice subdued. "Let's go. There's nothing left for us here."

Derrek activated the radio. "*Kismet*, this is Derrek; we're coming in."

"No, wait!" Thomas shouted. "We have to go back to the rendezvous. Christian hasn't arrived yet!"

"You gave Michael your transmitter, didn't you?" Derrek asked.

"Yes—I thought if he needed to, he could contact us. Why?"

"Well, he did contact us. It's about your son."

Thomas felt a sickening ache in the pit of his stomach. "What about my son."

"Michael said he's missing in action."

"Missing in action? What the hell does that mean?"

"Michael said when the cavalry returned to Zarmandokht, Christian wasn't with them. No one seems to know where he is. So he called me with the telecom ring to let us know."

"Quick, give me your radio transmitter," Thomas demanded.

"If you're thinking of calling Michael, forget it. His ring died shortly after we talked."

"Goddammit, Derrek!" Thomas thought for a moment. "Well, one more reason why we should go back to the rendezvous. Most likely he left the cavalry to come here."

"Okay, Thomas, but we have enough energy to wait for maybe two more hours, no more."

"I don't care. I'm not leaving Christian behind."

"I have an idea," said the small, dirty man sitting in the far back of the pod. "Why don't you head back to the *Kismet* as Derrek suggested? You could pick up a wireless camera, jump into another fully charged pod, and return to the rendezvous. Then find a nice tall tree to place the camera. This way you could have someone look out for him around the clock. At the same time, you could drop me off so I could take a shower and have something to eat."

Thomas walked back to the man. "And who might you be?"

"Brody," the man said. "Brody Powell."

"Where is Nicolas?"

Brody turned his head away.

"He's dead," Derrek answered.

"Fine," Thomas said. "Let's do what Brody said."

CHAPTER 45

Olivia Washington spotted Thomas in the cafeteria, where he sat at a table with his head buried in his arms. It was three in the morning. She assumed he had been up all night since the dining tables were shoved to one side. His famous Komodo files were laid out on the open floor. He also had next to him a laptop computer displaying a video feed of the rendezvous point. He was watching for Christian.

Olivia approached the table and gently put her hand on his shoulder. "Thomas," she whispered.

Thomas lifted his head, blinking groggily. When he saw Olivia he stood up out of respect. He swayed. Lack of sleep was taking its toll.

"Please, Thomas, sit down before you fall over."

"Sorry, I must have woken up too fast." Thomas tried to regain his composure. "Can I get you a cup of coffee? Or a tea, perhaps?"

"Not now," Olivia said as she pulled up a chair. "You should get some sleep."

"I can't do that. I must crack this puzzle before the deadline or we'll have the rest of our lives right here in Persia to solve it." He glanced at the cafeteria clock. "I have three hours."

Olivia knew Thomas was right. She also knew the longer he went without sleep, the harder it would be for him to solve the puzzle. "How are you doing with the files?"

"In order to decipher the files I need two keys. I have one; it's 'baboon.' It was carved into the stela. But without the second key it is impossible to solve, even with a computer."

"It's almost like your son didn't want us to succeed."

"I'm hoping to ask him about that when I see him," Thomas said. "Perhaps he has a good reason for his actions."

"Perhaps," Olivia admitted.

"When I agreed to be part of this mission," Thomas explained, "I did so because I had nothing left to live for. I thought it would help me forget things that hurt too much. In time, however, I believed this mission might be for a greater good after all, even if my role was unknown."

"And now that you know your role?"

"Now that I know my role, I'm more convinced than ever this is nothing more than rich men playing with expensive toys. I now know this mission has nothing to do with God."

"You make a good argument, Thomas, but it might yet succeed. Maybe the sacrifices made by all those we've lost will not be in vain."

"Tell that to Kelile and Aldon. Tell that to my son Christian." Thomas stared into his black coffee. "Poor souls." He paused to reminisce. "I too bought into the doctrine. You know the saying, they repeated it often enough. The stones will cry out even if no one spoke the word of God. I also believed it referred to archaeology. If no one talked about God, do you think he would need us to go back in time to find evidence so the world could start believing in him again? Does that not defeat the purpose of faith?"

"Luke nineteen forty," Olivia muttered.

"What's that?"

"The stones will cry out—it's found in the book of Luke, chapter 19, verse 40. It says, 'I tell you that, if these should hold their peace, the stones would immediately cry out.' I have it written on a small round pebble in my office back home. Why would God have it written in his Word the Bible if he didn't intend to use it?"

Thomas was in no mood for a debate that would lead nowhere so he changed the subject. "Did you have a chance to read the note Aldon gave me?"

"Yes, I did. I found it interesting."

"That's all, just interesting?"

"I already knew most of what he said. I did not know, however, that Yetta was with us on the *Kismet*. Nor did I know she stole one of the pods to get down to Persia, and I had no knowledge of the frequency change, either. I did know this was not the first trip to Persia. In fact, it's the third."

"The third?" Thomas's eyes narrowed.

Olivia decided to explain. "Eleven years ago, when the mission pioneers had their final breakthrough and they realized they could travel back in time, they built the mission training facility along with a miniature version of the *Kismet*, made for a handful of mice. They also intensified their efforts to find the Persian stela.

"Even though they failed to locate the stela and despite the misgivings expressed by the religious contributors, two years later the governing body decided to send forty-five people on a three month trip to Persia. We don't know what happened to them. They all either died or got lost in Persia.

"Four years after that disaster, we upgraded the facility. We introduced a one-year training program that included the Persian language, religion, culture, and history. We also thought it a good idea to add physical training with military combat skills. We were convinced that this time, nothing would go wrong. Despite not having the stela, the advances in technology were encouraging. We thought we would not make the same mistakes made on the first trip.

"At that time we uncovered a small group of loyalists who believed the mission would fail without the stela. We called them the resistance; who knows what they called themselves. They kept trying to delay the launch of the *Kismet* with minor but annoying sabotage tactics. Despite their attempts, the *Kismet* made a second three-month trip one year later. Your son Christian, the mastermind behind the program that ran the ship, was on that trip.

"Well, you now know the second trip did not go as planned either. All those on the ground were lost. We gathered no information and those on the ship made it back in humiliation.

"The mission's captain during the second trip was Callahan Rye and Major General Nathan Kirkpatrick was second in command. After the second failure, all but nine percent of the sponsors withdrew their support. They agreed to come back if the Persian stela was found. We'd underestimated the spiritual persuasions of our sponsors.

"It was only a few months after the second trip that the long sought-after stela was discovered. Immediately afterward, the training for the third trip began. This time we extended the training to three years and introduced a completely new team from the ground up.

"I believe you know the rest of the story. The stela renewed the interest for another mission and the investors came back in force. That was the mission you were on."

"Why did you lie about the other two missions?" Thomas asked.

"Because we needed everyone to believe this mission was blessed by God. If we told the new recruits we had two failed missions, we would not be able to guarantee their loyalty."

"How many people knew about the other two missions?"

"Professor Barnaby Lancaster, Major General Nathan Kirkpatrick,

Lieutenant General Commander Callahan Rye, Professor Ridley Walker, and me. Of course the governing body, most of the investors, and Yetta and Aldon knew as well."

"Don't forget Christian and the so-called resistance," Thomas said.

"Yes, Thomas, the resistance." She hesitated for a few seconds. "One thing is for sure, the deceptions and lack of respect for the lives lost will most certainly end any attempts at further missions.

"Your son believed the real goal of the governing body is no different than that of evil rulers of our dark past: world domination. He wanted to expose the ULRA so the science of time travel could be used for the good of mankind. Christian and his resistance felt the League should be in the hands of the public, managed by a committee where all decisions are voted on like a democracy. This way, no one could attempt a coup d'état, as Yetta and Aldon did.

"It's true that I'm not proud of what we did, but I still believe it was for the glory of God. As for the first two failures, it must be God's way of testing us. I have to believe the ULRA as a league represents everything good."

"I wonder if God feels proud of what was done in his name." They both eyed each other like two children playing a game to see who would blink first. "Anyway," Thomas finally said, "I need to get back to these files. They won't decipher themselves. Can I get you something to drink before I continue?"

"What you have looks good."

Ten minutes later, Thomas returned with Olivia's coffee.

"I was looking at your sheets laid out on the floor," Olivia said. "It reminds me of a field trip I took as a youth to a small museum in Washington. The theme was Nazi concentration camp survivors. Halfway through that guided tour we entered a large room where photographs of Jewish survivors hung on three walls. The wall facing the entrance had a large photo of the badge the Jews were forced to wear on their clothing. At first glance, it resembled a painting, but as we approached it we realized it was a photo mosaic. The background was made of thousands of mini photos of the concentration camp victims who died. The yellow Jewish badge was made of mini photos as well, but those ones were made of photos representing the survivors. It showed that the Nazi regime failed to wipe out the Jews. God preserved them. It's a lot like what Haman and his followers tried to do here in Persia."

"What made you think of this now?"

"While you were gone to make my coffee, I removed my glasses to clean them. While cleaning them I glanced at your sheets laid out on the floor.

With my cloudy vision, I noticed what appears to be a zero composed of those sheets over there." She pointed to a group of three sheets.

Thomas looked at them, then turned and said excitedly, "Olivia, stand on the table."

"I beg your pardon?"

"Sorry—please, stand on the table."

"There's no way I'm standing on any table," she insisted.

"I need you to look at my sheets from on top of the table. If this is a photo mosaic, you should be able to see more text."

Thomas examined the sheets. "Look at those." He pointed to three corners that met in the center, all with the same text character. He moved forward, searching the arranged papers, and suddenly bent and picked one up. "This one has the same character in its bottom left corner—it makes the fourth corner." He placed it in the empty upper right spot with the other three papers. It was a perfect match. He turned to Olivia, who was still sitting on her chair.

Thomas climbed onto the table. "Can you please do something for me?"

"As long as you don't want me to climb on anything."

"Can you get Derrek, Quincy, and Anna for me?"

"Won't they be upset?"

Thomas smiled grimly. "Actually, they'd be upset if I didn't get them."

Olivia left to wake them up.

●●●●●●●●●●○○○○○○○○○○○

Thomas was still on the table making notes on a notepad when Olivia returned with the others.

"Did you crack the password?" Quincy asked.

"I think so, but I need your help." Thomas jumped off the table. "Captain Washington figured it out. Come look at this." They all gathered around the table.

"The files were never meant to be deciphered as such," Thomas explained. "They were meant to be a photo mosaic. After matching all the corners with their respective symbols, it gave me these numbers: nine, fourteen, fifteen, zero, eleven, and one. This is the second key. The stela gave us the first key—baboon."

Thomas stared at his notes, thinking out loud. "No, it's unlikely Christian would use letters for one key and numbers for the other. We need to find something they both have in common."

"Everything on the Persian stela had to be converted from binary to text, right?" Quincy asked. "Is it possible that the same thing needs to be done here?"

"That's right," Thomas said. "It would make sense." The binary conversion skills Thomas possessed made this easy. The others watched him convert each letter into its binary equivalent one at a time, starting with the numbers from the files:

9 = 00001001, 14 = 00001110, 15 = 00001111, 0 = 00000000, 11 = 00001011, 1 = 00000001

Then the key from the stela:

b = 01100010, a = 01100001, b = 01100010, o = 01101111, o = 01101111, n = 01101110

"There. Now the next step is to add the two binary results together."

"Which formula do we use?" Derrek asked.

Thomas glanced at the stela. "We should try the AND formula since Christian would have been familiar with it."

"What's the AND formula?" Anna asked.

"It's quite simple, actually. We line up the binary code one on top of the other and look for all the matches that have a one both on top and at the bottom. These have a value of one. All the others have a value of zero. Then we convert it back to text or numbers, whichever come up." Thomas began the conversion.

AND formula

0 X 0 = 0
0 X 1 = 0
1 X 0 = 0
1 X 1 = 1

9	14	15	0	11	1
00001001	00001110	00001111	00000000	00001011	00000001
b	a	b	o	o	n
01100010	01100001	01100010	01101111	01101111	01101110
0	0	2	0	11	0
00000000	00000000	00000010	00000000	00001011	00000000

"That's not right," Thomas concluded, staring at the result. "It's too simple for a password. It's not what Christian would have done. Any simple password recovery software would have been able to figure this out in seconds—it's too easy."

"Maybe the stela has the answer," Anna suggested.

They all stared at a photograph of the stela for a good long time. Olivia looked at her watch. "Ninety minutes left before the password virus destroys the servers."

"Of course!" Thomas exclaimed. "Why didn't I see this before? Look at the last five entries."

> *Step one, two, three, now we are ready*
> *Five, eight, and twelve*
> *Two is better than one and three*
> *Baboon*
> *Rh!noc8ros*

"I already figured out that 'step one, two, and three' refers to the training I gave Christian when he was age five, eight, and twelve. But 'two is better than one and three' puzzled me until now. What cipher did we practice in the second part of his training that might be better than the first or the third? It's not something better, per se, but rather something that fits this mission more than the other two."

He looked around at them. "The answer is genocide. Haman tried to wipe out the Jews in Persia much like Hitler tried to wipe out the Jews in the twentieth century. When Christian was eight I taught him Hitler's cipher or at least one of them. It's easy to learn because it has to do with binary, so we used it extensively.

"When Hitler communicated with his generals he used different ciphering machines for secrecy. One such machine was called the Lorenz SZ40. It's a larger and more efficient machine than the smaller and more popular Enigma machines used before 1941. Christian and I used one of these machines. Well, not the machine itself, but the science behind it. It's named after Schlüsselzusatz—the SZ.

"The way it works is, each letter of the alphabet is represented by five binary numbers, combinations of ones and zeros. To decipher the message you need to have a key, also in binary form. The trick, however, is to add them up as we did earlier, but using the exclusive-or—XOR—formula. Here, let me write it down."

Thomas paused and scribbled code on his notepad. "We line up the binary code one on top of the other like before. This time, however, we look for all the matches that have a zero both on top and at the bottom, as well as those that have a one on top and at the bottom. These have a value of zero. All the others have a value of one." He scribbled some more. "There. As you can see, it's quite simple."

"I suggest we try it," Olivia cut in, "and leave the math lesson for another time."

"Yes, of course." They all watched as he added the two lines of code.

```
XOR formula

0 ⊕ 0 = 0
0 ⊕ 1 = 1
1 ⊕ 0 = 1
1 ⊕ 1 = 0

9          14         15         0          11         1
00001001   00001110   00001111   00000000   00001011   00000001

b          a          b          o          o          n
01100010   01100001   01100010   01101111   01101111   01101110

k          o          m          o          d          o
01101011   01101111   01101101   01101111   01100100   01101111
```

They stared at the results in disbelief.

"Komodo?" Anna said.

"It would appear so," Quincy confirmed. "But we already tried that, both with and without a capital K."

"There's still one final step," Thomas said. "I know what the password is. I'll tell you as soon as Christian arrives." He took a deep breath. "Or if I'm convinced he's not coming back."

Olivia edged close to confront Thomas. "I understand you want to save your son, but we need to think of the others on this ship first."

"I will not jeopardize the ship and its crew," Thomas said.

This assured everyone but Olivia. "You need to trust us with this password," she insisted.

"No. I have witnessed enough lies in the name of this mission to know better than to trust anyone associated with it." He turned to the others. "You'll get the password in time, I promise. But for now, I have to look after Christian. I will not allow someone to betray him as they did on the trip he was part of. I will give the password to Anna when the time is right. So, this is what we're going to do." He looked at his watch. "How long will it take to leave the ship and land on Persian soil?"

"About ten minutes," Derrek said.

"What if I wanted to go alone, can I do that?"

"I can put the pod on autopilot if you want."

"Good. That gives me about seventy minutes. Derrek, you will send me down and program the pod to come back with five minutes to spare. Whether or not I have Christian, you'll get the password at that point. So I suggest that Quincy station himself at the terminal, ready to input the password."

"What if something goes wrong and you can't make it back?" Olivia asked.

"Then you'd better make sure the communication system works."

They just stood there staring at Thomas. "Shouldn't you get moving?" Thomas urged. They scattered to their positions.

Olivia stood there a moment longer. She shook her head, then left without a word.

Anna also stayed behind. Thomas was hoping she would. "Anna, I need you to stay aboard the *Kismet* in case something happens to me and I can't get back on time. You're the only one I can trust with the password."

Anna blinked back tears. "Don't do this, Thomas," she pleaded. "You must accept that Christian may not be coming back."

Thomas embraced Anna, holding her tight in his arms. "I know that, Anna. But I will always wonder what would have happened if I gave up now."

Anna leaned back and studied his face. Then she stepped back, wiping the tears from her face. "You're not coming back, are you," she said in a tight voice.

"I promise you, Anna, I'm coming back. We have so much planned together. I still have to teach you to scuba dive, remember?"

Anna giggled, sniffed, and nodded.

"I need to do this first," Thomas said. "Or we have no future at all. There will always be doubts."

Anna managed a wan smile. "Then you'd better hurry back."

Thomas opened Anna's hand and placed a piece of paper in. "Just in case, here's the password. Now come; let's go, and I will explain on our way the last clue on the stela, the one that looks like a garbled 'rhinoceros.'"

They left the cafeteria. Anna hooked her arm through Thomas's as he lifted his notepad and wrote on it, *Rh!noc8ros*.

"Here let me explain, every time Christian and I created a new password," he said, "we would use the same pattern. First, each password started with a capital letter, then each vowel that followed would be modified according to a predetermined pattern. The first vowel would become a special character resembling the vowel; in this case, a commercial *a*" —he wrote @ on his notepad. "The second vowel stays as-is, so in Komodo it would remain *o*. Finally, the third vowel would be changed to a number that looked closest to the vowel. So the last *o* becomes the number zero. That's why I know the password is—" He wrote on his notepad: *K@mod0*.

• • • • • • • • • ● ○○○○○○○○ ○ ○

To avoid unwanted attention, Thomas stayed inside the pod with the invisible shield on. The waiting was excruciating. With only ten minutes left, Thomas resigned himself to the inevitable. He would never see home again. He would never see Anna again.

He stepped out of the pod into the open. Lifting a pair of binoculars, he surveyed the road leading to the rendezvous point. He glanced at his watch. Five minutes left. He looked again down the road, and his heart leaped. Someone was coming.

He started walking toward the road, keeping the binoculars in front of his eyes. *It's Christian, but why is he walking so slow? Why is he taking his good old time?*

Four minutes to go. He turned to the now visible pod, then looked at the camera in the tree. In his mind's eye he could see Anna's anxious expression. He turned to look at Christian, still very far away. Dropping the binoculars to the ground, removed his shirt and waved it back and forth like a battle flag. Christian noticed the flag, but all he did was wave back.

Thomas looked at his watch again. Three minutes left. *He's not going to make it.*

What happened next was all Thomas could do. He walked slowly toward the camera. He lifted his transmitter. It didn't work. He wasn't frustrated; he was too numb. He let the transmitter fall to the ground. Using his hands and his lips to gesture in universal sign language, he said, "I love you."

• • • • • • • • • ● ○○○○○○○○ ○ ○

Anna realized this was the last time she would see Thomas. She reached to touch the monitor. "I love you too," she whispered.

"We're screwed," Olivia said, looking over Anna's shoulder. "I should have beaten the password out of him."

With her eyes still glued to the monitor, Anna handed the password to Olivia, who stared at it for a moment. "Is this the password?" Anna said nothing. Olivia handed the paper to Derrek, who called it in.

•••••••••●○○○○○○○○○○○

Thomas turned toward the pod as the door automatically closed. Seconds later it disappeared into thin air. Thomas removed his watch from his wrist. "Five minutes more and Anna will be back in the twenty-first century," he said, then with all his strength, he threw his watch deep into the woods. "I won't need that anymore."

He walked toward the road just as Christian entered into the open field. They embraced for a long time.

"Thanks for coming, Dad."

"You didn't make it easy, son."

"Yet you figured it out."

"Yes I did, son. The mosaic was a great idea."

"So you didn't waste time figuring it out then, right Dad?"

Thomas smiled. "We'll talk about that some other time. Come on, let's sit for a while."

They found a nice dry spot on the grassy ground.

"Will we see anything when the *Kismet* leaves?" Thomas asked.

"From down here, you mean?"

"Yes."

Christian thought about it for a moment. "I'm guessing we would see some sort of flash in the sky. It would last less than a second, but it would be noticeable."

They both stared at the blue sky.

•••••••••●○○○○○○○○○○○

"Pay close attention, Quincy; it's complicated," Derrek said in his call to the wheelhouse.

"Just give it to me, Derrek."

Derrek spelled it out for him. "K-@-m-o-d-0. Now repeat it to me."

Quincy repeated the password. He typed it in but didn't press the Enter key. "What if it's the wrong password?"

"It's not. Anyway, if it is, there's nothing we can do about it now."

Quincy looked at the countdown clock on the top right corner of the monitor screen. Ten seconds left. He still failed to press the *Enter* key. Five seconds, four seconds, three, two—he pressed the key.

Everything went dark. The constant background hum of the computer terminals stopped. The air filtration system shut down.

"What happened?" Anna shouted. She could no longer see Thomas. The emergency lights came on, but nothing else. She turned to Derrek for answers, but he had none.

"What have you done?" Olivia yelled as she marched into the wheelhouse.

"I don't know."

"Are we not supposed to faint or something before we reappear in the twenty-first century, like what happened when we arrived here?"

Quincy turned to face Olivia. "I don't know. I just don't know, okay?" He turned back to the terminal.

Everyone held their breath.

The annoying hum came back, followed by the lights. Quincy stared at the terminal. Minutes passed before a BIOS message appeared.

"Is that good?" Olivia asked.

Seconds later a string of white text appeared on a black background. It rapidly scrolled up the screen, much too fast for anyone to read.

"Yes, Captain," Quincy said, "this is good—this is very good!"

After what seemed like an eternity the scrolling text stopped to display one word: *User.* Quincy entered the username root.

Olivia looked horrified. "Not another password."

"No—I mean yes, but this time I know the password."

"But I said no passwords allowed," Olivia protested.

"A password is mandatory in this version of UNIX. We had no choice. But don't worry, the technicians all know it." He entered the password: ULRA. A graphical user interface appeared with the familiar icons in all the right places, including the countdown clock in the top right corner. "Well I'll be damned," Quincy said and burst into maniacal laughter.

Olivia moved closer to the monitor. "What does that mean?"

•••••••••●○○○○○○○○○○

"Was it the tomb inscription, the stone stela, or the wall engraving that got you here?" Christian asked.

"You sent three messages?"

"No, I was thinking of one of those three. I haven't made up my mind which one yet."

"The stela," Thomas said.

"I see. I was leaning more toward the tomb inscription. I wonder why I went for the stela." He thought about his choice for a moment. "Did you find any of my staffs?"

"I knew you made more of them!"

"I made three, with three more to come. Two here in Hīt, one in Babylon, and the other three, when ready, I would have put in Susa. Which one did you find?"

"The one in Babylon, but how did you know I would catch on? It's not that obvious."

"Dad, come on. Komodo has been part of our IT strategy since I was a boy. So I placed them where you would look, following the mission's objective of relic hunting. I knew if you saw one, you'd understand. It worked, didn't it?"

"It sure did, son, it sure did."

Christian stared at the still empty field. "So when is the pod coming to pick us up?"

Thomas had difficulty swallowing. How could he tell Christian he wasn't going home, after everything they'd been through? "Well, son, I'm afraid I have some bad—"

"There it is," Christian said with delight. "Isn't that the most beautiful piece of technology you ever laid your eyes upon?"

Thomas was speechless. *How can it be possible?*

Christian turned to Thomas as they walked toward the pod. "What was that you were about to say, Dad?"

"Oh nothing, it can wait."

• • • • • • • • ● ○ ○ ○ ○ ○ ○ ○ ○ ○ ○ °

Thomas and Christian made it back to the *Kismet* safely. They walked out of the pod to rounds of applause. Anna was the first to approach Thomas. As he opened his arms to give her a huge hug, Anna slapped him across the cheek. Then she jumped into his arms. "Don't you *ever* do that to me again."

"Whoa," Christian said, backing away. "What's that all about?"

Anna smiled at Christian. "It's nice to finally meet you, Christian."

"Stay right where you are," Callahan Rye ordered. Kirkpatrick was right behind him. They approached Christian and each grabbed an arm.

"Let him go," Olivia said as she entered the room.

"But he's the reason for our failed mission," Rye said.

In a slow, deliberate voice, Olivia repeated her order. Reluctantly, they released Christian. "Welcome aboard, Mr. Faraday," she said. "Sorry for the unpleasant reception, but you sure gave us a great deal of anxiety with your password."

Christian stared Olivia down. "You and those two over there knew what happened to us on the last mission, yet you still came back. I had to make sure this trip won't be a repeat of the last one."

"So you were ready to sacrifice everyone, including your father, for this purpose?"

"I knew if my father came, he would figure out the password. If he didn't come, then yes. Better stuck here forever than to have more men and women sacrificed in the name of God." Christian stepped up to Olivia. "Rest assured, Captain, this is just the beginning. When I get back, the whole world will know what happened here. I'll make sure this is the last trip operated by this governing body of yours. And if you and your two gorillas ever try to stop me, there are others ready to take my place."

Olivia looked at those around her, then sighed. "No Christian, I won't get in your way. It would appear you have already accomplished your goal anyway. It's unlikely any more missions will be sanctioned now. I am curious about one thing. We were forced to put in the password with seconds left on your countdown meter. What would you have done if we failed?"

Christian looked confused. "Seconds? I don't understand. There should be another three days before we head back. There's no negotiating the time for the return trip."

"I know what happened," Thomas said. "You had no way of knowing we were accidentally sent here three days premature."

"Three days premature?" Christian thought about this for a moment. "I know what happened, Dad. The *Kismet* has a five-day window for launching from the portal back home. We have control over its environment so we can make the necessary adjustments for a launch. But for the return trip we can't make adjustments without knowing precisely when the *Kismet* will show up. With no way of communicating back and forth, we need to have a precise day and time predetermined for the return trip. When I programmed the countdown clock, I presumed you would leave as planned. That's why the time limit for the password I programmed ended." He thought about it. "Less than thirty minutes ago."

Olivia had heard enough. "Anna, have an announcement made for everyone to come out of the launch chambers and report to the auditorium in one hour. Derrek—and you too, Quincy—get all the uploaded data from the foot soldiers and compile it in one place for easy retrieval when we arrive back home." Olivia made sure Thomas was paying attention. "As for you, Christian, I want you to get a full physical at the infirmary. I'll let Dr. Patterson know you're coming. The rest of you know what to do."

Everyone scattered to their various assignments.

"It's finally over," Anna told Thomas as they accompanied Christian to the infirmary.

"Not quite yet, Anna. There's still one last thing to do to put an end to the ULRA forever, and I think you know what it is."

"Yes, Thomas, I sure do. And how convenient it is that all the video data is being stored in one easy to access location."

If you enjoyed reading this book,
would you consider leaving a review at your place of purchase?

Thank you

ABOUT THE AUTHOR

For over eighteen years Michel Cloutier has taught computer networking environments in Montreal, Canada. Occasionally, he manages to tear himself away to scuba dive the many local shipwrecks that dot the bottom of the Saint Lawrence River. His love for history has also moved him to travel to exotic and history-rich countries such as Italy, Greece, Turkey, Israel, Egypt, and many other areas in Europe, the Middle East, and Central America.

In the pages of this novel, Michel has merged his two passions for network security and ancient history to create an adventure sure to hold your interest until the climactic end.

www.ingramcontent.com/pod-product-compliance
Lightning Source LLC
Chambersburg PA
CBHW011425200626
46814CB00017B/2944